a Tyler Bedlam novel

by Jon A. Hunt

Adams: 2009.
Denali: 2009.
Baker: 2010.
Aconcagua: 2011.
Rainier: 2007, 2009, 2011, 2012.

This book is dedicated to Mark,
who appreciates a panorama when he sees one.
He's earned his.

This novel is a work of fiction.

No characters herein are real, except for a few who died centuries ago and won't care if dramatic adjustments are made to *their* stories for the sake of *mine*.

The places are more complicated. Many exist, more or less as described. These essential components of the region's personality shouldn't be generalized. Modern residences and businesses in the novel are fictitious.

The organizations are also a mixed bag. Law enforcement entities mentioned are real, but their hierarchies and operations are literary guesses only. Other organizations mentioned specifically by name are imaginary.

Copyright © 2019 by Jon A. Hunt
All rights reserved.

ISBN: 978-1-0878-1884-9

FLINTLOCK

Prologue

A nasty garbage truck funk hauled me into the living room by my nostrils. Not just a person, but the whole house, had died.

Furniture, lamps, pictures, drapes, everything was demolished. Wallboard had been ripped from the studs. Carpet curled up at every edge. Debris lay in categorized heaps in the middle of each room. Books and magazines occupied separate piles, one for pages, one for the gutted bindings. I'd never seen such a ransack job.

"Don't touch," Lieutenant Rafferty cautioned.

"What? And screw up the system?" I said.

He grimaced without inviting his eyes to the expression. Jerry Rafferty would look tough even if he wasn't six-foot-six and built like a bridge pylon. He wore his rusty hair cropped flat and tight as a Belle Meade putting green, and in the year and a half I'd known him he'd rarely cracked a convincing smile. We saw eye to eye more often than not, a rarity between cops and for-hire snoops like me. That didn't mean he liked me enough to invite me to crime scenes for giggles.

Blue-gloved forensics technicians parted so we could enter the kitchen. Similar wreckage waited there, different ingredients. A man-sized twist of plastic baffled me till I recognized it as the inner lining of a refrigerator. The appliance's door teetered against more denuded wall studs. It

1

was folded in half.

"Tell me this guy found what he was after."

Rafferty stepped around the carcass of an electric range without answering.

I paused to consider tiny magnetic lettered tiles, the kind households with intact refrigerators use to spell cute messages to each other. Five of the letters persisted in a row near what had been an upper corner of the door:

ARTIC.

Maybe I'd been snared by the irony of a one-person household with no one else to read the cute messages. Maybe it was a spelling handicap taken unnoticed to the hereafter. More likely, the finger marks held me. They were huge and impressed deeply in the stainless steel the way a naughty toddler's hand might mar a cube of butter.

I rose from my crouch before the blue-gloves got antsy and followed the Lieutenant.

Steps descended from the kitchen to a converted den that had started out as an attached single-car garage. Less searching and more smashing had happened here. Dark-edged holes pocked the walls on three sides, breaches the size of a man's head, because that's what had made them. Handprints in dried blood splayed beside the holes. The wrecking ball had put up a fight till the fourth wall, which was brick. Nobody's head is that hard.

The body hadn't yet been moved. Before grittier details coalesced, I sensed something more immediately disturbing. All of the *things* in the house had been crushed methodically, sorted, tested for value. The *man* had just been crushed. His broken shell huddled at the base of the last wall, arms angled incorrectly, as if the killer had found their flailing tiresome and snapped them to make it stop. A grisly pulp merged defeated

Flintlock

shoulders with the bricks.

I recognized the suspenders. They had been black and white before the blood, a kitschy crossword pattern with letters facing all directions. Not many men wear suspenders these days. I'd only known one living man with that kind of taste. Now I didn't know any again.

"Cell phone was under a cabinet over there," Rafferty said. "Apparently not worth taking or busting. Guess whose number was dialed last."

"Mine," I said flatly.

The Lieutenant growled affirmation. "Client of yours?"

"Almost."

Today was supposed to be my first on the job.

Chapter One

The man in suspenders used to be Mitch Braunfelter. We'd met two days ago at my usual coffee joint.

I can afford as nice an office as the next guy. But offices come with drawers to organize, wastebaskets to empty, and swivel chairs that make you heavy and slow when you're better off lean and quick. Worse, every office I've ever seen includes the ubiquitous plastic appliance that only brews mud no matter what you pour in the top. I'm fine interacting with strangers for a living. I just don't care to meet them in offices and I'm all for a decent cup of joe.

I'd walked over from my condo. November had been almost balmy. December, not so much. Nashville temperatures barely crept above the teens all week. I nursed a second cup of fair-trade Peruvian and tried not to think about the walk back. My next client was late.

So-called alternative music with thumping bass and intrusive lyrics set my nerves and the concrete floor on edge. I suppose the racket appealed to college students who stamped red-faced through the door to join others around tables or stand in line to order. Everyone stayed close to the back wall. A plank bar and metal stools along frosted storefront windows had no takers. The winter haze limited what could be seen outside, anyway, to cars passing on the street. A city bus dragged diesel exhaust uphill as if the fumes had weight. My man stumped into view

Flintlock

with somewhat more enthusiasm than the bus.

He got indoors as quick as younger customers, though he looked the type who'd take his time on a warmer day. Late middle-aged, average height and build, balding, all the stereotype lacked for completion were round eyeglasses. His overcoat was expensive but a size too large, probably a gift. The red acrylic scarf swaddling his chin came straight from a dollar store bin. I'd have pegged him for a university professor, except none of the students appeared to recognize him.

The barista at the counter caught my gesture. She turned with a mug toward a chrome urn containing the featured drip. The newcomer wasn't as easy to reel in.

"Mr. Braunfelter? Mr. Braunfelter?"

He pivoted toward my third hail the way people do when they hear their own names, which was reassuring. I'm fed a lot of funny aliases. I nudged a chair back with a foot. Braunfelter and his gourmet caffeine arrived simultaneously. He nodded to the girl, greeted me with a handshake and plunked himself down. Slender fingers with neat nails and arthritic knuckles encircled the warm mug. His eyes came up and jolted me with blueness.

"Mr. Bedlam, thank you for meeting me." His voice traveled on the low side of tenor and he enunciated too crisply to be a native. "You aren't quite what I expected."

"Just a regular guy."

"No, I don't suspect you are. I've read some—"

"Journalists exaggerate worse than novelists." I passed my business card over like it was the whole autobiography.

Tyler Bedlam
Private Investigations

A willowy forefinger touched the cardboard rectangle. Blue eyes dipped briefly. He seemed as impressed as anybody ever

Jon A. Hunt

was. I needed flashier business cards.

"We discussed *protection* over the phone."

"I do that. Just didn't want to clutter up my card."

"Are you...armed?"

"Not unless I need to be. Make yourself comfortable, Mr. Braunfelter. Nobody's been accosted here since I started showing up."

"Please, just Mitch is fine." If the red scarf and blue eyes hadn't charmed me, his sheepish smile did. You couldn't help but like the guy. He squirmed out of coat and scarf and draped both over his chair. That's when I noticed the two-inch-wide crossword suspenders.

"Mitch, you aren't what I expected, either," I said.

His smile blossomed to a full-on grin. He hooked knobby thumbs under the cartoonish straps. "Thirty-eight years with the water company got me a pension and these!" He might well have been given the last such things on the planet. Sufficient pride buoyed his words, however, that I knew Mitch Braunfelter didn't see those suspenders as a gag gift, even if the givers had. "I was the company problem solver. If there was a glitch, I'd find the source when no one else could. That's my calling, I suppose, solving puzzles. Like what you do, except with water pipes, eh?"

I nodded. We might not be all that dissimilar, though I hadn't yet earned my suspenders.

"...that's why I want to hire you," he continued. "I tripped over a doozy of a puzzle and I think I can solve it. But— possibly just my imagination—it seems somebody is following me. I promised a friend I'd find help."

"You're retired. Why not let the company figure out its own problems?"

Nothing in those blue eyes resembled a retiree's weariness. "This has nothing to do with plumbing."

"I had to ask."

Flintlock

Braunfelter tried a sip of coffee. The overhead speakers got thoughtful for a few seconds, and other conversations became audible around us. Then the musical assault resumed as he opened his mouth. Annoyance showed briefly—this noise fit *his* definition of music even less than it did mine—and I wondered whether I should apologize for not having an office with swivel chairs and file cabinets. He leaned in over his mug to compensate.

"That's reasonable. But this is my personal trouble. If it's trouble at all. See, I brought something home I wasn't meant to. It's very old and must be quite valuable. I wasn't charged for it, just found it tucked in with ordinary things. A lot of people were hurrying to the door the same time I was and maybe it fell into my bag by mistake. I can't imagine the nice girl who rang me out would have missed it. I mean to return the item to its rightful owner. But, well, I don't think the rightful owner was ever the *store*."

"I'm good at finding people," I said. My professional description on my boring business card implied as much.

"I bet you are! But I'd rather handle that myself. The puzzle intrigues me. I've got time."

I shrugged without asking what he'd acquired by accident. He had no intention of telling. An ache in my right shoulder urged caution. The cold bothered it ever since I'd collected a .38 caliber weather detector from the last clients who weren't completely straight with me.

Braunfelter eyed me intently. I was a riddle for him as well, a big inscrutable tough guy with a five o'clock shadow before noon, questionable business cards, no office. Something or someone had worried him enough to find me. I might be just as dangerous, though.

"I, uh, I don't know how the process works," he said at length and the embarrassed smile returned. "I've never hired a bodyguard."

Jon A. Hunt

I ignored my shoulder and dove in like I always do.

"That depends on how obvious you want me to be. I can follow you around like an old dog. Might scare off anyone watching you. It'll get on both our nerves, too, and may just make us both targets. Or I can stay out of sight, keep an eye on you from a distance. If someone *is* after you, they're less likely to know I'm involved that way. The downside is I might not get to them—or you—quick enough. Nothing's foolproof. I'm just one person."

His smile evaporated. The reality of paying a stranger to watch your ass never sinks in when you first come up with the idea.

"The second way sounds better, I suppose." That hurdle crossed, Mitch was all business. "I'd like to start this Friday afternoon."

"I'm able to start now if you prefer."

The smooth head wobbled negatively. "Thank you, but I would rather put together the funds first. No sense in starting up new debt right after retiring."

"I'm not hurting for money—"

"I know." This was backed with a more serious blue-eyed look than had seemed possible from his sort. "I imagine a billionaire would be difficult to bribe."

I beamed across the table. Not many were able to offer me what I couldn't just buy on a whim. That was my father's wealth; I hadn't asked for it. Meeting strangers in loud coffee shops to help them with their problems was what I wanted to do.

"So, let's meet here again on Friday. One o'clock? Start then?"

"Of course," I said.

I watched him to stand and squirm back into his oversized coat and chintzy red scarf, then I picked my card off the table to give him.

Flintlock

"Please keep the card, Mr. Bedlam," he said. "I'm very good with numbers."

With a wink, Mitch Braunfelter turned, dodged politely through the drink line and exited into the cold. Our encounter hadn't lasted ten minutes. He caught the next Hermitage Avenue bus in no time.

He didn't live to make our Friday appointment.

Chapter Two

"Not his home," Rafferty said as we watched techs stretcher the bagged corpse down the front steps. He'd have gotten a bouncier send-off if he was still breathing. We're taken better care of when we can't complain.

"Huh?"

"He didn't live here. Had a place in Columbia."

The Lieutenant also told me Braunfelter was single and had the house to himself when his killer arrived. The refrigerator magnets made even less sense now.

"This doesn't look like a rental," I said.

Rafferty's shoulders lifted. "Already questioned his real estate agent. Bought the place last month, she never knew the reason, just that he had no plans of moving here himself. Furniture was delivered brand new this morning. Could've saved his bread."

"What do they know?"

He traced my gaze across the street. People shivered there in hastily donned jackets, caps and slippers. Eyes stared through clouded breath, except a few that stayed downcast as they waited to share their versions of what they hadn't seen with officers. Blue roof lights on the police cruisers sapped any natural color from their faces.

"I doubt much," Rafferty admitted.

My head was cold. I had more hair than the Lieutenant and

Flintlock

no reason to act especially tough. I put on my hat. "Are we finished?"

"For now."

"Tyler..."

I paused at the concrete walk.

"Said yourself he wasn't a client. How about just letting me do my job?"

"Mind my own business, you mean."

Rafferty jammed big paws into his coat pockets. Even characters too tough for hats can respect a twenty-degree day. "Yeah," he said.

My scowl as I walked around the cruisers to my car wasn't anything personal, just a reflexive thing that happens whenever anyone suggests I butt out. Jerry Rafferty knew me better than that.

• • •

Mitch Braunfelter's final going-away party happened at Arbuckle Brothers Funeral Home in Columbia, on a bitter Saturday afternoon, a week and a day after he and I were supposed to begin our business relationship. This appointment he kept.

Columbia, nicknamed "Mule Town," is thirty miles south of the big city. Its primary claims to fame are a house where James K. Polk once lived and the annual spring Mule Day celebration. The historic town square has charm. Impressive old homes can be found in the right neighborhoods, less impressive shacks in the wrong neighborhoods. The population is around thirty-five thousand, more during Mule Day. I've never seen a single mule inside the city limits any other time of year.

The funeral home stood a hundred yards off the street on a wooded hillside. It boasted faux marble columns and vinyl decorative shutters on the windows. I idled into a space on the lowest tier of terraced parking, which suited me fine. My winter car was in the shop and I'd driven the less discrete one.

Jon A. Hunt

One symptom of inherited wealth was my predilection toward loud expensive sports cars like the Viper. I compensated for this dearth of subtlety with my best jacket and tie.

Mists spilled through bare elms in a lethargic gaseous avalanche. The fog tasted like snow. So far, the roads were dry and I was glad. The ten-cylinder monster I drove tended to want to kill me when the pavement turned slippery. One funeral per December was enough.

I struggle with December funerals. I'd buried my father two Decembers ago. We'd never been close and his passing left me with more money than I could spend in ten lifetimes. Yet both winters since had been poisoned by a vague sense of loss.

Regardless of month or weather, I couldn't have parked closer to the building if I wanted. The majority of vehicles were cheap commuter cars and pickup trucks, a lot of them. A phalanx of utility service trucks with lift buckets stood guard in front of an expectant hearse. Mitch had been with the company for nearly four decades. They don't give suspenders to just anyone.

A heavyset gentleman opened a pseudo-mahogany door for me. His suit fitted perfectly over a well-fed belly. Empathy showed in his quiet eyes. He'd held that door for thousands before me and would hold it for thousands after me, till the day he was the main attraction himself. One of the Arbuckles, I presumed.

Someone with thinner blood than mine had gotten hold of the thermostat. The foyer was oppressive. I added my hat and overcoat to an alcove brimming with outerwear. My suit jacket stayed on and buttoned. Every other male there sweated in his somber dignity. Judging by the cut of their lapels, they'd relied on the same suits to get them through weddings and funerals since Reagan held office. If they could do it, so could I, and my semiautomatic stayed respectfully out of sight.

No one migrating from foyer to chapel was familiar. I barely

Flintlock

knew the man in the box in the next room. People I didn't know died every day and I didn't owe them a thing. What made Mitch Braunfelter different? I followed everyone into the chapel to find out.

• • •

Architectural magic attempted to make the room grander than it was. Stained glass windows marched along the aisle walls, not real windows, only panels with fluorescent bulbs behind them. The pews creaked like honest wood, at least. A choral rendition of *Nearer, My God to Thee* sifted from unseen speakers. The pot-bellied fellow with the tailored suit pulled the doors shut. I leaned against a wall in the back. Nobody spoke above a whisper. Sobbing was audible. The occasional cough was stifled. All eyes were forward.

Mitch rested there in a polished ebony casket. The lid was closed. Nobody wanted to see what morticians couldn't fix. His image smiled instead from a frame on a wire easel beside the casket. The photograph had been snapped at his retirement party. He held those crossword suspenders. I wondered if he'd been allowed to wear them today and forever. I hoped so.

The funeral director maneuvered to the pulpit past hothouse roses, lilies, glossy leaves of condolence. He shared a few soothing words after the recorded hymn faded. He led us in a prayer. The usual one. *Yea, though I walk through the valley of the shadow of death...* The familiar verses comforted him as they comforted his audience. He'd never met the breathing version of Mitch Braunfelter, but I bet he'd seen inside the box.

I turned my attention to the gap between us before my thoughts soured further.

Most in the pews were far younger than Mitch. Seating had been first come, first served. Any living Braunfelters were shuffled in with the rest. I searched without success for family resemblances. Then the man up front invited the congregation to share memories of the dearly departed.

Jon A. Hunt

A woman, formerly a single mother with her toddler fleeing westward from an abusive home back east, shared a story of a utility worker who stopped to help when her car broke down. He'd given her a reason to pause in Mule Town. Her boy was finishing college now. She had a job here. She'd stayed for twenty-three years.

A Cumberland-Presbyterian preacher told how Mr. Braunfelter helped re-roof the church after a storm. Mitch brought along any office staff who could be spared during the cleanup. He wasn't a member of the church.

Several in the pews joined in a thankful chorus with the once unemployed auto worker whose electric and water bills were covered by Mitch till he found new work. Mitch paid a lot of people's bills in the recession.

A regular in the town square, he'd supported every business with small purchases. He'd play chess with strangers outside the coffee shop. He fetched cats from treetops. He searched for lost puppies, and if the dogs turned up dead by the road, Mitch was the guy who brought them home to their owners with tears in his eyes. He helped his fellow humans whenever he could. Mitch Braunfelter's funeral didn't have reserved seating for family members because every person there was family as far as they were concerned.

Yet some monster had bashed his brains out against a brick wall. That's why I'd come. Mitch had gained one last family member on his way out, a brother to bring justice as a funeral donation. Because Mitch had promised he'd find some help.

We bowed for a closing prayer. Six power and water company men carried the coffin out through the double doors. The rest remained seated, stunned to silence by the cruelty of the world, two-hundred sorrowing souls in the pews, and me against the back wall.

• • •

The funeral coordinator inclined his forehead toward the

Flintlock

front pews. People rose and filed numbly out to the foyer again. Nobody said anything: I'd have noticed because I exited the room last.

Funerals aren't for questions. You can crash a family reunion and play off everyone's dread of having forgotten about you when they're sure they ought to know your life story. I've collected a lot of information at reunions, also some excellent recipes. Corporate parties can net similar results. Not funerals. Today was for observations. I made note of who gravitated to or avoided whom, who had to drag their eyes from Mitch's grandly packaged remains, who couldn't get away quick enough.

I wasn't the sole watcher. The other guy slipped outside as I entered the foyer, a little too fast. He steered clear of eye contact but I recognized him anyway.

Power and water company employees crowded one end of the foyer and put on coats and gloves simultaneously. A tight-knit bunch. I memorized faces. Names could be found later.

Then there was the couple who might as well have shown up on a dare. They didn't belong in Columbia. I'd spotted them during the service. A man and a woman, both slender and upright with jet black hair and a regal aura. Her hair was cropped as short as his, but even seen from the back there was no mistaking genders. When they got up to leave, I spied a haunted beautiful face there'd be no forgetting. They disappeared before I reached the lobby.

Mr. Arbuckle beat me to the front door and opened it again. He glanced up with the only unrehearsed expression I'd seen him wear: curiosity. He'd been doing this a while and he could sense something darker than plain old sorrow brought me.

Jon A. Hunt

Chapter Three

Outside the Arbuckle Brothers' dolorous sanctuary, the sky sagged. Crystalline will-o'-the-wisps that might or might not be snowflakes darted on a fickle breeze, touching nothing, pausing never, worrisome. People wasted no time getting to their vehicles. Any accumulation on the roads meant we'd be staying the night in Mule Town whether we lived here or not.

A police cruiser idled in the driveway amid billowing exhaust. Six big diesel engines fired with a unison clatter. Utility company service trucks would be joining the funeral procession. The patrol car's roof lights flared.

I allowed myself a turn to survey impending departures. The raven-haired man and woman opened the doors of a gray Mercedes. I changed my mind about leaving ahead of the weather. I wanted to see where the Mercedes went, as soon as I got rid of the other private eye who was leaning against a tree admiring the Viper.

Keller Ableman never bothered to dress the part. He wouldn't be caught dead in a trench coat and fedora, or standing in a rainy alley under a neon sign with a cigarette in his mouth and a flask of cheap bourbon in his pocket. All that Mickey Spillane horseshit belonged in the 1950's and he had no qualms about telling you so. Keller solved his mysteries with computers. Usually he solved them quicker than I could. But technology hadn't entirely spared him from getting his shoes

Flintlock

dirty. Right then, he was dirtying his shoes closer to my car than I liked.

"'Afternoon, Bedlam," he said. Not *good* afternoon. We were at a funeral.

"Why're you here, Keller?"

He finished tapping on the screen of a shiny new mobile phone—only the best equipment would do for the Keller Ableman Agency—then fed the device to an inside breast pocket of a hand-stitched Lanvin suit jacket he'd never worn before today. Keller was a clothes horse. He was good-looking in a classic Cary Grant sort of way. Diamondbacks come in pretty wrappers and I don't trust them, either.

"Paying respects, same as you," he said.

"You knew Mitch?"

He smiled and straightened onto both feet, carefully, to avoid snagging the fine European fabric on elm bark. All that style couldn't be especially warm: the jacket was thin enough I spotted the outline of a shoulder holster.

"I hadn't realized you were back working after that dust-up in Green Hills," he said, avoiding my question. Again.

"Who said anything about working?"

The police car started toward the street. Service trucks clunked into gear. The procession was beginning. I unlocked the Viper's door.

"How's the shoulder?"

"Never better," I lied, settled into the driver's seat and shut the door. The V-10 obliterated any further attempt at conversation on Keller's part. If he tried. He grinned at me via the side mirror and brushed a snowflake off his sleeve.

I wasn't crazy about the guy. People of Mitch's caliber certainly wouldn't be. And he was more expensive than me because he needed to make a living. Who'd invited him, then?

The Viper found a place in line, three cars back from the Mercedes. I thought about Keller Ableman as we filed onto the

Jon A. Hunt

street and slowly motored through town. I bumped my wipers to clear the windshield.

• • •

We paraded through intersections behind the pilot car, large white bucket trucks, the hearse. Running lights pulsed out of sync, muted by blowing snow. The pavement thus far was only wet, but trees and lawns were white and fuzzy. The Mercedes glided briefly into view before it was hidden by a white-flocked forsythia bush. I disobeyed the stop sign like the rest and then the only flashing lights I saw were in front of and behind me.

And inside my car.

My phone flickered on the passenger seat where I'd left it during the service.

Keller Ableman would've been envious of my phone if I let him see it. He hadn't inherited any international technology companies. The device had all the usual gimmicks: voice recognition, high-resolution cameras, solitaire. It also had the ability to scan for electronic lock codes, open garage doors, and tie in directly to Cool-Core's mainframe computers via encrypted channels which were a hell of a lot better at finding information than Google. The phone knew whether someone besides me picked it up and would lock down till I promised it everything was okay. Once in a while, just for fun, I used the thing to call people. But the fluttering LED was new: I'd never seen *purple*. I'd have to call Danny Ayers, the Cool-Core whiz-kid who'd built the phone, and get him to explain.

Brake lights recalled my attention to the cars outside. We'd reached the cemetery.

• • •

When the Army of Tennessee threw itself against Union breastworks in Franklin in 1864, Columbia's Rose Hill was already an established cemetery. Confederate dead lay there a

Flintlock

century and a half later beneath lumpy sod and simple markers, around a stone monument taller than the ancient magnolias. A soldier's weathered likeness stands atop the monument. His hands rest on the butt of a rifle with its muzzle planted on the toe of his left boot. The weariness in his chiseled face is convincing.

Today the stone soldier had diminished to an apparition on the hilltop, blurred by flying snow. I parked half on the asphalt of the entry road, half on slushy grass. Generations of interments had left no room for Mitch Braunfelter up on the hill. His grave waited down lower, near a limestone wall beside the train tracks. He wouldn't mind the noise.

Reflections of utility truck drivers stumped into my side mirrors. They'd parked across the street and walked over. Veteran linemen, every one, I could tell by their permanent squints and casual disregard for what spiraled from the sky. They'd been out in worse.

The hearse was an inkblot against a whitewashed backdrop. Rorschach might have overanalyzed my first impression: to me it just meant someone had died. A copy of the man back at the funeral home was closing the rear hatch. The coffin had been transferred to a chrome-plated lowering device that straddled Mitch's six-foot-deep portal to Eternity. Mourners assembled one last time beneath a white protective awning.

The scene resembled a black-and-white newspaper article. Beneath the grainy image would be a few paragraphs in neat-edged columns about a beloved citizen whose head had been caved in for unknown reasons. Sad. Colorless. A December funeral.

My phone winked purple from the passenger seat. I left the irreverent thing locked in the car.

The Cumberland-Presbyterian preacher took charge of the graveside prayer. Mitch hadn't been a church member. The preacher wished he had. Certainly no one questioned Mitch's standing with God. The preacher simply would have appreciated more time to get to know him. We all want more time.

I listened, hat low, not much different from the stone sentry up on the hilltop.

People wept openly now. Mitch's mortal husk hovered too near the dirt for emotions to stay contained. Folding chairs squeaked as the living stood. Shivering hands touched the casket's cold polished ebony. Flowers and mementos were laid on its beautiful, horrible lid, hints of color in an otherwise monochromatic setting. Among rose reds and lily yellows, a rectangle of orange appeared. It was a magazine, like others I'd overlooked in drugstore checkout lines, decorated with alternating black and white squares, like the magazines I'd seen shredded in Mitch's ravaged Nashville house. A crossword puzzle book.

I stepped forward, because the book had been set there by the gorgeous aristocratic woman with coal-black hair, because Mitch had promised to find help, and no man makes that kind of promise just to himself.

• • •

Mitch's coffin was ratcheted underground. Assistants retrieved the straps which had supported it, disassembled the lowering machine and took the pieces away. Others took up shovels and began filling the hole. They put their backs into it. Weather this cold freezes Tennessee clay into iron.

Mourners dispersed, parsed into smaller groups by slithering curtains of snow. With no better plan, I approached the dark-haired couple directly.

"Miss?" There was no telling whether a ring hid inside the sleek black gloves clutching her collar. I'd come looking for a hunch to play, why not guess double?

She stopped walking. More immediately, her companion put himself between us. He was all of five-foot-two, fierce as a

Flintlock

Bantam rooster and soft as a leaf spring on a one-ton pickup. I could knock him down if I wanted, but he'd pop right back up again. His eyes weren't as dark as the rest of him; they were pale gray iridescent pools of anger.

"Why'd you leave a crossword book?" I persisted.

"That is between her and the deceased." The man's voice suited him, taut, focused, spiced with warning.

Looking over him wasn't difficult. He must have endured being looked over since middle school. Probably that accounted for the ferocity. I found the girl's eyes, which were neither pale nor gray, but deep wet blue, with lids swollen from crying and mascara starting to run. She was worth going to a funeral to see.

"Grief is only as private as you want it to be," I said, to her, not him.

"Look, Mister——?"

Here was the opportunity to present my lackluster business card. The little shit made no move to take it.

"Tyler Bedlam. Mitch interviewed me for a job but before he could...well..."

"Mr. Bedlam, this is hardly an ideal time!"

"It's an awful time. Sorry about that. It's just Mitch said he'd promised to find help."

The girl's blue eyes brightened with surprise, alarm, maybe something else.

"I think *you* were who he promised," I said. "Otherwise, you'd have brought flowers."

The bantamweight twitched toward me. I was going to have to test my theory about his bouncing back to his feet. She outmaneuvered us both and reached past him for my card.

"Eli, stop!"

Her whisper didn't carry much confidence Eli would listen, but he simmered down.

She brought my card close, gently blew clinging snowflakes

Jon A. Hunt

away. I bet it was fun watching her put out the candles on her birthday cake, something which couldn't have yet happened thirty times. Big sapphire eyes measured me from beneath her lashes.

"You're a bit late."

"Mitch wanted to wait till Friday afternoon. He only had till that morning. I'm still here to help. You, maybe. I don't need a dime. Just a phone call."

Eli fairly quivered. Restraining himself wasn't easy. We were both looking over him. Her eyes moved away then returned to me, shining with fresh tears.

"I'll think about it," she said.

Flintlock

Chapter Four

I found a hotel, across from the remnants of Columbia's mall, that had one unbooked twin room. The man at the counter told me a convention down in Hohenwald had consumed that town's available lodging and spilled into Columbia. Still, few parking spaces were occupied outside the mall. If the Viper hadn't traveled most of the last blocks sideways, I'd have gone and bought a pair of shoes out of pity. As it was, I left the car parked slightly askew outside the hotel, hoisted the overnight bag I kept ready in the trunk and checked myself in for a reflective evening in Mule Town.

The room was clean and simple, a little heavy on the earth tones. I tossed my jacket and tie onto a beige desk chair. My clothes weren't as fancy as Keller's but did a better job of concealing a shoulder rig. I shrugged out of that and laid it strategically on the second bed. The leather fit right in with the rest of the place, or would have except for the black Smith & Wesson semiautomatic jutting from the holster. I found a receptacle under the nightstand lamp for my phone charger, unlocked the screen. No missed calls. I hadn't gotten the woman's name at the graveside, just Eli's, who interested me less. The purple blinking had quit. A software update, maybe. I'd give Danny a call on Monday to be sure.

Drawing the brown drapes aside revealed descending flakes that obscured the view twenty feet from the window. I settled

Jon A. Hunt

into the beige chair and propped my feet on top of the air conditioner to watch the snow fall.

The fresh-turned sod over Mitch Braunfelter's grave wore a layer of clean white by now.

• • •

I had no such opportunity for private contemplation over breakfast. The hotel common areas brimmed with competing conversations and an abundance of coonskin caps. A loquacious fellow in head-to-toe furs at the bagel bar explained. They were there for the Second Annual Meriwether Lewis Exhumation Convention.

"We're gonna get together and make whatever noise it takes, so's the government allows the proper recognition and funeral such a great man deserves. Every year on the 28th. That's the anniversary of Guv'nor Lewis' arrival in D.C. in 1806 after the Expedition, you know."

"Wouldn't the anniversary of his death be more appropriate?" I asked.

He muttered something about members not having vacation time in October, lost interest in furthering my education, and left me alone.

By the time I poured out the rest of my coffee, sunlight made every window in the dining room sparkle. People began to rethink wearing coonskin caps indoors. A weatherman on the lobby TV promised highs in the upper fifties, though he was the same slippery character who swore last night we'd wake to six inches of accumulated snow. Nothing remained of his supposed blizzard except puddles and soggy lawns.

I settled my bill and decided I might as well go see Mitch's real house. My phone resumed its purple strobing as I punched the Viper's starter button. I turned the phone off again. I'd already looked up the address. No two places in Mule Town are especially far apart.

The house was an updated craftsman, white, with a green

Flintlock

shingle roof and a gravel driveway, on the opposite side of Riverside Drive from the Duck River. The yard was unmowed and unfenced. Mitch hadn't owned a pet. Probably the Dachshund yapping and lunging against the end of a chain next door had convinced him pets were a bad idea. I could hear the dog over the engine.

But the dog did clue me in on the fact that Mitch's place was watched.

The city had turned the space between the flood-prone Duck and Riverside Drive into a walking park with concrete paths, vista points and pedestrian bridges. Just downstream from Mitch's empty home, an old concrete dam carved the stream into twenty-foot liquid stair steps. A small parking lot accessed the footpaths, the riverbanks below the dam, and a concrete catwalk to the dam's control house that was fenced and padlocked. A newer metal shed, with an electric transmission yard inside a chain link enclosure, had taken over generation duties once performed within the older structure. High-voltage lines swept from the shed across the river between ponderous steel towers on either bank. A gravel track with dead crabgrass for a center stripe looped around the TVA yard on the river side, then rejoined the street directly opposite Mitch's house.

Gates ordinarily closed both ends of that road. Today, however, the gate facing the house hung open and a black Crown Victoria sat in the opening. I wouldn't have guessed Columbia had undercover cops. A man's head swiveled behind the windshield to watch the Viper growl past, likely his most entertaining sight all morning. He had the driver's door open with one foot outside. The end of a lit cigarette flared briefly in the breeze.

I kept the speedometer five over the limit. He wasn't there to nab speeders.

• • •

I parked in the empty lot and got out to stretch my legs. I hadn't been outside with my jacket unzipped for weeks. The icy steps down to the river's edge discouraged casual investigation. I drifted uphill instead. Signage on the catwalk gate warned of danger to unauthorized personnel and prison time for aggravated criminal trespass. I made a mental note to look up the legal definition; I'd probably done it once or twice. The river sloshed under the catwalk, rolling in equal parts through six concrete arches. The water looked how it always did: brown.

How often had Mitch come down here?

Meandering up Riverside Drive would be a surefire way of adding myself to the undercover guy's stakeout notes. I wanted another look at Mitch's home, anyway.

The dog had shut up, though I stood in plain view of its sovereign territory. The Crown Vic hadn't moved. Knowing what I did of Dachshunds, this combination felt unnatural. A quick glance couldn't hurt.

The car's door remained open. A fresh cigarette fizzled at the edge of a puddle. The cigarette wasn't odd in itself except that it had been lit and not smoked.

A white minivan with tinted windows appeared on Riverside Drive heading toward town. I looked down at melting slush on the sidewalk where it crossed the mouth of the gravel road and tried to appear uninteresting till the minivan was gone. New footprints crossed the slush. They traveled away from the undercover car, toward Riverside Drive and Mitch's house. They were the largest footprints I'd ever seen made by anything wearing shoes.

All was quiet across the street.

The Dachshund didn't bark because it was swinging, dead, on the end of its chain, which had been thrown over a tree limb ten feet above the doghouse.

The man in the Crown Victoria wasn't going to turn me in.

Flintlock

He had both feet inside the car and both hands on the wheel, but he wasn't going to drive anywhere, either. His head was twisted like a bottlecap, ninety degrees too far. Unseeing eyes stuck to the headrest. The lower jaw hung permanently open, drooling.

I sprinted across the street and up the front steps and tried the door without permission. The knob turned loosely, its inner mechanism snapped as effortlessly as the man's neck on the other side of Riverside Drive.

I trespassed.

I wasn't the first person to do so. The Smith & Wesson went in with me.

• • •

The door might as well have opened into another house forty miles away and a week in the past. I'd seen this before: curtains and walls torn down, carpet pulled up, everything in the kind of disarray a tornado leaves, except the roof was still on and tornadoes don't sort debris into piles. Tornadoes aren't looking for anything.

Metallic racket spilled from another room beyond a half-demolished wall. Saucepans. One after another. Bouncing off a tiled kitchen floor.

The gun's checkered grips dug into my right palm. My left hand couldn't be persuaded to let go of the doorknob behind me. While I hovered in the entry between my semiautomatic and my hardwired desire for self-preservation, two new sounds joined the fray. A warbling shriek told me the neighbor had discovered her strangled Dachshund. And a rending boom, that made the floor jump underfoot, must have been another refrigerator toppling. I trained the gun's front sight on a hallway that led to the kitchen. King Kong was in there, folding appliances.

"You won't find it," I said. "It isn't here."

The commotion in the next room ceased. Outside, the

neighbor lady hadn't stopped screaming; owners tend to share personality traits with their pets. The mangled living room was dark for daytime—untended hedges blocked the bare picture windows and the ceiling light had been slapped away—but I had enough light to shoot.

"Let's talk. I'll be nice if you are." My gut told me diplomacy was the only option that might not require another December funeral.

The big guy wasn't a talker. But he did come to the living room. Not nicely. Not via the hallway. He came through a wall. Plaster exploded and sprayed the room, stung my eyes, disoriented me. Boards snapped, structural timbers, the ones you're supposed to leave alone when remodeling. A table-sized chunk of ceiling collapsed into the space. I'd lost track of the front door, so my left hand joined my right to steady my aim. I fired point blank into a raging mass that shoved wall studs aside on its way to crush me. Muzzle flash briefly illuminated a heavy-browed face, hideous, sort of human.

At that range a .45 slug ought to have knocked a normal man down. This one roared back at me. He kept clawing the wall away. One of those colossal feet kicked through. I jerked the trigger again. The Smith & Wesson bellowed. At least I was louder.

This time my assailant doubled over with a grunt. Then he straightened again and came on. I'd pissed him off. Some diplomat I was.

A third party settled our argument. The house decided matters by letting go of the rest of the living room ceiling. Plaster and wood joists and blown-in insulation crashed over us both. I groped for the front door, never found it, dove instead for a picture window.

Bashing down walls must have been the one-man wrecking crew's confrontational style. He didn't follow me through the window. He went out the back, by a door or through another

Flintlock

wall, and he made a godawful noise going. A dog in the alley lost its cool, then more distant yards contributed with baying and howling. For the dogs' sakes, I hoped he kept running.

The hedge that tried to catch me was as sharp and brittle as the window fragments. Leafless twigs snapped and deposited me onto cold wet grass. I let my .45 go to ground without me. My shoulder hurt—doctors hadn't thought to forbid jumping through windows—but I still lifted both hands slowly over my head.

A bunch of Columbia cops were watching me sit on my ass on Mitch Braunfelter's lawn. They watched me over their gun sights.

Chapter Five

He introduced himself as Tug Moran. Whether *Tug* was a nickname or his parents had a sense of humor, anyone that solidly built needn't worry about it. I watched the upper portion of his face in the rearview mirror, sapphire-hard eyes that mismatched a lot of boyish freckles. His military mow-job barely left sufficient stubble to confirm he was a redhead. He didn't mention being the Chief of Police. He didn't need to. Mule Town is small enough the big brass occasionally roll up their sleeves and do the little jobs.

"In town long, Mr. Bedlam?" It was a funny question to bounce off a guy wearing handcuffs in the back of a squad car.

"I'm not sure."

When Chief Moran grinned, he looked his age. A man doesn't earn those kinds of laugh lines till he's survived long enough to laugh as his own seriousness.

"I know you didn't lay a hand on my man in the car." The corners of his eyes smoothed. "Your feet are too small."

"I'm glad you noticed."

"Nobody invited you inside that house."

"Who invited the other guy?"

Chief Moran continued as if I hadn't made any smartass cracks. He'd heard worse from that back seat. "In light of circumstances and your unwarranted... assistance...trespassing charges might be dismissed."

Flintlock

"If——?" I said.

Hard blue eyes flitted to the mirror with meaning. "No more trespassing. No altercations. No loitering, no running lights, no double parking, nothing. As long as your name doesn't come over dispatch, you won't bother me and I won't need to bother you. But if it does…"

I might be more than just a little job for the big brass. Tug Moran already had a town of thirty-odd thousand potential problems to justify his existence before I showed up.

"Point taken," I said.

"Good. A friend's going to take you for a quiet drive till news crews are finished with the place. Columbia doesn't need that kind of publicity. I'm sure you understand."

• • •

My friend for the quiet drive was none other than Jerry Rafferty.

"I thought only pimps drove these."

"Keep on if you'd rather spend the night in Maury County Jail." The Lieutenant left me to open the front passenger door for myself. His midnight blue Cadillac had so little company at the curb, I suspected other cars were intimidated. "Your stuff's in the back."

A trash bag over the heated leather seat-back yielded my belt, wallet, keys and empty shoulder rig. Rafferty's eyes held the road better than the Caddy, which preferred an extra lane when it could get one.

"They kept your gun for ballistics."

"I've got a backup."

"You *had* one, if you mean that Glock stashed under the driver's seat."

At least my phone hadn't been retained. I lifted that from the bag last.

"Battery's flat."

"Who went through my things? Them or you?"

Jon A. Hunt

A corner of Rafferty's mouth twitched. The phone lit up when I pressed the power button, because it only ever turned on for me, my one perfect relationship. No purple blinking now. I let him see the screen glowing then plunked the device in my otherwise useless holster.

"Tug said he'd leave that toy car of yours where you parked it till I brought you back."

"He's a great guy," I said, "looking out for me since I got to town."

Rafferty's trademark inscrutable growl preceded: "He's too busy to arrange for a flatbed. Whoever you ran out of Braunfelter's place vanished when the cops showed. Somebody saw a white van, no one's sure. No Columbia cops are going home till they're certain he's really gone. If you mean Moran watching *you*, you're half right. You weren't on his radar till you busted in there. Columbia guys had an eye on the *house* all week."

"Jerry, you didn't drive this living room on wheels down here to gossip."

"You didn't mind your own business like I asked."

"Columbia isn't in your jurisdiction," I countered. "What's up?"

"Lots," muttered the Lieutenant.

• • •

A mere drive around the block wasn't sufficient for Rafferty's explanation, and nobody hates loitering in parking lots more than a cop. He found a scenic route. Automatic climate control pegged the cabin temperature at seventy-two degrees. If any bumps passed under us, no indication of them reached my seat.

"Your client—"

"Mitch never finished hiring me," I reminded him.

"Yeah. You said that. Why're you here, then?"

Arguing with Jerry Rafferty was usually productive that

Flintlock

way. Like pissing into a tornado. He waited for me to realize it, then: "Braunfelter isn't the only dead guy we found with a house remodeled around him."

"All the neat little piles?"

"Uh huh. First up in Louisville in September. Same mess, owner flattened under a piano. Like in cartoons, only nastier. Second was in Belle Meade. Missed Thanksgiving Dinner for it. Antiques collector named Jorgensen. He wasn't popular, or I'd have gotten the call when he was fresher. A lot of the stink was money."

Rafferty wouldn't toss around adjectives about wealth idly. He knew my financial standing. That meant this Jorgensen had belonged to the upper one percent.

"Did Bigfoot use his head for a battering ram, too?"

"'Bigfoot'?"

"Have a better name?" If you talk about people behind their backs, you have to call them something.

Rafferty grunted. "No. Jorgensen had a .60 caliber tunnel blown through his face."

"Sixty!"

"They used man-sized bullets back in the day. Black powder, close range. House is a regular war museum—he owned hundreds of old guns—whoever offed him probably used one of those. Weird part was he'd been dead a couple days *before* his place got turned upside down and the alarm system dialed out."

"Separate incidents? Or the killer might have come back for something."

"Don't know," said the Lieutenant. "Maybe. Alarm didn't go off the first time. Place is airtight, except for a back gate not visible to neighbors and an owner who was allergic to cameras. Apparently, he worried someone might tap into them from outside."

I nodded. I'd seen it done. Rafferty continued.

Jon A. Hunt

"Nobody saw a thing. We have an idea what *might* have been taken but aren't sure what was supposed to be there in the first place. Getting Jorgensen's insurance company to share information takes an act of Congress. Meantime, we have the next best thing: museum-class antiques expert. Guy knows his shit. If the gun we're looking for is on site, he'll find it. Jorgensen had muskets, dueling pistols, you name it. A lot haven't gone bang since Gettysburg. But a killer coming back for a dropped weapon can't explain the mess, or the other places upended before and since. Counting Braunfelter's two houses, that's *six* around Nashville, plus the other in Kentucky. No one was home the other times."

Mitch's words revisited me from a noisy coffee shop, on a Wednesday morning, already prehistorically distant.

I brought something home I wasn't meant to. It's very old...

None of this was really my business. Why was I here?

Why was *Jerry Rafferty* here?

I grinned across a plateau of burled walnut and stitched leather.

"Don't look at me like that."

"What do you need, Jerry?"

He flicked a big forefinger at the turn indicator lever, which darted in the intended direction out of self-preservation. The Caddy surged around a short-haul semi and reclaimed its original lane. I didn't hear the engine.

"You're gonna snoop. I could use extra eyes."

"You hiring me?"

"Saving you bail ought to be worth a few days."

"Fair enough," I said.

"I'll expect you to keep this conversation out of any *other* conversations."

"Standard client confidentiality applies."

That was the best promise he could expect. Rafferty had tried unsuccessfully to coax information from me about my

Flintlock

clients in the past. He percolated a while.

"I'm supposed to drop my best lead," he said finally.

"Supposed to?"

"Been told. Explicitly. Leave it to TBI, at least for a few weeks. The unemployment office was mentioned. On administrative leave now. But it's the only trail we've got that isn't a dead end and I'm not convinced the Bureau is pursuing it with urgency. My team just stepped where they shouldn't have, before the lead panned out."

"Since when do you worry about people's toes?"

"I arrested the DA's kid."

"Oops."

"Shit yeah, oops! He wasn't breaking any law as far as we can tell. Just in the wrong place at the wrong time. You're not the only person with that talent."

"You want me to take over while you're in the penalty box."

"Yeah."

Fields of dead corn stalks swept by, gray twiggy rubble. White slush clung defiantly to the broken dirt.

"Tell me how we got here, then. You haven't given me any secrets to keep so far."

"I'm going to. This goes back months, a string of targeted burglaries across the state and up into Kentucky. Colonial American antiques. I'm not talking quilts. I mean one-of-a-kind things, legal papers, diaries, letters, from the United States' formative years. When the stuff's insured—most isn't—you need special appraisers and there's only a dozen in the country. Not just any hack can tell you what Ben Franklin's bank statements are worth. That consultant checking Jorgensen's arsenal is one of them, or used to be, before he started working for TBI. Regional guy, sort of a cross between forensics guru and archeologist. Weird but whip smart.

"Someone's stealing stuff nobody knows how to insure.

35

Jon A. Hunt

Guards, dogs, fences, security systems, doesn't matter: they get away clean, whatever they take is permanently gone. No pawn shops. Never hits black markets here, never shows up overseas. I've learned since that happens a lot with museum pieces. The burglaries aren't making the news. Regular people have no clue the items stolen exist, and victims usually report only the *break-in*, not what's been *taken*."

"Victims might be thieves themselves," I mused. "And if it's other collectors who reel these things in, maybe they just want to hang onto what they took."

The Caddy swooshed around another slower car. *All* of the other cars were slower. I wondered aloud what might tie Mitch to a billionaire like Jorgensen. He hadn't struck me as particularly crazy about Colonial Americana. Rafferty expected the question.

"Know that bookstore off West End, the one with all the Civil War trinkets?"

I did. Shoehorned into a constricted block within walking distance of Vanderbilt's main campus, the place had claustrophobic aisles, sagging shelves and a chronic cobweb problem. Between the shelves were display cases full of notched bayonets, Minié balls, uniform buttons, and tatters that were either Confederate battle flags or abused dish towels. Few institutions this side of the Mississippi had better access to rare old books. The same family had run things without notable interruption since Prohibition. They were tremendously successful, and the color of their skin hadn't seemed to be any hindrance; their chief concession to the whiteness around them was a somewhat misleading surname.

"O'Dell's," I said. Nothing Irish about it.

"That's the one."

"And the connection to Mitch Braunfelter…"

"Team working the burglary angle have it in their heads O'Dell's is a transfer point for misappropriated antiques. Not

Flintlock

tough to believe. Remember those articles last year about the store buying stolen textbooks and selling them back to students? Old man O'Dell swore it was just a ploy to sell papers. He demanded a retraction. Paper stuck to its guns, even ran its own undercover investigation. O'Dell started a defamation suit, but he was too old and sick to deal with lawyers and the whole thing blew over when he died. But once a suspect, always a suspect. Why not bigger things than textbooks? No one denies damned valuable material moves through there. I don't guess you read about the Shakespeare First Folio?"

I confessed ignorance clumsily. Hearing the name *Shakespeare* from Jerry Rafferty rattled me a little.

"The First Folio is a book of plays from the 1600s. Not my thing. But there's just a couple hundred copies and a few rich nutjobs will pay anything for them. Paul Allen from Microsoft let go of six million and change for his. O'Dell's briefly had *two* on hand."

"That ratty little store?"

"Happens more often than you think. And they've got next to no security. Go figure. So, a tip comes in about a hand-off of potentially old, valuable parcels. This was right after we found Jorgensen missing most of his brains and odds were fair his things might be in the deal. Not the kind of opportunity we take lightly. Sent my guys to join the crew working the burglary cases, we set up a raid, right in the store, normal business hours."

"And?"

"I should've listened to my gut. Too easy. Wasn't the same people who always vanished without a sign. This was an inept attempt to offload who-knows-what to Nashville small-fry. Maybe even an intentional set-up to make us look stupid. And boy, did we look stupid.

"The real perpetrators and the real goods—if there were

any—split with ordinary customers. We couldn't detain *everybody*. Braunfelter may have been one of the shoppers who left just before we jumped five guys."

"What did he buy?"

"Beats me. Receipts are sketchy. Cameras weren't working that day. Tough to believe anybody at O'Dell's even if they told me."

"What about the five guys?"

Rafferty glared at the dash. Big quiet cars don't make a fuss about doing ninety. He lifted his foot slightly. The guard rails became less blurry.

"Five wrong guys," he rumbled. "One a lot wronger than the rest. DA Langston chewed my ass for an hour. He only agreed to stop his son from pressing charges *if* my team steered clear of O'Dell's till after New Year's and I took this unscheduled time off."

"His son agreed, too?"

"Only just. Kid's got anger issues. He was at the funeral, by the way, the son. Eli."

Suppressing my smirk wasn't easy. "We met. DA Langston has more than one kid?"

"Probably. Married three or four times. Hell, I didn't know who Eli was till we had him face down on the floor in cuffs. Why?"

"Eli didn't look like the only Langston there."

"Uh huh. You helping me, then, or not?"

"Might as well." Rafferty was right, I was going to look anyway.

"All right. I have a couple angles for you. Obvious one is O'Dell's. Still something fishy about the place and the DA's kid shopping there doesn't improve the aroma. We got shut down before we could dig deep. If you can find out what we couldn't without making a nuisance of yourself, do it. If you can't be discreet, I'd rather you stayed away. I got a mortgage.

Flintlock

"All we know about Jorgensen's will so far is he was an asshole. Left his entire collection to museums, not relatives. None of the relatives are in the States, anyway. The insurance company is keeping a low profile because they're sick of us asking for information they aren't obligated to share—and TBI already hired the same expert the underwriters want to talk with when we're finished. He's overseeing the crime scene and he's the only person qualified to shoot those old guns for ballistics. He's your second angle.

"He says he could use a hand, especially now that none of my people except Poole are allowed on site. Tremaine Gering. Goes by *Tipper*. He's an independent consultant, so he isn't on Metro's or TBI's regular roster, and he isn't held to the limits Langston slapped on the rest of us. I'll let him know you're coming. He'll tell you more than you thought to ask."

Scenery traveled past my window at a leisurely pace now, familiar scenery. The Cadillac shushed down Riverside Drive. Mitch Braunfelter's home had four police cruisers out front. Water spilling over the old dam had gotten higher. Otherwise, the neighborhood was living another typical Mule Town Sunday. Rafferty steered into the lot by the dam, which now held more pedestrians than vehicles. The Viper brought more attention than a dead cop up the road.

"Watch Eli," the Lieutenant cautioned as I undid my seatbelt. "Kid wants me canned. I'd appreciate it if you didn't give his dad reasons to do it."

I grinned back at Rafferty.

"Don't look at me like that," he said and pulled the door shut.

Jon A. Hunt

Chapter Six

Danny Ayers wasn't old enough to rent a car without a cosigner. But blindfold him and give him a box of loose wires and old computer chips, and he'd build a mobile phone. Or a rocket guidance system. That's why NASA snatched him up before the ink dried on his high school diploma. He breezed through MIT quicker than all the ordinary geniuses and Uncle Sam giddily footed the bill. Like many federal expenditures, however, Danny proved to be a bad investment. This wasn't because he failed to live up to his potential. It just doesn't take a rocket scientist to follow big money. My father outbid NASA's compensation by the cost of a lunar expedition, and Cool-Core Technologies had owned Danny ever since. When Dad was gone, I inherited Cool-Core and Danny.

Danny had made and programmed my fancy phone. Out of brand-new parts, with his eyes open. When the thing acted strange, Danny was the person to call on Monday morning.

"Wha-huh?"

"Coffee fixes that," I said.

Muffled noises of a person fumbling into wakefulness found my ear. I tipped a dose of my own prescription into a mug from a French press, because the coffee shop down the street wouldn't be open for another hour. Danny rejoined me with a few more synapses firing.

"Kinda early, Ty. Everything okay?"

Flintlock

"I'm fine," I said. My weather shoulder hardly bothered me and I'd slept well. "The phone's being weird. I thought firmware updates were a green LED."

"They are. I haven't scheduled anything since last month. When did it start?"

Danny always initiated my phone upgrades directly from Cool-Core's central network. It was more secure than an unsupervised overnight download, he insisted.

"Last Saturday," I said, "but the blinking isn't *green*, it's purple."

"Where are you?"

"My kitchen."

"Is it blinking now?"

I held the phone at arm's length, then pressed it back to my ear. "No. It's sporadic—"

Was it sporadic? I considered the instances: en route from Arbuckle Brothers to Mitch Braunfelter's graveside, no blinks in the hotel, again as I drove through Columbia Sunday, not in Rafferty's Cadillac, then as soon as I got back in the Viper—

"It only happens in my car," I realized.

"Your phone's okay." Danny sounded fully alert now. "There's a low-frequency transmitter in the car that didn't used to be. The phone picks up the signal and the purple blinking light is a warning."

"The Viper's bugged?"

"No. You get a text message for that. A little angry ladybug picture. This isn't anything complex. I bet it's just a GPS tag."

"A homing beacon."

"Sorta." My grasp of his native jargon failed to impress. "Wanna bring it by and I can find it for you? Probably has to be next week, though. I'm at Vandy till Thursday, helping with their new security software."

"No hurry," I said. "I'm sure Griffin's still simmering about last time."

Jon A. Hunt

Brad Griffin was Danny's supervisor at Cool-Core. Danny was close to being a millionaire if he ever stopped to think about it; Griffin's job was to keep him too busy for extraneous thinking. He'd never taken kindly to my borrowing his lead engineer.

I thanked Danny and let him get back to whatever constituted his pre-work routine. Frigid grayness spilled into my living room through floor-to-ceiling windows. From nineteen floors up, nothing about Monday promised to be close to Sunday's unseasonal warmth. It was a safe bet Keller Ableman would just track my movements from his office computer, instead of freezing his trendy ass off following me the old-fashioned way.

Of course the GPS tag was Keller's. He loved shit like that.

• • •

I'd have found Erik Jorgensen's place without Rafferty's directions. Eventually. I didn't know my way around Belle Meade half as well as I thought. My phone's navigation was equally clueless; I left the thing face down on the passenger seat, blinking purple. Somewhere, Keller was trying to decipher a lot of circles I made on his computer screen. It didn't help that most of the fancy Belle Meade street signs were absent, as if someone had paid to make sure the signs weren't installed. People with too much money can spend creatively.

A massive granite wall came into view. Constructed of polished slabs the size of billiard tables, the structure utterly failed to hide behind rows of leafless pin oaks. Pretentious brick homes glared at the Viper's passage, watching through tall windows across well-groomed dead lawns. The homeowners assuredly held similar opinions about their wealthier neighbor across the street. Not that guys who shut themselves inside twelve-foot stone walls give a rat's ass what the neighbors think.

The front gate was simple. One black scrolled iron section,

Flintlock

with minimal ornamentation yet as high as the walls, had been left rolled aside. Jorgensen was dead, the estate robbed. No point remained in shutting the gate now. I didn't see the back entrance Rafferty had mentioned.

The Viper rumbled inside and gave the neighbors something to wonder about. Maybe the person in the colorless sedan, by the curb a quarter block beyond the entrance, wondered along with the neighbors. He was no local. His car wasn't nice enough. And locals didn't sit in their cars at the roadside. People talk.

Beyond the gate sprawled a sizeable lot. The trees inside had an unrealistic appearance; they'd learned better than to sprout twigs in unapproved directions. The grass hadn't grown since Erik Jorgensen lost his stare-down with a vintage firearm. Aside from groundskeeping expenditures, all that made the place ritzy was that looming granite backdrop beyond the trees. The house was large and continued the granite motif at the corners and around doors and windows, nice, just no grander than others in the area.

A vehicular quartet occupied the roundabout in front of the house: a police cruiser, a white utility truck with blue stripes and TBI markings, a vanilla Nissan, and a rusted pickup truck no self-respecting salvage yard would accept for scrap metal. The truck's owner perched on its tailgate, beefy shoulders hunched, his face tipped to peer through clouded breath at an open paperback on his knees. I knew the truck and the man. He glanced up unconcernedly while I parked the Viper. He was a looming hard-as-nails plainclothes detective with an embarrassing library and a cute name.

"What are you still doing here, Smally?" I said.

He snapped the paperback shut with one bear paw of a hand. The drugstore smut Smally preferred hardly required a bookmark.

"Babysitting," he confided, "till you showed. Metro crew's

Jon A. Hunt

supposed to bug out and leave the TBI people alone by end of the day. Except Poole. He's inside with the Professor."

"They wouldn't let you read in a corner?"

"'Stay the fuck out,' the boss said." Smally slid off the tailgate and brushed rust from his backside without needing to look to see if rust was there.

The tailgate required two tries for the latch to catch but I counted *three* bangs. Smally stopped me from hauling that morning's new .45 caliber purchase from under my arm.

"Not what you think," he explained. "Just the Professor test-firing antiques. Indoor range. None of us knows how to load the things. TBI lets him do it. Kinda interesting till he starts droning on about it. Go on in."

• • •

Not surprisingly, the front steps were chiseled granite. The estate was lousy with the stuff. I'd been told Jorgensen was the sort who expected people—employees, family, guests, staff—to go elsewhere when he was finished with them. He'd been killed on a Friday night and no one bothered checking in on him before he was found on Sunday night. Being dead, Jorgensen was as finished with everybody as a person gets. I let myself in.

Only the left-hand ironwood entry door swung inward. Rubble against the other door's warm side held it securely as any deadbolt. The grand foyer impressed me. Not in a good way. Mitch hadn't owned enough things in *both* of his houses to fuel a mess on this scale.

What remained of the interior occupied dozens of familiar piles. They marched perpendicularly away from the doors, with slender footpaths between them that lay bare to the granite floor. The paths resembled miniature city streets, a small rendition of London during the Blitz. Police work hadn't progressed into the foyer, although the TBI crew industriously prodded more heaps in an adjacent room. I watched them through an opening with ragged edges that might have been

Flintlock

gnawed by a teething Tyrannosaur. The forensics techs' smocks contrasted violently with filthy surroundings. Work lights on portable stands were everywhere: all that was left of the ceiling lights were broken wires spilling from holes.

I cleared my throat. A tech glanced up in annoyance then left the room. I pressed the door shut behind me with the sole of a shoe. At least the heat was working.

Officer Poole entered via another damaged archway. Stepping between wall studs was a more direct route, but civilized people use doors. He was lean and wiry and his face had a youthful smoothness, except for starter wrinkles at the outer corner of each eye. He reached forward to shake my hand.

"Welcome to Ground Zero, Mr. Bedlam."

He said it like we'd been joking about such things our whole lives. But Poole's uniform still had factory creases, and I'd only known him six of his seven months on the force. In that short time, he'd already witnessed first-hand how contemptable and undeserving the public he'd sworn to serve and protect could be. He showed up for work anyway. He'd be a damned fine cop in another couple years, provided a bullet or an overwhelming sense of irony didn't interrupt his advancement.

"Have they made any progress?" I asked Poole because he'd give a straight answer without bridling like the specialists in the other room would. My existence seemed to insult them on principle.

"Not in here," he said, "but you have to see the rest of the house to get an idea what they're up against. You'd think whoever did this had twenty helpers and——"

Another muted gunshot cut into the conversation from behind him. The Professor test-firing another antique. Poole scarcely reacted beyond a mid-sentence pause. The sound was oddly compartmentalized, more like two close-set explosions rather than a single blast, so he had a split second to prepare.

"Good timing," Poole said afterward and waved me into the next passage. "It'll be a bit before he shoots again. I'll introduce you. Watch your step!"

• • •

By no means a modest residence, the home took on especially cavernous dimensions now that only studs were left for the interior walls. Sunlight from windows and antiseptic flares from work lights stabbed past vertical lumber, ignored ineffectual boundaries, blended each room unevenly into the next. It was disorienting. Poole had gotten used to navigating the avenues between cairns of gypsum board, insulation, furniture fragments and other debris, rather than trying to find hallways. The foyer hadn't been that bad in comparison. I expected when the investigation wrapped, they'd bulldoze the mess to its granite foundations.

The back third of the first floor used to be a sort of trophy room. Not much of the wreckage appeared modern. Windows with UV-tinted glass looked out across a still pond, manufactured hills, leafless trees. The omnipresent stone wall punctuated the little panorama. Too bad Jorgensen hadn't been much of a window gazer. From what I'd been told, his attention was always inward and backward.

The carpet here had *not* been pulled up. Divots embossed the shag to show where heavy display cases once rested. Those cases were reduced to oak splinters and glass shards, and everything from inside them occupied a phalanx of squared-off mounds along the window wall. Ignoble heaps of old wood and iron, these were the bones of Jorgensen's priceless small arms collection. Half the piles had since been removed. TBI's crew had set yellow numbered reference markers in their stead. They'd been busiest here, with good reason.

This was the room where Erik Jorgensen died.

The worst evidence was gone. Buried, I presumed, same as poor Mitch. But persistent stains left little to the imagination.

Flintlock

Jorgensen had been blasted from the point where Poole and I entered the room, then he'd pitched onto the carpet parallel to the windows.

"Did you see the—"

"No." Poole wagged his head. I could tell he was glad about that.

White-coated specialists watched intently as we continued through the space. I kept track of my feet. Tripping over evidence wouldn't earn me any gold stars.

Where the wall turned toward us, four paces to the right of the last spattered picture window, a metal door waited, partially open. Fluorescence gushed from the other side. Poole started through. Before following, I mortified the TBI guardian with a direct question.

"Which direction was he facing when he got shot?"

This was the forensics guy's area of expertise, his thing he did better than me, and my asking was as good as an admission to his superior skills. "Straight at the killer," he said.

"That's what I figured," I said and ducked through the door after Poole while the professional in the smock puzzled over what I meant.

I love messing with them.

Jon A. Hunt

Chapter Seven

Prior to his .60 caliber headache I might have envied Erik Jorgensen. He could shoot heirloom guns whenever he wanted, in his skivvies if he wished. A first-rate indoor firing range waited a minute's stroll from his dining room.

Past the metal door was an eight-by-eight anteroom and another metal door. A sign over the second door read *ENTER* in glowing green letters, which we did. A rubber-tiled staging area beyond crossed the ends of three lanes, two twenty-five yards deep, the third a full hundred-yard rifle lane. Each lane boasted sound deadening and an electric target conveyor with touchscreen controls at the bench—a twenty-first century proving ground for eighteenth century hardware. Spent black powder fowled the air in spite of whirring exhaust fans. Shelves with suede padding filled the upper half of the back wall. Cabinets underneath held targets and supplies. Whoever trashed the rest of the house had stopped short of the shooting gallery.

Poole let me enter ahead of him. No one else there seemed to notice us.

Real estate in front of the rifle bay was full of a large stainless-steel box that wasn't native. The contraption resembled a refrigerator on its side with the door open, coffin-like, except for eight steel legs that elevated it so the top was four feet above the floor. A forensics tech morosely crammed

Flintlock

squares of cotton batting edgewise into the opening. Cellophane-wrapped cubes of the batting were stacked behind him, nearly to the ceiling.

"Portable ballistics testing?"

"Yessir. Shoot into a hole on the end, cotton stops the bullet, tech unloads the cotton and finds the bullet, then he reloads new bats for the next shot."

"A college education gets you that."

Poole chuckled.

At a table between us and the bullet-catcher sat Tremaine Gering. The Professor tilted precariously on the edge of a chair, his back to us, lost in concentration. Yellow hearing protectors clamped either side of his head above the ears. The near cheek of a ruddy face gleamed in the blaze of two swing-arm desk lamps with their hoods pressed almost to the tabletop. Light flared from the multiple lenses of jeweler's glasses with flip-down sequential magnifiers. A hurricane of curls dodged over and around the earmuffs and shone like flames. The man looked either sorcerous, or like Harpo Marx in the headlights. His left hand leaped up, though he'd never turned toward our entrance, and an index finger extended in the universal request: give me a minute.

"No reason both of us should wait," I told Poole.

The officer grinned. He presented me with a package of disposable earplugs and retreated through the metal door. I pressed the door till the latch engaged and, I presumed, the *IN USE* sign lit up in the anteroom. I parked myself in an extra chair while the Professor used his requested minute several times over. The man stuffing cotton into the steel box didn't say "hello." I generally tolerate being ignored. It's the people who pay attention to you who cause most of your troubles.

Arrayed on the padded shelves were dozens of old-fashioned rifles and twice as many clear plastic evidence tubs. The tubs contained one antique pistol each and, like their larger

49

Jon A. Hunt

brethren, the pistols all wore a faint chalky dusting of fingerprint powder. Several were damaged. Guns hadn't changed so much in the last three centuries that I couldn't tell when parts weren't connected how they ought to be. Tremaine's responsibilities probably included field repairs where possible, before loading, firing and cataloging. Whatever kept him busy now bore scant resemblance to ballistics testing I'd witnessed elsewhere. He wore no gloves. Doubtless TBI had his prints on file and could discount them if they turned up later on weapons he'd tested, but that seemed sloppy handling by TBI standards.

"Bring your chair on over, Mr. Bedlam," he said without yet turning. "You'll appreciate a closer look."

I carried my seat across the room and sat again at the table to Gering's right. He beamed a toothy lantern-jawed smile at me from beneath the jeweler's glasses. Especially on the right side with both the five- and ten-power lenses flipped into place, his pupils showed grotesquely huge, with striations of green, hazel, brown and gray. Probably no two people who ever met him would easily agree on the color of Tremaine Gering's eyes, except that they were not blue.

"You're acquainted with firearms?"

"I am, just not any like these."

"The differences aren't as profound as people make them out to be."

The outsized gaze returned to the table and dragged me along with it. An ancient dueling pistol rested there on a commandeered batt. Every atom of fingerprint powder had been brushed away. A thick octagonal barrel reluctantly echoed the lamp light. Embellishments adorned the side-mounted action, which included a chiseled bit of flint swaddled in rawhide and gripped in a tiny clamp at the end of a short curved armature. The polished hardwood stock put any Louis IV chair leg to shame. I felt embarrassed for the brand-new lump of

Flintlock

Smith & Wesson pig iron under my left arm.

"Very pretty," I said.

"And deadly."

"Jorgensen?"

Gering plucked the complex eyewear from his face. His eyes seemed suddenly tiny, no less electric. "No," he said, "nobody's found that one. This gun's caliber is too small. But it isn't innocent. One must admit there's irony in trying to find this year's murder weapon in a house full of the last few centuries' murder weapons."

"I'm not sure I follow."

"Lieutenant Rafferty promised you would," returned the Professor. "Oh! Tremaine Gering, pleased to make your acquaintance."

I shook his offered hand, which in addition to being ungloved was strong and dry. He already knew my last name, so I just gave him my first. I asked if he was really a professor. He laughed warmly. Actually, everything about the man was warm, his handshake, his expressions, his hearty baritone. Veritable human sunshine.

"PhD," he admitted. "Colonial American history is my specialty, but Professor is more of an honorary title: it's hard to find time to teach. I lectured a couple courses at Vanderbilt. I'm more like an insurance adjuster for really obsolete things. Please, just call me Tipper."

"'Tipper'?"

I'd never seen a person shrug with just his eyes till that moment. "Not a clue. The kids came up with that, and it stuck."

I motioned toward the pistol. "This is a long way from the classroom."

"It is! But the authorities decided I'm a better choice to handle these old things than their own people. Metal gets tired, barrels and chambers can develop tiny fractures, and any of the weapons in the collection will explode if loaded improperly. I was hired to look over documents but having me do this is quicker than training someone else. There's really no point I can see in testing *every* gun here. They're insisting on it anyway. Just want to be thorough, I suppose."

"How many do you get to in a day?"

He brought the pistol off the table, cradled affectionately between the fingertips of both hands. "That depends on the condition of the weapons. Many of these were so overbuilt to begin with they can be tried after a quick check. Several were damaged in the break-in. I can put some back together. Some will never be usable again. A few, like this beauty, require an exta going-over and turn out fine in the end."

"Shouldn't you wear gloves?" The question was going to gall me till asked. Tipper's reaction surprised me.

"Absolutely not! Everything's been fingerprinted. But unless you're flipping pages in a Gutenberg Bible, history is meant to be touched! Sure, I'm better able to detect a structural flaw with bare fingers. There's more to it than that." His eyes shimmered with enthusiasm. "People only get bored with history because they're beaten over their heads with the disconnected versions between textbook covers."

He extended the pistol butt-first toward me in a way that invited no refusal. The TBI tech shot us the stink-eye. I took the pistol.

Heaviness I expected. My expectation was a couple pounds shy of reality. An inescapable thrill seeped from smooth wood and cool iron into my skin. Gering's smile hardened slightly with an understanding we both felt.

"*Reading* history isn't the same as *holding* history, is it, Mr. Bedlam?"

I shifted the weapon to my right hand, sighted down the barrel, out beyond the table into the darkened firing range. A white torso showed twenty yards away, one of Jorgensen's own

Flintlock

paper targets, suspended in the lane he'd never again use.

"How much history am I holding?"

"About two-hundred years."

Muscle memory elevated the gun at arm's length. The thing balanced nicely despite its heft. There was even a rudimentary brass front sight. How concerned ought a real human be at that distance?

"Would you be interested in shooting it?"

This was too much for the tech. "Mr. Gering—"

Tipper poo-poo'd him good-naturedly. "Come on, Allison. You know as well as poor Mr. Jorgensen did this isn't the gun that killed him."

I hadn't thought about it that way. If he'd faced his killer, Erik Jorgensen had known exactly what hit him. And of course I was curious.

"I wouldn't mind squeezing off a shot or two," I said.

Jon A. Hunt

Chapter Eight

The Viper departed Jorgensen's granite garden with the aural subtlety of a Rottweiler guarding a stolen ribeye. Exhaust twisted from the side-mounted pipes and piled like shaving cream in the gateway, where my taillights tinted it crimson. The headlights carved a path out onto the street through early evening fog. The temperature had bottomed out again and no one waited outdoors to be impressed, not even the person in the unremarkable sedan I'd noticed earlier. I seemed to have Belle Meade to myself, at least the parts without central heating. Streetlights began to flicker. Window rectangles across the neighbors' lawns leaked an uninviting glow. None of the fancy houses had Christmas lights burning. I left the transmission in a low gear so the car snarled inconsiderately on its way back to friendlier quarters.

On the passenger seat beside a paper-wrapped book Tipper had given me, my phone lay face down, off. It hadn't helped me find my way here, and I could do without a constant blinking reminder that every wrong turn would be remotely cataloged while I tried to get back home. Otherwise I didn't mind driving in circles. Getting lost is one of those things I've always been able to do while thinking, like peeling labels off empty beer bottles. Since Mitch's funeral I'd collected several new angles to consider.

Tipper Gering had added to that list. His assessment of Erik

Flintlock

Jorgensen's character differed little from Rafferty's: Jorgensen had been rich and aggressively unfriendly, and plenty of people wouldn't have minded firing a small cannonball through his face. Tipper also gave me a crash course on antique pistols. His only requested favors before we next met on Wednesday were that I return a reference book he'd borrowed from, of all places, O'Dell's, and fetch some drawings for one of Jorgensen's exotic pieces from another area expert. Black powder connoisseurs weren't as rare as I'd imagined. After a couple hours "test-firing" evidence in a dead man's private gun range, I understood the appeal.

Sootiness lingered on my tongue like cheap whiskey sipped by a campfire, not especially tasty, just a reminder. Each time I grabbed the shifter my right hand remembered the heavy lurch of undamped pistol recoil. Every streetlight was a still-frame memento of the duplex flash of a booming chunk of history. Tipper had loaded nine weapons for me. He was absolutely correct about touching the past. The sensation was almost spiritual.

"Mr. Bedlam, you're a fine shot!" he'd said. "If that piece's first owner had been half the marksman, he'd have lived longer."

"This one, too?"

"All of them. Jorgensen only collected death weapons."

"Cute hobby," I'd said.

A familiar intersection filled the windshield. I wasn't lost now. My brain returned to the question I'd brought with me to Belle Meade: what did any of this have to do with Mitch Braunfelter?

According to the dash clock, the day wasn't as far gone as December liked me to think. Tipper's firearms guru lived forty minutes away in Hendersonville. *Art's butler said swing by any evening between six and eleven.*

I wondered what kind of music Mitch had listened to. Dumb, useless question. I should at least guess.

Those crossword suspenders had *big band swing* written all over them.

I tapped up the satellite station. A scratchy recording with thumping two-four string bass sparred over the speakers with the car's exhaust rumble. Brass joined in, bee-bopping a riff older than my grandparents, building in volume and complexity.

Tuxedo Junction.

The poor guy could've been a Nickelback fan for all I knew. I wasn't going to subject myself to that, and in my mind Glenn Miller seemed a good fit.

I upped the volume and toed the accelerator.

• • •

My downtown condo was on the way. I didn't need anything upstairs, just the well-lit underground parking garage. I'd started to miss my phone and didn't feel like advertising my whereabouts much longer. Now was as good a time as any to see if I could find that homing beacon Danny Ayers said was attached to my car.

The garage consisted of more concrete than automobile. Tenants had Christmas shopping to finish. I lived in a twenty-story den of procrastinators. The Viper rumbled to a stop between its assigned stripes. I powered on my phone and set it on the dash where I could see it from outside, retrieved a penlight from the glovebox and got to business. The purple LED pulsed as expected.

I had no doubt at all Keller was who'd electronically branded my ride. I'd caught him near the car and computerized surveillance was his schtick. He probably had it printed on his business cards. I bet he had a swivel chair and a secretary who organized his file drawers, too.

The inner edges of the wheel wells earned me nothing

Flintlock

except grimy fingers. That wasn't where to look: Keller would never get his hands dirty. He hadn't been alone with the Viper more than a couple minutes. His hands and knees had been spotless. Most likely the GPS tag was magnetic for quick attachment to the average vehicle. Trouble was, a Viper GTS isn't an average vehicle. There aren't many places on one a magnet will stick.

I crouched beside the closed passenger door. Pretending my clothes were nicer than they were might help. The side exhaust pipes would have discouraged anyone from reaching underneath for the steel subframe, unless the car had been allowed to cool down...or if the car had been parked outside for a short time on a day cold enough to snow.

I let my knees touch the floor. The penlight flicked on. Heat from the pipe warmed the uphill side of my face, the concrete felt like ice on my downhill cheek.

There it was. A black rectangle, an inch square and a quarter inch deep, clung to the steel at an improper angle for factory work. It took effort to pry the stubborn thing free with my pocketknife, and then I had to stand on it and slide the blade from under my heel to get the magnet to let go. Afterward the GPS tag seemed docile as a perch out of water. My phone continued winking through the windshield. I brushed my knees and cheek off, returned to the car, drove out to downtown and Hendersonville beyond.

The little black rectangle went into a jacket pocket. I wasn't sure what to do with it yet. Force feeding Keller his own electronics crossed my mind but that would be unprofessional.

• • •

In the mid-fifties, the Army Corps of Engineers commissioned a dam across the Cumberland River where it ran through the DuPont factory town of Old Hickory. Old Hickory Road crossed the river's unaltered portion on a grand stone and iron bridge. Naturally, the ninety-seven-mile backup behind the

Jon A. Hunt

new dam was dubbed Old Hickory Lake. Tennesseans love catering to the ego of their favorite dead president. Lake homes, marinas and parks populated the reservoir's shores now, and locals considered the fattened stream a bona fide lake. But the Cumberland never completely changed character just to humor a concrete speed bump. It still followed its original sinuous track, merely wider and edged with tapered inlets where old tributaries flowed in, looking from the air like a Chinese dragon. Arthur Fontaine owned one of the larger curves along the dragon's back.

The car's navigation screen saw things that way. My view through the windshield was less expansive. I inched through a syrup of lake fog. Street signs were swallowed by the atmosphere, along with everything else higher than six feet. Eventually meager glimmers resolved into gas lanterns atop sturdy posts. Brass numbers affixed to each post corresponded with Tipper's directions. I pointed the headlight beams between the posts.

No gates waited. This rich gun nut was less obsessed with privacy than the dead one back in Belle Meade. The exhaust rumble faltered to a leaden thump. The world collapsed like a gray fallen tent around me. A platoon of lanterns materialized to reclaim a semicircle of dormant lawn from the mists. Their incandescence also delineated the driveway's end, low aggregate steps, the front doors. I saw little else beyond the doors, but they stood tall enough and wore fine enough hardware to belong to a mansion.

By the time I killed the engine a man in a jacket and tie stood beside the car. He'd simply appeared as the lamp posts had. In their glow I saw a suggestion of dark hair slicked sideways across his round head. His breath hung in lacy tendrils. I had the impression he'd open my door for me if I only asked.

"Good evening. Mr. Bedlam, is it?"

Flintlock

"Word gets around?"

He shared a smile more subtle than his hair style. "I cannot attest to that, sir. However, a description of your rather charismatic transportation was provided."

I liked him. I held out my hand. "Tyler."

"A pleasure, sir. I am Gerard." His gloved grasp was precisely as firm and lingering as discretion permitted. "Mr. Fontaine is expecting you."

• • •

Arthur Fontaine's lakeside manor resembled Erik Jorgensen's home the way a Kentucky thoroughbred resembles a 'possum. Even allowing for vandalism, this place had been better designed to impress from the get-go. Gerard glided ahead of me down a long foyer with no practical function. A muscular framework of cedar posts and arched cedar trusses held the vaulted cedar ceiling aloft. Rustic gas lanterns hung overhead. Between the posts on either side: uninterrupted glass. Tonight, the windows batted our reflections back and forth, multiplying us to infinity. I could only imagine the drama when morning sunlight streamed in from across the lake and defeated the reflections.

The foyer terminated at floor-to-ceiling glass panels. These swept aside with a scarcely perceptible hydraulic hiss. Gerard paused to accept my hat before proceeding. I made no move to relinquish my jacket.

"You are armed, sir?"

"I am." I could hardly be the first, or he wouldn't have asked.

Gerard cataloged the information with a nod and we continued. Beyond the panels the roof soared higher in a room large enough to accommodate the Southeast Democratic Convention. Here, at least, walls separated expanses of glass. Mr. Fontaine couldn't very well hang his art collection on the windows. A fieldstone chimney extended from the room's

Jon A. Hunt

center up into shadows. Most of the lights were off, except for slim glowing bars on wire arms that reached from the walls above the paintings. I recognized works by Remington and Russell. The paintings followed common themes: cowboys roping steers, cowboys hunting bears, gun battles in dusty streets, fleeing cavalry soldiers firing over their shoulders at a pursuing Sioux war party. Fontaine seemed especially fond of representations of the lucky shot. I supposed the pony soldier pitching off his horse with an arrow in his back held a different opinion.

The next door relied on an old-fashioned manual knob. Gerard operated the mechanism without complaint and waited for me to enter first. Arthur Fontaine's office had more lights burning. Its owner leaned against a colossal desk, reading his mail.

"You stink like a gun range, Mr. Bedlam." He had yet to glance up from a typewritten page in his hand. "Gerard, I'm sure all that smoke made him thirsty."

"What would you care to have, sir?" Gerard asked dutifully from the doorway.

I said *scotch, neat, please* and *thank you*. Fontaine might not be the only person in the room with money, but one of us had manners. Gerard left. The door clicked shut after him.

Fontaine deposited his correspondence on the blotter and faced me. His physical appearance matched his butler's to a startling degree. Aside from a predatory meanness in his eyes, Arthur and his man Gerard might be twins. Their personalities didn't match. Fontaine never offered a hand. And how he detected black powder on *me* when *he* wore the aroma of a bourbon mill on bottling day, I couldn't guess. I estimated him to be at least three glasses in.

"Tremaine said you've got blueprints of an old pistol to lend him," I said. Regular salutations were pointless.

"*Tipper*," Fontaine corrected. "Nobody who knows him calls

Flintlock

him Tremaine."

"I'll make a note of it."

The eyes regarded me with impressive sharpness for being half pickled. I showed him my most cherubic smile.

"Wait here."

He glanced at the wall behind me, then carried the shell of his drink with him. Gerard came in as his master went out. One of the crystal tumblers he carried, brimming with amber liquid, was deftly exchanged for Fontaine's empty as they passed. The switch would have embarrassed an Olympic relay runner. I thanked Gerard for the remaining glass, then I had Fontaine's office to myself for a few minutes. I looked around. It's what I do.

Only one wall had a window, though it extended to all corners on that side. The night had nothing to share and the window became another mirror. The rest of the room glowed with rich light from seeded glass sconces, two per non-window wall, and a banker's desk lamp with a green shade. Fontaine's mail lay fanned on the blotter like a poker hand. The envelope on top had that stiff formatting you typically see coming out of lawyers' offices and an embossed logo of an anvil and hammer. *The Colonial Societists.* I couldn't read much without picking the envelope up. I turned my attention elsewhere.

Above the door was a framed metal plaque, etched with a floorplan of the house. Room names were laser-cut so amber indicator lights could shine through whenever the security system detected a person in that room. According to the glowing letters, the kitchen, a vault, and of course Fontaine's office, were occupied. The office's infrared detector watched me from the corner of the ceiling nearest the door.

The wall behind the desk was a forest of plaques and trophies, brass and lacquered hardwood, adorned with representations of single or crossed pistols. The majority were for first or second place. *A. Fontaine* was engraved on every one.

Jon A. Hunt

Several trophies wore two names, proving Fontaine had found people who could stand him long enough to shoot *with* him instead of *at* him. I spotted *T. Gering* a couple times. The most interesting award was the largest, two feet tall, topped with brass pistols similar to those I'd spent the afternoon firing at the Jorgensen estate. In fact, *A. Fontaine* shared billing here with none other than *E. Jorgensen*. The trophy was three years old.

Chattanooga Black Powder Pistol Invitational
Twenty Yards
First Place

"Yes, I'm a hell of a shot."

Fontaine had gotten back into the room without hitting the door jamb. I had to give him credit.

"Tipper hadn't mentioned competing with you." I used his nickname this time, though like it or not, Fontaine was right. I barely knew the man.

My host narrowed his eyes, first toward the untasted scotch in my left hand, then at the letters left alone with me. He'd have remembered to stow his mail if I'd arrived on the first or second drink. He set his glass down, opened a top drawer, scraped the letters into it with the edge of a fat manila envelope he'd brought from another room, shut the drawer again.

"Just twice." His diction remained precise. I sensed his need to concentrate, though. "Excellent marksman."

"As good as you?"

Something like rage sparked in the eyes, but the liquor in there extinguished it before I could be sure. Fontaine smiled instead. Any simple drunk can smile. His displayed an inner ugliness that completed my assessment of his character. I loathed Arthur Fontaine.

"Almost," he said. "Neither of us has time for tournaments these days."

Flintlock

I wondered about that. For all of the antiques Tipper gave me to shoot, he hadn't sighted on a target.

"How about Erik Jorgensen?" I asked.

"I'd say he's done with tournaments, too. Tipper never mentioned an interview."

"Occupational habit. I ask a lot of questions."

"I've answered too many about Mr. Jorgensen already, for real detectives with metal badges. You'll understand if the topic wearies me."

"Of course." Metal badges. He wouldn't likely care for one of my lackluster paper business cards, then. "I can take those drawings and get out of your hair."

Fontaine watched me over the rim of his glass. He watched a lot of things over the rim of a glass. He finished the contents and pressed the empty toward the desk till it met the blotter. The manila envelope rapped softly against his thigh. For being weary of the topic, he didn't seem particularly willing to let it go.

"There's more to that estate than guns."

"Sure," I said.

"Tipper's making good progress?"

"I'm just the hired help, not at liberty to discuss an active crime investigation. I'm sure you understand."

Gerard made himself visible in the doorway and saved us from evading each other's further questions. He didn't carry refills. Fontaine tilted the wrist bearing the envelope to consult his watch, which took somewhat longer than a sober person needed.

"I've another appointment," he drawled, as much to the watch as to me. "Tipper should find what he needs here." He snapped the manila envelope with emphasis onto the desk for me to pick up after he left. He bobbed past me and still maintained an acre of separation.

I traded the tumbler I'd been holding for the envelope.

63

Hadn't tried a sip.

"Not to your taste, Mr. Bedlam?" Gerard asked.

"I'm not as thirsty as Mr. Fontaine."

• • •

Gerard released me back out into the fog with an apologetic bow and pulled the cedar front doors closed behind him. Another car was parked in the gloom next to mine. This guest might actually drink some of Fontaine's poison. Gerard needed to be there to take the order.

The second car matched the sedan I'd seen outside Jorgensen's granite walls. The thing was pretty generic. I doubted this was a coincidence, though. Fontaine was mighty curious for a weary drunk guy. He could afford to have his former shooting partner's house watched.

For grins, I fished the tiny magnetic GPS tag from my pocket. It made a satisfying click when it grabbed the inside of the sedan's right rear wheel well.

My phone only blinked purple for the first minute as I drove away, then stopped.

Flintlock

Chapter Nine

The fog relented a mile from the lake. Cars and traffic lights reappeared with clarity beneath black skies and brittle stars, and just like that I was driving through Hendersonville. Ephemeral puffs of exhaust chased taillights in front of me, toothless ghost dogs that never quite caught their prey. I turned left onto Gallatin Pike and took my time going home. I told the hands-free system to dial Jerry Rafferty's mobile number.

"Yeah?" he growled after two rings.

"How much have you looked into Arthur Fontaine?"

"We made sure where he was the night Jorgensen bought it. Wasn't what you'd call a fan of the deceased."

"I'm not convinced he's *anybody's* fan."

Rafferty's chuckle was unmistakable this time. "A toss-up between which was the biggest prick. Used to get along fine, had a falling out a couple years back. Tipper can tell you the story, antique gun nuts run in the same circles. They eventually patched up their differences enough to discuss common interests. Both men turn up on O'Dell's security footage. Never at the same time, of course. But Fontaine's alibi is better than yours. Had half the city council over for drinks when forensics say Jorgensen got popped. Why?"

"Gering had me pick up some papers from him," I said. "Fontaine's pretty curious about the investigation."

"Aren't we all?"

65

"He hinted there's more to this than old guns. I don't like him. But I believe him."

"Of course there is. Since you brought it up, I'll tell you this much: there could be some old documents missing from the estate. Just can't be certain till the whole mess has been searched. Let's not be mentioning that anywhere, okay?"

"Not a word. How do you know about the documents in the first place?"

"Tipper's been tracking them. TBI hired him for it."

The Viper snorted away from a green light and conversation wasn't possible till I cruised again at lower RPMs. Then I asked if Rafferty ever meant to tell me more specifically about those old documents.

"You're needy."

"Remind me who's helping who again."

Rafferty employed some colorful language. He disliked sharing. But then he said: "Ask Tipper about the red journal. Tell him I said it's okay. I'm the only way you'd know to ask."

"*Red journal.*"

"He can explain better than me."

"All right. Hey, by the way, where are his relatives?"

"Why the hell do you need to know about Tipper's family?"

"Braunfelter's."

"Oh. He doesn't seem to have any. There's a will, but it's in the courts where we can't see it yet. I'll call if I hear anything and feel like gossiping. Satisfied?"

An unfamiliar number began scrolling across the dash display. Unlisted.

"Yeah," I said. "I've got another call."

Rafferty grunted and hung up.

I tapped the dash touchscreen. My peripheral vision caught the phone blinking purple on the passenger seat.

• • •

"Mr. Bedlam?"

Flintlock

The voice on the second call differed drastically from Rafferty's forty-grit persona. Feminine uncertainty and silk had never been more perfectly blended.

"Yes," I said.

"Aubrea Langston. From the funeral?"

I lifted my foot and let the Viper's engine simmer. She hadn't needed to add her last name: I'd cataloged the sound of her at the graveside in Columbia, when she promised to think about calling me. Those business cards had been a worthwhile investment after all.

"You said you could help."

"I'd like to try."

"You never mentioned *why*."

A red-light bleeding over the intersection represented just *one* of the crossroads I'd reached. I glared through the windshield and considered my next words carefully. Aubrea Langston sounded less comfortable with the idea of calling a PI than most. Say the wrong thing, she'd hang up and that would be the end of our association. The only Langston I'd stand a chance of bumping into afterward would be furious little Eli or, worse, their District Attorney father.

"It's what Mitch would have done," I said.

This response earned a full minute of dead airwaves. Her number still showed on the dash display. A puddle of green radiance beneath my phone on the passenger seat indicated the call remained active. The pulsing purple reminder that Keller's GPS doohickey liked me so much it had run after me with a whole car attached, clashed with the green. One of the headlight pairs in my mirrors had only driven into Hendersonville because I had. At least I had an idea who was following me. Mitch hadn't.

"Yeah," the woman on the call finally agreed. Her informal shift felt so natural I wondered whether her grown-up tone was the act. "Mitch would offer, even if he didn't understand the problem."

I warned her my approach to problem solving probably lacked Mitch Braunfelter's brand of diplomacy.

"You seemed polite enough at the funeral," she said.

"Your companion didn't think so."

The silk left her voice. So did the hesitation. "Eli is my older brother, Mr. Bedlam, not a 'companion.' He thinks I need a second opinion when gauging character."

"You must have had Mitch figured out fine. He listened to you enough to look me up."

"I...I suppose so."

"Would you be willing to meet in person? Someplace safe, public, wherever you feel comfortable. I'd love to hear more about Mitch."

"Men typically only want to hear about *me*..."

"I'm a better listener than the average male."

I hadn't heard soft summer rain on leaves for months. Aubrea Langston's short laugh came pretty close. "All right," she said. "How about tomorrow?"

All silk. No uncertainty.

• • •

Once the only person to talk with was myself, the purple warning pulse got on my nerves. A quarter mile east of the ramp to 386, I downshifted to a chortling crawl, let other drivers who *weren't* tailing me zip irately past, and floored the gas pedal at the last second to send the Viper rocketing up the ramp. The sedan bearing Keller's magnetic beacon missed the turn and continued eastward on Gallatin Pike. My phone quit blinking.

• • •

My condo lorded over Nashville's jostled core from a nineteenth-floor perch the average guy in my profession couldn't begin to afford. I'd dropped a deposit on the place a

Flintlock

few years earlier, when it was half built and I was reeling from the sudden inheritance of an international company that demanded, among other sacrifices, a local mailing address. When the hammers and cranes quit swinging and I'd found no better options, I moved in and started reading my mail where it was delivered. All that prevented me from settling in completely was a dim suspicion the building had never been actually finished.

Hardwood floors and granite countertops tried to offset high undisguised concrete ceilings with bare metal pipes and contractor's pencil marks. The stone-trimmed fireplace blended into this setting the way a tuxedo does in an iron foundry. Every exterior wall consisted of only undraped floor-to-floor plate glass. Nighttime views were staggering. But cranes and hammers don't stay still for long. Another new tower had begun to claw skyward to shut out the panorama I'd purchased. Maybe they'd finish this one.

I leaned against the living room glass while the fireplace fluttered behind me, and peered past reflected flames across a skyline I scarcely recognized. Nashville was changing. The unassuming charm that had lured me into staying was being swallowed by metropolitan steel. It remained Music City, USA. For how long? It bothered me that transplants like myself were responsible.

Normally I treat moody spells with something from the liquor cabinet. Not tonight. I didn't care to smell like Arthur Fontaine.

I would see him again, however, if that's what it took.

Aubrea Langton's call couldn't have been better timed. The self-focused lush on Old Hickory Lake's foggy north shore had disgusted me nearly to the point of calling Rafferty back and telling him he and Tipper were on their own. I didn't technically owe anybody anything. I'd been asking myself where in a world full of Fontaines and Jorgensens I expected to

Jon A. Hunt

find anything good. And who would care if I did? Then a girl who only knew me from a cemetery encounter and a hokey business card had called, because *she* cared.

The girl had no way of knowing she'd refocused me on my original goal. I'd been diverted by extraordinary characters: Tipper Gering, with his passion for a history that could be heard and felt in the present; Arthur Fontaine, who'd never fully obscure self-loathing beneath a sea of liquor; Gerard, the sober reflection of his employer who possessed a regality his master couldn't comprehend; the nameless bullet-resistant behemoth who crushed appliances and skulls and liked to stack the guts of people's homes in little piles; Erik Jorgensen, a corpse I'd never met in the living world, whose last splattered thought might have been of the very missing thing that kept Jerry Rafferty up nights. None of them were the reason I'd waded into this swamp.

Aubrea Langston had reminded me of that.

Tomorrow, I'd add more characters to the stew. Miss Langston, certainly. Probably others. My next logical step might keep Rafferty up at nights even later, though he'd suggested it. He'd nearly lost his job over the fiasco at O'Dell's bookstore.

But I wasn't working for Metro.

Until my gut said otherwise, I worked for Mitch Braunfelter.

Flintlock

Chapter Ten

Tuesday morning was miserable. The high rise going up across the street had diminished to weird vertical lines stabbing the blurred bottoms of clouds. Droplets tracking across the living room windows trembled in the wind yet held their ground, as if they had half a mind to just stay put and freeze. My weather shoulder ached.

The forecast on my phone said highs in the low twenties, with a wintry mix changing to ice in the afternoon. I decided to skip the coffee shop. I hadn't much desire to go there since Mitch died. After a microwave breakfast sandwich from the freezer, I called a taxi. O'Dell's bookstore had sparse curbside parking and notoriously short-running meters, and a shiny black Viper wasn't the kind of low-key approach Jerry Rafferty appreciated. I tucked Tipper's book inside my overcoat and stopped to confirm the tilt of my hat in the hall mirror. Momma would've been so proud.

Little traffic moved between the condo and West End, neither on streets nor sidewalks. Any suggestion of freezing rain tends to confine locals to their homes or, counterintuitively, the interstates. My cab deposited me a block from the store. I walked the rest of the distance with my head down to keep the sleet out of my eyes. The bookstore's entrance waited beneath an old-fashioned orange neon sign that was as universally recognized as those on Broadway. A flock of middle-schoolers scattered like free-range chickens. Unless school was cancelled there shouldn't have been anything free-range about them. The door bumped halfheartedly against its frame behind me, so I had to tug it the rest of the way shut. An electronic chime thanked me.

Nothing had changed since my last visit years ago. The place didn't have *aisles* so much as claustrophobic *canyons* jammed with more bound pages than the stacks could reasonably contain. Cardboard boxes cluttered the footpaths, stuffed with out-of-print reference books and paperbacks that had no business sharing vertical space with the classics. Attempts at merchandising consisted of the odd volume wedged flatwise between shelf-mates so its front cover faced into an aisle. Beyond general category sections—literature, Civil War (a specialty), mysteries, cookbooks, and so forth—only the staff's collective memory served to pinpoint any particular title. One didn't merely browse at O'Dell's; finding what you sought was more of an archeological expedition. People came in every day to dig, though.

I paused on a soggy doormat to tug off my gloves and put Tipper's wrapped book under an arm. Steam gurgled through pipes to grumbling iron radiators. Fluorescent tubes hummed overhead, noticeable, not sufficient to mask the arrhythmic flip of dry pages. Patrons glanced briefly over their reading glasses to see who'd made the door beep and the room colder. I probably didn't strike them as the bookish type. There were employees—somewhere—to tend to me if necessary. A skinny boy, maybe fourteen, wearing dirty jeans and dazzling white Reeboks with the laces dragging, watched me a beat longer than the others. His demeanor was less free-range and more feral; whether school is cancelled makes no difference to a homeless kid. But when he turned back to the shelves, I could tell he was reading titles. Recently homeless, then. I silently wished him luck.

Flintlock

My properly laced shoes carried me deeper into the labyrinth. I had less of an idea what to expect than the kid, yet, like him, I figured I'd know when I saw it.

Low voices emanated from the room's center. Management at O'Dell's famously held few reservations about expelling shoppers with underdeveloped library manners. Regulars were aware of this. The female voice was most intelligible, not louder than the others, just clearer. Her drawl was the kind that softened the edges of words instead of plucking them like banjo strings.

"We have nicer editions in back, both volumes, sir, already down where you can see——"

None of the masculine responses reached my ears. Mutters never carry.

"——oh," the girl said, "okay, not a problem."

I found the show one more aisle over. That's exactly what it was: a show, a slow burlesque for dirty old men who lacked means or knowledge to get their jollies at home. Four octogenarians crowded the bottom of a five-foot folding ladder and craned their wrinkled necks to goggle upward. It doesn't take that many men to steady a ladder. Their enthusiasm had less to do with anyone's safety than with the shape of the girl on the top rungs.

I saw just her legs. But I saw *all* of them, exquisite calves and thighs, taut as she leaned precariously over the top of the ladder in a maroon skirt that must be scandalous even when she stood flat-footed. The view certainly had my attention, and I wasn't so old I couldn't find nice legs outside the Biographies section. December hadn't persuaded her to consider stockings, and chestnut skin that smooth hardly needed them. A sliver of festive purple winked from beneath the skirt's immodest hem. A tiny mystery remained for the imagination.

I stepped around the lecherous quartet and reached for the leather spine an inch beyond dainty brown fingertips with a

Jon A. Hunt

French manicure. Being tall and far south of AARP eligibility has advantages.

"This one?"

The girl let her hand drop back to the ladder. My view from the front was just as enjoyable. A graceful neck and jawline reminded me of Marilyn Monroe, otherwise her features were exactly the type of African American that would distract men regardless of skin color. Her smile was bright and infectious. Her eyes were large, liquid bronze, framed with purple eyeshadow to match the panties her geriatric audience so admired. More lace of the same hue traced the outer curves of each breast, both ample and scarcely hidden while she rested her stomach on top of the ladder and her scoop-neck sweater gaped. A plastic rectangle with engraved letters was clipped to the sweater's collar; whether by art or accident, the nametag might just as well serve as an exit ramp sign for décolletage. The letters spelled *Darlene*.

She mouthed a "thank you" that only I could see.

Determination alone seemed to hold the book's pages together. The cover nearly came apart in my hand. Anyone looking up from below could not have seen the title, which was barely visible on the worn front cover. I grinned at the old-timers.

"I'd have pegged you as Lee or Forrest fans." I said it to the group, since none stepped forward to claim the prize. "At least one of you already owns the first book?"

I held the *Personal Memoirs of U.S. Grant, Volume II*, toward them. Four pairs of rheumy eyes challenged me, four self-righteous old white Confederate roosters caught peering under a pretty black chick's petticoat. Either all of them owned up to the ruse, or one of them was going to leave that store carrying the final musings of a despised Union general. The sourest of the bunch finally snatched the tome and they shuffled en masse toward the sales counter at the back of the store.

Flintlock

The girl touched her feet to the tile floor beside me. I'd been dead right about that skirt.

"Thanks again, Mr.——"

"Tyler Bedlam," I said. "Not a problem. But I'd hurry and make sure they pay full price."

"You're not shopping?" Her pout was adorable.

"Sorry. I'm just returning something Mr. Gering borrowed."

"Oh! Tipper!" Her pout dissolved into another smile.

I presented the parcel from under my arm. The girl accepted it, pirouetted and sashayed toward the business end of O'Dell's. Her shameless skirt beckoned, a velvet enticement, left and right edges flipping up in time with each step. Nothing in the place quite appealed like keeping up with Darlene. But I'd made too good a first impression not to stop the kid with the wayward shoestrings before he made the front door.

His mistake was risking eye contact a second time. Overdue for a meal, he'd nonetheless gained recent weight, visible as a rectangular lump under his jacket. He must have grabbed the book during my interaction with the pervert quartet. I wouldn't have made him my business if he'd kept his face down. People steal all the time and it's rarely up to me to stop them. Ordinary shoplifters just don't look *that* scared.

I moved quicker because my shoes were tied. We reached the door simultaneously and he'd pressed it open a crack before I caught the upper portion of the handle and hauled it shut again with a bang. The electric chime chirruped like an angry tree squirrel as we battled for ownership, but weight and strength were on my side. Our contest spawned movement on both sides of the glass: rapid footfalls sprinted toward us from within the building, and the truants on the sidewalk dispersed. The boy whirled. Three pounds of leather, paper and ink thudded onto the wet mat between us. His hand darted inside his jacket. My right shoe stamped onto loose Reebok laces, tight to his ankle where he'd feel the pressure. The wrist I snatched might have been kindling in a coat sleeve, thin as he was.

"Whatever you've got in there is only going to add broken bones and an assault charge to an already bad day." I kept my warning low, so only the boy heard.

His free hand dropped outside the jacket, empty. The stick arm in my grip trembled.

"Please, mister..."

I didn't lecture, didn't demand a name. I didn't tell him not to steal again. He knew no better way of living at the moment, and I sensed his more immediate concern was dying. I gave him *my* name.

"Tyler Bedlam. Look me up. Maybe I can help."

Whoever ran from the back of O'Dell's was nearly there. No words, no nod from the kid, all I got was that expression of hopeless terror. I let the scrawny arm go.

The kid was gone in less time than the door needed to close. His compatriots outside were gone, too. The chime continued to squawk at three-second intervals. I crouched to retrieve the book and was standing again when the man from the store's depths arrived.

"You let him go?" His demand came in explosive puffs. He was winded and upset.

Unlike Grant's memoirs, this volume felt solid. The binding was supple green leather with spine ridges and embossed foil lettering. *Edgar Allan Poe, Tales of Mystery*. A deluxe edition. And I'd thought middle school thieves had no class. I brushed dirt from the cover, tapped a loose page back in, and handed it over.

"You rely on customers to handle loss prevention?"

The man snapped up the book like cheese from a rat trap. He was slightly stooped, similar enough to the lovely Darlene to be related, yet nowhere near as easy on the eyes. His forehead continued to the top of his skull before tightly

Flintlock

constricted black and gray curls started. Silver reading glasses on a chain swung from his rush to the door. Another plastic nametag on his off-white sweater vest introduced him as *Raleigh, Vice President*. Surnames apparently weren't advertised around here.

"We have security," he snorted loudly enough to compete with the incessant beeping, "but we hope every customer will do the right thing. You could have detained that boy."

Lectures never yield good results with me. Raleigh was correct, I could've kept the kid there. It wouldn't necessarily have been the *right thing* for anybody. The police would give the boy a square meal. They'd take away his white shoelaces. Then there would be no one to claim him and he'd be back on the streets in days, stuffing unpurchased merchandise under his clothes. Unless whatever had him so terrified caught up with him first.

"You have your book. You're welcome. He didn't get out of the store with anything of yours."

"How do you *know?*" Mr. Vice President bridled.

"You wouldn't have popped up here so quick if you weren't watching. You tell me."

It was a double-edged bluff. I didn't honestly know what the shoelace bandit might have had in his pockets. And Rafferty had mentioned problems with the security cameras, even if I could see three of them staring our direction from strategic locations in the stacks. I netted an interesting response, though.

Raleigh stood up taller and his eyes glittered with what counted for menace in his type. His tone bore nothing akin to bookstore etiquette.

"Our security systems and our customers' privacy will not be compromised to satisfy petty arguments! Perhaps it would be best if you left the building——"

"Ssh," I said, "people are trying to read."

I almost wanted him to go ahead and try heaving me out

Jon A. Hunt

that damn chirping door. The Vice President of O'Dell's needed some attitude adjustment, which happened to be another of my many unadvertised skills. But then Rafferty would need to find somebody else to do his snooping and I wouldn't be doing my own cause any favors, either. Mr. Raleigh's superior interceded and spared us both the trouble.

"Raleigh!"

He didn't turn. He settled back into his original hunch, tore me apart with his eyes. If his grip on Poe's *Tales of Mystery* tightened further the spine would snap.

"Go back to your desk," insisted the voice, not dissimilar to Darlene's, though raspier. "I wish to speak with Mr. Bedlam."

Raleigh's clapboard wall of a forehead never shed its frustrated creases. He stalked around me to press the door fully closed so the chime quit, then retreated into the leather and paper canyons of his lair. Darlene had been hovering in what must be an unaccustomed position for her—outside anyone's attention—and reclaimed the book as Raleigh stomped past.

I conquered a tremendous desire to grin after him and was glad I did.

The small stern seventy-year-old woman left standing in Raleigh's place would tolerate none of that.

Flintlock

Chapter Eleven

O'Dell's had no second floor. High above the shelves spread a network of structural iron and cables that thus far had kept a roof up. Modern steam pipes and fluorescent lights dangling in the void on dust-furred chains hadn't been figured into the original design, and a true second level with furniture, people and swivel chairs would have been pushing everybody's luck. There was, however, a mezzanine in back. Raleigh's Vice-Presidential nest hid under it. He *ran* things from a pine desk buried under an ancient typewriter and teetering stacks of books; he *watched* things from two flat panel monitors on a newer steel table. Data cables wormed around the table legs so chaotically Raleigh must have lost time extricating his feet before scrambling out to confront me. He sat there now and never raised an eye as we passed. No doubt he glared instead at my pixelated likeness on one of the screens.

The store's surveillance network couldn't be as sophisticated at it appeared. There'd been no video available the day of Metro's ill-informed raid.

The old woman continued past Raleigh's space and climbed a grate stair quicker than I'd have expected. A door with glass in its upper half waited at the top. A brass plaque hung above the door, *Meredith O'Dell* engraved thereon. The door closed on a spring behind us and she motioned for me to sit while she circled to the driver's side of another pine desk, identical to

Jon A. Hunt

Raleigh's except completely bare. I took a chair in front of the desk. The room was twenty by twenty, with white walls and tan Berber carpet. Family photographs in chrome frames filled the walls from four feet to the ceiling. Most of the pictures had been taken in the store, starting decades before Kodachrome. A handsome black man in a suit, his arm locked possessively around the slim waist of a dead ringer for Darlene downstairs, had to be the Mr. O'Dell who'd married my host fifty years ago. The shelves didn't look any different. Mrs. O'Dell's skirt was a respectable length. There was even a preschool edition of the current Vice President. Raleigh had not been a photogenic child.

Otherwise, I saw four gray metal filing cabinets with locking drawers and typewritten labels, *Ab-At*, *Au-Bl*, *Bo-Cr*, so forth. A black multiline phone hung on the wall beside the filing cabinets. A wire wastebasket waited beside the desk, half full of discarded junk mail. That was all. Not a single bookcase.

"I'll save you from asking," said Meredith O'Dell. "No books in here. You think that's odd."

I set my damp hat on a near corner of the desk. It needed something.

"There's plenty to read fifteen steps down if you're in the mood," I said.

Meredith O'Dell nodded soberly. "Precisely, Mr. Bedlam. Thousands of books. And old newspapers, treatises, chapbooks, poetry, history, literature, smut. It's printed in English, Spanish, German, French, Italian, even Latin. We have four-hundred and five different English versions of the Bible, twice as many theology books to argue about which of those versions is best. I am surrounded by books all day. But not in this room."

My own library was pitiful in comparison, and I hadn't spent my adult life depending on the printed word for much, at least not directly. Books weren't the escape for Meredith O'Dell that they were for others. Books were the bricks of her

Flintlock

prison.

"What was it you wanted to discuss, ma'am?"

Her upholstered leather chair outclassed the rest of the room. She settled back against the cushions and her grizzled hair feathered around her like a halo.

"Details," she replied. "Raleigh's my oldest and he's a smart man most of the time. He can be an idiot about small things, though. *You* counted the steps up just now, I assume out of habit. You didn't just come to bring back a book from Mr. Gering. He usually returns what he's borrowed himself. You might be here on his errand but you're also looking for something."

"Who isn't?" I said.

"Don't get flippant with me. I've outlived a lot of bullshitters."

I didn't apologize. That would show weakness.

"Mrs. O'Dell, I'm not sure what I'm trying to find. A...friend...used to shop here, before he died. Maybe he bought something that will help answer questions I have about him. That's all I can say at the moment."

She asked for nothing more. A woman connected to the printed world as she was certainly knew of Mitch Braunfelter's grisly passing, but then uncounted others passed through O'Dell's chirping front door each day and I could be curious about any of them.

"You aren't with the police."

"No, ma'am. I'm here on my own." That was as much bullshit as I dared.

"A cop wouldn't have turned that boy loose."

"You seem less concerned about it than Raleigh. Would the store have pressed charges?"

"Raleigh would. That won't fix the problem, will it?"

"No. Homeless kids can find more profitable places to shoplift than a bookstore. The market for hot books must be

81

Jon A. Hunt

pretty specialized."

"Oh, it is!" Meredith O'Dell pivoted forward in her fancy chair so her rail-thin torso hovered over her side of the desk. "I can tell you who the main buyer is for items stolen from this store. The police aren't as clever about it as they like to think."

"Who, then?"

"We are." She sank resignedly into the suede. "They're half right, the police and that damned paper. O'Dell's *does* buy stolen books. *Our* stolen books. We buy them back all the time, because we stand to lose a great deal more if we don't."

I didn't feel any cleverer than the police. DA Langston had basically shooed them out of the place for a dumb mistake. I might be equally clueless. I also doubted Rafferty had been invited to the mezzanine office.

"They come looking for *sets* of rare books," Mrs. O'Dell explained, "like the Grant memoirs Darlene just sold. How she managed it, I'm sure I don't want to know. The first volume is gone, the one with Mr. Grant's signature, so the remaining volume is worth a fraction of the complete pair's selling price. These kids swipe one or two from a set and leave the rest. When the missing pieces come back, we have a brief chance to recover them by quietly paying whatever is demanded to whoever brings the books in. I told Raleigh to refuse and call the police once. We found what was left of that mistake burning in a trash can out on the sidewalk."

"Like kidnapping a twin," I said.

"A bit. What is left still has value, but greatly reduced. There's a bottom line to consider, and O'Dell's reputation for *intact* rare collectibles. Whoever does this knows the books and the market almost as well as I do."

"Pricey collections aren't just stuffed into the shelves with regular books," I said.

"Of course not. The Grant volume was today, because it's nearly worthless by itself. We've discovered that moving the

82

Flintlock

remainders into the open signals the thieves that we are interested in dealing. But even items stored in back aren't safe. The store's not built to be Fort Knox. Raleigh's had some luck with the security cameras, not enough to justify their cost or his time lost staring at computer screens. Just because you have video footage doesn't mean you ever see your merchandise again once it leaves the building. The young man with the white shoes has been here before—Raleigh recognized him, that's why he ran up front."

"That wasn't part of a set the kid had. It looked like a standalone book."

"You're right," she said. "It's mostly a pretty cover. Sells for $85. It's the type of book an untrained person might *think* is valuable."

I caught myself fidgeting with the brim of my hat as it perched on the desk's edge. This wasn't about one kid I tripped up on his way out. Bigger fish were calling the shots, or had been till today. Today, the kid was flying on autopilot. Terrified about it, too.

"I usually work harder to gather information."

The old woman smiled conspiratorially. I was reminded by the contrast of her teeth to her dark leathery features that I was speaking with a woman of color. Most successful Nashvillians I knew were as Caucasian as people can be. Few had impressed me with Meredith O'Dell's brand of toughness. Achieving what she had required a steeper climb than the white folks got. She wouldn't accept anyone siphoning away what she and her late husband earned. She'd fight for every penny.

"My grandfather didn't get this place the way people think. The first Mr. O'Dell caught him stealing a book. It was the Depression. Not many could afford a meal every day, let alone anything to read, black or white. Mr. O'Dell never pressed charges. He hired the boy, paid him to stay honest, which wasn't much because Granddad was more desperate than

Jon A. Hunt

criminal. Mr. O'Dell knew the best guard against thieves was another thief. Granddad stayed on the job his whole life. He swept aisles, stocked shelves, kept watch, became one of the family, married Mr. O'Dell's daughter. Oh, people talked! But the old man kept their ugly words from becoming actions. It may have helped that Granddad took the O'Dell name. When the old man died, the store passed to Grandma and Granddad, and we've had it ever since. All because of that second chance.

"Raleigh doesn't know the story. I haven't told him because he'd work himself up to return to an original family name he didn't even know existed. He doesn't understand. *You* understand, though."

"I understand you have a larger problem than just one hungry boy."

"I do. What does it cost to hire you, Mr. Bedlam?"

Flintlock

Chapter Twelve

I left the bookstore owning yet another job I hadn't asked for. Meredith O'Dell had made me an outside security consultant. My regular rate applied, four hours per evening unless exceptions were granted beforehand, and no less than two of those hours were to be spent on premises. She'd paid cash for my first shift, which would be tomorrow night. I hadn't argued. Even a rich guy who doesn't need financial motivation appreciates being valued. Mrs. O'Dell checked my references more thoroughly than Mitch had. She kept a business card.

Customers were conspicuously missing when I returned to the main floor. Raleigh and Darlene had closed the store early due to weather. The front windows wore stippled layers of ice. Important matters kept the Vice President from seeing me out, but Darlene (his niece) didn't mind unlocking the door for me.

"Y'all be careful." She meant it. She wanted me to come back soon. If anything, the scoop neck of her sweater drooped lower.

"Always," I promised as the door beeped open and ice water splashed both of us. I tugged my hat brim low and sidestepped out into the sleet.

Conditions had definitely gotten worse. The sidewalk sparkled like orange glass under the store sign, and offered all the traction of a hockey rink. Cars moved on the side street,

Jon A. Hunt

with tails slithering and drivers wide-eyed after having escaped the horrors of West End. Sirens echoed off glistening bricks. Expecting a taxi now was absurd and no one except me was dumb enough to walk.

A recessed entry to a law firm provided a hint of shelter. I could make out other legal-looking signs through the slanted downpour, two names and an ampersand apiece. *So-and-so, So-and-so & Associates*. Nobody eschews catchy business titles like attorneys. I hauled my phone from the depths of my jacket.

No missed calls. Aubrea and I had discussed the forecast when we made our appointment. She had been certain about Tuesday afternoon and promised she'd call if she wanted to reschedule. Once the girl got around to making up her mind she seemed to stick with it. The purple blinking light had found me, though.

I stowed the phone and ran my eyes up and down both sides of the street. Cars parked curbside had that neglected look cars get when their owners are afraid to drive them. Glazed meters winked expiration warnings. One of the ice-crusted cars was the plain Ford that had dogged my tracks since Jorgensen's place. Keller's man wasn't in it. He wouldn't be far, though.

Keller surely knew his electronic wizardry wasn't still attached to me. I wondered why he hadn't deactivated the thing. I wondered if *he* had any idea what he hoped to find here.

I could wonder as easily walking as standing. Off I went again, shuffling down the perilous shiny sidewalk toward Vanderbilt's campus.

• • •

My face-to-face with Aubrea Langston varied significantly from our plan.

We were supposed to meet after her yoga class, in a restaurant on the third floor of the building where her class was held. A girl ought to feel safe with the lunch crowd. I had time to walk there in spite of the weather.

Flintlock

But crossing West End proved more complicated than normal. Ice shorted out traffic signals and the thoroughfare was a battlefield of violently conjoined metal, glass and strobing lights. When I finally spotted an opening and stepped off the curb in the middle of the block, momentum carried me most of the way to the opposite side across a glossy surface no tire could grip. The sidewalk was no better, it just had fewer cars on it. Sirens ricocheted off the buildings, no nearer than they had been earlier. Whoever needed help was going to have to wait for it.

I skated across 21st South to the six-story student apartments without quite falling. The red bricks had paled to pastel pink, coated in ice like milky glass. The footpath between the apartments and older Wilson Hall were similarly glazed. From there on, I stayed off streets by crossing the parklike commons, tramping under the trees *beside* the walks. The ground under the crunching grass hadn't yet frozen and my shoes gained purchase.

Crystalline hulks sagged over me, trees so ice-bound they drooped completely to the whitened lawn. Several Bradford pears had split and fallen in ruin. It was impressive in a Dickensian way, lovely, perilous. Every sound, from far-off sirens to the rattle and smack of a trillion solidifying raindrops, came distinctly to my ears. You don't expect noises like that to hurt, but if your ears get cold enough, they do. I jammed my hands deeper in my pockets and quickened my pace as much as I dared.

The Sarratt Student Center metamorphosed from darkness to an ungainly block of brick and glass. Once it had been two or three separate buildings. A yellow and red fold-out barrier across the sidewalk made me rethink my shortcut. That route sparkled with menace. I continued around to the doors facing West Side Row.

A compact pickup with university markings and fluttering

Jon A. Hunt

roof lights crept along the street. A bin in the bed spat salt and grit from a chute at the back. This was the only mechanical life I saw, except for a dirty white minivan idling in the lot across the street. The van's windows collected no ice because the driver had the defroster cranked. The van reminded me of one I'd avoided looking at outside Mitch's house in Columbia. Hadn't Rafferty mentioned a white van? There couldn't be more than a few thousand similar rides in the metropolitan area. I let the thought go.

A lot adjacent to the building held another more recognizable van. I almost couldn't see the big sign on the wall beyond it that read *No Unauthorized Parking Beyond This Point*. I'd forgotten Danny Ayers was on campus today. Cool-Core had loaned him to the university to help with upgrades. His baby blue Volkswagen microbus probably had no relations within a hundred miles.

More barriers steered me toward the main entrance. The steps swept around a venerable oak that predated the building; most days their approach easily accommodated herds of students, with steel handrails and wide landings, all ascending gently from street level. Today, the stairs seemed less inviting. The rails wore a slick semi-transparent crust. The tree had transformed into a morose, drooping ice sculpture. A worker in overalls and gloves shoveled rock salt onto the steps from the top landing. He'd created a crude path upward. The rest of the stairs were glossy, a quick way to break your neck.

Another man leaned against the glass beside the entry doors and watched the worker. He had no affiliation with the university. He wore a leather jacket and a low-set Fedora. The red end of a cigarette burned in the shadows under the hat where rain couldn't extinguish it. This character had me beat hands down at looking tough.

The worker grunted a friendly hello as I passed, jabbed his shovel for safekeeping into the bucket of salt, and went in with

Flintlock

me to recover circulation in his fingers. We commiserated about the weather on the way. The smoker said nothing. I glimpsed his reflection in the door glass, putting the glowing rectangle of a mobile phone up beneath the hat where an ear would be.

The glass vestibule opened into the building's second level. Sappy Christmas carols permeated the interior. Not even university campuses are immune. The worker disappeared around a corner, but I hardly had the place to myself. Even if classes were cancelled, Vanderbilt remained busy. Students and staff moved to and fro, gathered for impromptu corridor meetings, discussed exams, term papers, holiday plans. I found the stairs and followed them around the glass elevator shaft to level 3U. The treads were slick underfoot. My ears throbbed and felt as if they'd been lit with a blowtorch.

Cross-beamed ceilings imparted an old-fashioned ale house atmosphere to the Overcup Oak Pub on the upper level. The taps open after six and they'll pour you a beer to go with that burger, but I'd never considered the place a serious drinking establishment. How much trouble can you really get into where the doors are locked by nine? My opinion didn't count for much on a college campus, however, and weather hadn't diminished the lunch rush. People in line for seats crowded around a pair of threadbare billiard tables and a foosball table.

One person just outside the doors had no interest in lunch. He could be the other bookend to the unsociable smoker downstairs. Lighting up wasn't permitted here and looking tough without the requisite cigarette required more effort. His concentration slipped to allow eye contact, which meant he knew I'd spotted the glimmer of a hastily stowed phone inside his jacket. I'd seen the automatic under his arm, too. He wasn't a cop. I didn't like turning my back to him, but that was the only way to get into the restaurant.

Coeds dangled their legs off bar stools around high-tops.

None were Aubrea Langston. She wouldn't blend in easily. I brushed past a blonde who'd have been happy to take my name for the next seat. The only thing dumber than telling her who I was within sight of the hard case with the artillery would be saying I had someone waiting for me.

Either way, Aubrea wasn't there.

And the bar in Nashville least likely to require bouncers suddenly had very serious door-minders, upstairs and down. Why?

I stopped in a corner next to a fireplace with gas logs and a cheap garland draped over the mantlepiece, tapped up Aubrea's number on my phone, redialed.

I didn't expect her to pick up. One of four football players at a table twenty feet away did. He'd noticed the unattended phone lighting up next to his size fourteens on the floor. While all four of them stared at the thing he'd set on the table between platters of fries, I stepped up and asked if they'd seen who left ahead of them.

"Yeah, an older man with glasses and a hat. Like yours. And a girl. She seemed sort of upset, but, you know…finals."

"Pretty?" I pressed.

All four of them grinned. "You know her?"

"Sure," I said and picked up the phone. I exited the Overcup Oak in a hurry.

The heavy out on the landing had vanished. The glass elevator cab was on its way down with two men and a girl inside. I took the stairs, two at a time.

Flintlock

Chapter Thirteen

I made a sufficient spectacle of myself for students on the steps to move aside without being asked or knocked over. I skidded into the elevator wall on the second-floor landing and whacked the recall button. The button lit up too late. The elevator continued downward. So did I. Onlookers applauded.

A vestigial fifth-grader's terror of looking stupid scrambled with me to the ground floor. This could be epic overreaction. I'd been stood up before. Except I'd never met a woman so desperate to avoid me she forgot her phone, and the last person who'd failed to keep an appointment with me had a brutally forgivable excuse I didn't want anyone else to re-use.

Unfounded paranoia wasn't a problem I had to live with beyond the second floor. The smokeless tough guy waited there to reassure me with a comforting right cross. No introduction, no warnings, just a knuckle sandwich served as fast food. I wouldn't have come back for seconds if I'd been standing still when he punched me. Instead, he connected with just enough of me to guarantee a fight. I let momentum carry my hip into his ribs and we hit the wet tiles hard.

The elevator chimed just like the doorbell at O'Dell's. It was a regular jingle-bells sort of day. Metal doors whooshed open. My second-floor greeter and I were too preoccupied with pounding the hell out of each other to pay much attention. New shapes sped through my peripheral vision, a slight feminine form herded from the elevator toward the rear exit by two larger forms. Then a fist distracted me and I had to duck to keep my teeth. While low, I hooked a knee and sent my foe cartwheeling across his compatriots' path.

"Keep moving!" one of them snarled.

An elbow found my gut. The three shapes kept running, an action I barely registered as I crashed my left fist into the non-smoker's nose. Cartilage popped. He staggered and I shut him down with a knee to the groin. When I pivoted toward the front doors his face provided a springboard for my heel. No apologies from me. He'd started it.

Weight against my left side begged for attention. I ignored it. *You* try hauling a gun out on a college campus and see what it gets you. The bad guys hadn't yet dared.

Aubrea Langston's blue eyes flashed my way for half a second, then the men dragged her outside. The vestibule's outer doors didn't finish closing before I blasted through.

Four of us didn't fit on the six-by-six patch of salted concrete the maintenance worker had left. One man slipped on the ice without my having to touch him. He went down and took the girl with him. The other guy rocked on his feet at the edge of the top step, facing me across the bucket and the shovel handle. The bad-ass who'd been hovering outside still had a cigarette glowing under his hat. He reassessed the arguments against using firearms on campus and a hand went inside his coat.

I couldn't outdraw him. The shovel was closer. I wrenched it two-handed from the bucket in a salty spray and swung for the fences.

The gritty blade bashed through bone. His gun went off inside his coat and fire and stuffing exploded from his side. Then he was bouncing head-first down the icy aggregate steps. He missed the oak tree and made it all the way to the street. I watched him go with my chin in a pile of rock salt. My battered

Flintlock

midsection had had enough and folded me in half.

"Mr. Bedlam?"

Hands took hold of me. Not rough hands. The girl's hands. Somehow, she'd returned to the top steps.

The third man, the one who'd fallen with Aubrea, flopped around a steel railing below us, struggling to disentangle himself. I could still smell the cigarette because it fizzled in the rain on the step next to my face.

"Can you get up?" she hissed in my ear.

The dirty white minivan appeared. The thing actually bounded right up onto the bottom landing. It looked like the one I'd seen in Columbia. The van's doors started to open before it finished sliding.

"Mr. Bedlam!"

"Yeah, I hear you!" I wheezed.

My lungs processed air again. I wasn't dead, my belly just hurt. Ice bit into the heels of my hands as I heaved myself up. The guy halfway down the stairs had gotten to his knees. He flashed me a bloody smile. Rain drilled into the back of my neck like wet ice picks.

"Let's get back inside," I suggested.

• • •

Our welcome in the lobby was mixed. A third of a football team rummaged desperately for furniture to barricade the doors. Chairs and tables there were too lightweight, the doors opened outward, and there was too much storefront glass to resist any determined attack. But the chairs that had been jammed in front of the doors wouldn't have been moved for me; I looked like one of the characters they wanted to keep outside. Aubrea banged on glass to convince the ball players to let us in.

Furniture was scooted back in place behind us, better than nothing. Then we were enveloped by a tense crowd. Most asked if we were okay, said they'd called the police—dozens of

Jon A. Hunt

phosphorescent rectangles clung to ears still—nobody was sure when the cops would arrive. Others maintained wary separation from us. I didn't know any of them and distrusted the lot equally. Aubrea found my arm. Even through a wet jacket she felt warm.

"What now?" she whispered.

I dug her phone from my pocket. A crack split the glass. That made us even, since my knuckles were bleeding and had rock salt under the skin for her sake. It kept me from dwelling on what the smokeless tough guy had done to my stomach.

"We can't stay."

A retreat into the student center had been our only option half a minute ago. But I'd already spotted my man with the bloodied nose outside the stippled glass of the back exit, past the elevators. He stood a few degrees off vertical, but he was upright. His friends must be regrouping out front.

Cops hadn't shown. Till they did, there was time for us to suffer more.

"Who *are* they?"

Aubrea pressed into my side, sapphire eyes darting. Something about her reattuned me to the holiday tunes that still filtered through the space. A dirty cut marred her chin and she was paler than she'd been at the funeral. She was still gorgeous and regal.

"I'm not sure," I admitted. "They might be involved with what happened to Mitch." Louder, to the bystanders: "Can we have some space, please?"

A student peering around a window's edge into the rain muttered "Jeezus, dude's huge!" I recognized him; he'd picked up Aubrea's phone in the pub. I worried I might recognize the huge dude who must be on his way up from the street, too.

White van.
Three-by-three debris piles.

Flintlock

Mitch Braunfelter's pulverized shell with the gory crossword suspenders...

"Can't we—"

"We wouldn't get far," I said.

The second phone in my pocket had survived unscathed. I wiped the blood off my thumb and tapped the phone number of the only person who might be able to get us off campus quickly.

• • •

Danny Ayers came downstairs nearly as fast as I had. He wasn't dressed to walk home in the weather and had no inclination to try driving in it either, till I'd shot his afternoon to hell with a phone call. The kid never could hold his own in an argument. He found us near the closed cinema ticket counter. He carried a ring of university keys. This wasn't the first time I'd cajoled him from the safety of his microprocessors and algorithms.

Introductions were limited to first names. I asked if he knew of any less public exits from the building.

"There's the doors they hauled that new UPS cabinet in," Danny offered.

"How far from them to your VW?"

"Uh, ten yards? Are we bringing something in?"

The lobby suddenly emptied except for us. People lost their curiosity when the gorilla I'd tangled with at Mitch's place ducked through the front doors. He swatted chairs aside like flies. I couldn't see eyes beneath the looming brows, though it was easy to imagine them boring through the air between us. Any .45 caliber holes I'd added to his physique didn't show. The girl's fingernails bit into my arm.

"Don't stare," I warned her. "He won't like it."

• • •

We made the most of our head start while we had one, and

Jon A. Hunt

half fell down a last flight of steps. Bigfoot stamped fully into the lobby. Christmas music didn't at all fit the mood. Bigfoot's cohort with the dented beak came in from the opposite side of the room. Funny, no one had thought to barricade that way.

Danny used a passkey on a door with an *Authorized Personnel Only* sign. A dim passage beyond contained no personnel, authorized or otherwise, and overhead carols were barely audible. Danny stopped to test the lock.

"That will slow *us* down more than *him*," I said.

Uncombed blond hair exaggerated his emphatic nod. He sprinted ahead of Aubrea and me, keys jangling. For a computer nerd the kid could move.

The hall ran straight for eighty feet. Doors sped by at regular intervals. The doors wore black plastic plaques with office numbers and names that trailed important-looking clusters of letters. Narrow windows in the doors were dark. All of the other staff had called out for the day and left one schmuck to sprinkle rock salt. Then came a brief downward flight of steps and a left turn. A pair of double steel doors interrupted the corner beneath a glowing red exit sign. Danny and Aubrea's hands found the panic bar but I stopped them.

"These aren't the doors you mentioned, are they, Danny?" Heavy deliveries surely had routes with fewer stairs.

"No, that's in Receiving. This way is quicker—"

"If it's a regular exit, it'll be watched."

Danny's eyes opened wider and reflected more of the red aura. He hadn't been aware of the scope of Aubrea's problem—now *our* problem—but he'd hung around me often enough to trust my judgment. As if to reinforce my wisdom, a savage bang and metallic crashes behind us verified the futility of locked doors.

"Please hurry!" whispered Aubrea.

"Right! C'mon!"

Danny hurried around the next corner. The girl and I stayed

Flintlock

hard on his heels. The lights never changed. Insipid holiday music had been displaced by our labored breathing, our pounding feet, the feet of our pursuers. A couple of those running feet might as well be pile drivers. The next set of double doors had another plastic tag with nobody's name, just a number and the word *Receiving*. Danny wrangled the keys. None seemed to fit. The buffalo stampede coming after us didn't do his motor skills any good. He dropped them.

"Get behind me," I said and yanked the shiny new Smith & Wesson from under my arm.

Nobody loves using guns in tight spaces. Every time I've done so, another part of some favorite song becomes lost to my hearing forever. A splintering explosion and flame half obliterated our senses. Aubrea's startled scream somehow made it through.

The right-hand door bucked against the frame and bounced open, minus the knob and deadbolt. Brightness spilled through. In unison we sprang to join with it.

But we weren't out of the building yet. The next room had no proper ceiling, just structural beams and industrial lights that switched on via a sensor. We crossed a concrete floor between pallets and stacked boxes, squinting against what at the time seemed oppressive brilliance. Another set of doors waited on the far side. My companions hesitated.

The doors were cool to the touch, but no signs designated them to be a way out; they were for the loading dock. I went through first.

Even the dock doors had someone guarding them. The man had stationed himself too close. I barreled through and a door's edge spun him. He was thick and brutish and he reacted too quickly to be a regular Joe trying to find a place to light up out of the rain. Sight of the .45 in my fist sent him reaching for his own. I busted his jaw with the Smith & Wesson's butt. His backside skipped off the edge of the dock, and he flipped over

Jon A. Hunt

the edge and out of sight. A second later his prone form reappeared moving without his input at bobsled speed. He stopped face-down under the front wheel of a university maintenance truck.

Sleet stung my ringing ears. I suddenly missed my hat. A wonderland of glittering grass and ice-crusted trees marched away from the receiving lot. Nearer were a couple dozen cars and one vintage VW microbus. Overloaded limbs had drooped onto the lot to embrace the old van. Sirens brayed brightly now. The good guys were closer. Hints of blue brushed the crystallized trees. Aubrea clutched my arm.

"Police!"

"We can't wait."

Danny found steps off the dock down to the parking lot. He might have died trying without the handrail. I pulled the girl's hand from my arm, gripped it tightly in my left, led her as rapidly after Danny as we dared.

Fortunately, he'd only dropped the university's keys. He caught himself by the van's door handle. The guy I'd clobbered lay a few yards from us, not blinking when icy rain bounced off his eyeballs. I tried to keep myself between the live girl and the probable corpse.

Somebody shouted. A very large, very hostile man slapped the receiving doors apart so forcefully bricks shattered on either side. Danny furiously tugged on the Volkswagen's door handle. It had frozen shut. We combined efforts and I bashed the window out for a handhold. The door wrenched open. I apologized as the three of us piled inside.

"Everything else is already broken," Danny said.

While I slammed the door shut from the passenger seat, he stabbed a key into the slot on the column below a steering wheel broad enough to be a spare for a horse buggy. He yanked the choke knob out from the dash, stomped the clutch and gas pedals, twisted the key.

Flintlock

Bitter rain attacked my cheek. Wavy reflections of running men increased in the round side mirror.

The starter whirred. The bus gasped out a lot of blue smoke. The engine didn't fire.

Shit.

I pivoted in my seat with the .45. Aubrea sat directly behind me, a wide-eyed ashen rendition of terror. "Better get low," I suggested.

The starter motor ground again. This time the engine coughed repeatedly, belched more blue smoke, then the exhaust popped. Danny had woken all forty air-cooled horses under the back floorboards. He jerked the shifter against his knee and popped the clutch. The back tires grudgingly spun on ice.

Bigfoot was a slow runner. Another man who'd joined him moved faster. His silhouette darkened the back glass. I brought my gun around for the shot.

The tires grabbed.

The Volkswagen lurched. There was nothing quick about it, but the man behind us had even less traction. He thudded into the tailgate and disappeared.

"Oh my God, I hit him!"

"Just drive!"

Gears gnashed. The van lunged in a new direction, not exactly forward. The thing was far from agile on dry roads. Somebody or something slammed into the side and threw the front end onto another course. Tree limbs swept across the split windscreen. Lights flashed orange and red. A car alarm brayed. Another loud noise began to hammer inward, not the wheezing engine, more rhythmic, brutally intense. Electric guitar?

Gargantuan aftermarket speakers filled the spaces where the rearmost seats had been. In spite of the van's jarring wobbles, I could *feel* the damn things throwing sound at us. The volume must be cranked.

"Stereo's one of those things that's broken!" Danny shouted over a chorus of reverb and a familiar lead singer. "Can't shut it off!"

The microbus gained impetus and careened through the whitewashed lot, as out of control as the first Doors fan who owned it must have been. The mass I'd dubbed Bigfoot staggered after us and fell in the distance. I doubted asphalt would do much damage but hoped it at least hurt. We bounced off the front fender of a Mercedes, jumped the curb, and found a thin trail of the grit the maintenance truck had laid down earlier. The Volkswagen traversed half a block up West Side Row at a forty-five-degree angle.

But we left the Sarratt Center in the mirrors. And we treated every unsuspecting ear within a quarter mile radius to vintage Foghat at full volume.

....*slow riiiide! Take it eeeeeeeasy...*

Flintlock

Chapter Fourteen

Five blocks on West End were enough.

The rain slackened. Splashes from the missing passenger side window stung less. But washed ice still coated everything and even slow-moving vehicles bounced into each other like bumper cars at the county fair. Danny's damaged VW seemed to specialize in near misses. Maybe sound waves repelled the thing from obstacles. After a few slugs to the jaw my skull had little tolerance for being pummeled by thirty-two-inch subwoofers. I rapped Danny's shoulder—he hadn't heard my shouts over Aerosmith—and pointed to a parking lot. He cranked the wheel. The microbus altered direction one third as much as requested. A front tire struck the curb and the ass end whipped around into the lot first. The Volkswagen jolted to a halt against a concrete wheel-stop, more or less in a defined parking space. My ears were full of Steven Tyler for thirty seconds after Danny killed the engine.

Other cars in the lot gleamed as white as the skating rink under them. The air had cleared to reveal a cleaner version of the city, with high-rises and wrecked cars and blinking traffic lights, all glazed in sparkling ice. That Danny had maneuvered this far was miraculous.

"Do you think they followed us?" breathed Aubrea.

"I don't see how."

Danny shuffled warily across the ice to our side of the van.

101

He frowned at a man-sized dent in the rear panel.

"You didn't kill anybody," I assured him.

I suspected I might have, however, in front of who knew how many witnesses. Whining sirens had become the city's most prominent sound—I just hadn't regained full use of my ears till now to notice—but the odds were decent my violent acts weren't their top priorities. Yet.

Danny and I raised our eyes across West End simultaneously. The tallest of the glittering structures there was familiar.

"Um, you suppose..."

"Might as well," I said. "The sooner we get far from the bus, the better. Miss Langston, how'd you like a backstage tour of Cool-Core's corporate innards?"

She sounded doubtful. "You know someone who'd let us in?"

In spite of his unexpectedly dramatic afternoon, Danny laughed.

• • •

The Cool-Core Tower rivaled Nashville's better-known AT&T building in both height and flair. The architect had respectfully crafted a design one story shorter than the earlier landmark. Then my father had it built outside the city center on higher ground, so both structures shared the same overall elevation above sea level. Dad could be a real shit that way. He hadn't lived to gloat about it, and though his only offspring had every right to come and go at will, I shunned the place as religiously as Einstein shunned combs.

To the rest of the world, the skyscraper looming over the first block of West End was the pulsing heart of a multi-billion-dollar technology empire. To me? Thirty-two floors of swivel chairs and filing cabinets. But today I had sidekicks to worry about. Getting all the way to my condo or to police headquarters without breaking our necks, or having them

Flintlock

broken for us, seemed too long a shot. Cool-Core was close and the security was first-rate.

There was a watchman at every door. Always. He stood in every vestibule, his careful eyes supplementing twenty-four-seven closed-circuit security cameras. His jacket was pressed, his tie done in an impeccable double-Windsor. He would politely answer questions and politely ask questions, and when necessary he'd dissuade anyone who had no business in the building from going farther. He wasn't required to be polite for that.

I looked as rough as the last vagrant who'd been turned away, but the watchman merely nodded when we came in off West End. Danny and I had been recognized before the automated doors opened, our irises scanned discretely and compared to Cool-Core's personnel database ten seconds after we faced the entrance. Supposedly the system even saw through sunglasses.

I touched the button engraved with a glowing number *32*. No one except the night watchman and I had permission to use that button. I hadn't done so yet. Danny's excitement was palpable. His duties normally constrained him to the basement labs.

The girl's blue eyes dodged between us and the advancing floor numbers. She's spent all afternoon desperately running from questions, which made it awkward for her to press her own.

"I, uh, think I've got an office up here," I said.

"You *think...?*"

"He hasn't seen it yet," Danny interjected helpfully.

Aubrea crossed her arms and waited. Danny and I had done a sloppy job of getting her out of a rough place. She'd withhold judgment for now. The sparkling elevator cab lights transformed her into every inch of a runway model. This, in spite of torn jeans, a scraped chin, and dried blood on her denim jacket. We both realized I was staring at the same time. Her smile seemed ineffective punishment. The elevator stopped with a shiver and proclaimed the thirty-first floor with an electronic ding. I'd heard enough electronic dings for one day. The doors opened only because the button for that floor had scanned my fingerprint and correlated it with the pictures of my eyeballs from the first floor.

Aubrea held back, unsure. Danny let me go first. Of all people familiar with my recent past, he probably understood best what my coming here meant.

The entire top floor of the Cool-Core Tower should have been my father's executive office. He'd approved the floorplans. He'd chosen the carpet, furniture, wall finishes. He'd decided which way the windows faced. And the day before he was to lay eyes on his completed corporate aerie, my old man slid out of this world as tight to the ground as a man can go, face-first in a puddle of the whiskey he hadn't kept down, under a cheap barstool in Madison. Cool-Core had belonged to me for the two years since and I'd have avoided this level longer, given the choice. I stepped off the elevator.

You wouldn't expect a career drunk to have that kind of taste.

The lobby ended in a wall of seeded glass that curved inward on the left and right. After a thirty-two-story ascent, bubbles in the glass imparted an odd sinking sensation, as if we were settling toward the bottom of a clear weedless lake. Shapes beyond the glass resembled furniture. I led the others around to confirm this suspicion. A broad open space waited, not bright. There were windows surely. Dad would've expected his digs to do what they were told.

"Blinds," I said.

Voice-actuated motorized blinds raised in unison. Fresh sunlight lanced between breaking clouds and shot inward from three directions. On one side of the space stood a broad desk,

Flintlock

all aluminum and glass and burnished red leather. Neither keyboard nor mouse were visible, only a thin wide-panel monitor mounted so organically it might have grown there. The desk was open underneath, proving my aversion to drawers was genetic, though a matching swivel chair waited beyond the far edge. Red-stained cabinets with aluminum hardware rose beyond the desk from the chocolate-hued carpet. Every other vertical surface was transparent: a plexiglass veneer separated us from a four-hundred-foot tumble into Nashville's iced skyline.

The remaining items were several red leather chairs and a sumptuous red leather couch, which bracketed a horizontal expanse of seeded glass for a table. My command to the shades had also woken a frameless gas fireplace in the center of the room that tossed swaying flames nearly to the ceiling. It was all very dramatic. I couldn't see getting much work done here.

"*Your* office?" Aubrea breathed.

"I just inherited it."

Her blue eyes zeroed in on me. With a jolt, I realized what color was utterly missing from the thirty-second floor. Had my old man disliked blue so much? I sensed questions coming, the usual questions, the ones I could never satisfy. A quiver inside my jacket interrupted. I apologized and reached for my phone.

Rafferty.

"Danny? Would you please catch her up on matters Bedlam? I should take this."

• • •

"Where are you?"

Mine was the first butt to ever land in that swivel chair. It surprised me. A guy could learn to appreciate that kind of comfort even at the expense of his waistline. I blew dust from the glass desktop. Cleaning crews had never been admitted since their original boss's passing, but with as much sensitive computer hardware as the building contained, Cool-Core's air conditioning was supremely filtered. This had taken two years to accumulate. Beneath the dust lay a capacitive keyboard. The glass over the buttons glowed where I touched, nothing more; the interface waited for Dad's password.

"My office," I told the phone.

"You don't have an office."

"Funny, coming from you."

The Lieutenant muttered something ugly under his breath. His own desk held walls apart in a windowless downtown hole better suited to storing mop buckets.

"Dad's old office," I added, before he got uselessly aggravated. "On West End."

"Uh huh. How long?"

"A while. You've looked outside, right?"

"Quit being a wise-ass. You at Vanderbilt today?"

The question came with his job. I expected it. I just wished he hadn't asked. Lying to Jerry Rafferty always came back to haunt a person. Yet if I told him the whole truth, he'd be obligated to do his job, and I couldn't help him or anybody else from a jail cell. My thoughts wandered to my hands, which hurt like hell. I turned both palms up. A doctor would ask why I'd been slapping rock salt into bricks all day.

"Ask me about my new job at O'Dell's," I suggested.

His reaction was immediate. "They *hired* you?"

"Meredith O'Dell did. I'm her new security consultant. Tomorrow's my first night shift."

Not often could I tell one of Rafferty's chuckles from his growls. I'd plainly told him something funny.

"No shit! I'll assume you were too busy interviewing to have anything to do with a bunch of brawling on campus. Don't talk me out of this assumption."

"I wouldn't dream of it."

"I know you wouldn't be caught dead doing donuts in any old hippy vans."

Flintlock

"I'm far too self-important."

"Uh huh. Not one damn suspect or body. Where'd those go, I wonder? It'll take days to sort out. Camera system was down. One of your Cool-Core boys didn't finish installing upgrades before he split for the day—"

"I'll give him a stern talking to."

"—and college kids make terrible witnesses."

"So what happened?"

"Don't push your luck," the Lieutenant said, "or mine. Looks like my vacation's over."

Then he hung up.

• • •

I laid the phone on a wireless charging mat built into the desktop. A prototype two years ago, it worked fine today. The whole place was an accidental time capsule.

Danny rose from one of the chairs across the room where he and Aubrea had quietly talked while I played mouse to Rafferty's cat. Her seated form made a graceful silhouette against reds and pinks that doused the city as departing sunlight stained the undersides of clouds.

"She's up to speed. Hope I didn't share too much."

"If it was that private," I said, "I wouldn't have told you in the first place."

His relieved expression was all the more comical for being genuine. I felt guilty for having goaded him into vehicular assault, however justifiable. Danny was an innocent in a world that didn't deserve him.

"Let your van sit for a day or two," I said. "Once the hoopla dies down I'll have it towed to a shop to get fixed. My dime. Even the stereo."

Especially the stereo.

"Wow, awesome! Thanks! Okay if I go downstairs? I can finish debugging some code."

"Sure. Don't talk with anyone about this, though. Have the

Jon A. Hunt

cafeteria send up a pizza if they're open."

"Will do."

The elevator chime mimicked his cheerful tone, then the doors opened and swallowed him. The District Attorney's daughter and I had the thirty-second floor to ourselves. The sunset dimmed to French gray. Where there was electricity, artificial lights twinkled from the city's high points. After dark, from atop the Cool-Core Tower, things looked no worse than normal. The central fireplace washed Aubrea's features with warmth. I hadn't noticed light switches, but I knew how my father had liked things.

"Lights to half."

The suite brightened by fifty percent as commanded.

"Like a drink?"

The pretty face moved side to side. "No, thank you. I'm sure I shouldn't be drinking."

"Me, neither. I'm really just looking for antiseptics."

A stainless-steel sink with a high arched brushed nickel faucet had been installed in the cabinetry behind the desk. Dad wouldn't put himself out of reach of a well-stocked wet bar. I found what I was after in an adjacent cupboard. Scotch, gin, bourbon...vodka seemed the most medicinal. That bottle came out to rest beside the sink while I turned on the tap and tried to rinse rock salt out of my chewed palms.

"Let me."

She'd crossed the room without my hearing. Gunfire and loud music will do that to you. Slender, agile fingers took mine, massaged debris loose one agonizing particle at a time. Bits of aggregate and dirty salt clicked against the metal basin. I was glad to be rid of them and glad for her touch, even if the process stung like a sonofabitch.

"Should have worn gloves," she said.

"I took them off to call you. There wasn't time to put them back on."

Flintlock

The eyes that flicked up at me as she reached for the Absolut weren't as startlingly blue as poor Mitch's. They were more hypnotic.

"Thanks, by the way."

The hundred-proof bite rendered me less than gracious. What got through my clenched teeth wasn't appropriate for mixed company. She didn't appear offended, but she didn't apologize for my discomfort, either. She used my lapse as a springboard for a question.

"You said...those men might have something to do with what happened to Mitch?"

The wet fire gnawing my palms and knuckles subsided, and evaporating alcohol created a slight cooling sensation. Aubrea's fingertips burned like soft embers against me. I drew breath more deliberately and made a better conversational effort. "At least one of them did."

"The big one?"

"Yeah."

"He hurt Mitch?"

My fingers closed over hers. I could think past the pain if I wanted. I could ignore the sharp bouquet of vodka. My answer was delivered to her eyes as well as her ears. "He killed him," I said.

"That wasn't my question."

Flames from the artsy fireplace reflected in her welling tears. Behind the tiny copies of fire, I also found unexpected ferocity. She firmly believed she wanted all of the truth, not just the safe parts. I wasn't sure I could bring myself to add those kinds of details to her burden.

Bloody handprints.

Arms busted like twigs.

A crumpled headless heap that only resembled the living man because both versions wore the same crossword suspenders.

Jon A. Hunt

"Mitch died hard. I'm sorry."

Tears tracked freely over her cheeks now. The shape of the word "why?" formed on her lips without resolving into sound.

"You must have an idea," I said. "He called me because he promised you he would."

Her frame tensed. The fingers caught in mine might as well be sixteen-penny nails.

"He...he found something 'A puzzle,' he called it. By accident. Very old—he wanted us to solve the puzzle together—we used to do puzzles all the time. But he..."

I willed my grip to soften before the pressure hurt her. In spite of an effort to keep my voice sympathetic it sounded harshly insistent. "What was it?"

Blue agony flashed up at me.

"Mitch wouldn't tell me! He said it wasn't safe..."

She'd have collapsed if I hadn't caught her. I can't say I minded letting her press against me as she cried. But her grief needed a while to vent and after a few minutes I felt awkward. My gaze wandered. The glass desk glimmered. Swaying gas flames from the fireplace provided most of the light now that night had fully arrived. Distant rectangular stars peered in at us from beyond the glass boundaries of our sanctuary. If people in half of those high-rises had the means and any of my nosiness, Aubrea and I were performing live for their entertainment. What keeps goldfish from going nuts is beyond me.

Intervals between the sobs increased. Now she breathed shallowly, rapidly. Her head remained tucked under my chin. She clutched my shirtfront for support.

"Mr. Bedlam?" she breathed into my chest.

"Hmm?"

"I think I will have that drink after all."

Flintlock

Chapter Fifteen

She woke the next morning by bolting upright with a scream. A lot of designer furniture might have gotten broken if I'd crashed into the room with my .45 in one hand and my shirt untucked. Fortunately, I'd been up for an hour and was relatively lucid in a nearby armchair. Watching Aubrea Langston sleep through a Nashville sunrise wasn't the worst way to start a day.

"It's all right. You're safe."

She shrank back into the cushions. Her kind of disheveled sold perfume in magazines. A blanket I'd draped over her was crushed into an anxious wad between her fists. I'd found the blanket in one of two luxurious bedroom suites that bracketed the elevator lobby. I had no idea who Dad expected to spend much time up here, or where the maid staff had gone after two years with nothing to do, but there was a king size bed available for each of us. I hadn't roused her to risk the offer of a bed being misconstrued, and she hadn't stirred from the couch. Put away enough Jack and Coke, and you'll sleep equally well on a sofa, or huddled in the fetal position on a tile floor beside a commode. It's the waking up part that can be miserable.

Blue eyes surfed the room, paused to glitter in ruddy new daylight, came back to me calmer. "Awful dream."

"You've had plenty of fuel for them," I said. "No need to apologize."

Jon A. Hunt

"Do you ever have nightmares, Mr. Bedlam? Or does nothing frighten you?"

"Everybody has them. Mine just tend to happen when I'm awake."

She blinked a couple times before deciding I meant it. "How are your hands?"

"I won't volunteer to wash dishes for a few days. But better. Thanks. I'm going to run down and find us breakfast. Any requests?"

There was no leftover pizza. The same watchman from the West End lobby had brought up the box of stale crust and greasy pepperoni after Danny's departure. Now the only nourishment available was in the liquor cabinet.

We looked up coffee shops on my phone. The computer built into the desk might have impressed me more if I could make it do anything, and Aubrea's cracked device was gasping on its battery's last dregs. I found an old-fashioned charger for her while we searched for food. She retrieved her phone once we'd settled on some promising options.

"Oh," she gasped, almost guiltily, "I have a *lot* of missed calls!"

I hadn't stopped to consider who might worry about her, especially if news about yesterday's fun at Vanderbilt had gone public. Little Eli came to mind. So did Aubrea's father. I supposed I ought to mention this to Rafferty.

"Let them know you're okay," I said. "I wouldn't provide details about yesterday or mention where you are. Security here is excellent but we can't stay forever."

Her eyes widened. She juggled beautiful and exhausted well. "I have no intention of staying long. I didn't exactly bring a change of clothes."

"You had plans for the next couple of days?"

"I...well, I didn't say that."

"You aren't out of the woods. Whoever tried to grab you

Flintlock

yesterday won't give up easily. And Eli—or your dad—can't keep an eye on you the way I can."

She exhaled. "I'd be locked away like holiday china."

"I'm not putting myself in charge," I said. "But I can only help as much as you let me."

"And I haven't told you about Mitch yet."

"Not yet."

Her smile was altogether disarming. "Okay. I'll sit tight till you return. I won't tell anyone about yesterday or where I am. It's doubtful they'd believe me either way. Please go find us breakfast! I'll enjoy the view and make sure Daddy isn't in a panic."

• • •

The city tried its best to limp into an ordinary Wednesday. In fact, where sunshine touched walk or street, yesterday's wintry glaze did soften. Buses and battle-scarred cars churned through dirty slush, encouraged by such liberally applied traction sand that Florida ought to consider recounting its beaches. But sun, salt and sand had no effect where shadows persisted, and getting around was perilous. People risked it. We had lives to live and work to do. I allowed a few phone calls to keep me inside the main floor lobby.

The dealership had finally fixed my winter car. Nobody with access to the keys had made their way in. I told them I'd get there when I could. I also mentioned an old Volkswagen that would need attention.

The second number was Tipper's. Congenial as ever, his responses came a beat slower than usual. I asked him if he'd had any trouble on the roads getting to the estate. He yawned.

"Are the roads bad? I've been here since you left."

"Seriously?"

"There's a lot to do. The neighbors aren't thrilled..."

"They put up with Jorgensen," I said.

"Did all of them? I wonder..."

Jon A. Hunt

Cynicism struck me as out of character for him. The man hadn't slept for days and he was playing with guns.

"Give yourself a break," I suggested. "I won't get out to Belle Meade till tomorrow."

Tipper stifled another yawn. "You may be right—"

"Probably."

"I keep eyeing those cotton batts for the bullet collector. Who'd miss them for a couple hours?"

"I'll pick up sandwiches on my way over tomorrow."

"Okay. Get enough for five, including Officer Poole? Nobody's starving just yet. But if I never see another cinnamon granola bar it will be too soon."

I promised I would and ended our conversation. Tipper's dedication left me astonished. Poole and the forensics techs likely had other adjectives in mind if he'd kept them in that shithole for forty-eight hours.

A car horn blared out on West End and two large objects slammed together on the street outside. Those particular Nashville cabs wouldn't be collecting fares today. I decided to stay where I was a bit longer and make one more call.

Jerry Rafferty was going to learn the DA's daughter's whereabouts sooner or later. I might as well be the messenger.

• • •

I got an affirmative nod from the day-shift warden upon my return an hour and twenty minutes later. He'd been tasked with keeping an extra eye on the penthouse elevator security monitors. It was an easy fifty dollars: true to her word, Aubrea hadn't left. I admired the guy's stoicism. Here I had a gorgeous girl stowed upstairs all to myself, and some very upset person bludgeoning me with perfectly audible four-letter words over the phone on my way out; yet, at least in my presence, the doorman never exhibited a hint of amusement.

The *32* button did nothing when I rapped it with a knuckle. Knuckles don't have fingerprints. The doorman placidly

114

Flintlock

watched me shuffle plastic shopping bags to my left hand so I could apply the required pad of my index finger to the button. My scanned print coincided with data on record, the elevator decided I was the same swell guy I pretended to be, the doors hissed shut and up I went. The doorman could smile now if he wanted.

Cool-Core didn't subscribe to elevator music, thank God. I could use a minute of silence. Between yesterday's hallway gunfire, Danny's jackhammer sound system, and Rafferty's reaction to the news of my top-floor guest, I counted on some permanent hearing loss.

What pissed Rafferty off most was he had no better alternatives. If anything related to his department's investigation harmed the DA's kid, he was screwed. If I delivered the girl into protective custody, Rafferty was going to be blamed for that, too.

"I'm pulling Poole off the Jorgensen estate," he snapped. "He can watch her while you're working your O'Dell's gig."

"Smally's your usual babysitter, isn't he? This girl's got a pretty rough fan club."

"You have enough trouble keeping your own shit straight. I'll do my job how I say. Smally's busy tracking down new leads."

I didn't ask for specifics. My ears hurt bad enough.

"Any other cute surprises?"

"Nope," I promised.

"Better fucking not be."

The call ended with a fierce click. My friend downtown wouldn't likely be asking any more favors soon. That was fine by me. My hands were full.

My full hands hurt, too, especially the left one where shopping bag handles dug into the raw skin. I'm not ordinarily so tender. Skinning my paws on rock salt was just a new experience. I focused instead on the intriguing reason for my

Jon A. Hunt

pain, the girl who'd guided the healing process with gentle fingers and hard alcohol.

We'd avoided further mention of Mitch the rest of the night. Aubrea's injuries weren't visible, yet went deeper. Safer topics centered around me: Cool-Core, the ostentatious building beneath us, my dead parents. Mostly, though, we slumped into the designer couch, separated by the space propriety dictated, nursed amateur cocktails poured from bottles nobody'd cracked open in two years, and stared mutely out over Nashville's glittering skyline. The diorama hadn't much changed when I returned with my treasures, except now sunlight washed through the suite, Aubrea's hair was wet, and she'd wrapped herself in a terrycloth robe from one of the bedroom closets. Either she'd decided I wouldn't take advantage of her in my lair, or she was the kind of woman who found comfort in new surroundings quickly.

"You've been industrious," she said, eyeing the bags I dumped onto my father's impressive, useless desk.

"I wasn't sure which kind of bagel you liked, so I bought one of each."

"I could probably eat one of each," she said. It was nearer lunchtime than breakfast.

I left her to investigate the rest of my trove while I busied myself with the coffee maker on the wet bar, which was at least superior to most office coffee makers. Her fascination was childish, in a Christmas-morning way, as she rummaged. It was nothing exciting: fresh apples, junk food, toothbrushes, deodorant, t-shirts, socks, blue jeans—

"How'd you know my size?" she demanded.

"The tag on the waistband of the jeans you slept in," I said. "I get paid to notice things."

"Oh. No new underwear?"

"I, uh…"

Aubrea's laugh had mesmerized over the phone. In person,

Flintlock

it utterly incapacitated a guy.

"I'm kidding, Mr. Bedlam. Mine are washed and drying in the bathroom."

Knowing this didn't help my concentration a bit. "All right. But if you're going to tease me about underwear, at least call me Tyler."

She straightened and extended a delicate hand. I accepted the offered touch. If my ragged palms stung under that warmth, I never noticed.

"Aubrea. Very pleased to make your acquaintance."

"Likewise," I said, honestly.

"Coffee now?"

"Yes, ma'am. And we can talk."

Her smile paled. "Yeah, we can talk about Mitch."

• • •

A half dozen bagels didn't stand a chance against our combined appetites. We'd burned more calories in twenty-four hours than one midnight pizza could replenish. We barely conversed till only crumbs and an empty cream cheese tub occupied the desktop between our coffee mugs.

If Aubrea felt disadvantaged newly scrubbed and naked beneath a borrowed robe that tended to fall open at her slightest movement, her manner never betrayed it. She remained as achingly beautiful as the first time I saw her. Clothes might make the man, but Aubrea would come across as royalty wearing only a smile. I caught myself imagining this very costume and suddenly realized she'd started talking. How long? Minutes? An hour?

"...and he said 'You don't have to go back.' Out of the blue, a stranger sitting by himself in a coffee shop. It was the first thing he ever said to me.

"I didn't know how to react. Maybe my sunglasses didn't hide the black eye at all. Maybe he'd been waiting there since the place opened, just because I needed a friend. It was weird,

Jon A. Hunt

but not creepy. He got up and pulled a chair over for me, and I sat down and bawled."

Aubrea's blue gaze sought me from under long lashes. I hoped I didn't look guilty. I hadn't been thinking about anything Mitch would've called chivalrous. For all I knew, the shine in Aubrea's eyes blazed through leftover tears from her first encounter with the man.

"Have you ever known anyone that caring?" she asked. "They'd be there no matter who you are or what you've done, and there isn't any angle. I mean, even Jesus had an angle, right?"

I shook my head. The best people I knew still expected something for being nice. None of them quite deserved crossword puzzle suspenders, except Jesus.

She sniffed, lingered on a memory, plowed ahead.

"He was right. I didn't need a man who hit me. I never went back. I started over clean because that funny old man wasn't fooled by dark glasses. Instead of the string of rotten boyfriends whose best qualifications were that Daddy and Eli didn't approve of them, there was morning coffee three times a week with a friend who'd never hurt a soul. He couldn't, you know—" piercing conviction in her voice drove the point home "—never in a million years would Mitch do wrong by anyone. Why would anyone hurt him? You think any of my exes—?"

"I doubt it," I said. "Jealousy had nothing to do with Mitch's death. He was killed for some*thing*, not because of some*one*. And he wasn't the first."

"Tyler, I have to ask. You said it was that gigantic man from yesterday..." She faltered.

I took the lead before her emotions did again. "He was the killer."

"If you know, can't the police just arrest him?"

"It isn't that simple."

"I don't understand."

Flintlock

Why would she?

"Mitch's murder was part of something bigger. The lump who did it isn't the only person with dirty hands. He has a boss. He has people who shuttle him around. A person that huge doesn't drive himself. So if I, or the police, want to make a permanent difference, we have to bring down the entire group. Not just the one who killed Mitch. All of them. Otherwise, this happens again. Look at how many men were there to haul you off. You won't be safe till I figure what they're after and they're all behind bars...or stopped some other way."

The unuttered part of the truth tasted acidic. My real intentions didn't include delivering Mitch's killer to the meanderings of an inconsistent legal system. Dead men don't need a jury. Rafferty should have considered the risks of involving me once I'd made things personal.

Then again, maybe he had. He wasn't crazy about the inconsistent legal system, either.

"What do these men want with me?"

"They're trying to find what Mitch had," I said. "At least what they *thought* he had. You'd been with him before he died. It's logical to assume he told you."

"You had the same idea."

"Lucky for you," I said.

"But I don't know anything about...whatever it is."

"You may and just not realize it."

I recalled my conversation with Rafferty. *Ask Tipper about the red journal.* Old documents missing from the estate. Mitch came to me because he'd acquired something old. And he'd been in O'Dell's seconds before the disastrous raid by Rafferty's team. I should try on a few obvious assumptions for size. Avoiding snap conclusions hadn't gotten me far yet.

"Could it be an old book?"

Aubrea clunked her mug down. "Why would you ask that?"

"Mitch was in an antique bookstore before he met with me.

Jon A. Hunt

I'm guessing that's where he found whatever it is that worried him. A rare book might make sense."

"O'Dell's," she said, flatly.

I tend to grin whenever a puzzle piece snaps into place. It was all I could do to keep a serious face now. "You know the place."

Aubrea's expression shifted in an unexpected direction. She looked contrite. "Yeah. They've got a court order that says I'm not allowed within a hundred feet of it."

• • •

Poole arrived in the ground floor lobby at a quarter to five. His fresh looks and a lump under his jacket shaped like a service weapon said *cop* to knowing eyes; for the rest of the world, he wore jeans and a Predators ballcap. Rafferty and I had agreed subtlety was our best bet. I rode the elevator down, squared his credentials with the doorman, sent him on up. He seemed excited about his first plainclothes gig. I didn't have the heart to tell him he'd be wading through the same shit, just in different muck boots. I snapped a Granny Smith out of the grocery bag he'd brought, for my evening commute.

The city was quiet. Nashville had had a rough couple of days. The air still had a wintry bite and the sidewalks weren't a sure thing. Main streets wore plenty of salt by now, but drivers were done being brave and pedestrians were scarce. I had most of the walk to myself.

I wondered if Aubrea peered down from the Cool-Core Tower to try and see me, or if Poole had managed to stagger into conversation right off. The man was so painfully single, I'd have asked for a different officer, if Rafferty hadn't already instilled sufficient dread of any involvement with the DA's daughter. Poole would probably keep both hands in his pockets till my return.

The more time I spent with the girl, the more fascinating she became. Sure, this was partially due to the thou-shalt-not

Flintlock

nature of our relationship. She'd grown up shielded from guys like me, men who breathed the kind of trouble that kept her daddy employed. Then came college. A parade of bad boys who lured a girl who knew better into the shadows. She drank. She partied. Her grades suffered, the usual college first-year slippery slope, only Aubrea had come at it in a dead run. Fortunately, that ferocious brother of hers never let her sink entirely, and not all of Aubrea's passions were self-destructive. More than most things, she loved to read. She was simultaneously a mirror image and an antonym to Meredith O'Dell; and Meredith's store became the first tripping point to stop a downward spiral.

Raleigh caught her shoplifting.

Of course, he wanted to press charges. But Aubrea's parents had larger influence than an old bookstore. Everything was settled out of court. Restitution was made, the girl put in her community service at the Rescue Mission, the courts cleared her record—on the condition that Aubrea didn't set foot in her favorite store for three years.

The bad boy habit took longer to kick. Mitch Braunfelter and Eli Langston labored in unwitting tandem to steer her straight again. Mitch became the friend and level-headed influence she desperately needed. Eli pulled strings, and the boyfriend with the indiscriminate right hook found himself searching for a higher education in any other state besides Tennessee, whose schools suddenly wanted nothing to do with him.

After all that, Aubrea still loved her books. So Mitch and her brother shopped in O'Dell's on her behalf. The Friday after Mitch died was Aubrea's birthday. That explained the presence of both men, though neither knew the other by sight, in the bookstore the day of Rafferty's unsuccessful raid. They were looking for birthday gifts for the same woman.

"He was always buying me presents," she'd said of Mitch.

"Just little things. Everybody else seemed like they were bribing me, even Eli. Always the angle! Not Mitch. Usually it was a puzzle book. That's how we spent our mornings, solving those silly puzzles together."

"Was he as good at it as he told me?"

"Mitch was the smartest person I'd ever met, smarter even than Daddy, at least when it came to finding patterns in things or sorting riddles. Especially crosswords. He asked me for the words all the time, but I'm sure it was just to be nice. He always knew the answers. I bet he read dictionaries or competed in spelling bees when he was a little boy."

Something about this stuck with me hours after she said it. Halfway through both my walk and the apple, I realized why.

ARTIC.

The little refrigerator magnet word I'd spotted, in the ruined kitchen of a dead man in kitschy suspenders, wasn't the correct spelling of any word at all. I remembered being dinged for misspelling *ARCTIC* myself in grade school.

16 across. Six letters. Polar region.
C'mon, Mitch, you knew that.

Six different letters extracted me from my reverie, the buzzing sign over the front door to O'Dell's.

I pitched the apple core into a trash can next to a parking meter, wiped my mouth with the back of a hand, straightened my collar. Meredith O'Dell hadn't mentioned ties being required. There hadn't been time to fetch one of my shirts at home. Tonight's came from a department store four blocks away. I hadn't shaved.

First day on the job. No problem.

Flintlock

Chapter Sixteen

The old woman waited in back at the foot of the mezzanine stairs with her bony arms crossed.

"You seemed better composed yesterday."

"I was," I confessed.

"What happened to your hands?"

"I fell."

She took two deliberate steps forward and stopped inches from my chest. I'd been toe-to-toe with contract killers who rattled me less. She sniffed. Fortunately, I'd made use of the shower in my temporary penthouse office and hadn't touched Dad's liquor stash all day. I smelled cleaner than I looked.

"I expect my money's worth, Mr. Bedlam."

"Yes, ma'am. I'd like to look over the cameras."

A trace of yesterday's humor tugged at the corners of Meredith's eyes. "Raleigh will show you," she said, pivoted and ascended the stairs.

The Vice President of O'Dell's tipped his forehead my direction from behind the wall of security monitors. Clenched black and gray curls telegraphed a damned sullen mood even before I circled around to his side of the table. It was difficult to say which of us was least enthusiastic about working together.

"Good evening, Raleigh."

"I suppose," he muttered.

I let that slide and dragged an extra chair up beside him. He

123

Jon A. Hunt

hadn't boobytrapped it with thumbtacks, which disappointed me. I only needed a tiny excuse...

"Are those all of the cameras?"

He glared, at the monitors, not at me. He'd probably considered the tacks. I just scared him too much.

"Not all at once. The system cycles through cameras every fifteen seconds. I can pause the cycle, choose any camera, and zoom in if I want."

"What if somebody misbehaves between cycles?"

"What?"

"How do you know what happens when a camera isn't up on one of the screens?"

"You're the security expert, I'm told."

"I enjoy the thrill of asking questions. Humor me."

Raleigh's eyes rolled but he answered. "Every camera has infrared motion sensing. If there's movement, that camera's view skips the regular queue and stays on screen. They automatically record when they see movement, as well."

"You're able to keep all of them straight?"

He didn't dignify that with an immediate response. But unanswered questions were precisely the reason Meredith O'Dell was paying me for my time.

"Everyone is missing something," she'd groused, "the police, Raleigh, everyone. These thieves know exactly what to steal, where it is, when it's here. I want you to find out how."

I also had my own reasons for being there, which Raleigh's stubbornness wouldn't serve.

"I'll repeat the question, if you like."

This time his glare was direct. The dainty chain looping from his eyeglasses diminished most of the intended ferocity. "They're numbered," he said dully. "I know where every camera is in the store."

Flintlock

"Okay. Where's Number Seventeen?"

He blinked without turning to the computer screens. "Early American Lit."

"Why's it black?"

Camera Seventeen suddenly had Raleigh's attention more than I did. It ought to, he stared at the things all day. He snapped back to the offending monitor, with its Hollywood Squares grid of color images. Some of these were still life pictures of vacant aisles, visible for their allotted fifteen seconds only; others showed moving persons. The people in the little squares were distorted, their heads too large for their bodies because the cameras viewed them from above. A square two up from the bottom and three from the right showed nothing except a pulsing number *17* in one corner. Raleigh reached up to the empty square and tapped. A dialog box appeared and told us the camera was sending a signal but obstructed. He plucked a cordless phone from the tabletop and stabbed the keypad to death with an index finger.

"Who's in Am Lit?" he demanded.

A tiny voice emanated from the handset. I couldn't hear it as plainly as Raleigh. I did recognize Darlene's lilting drawl, however.

"We talked about those top shelves, didn't we?"

The little voice sounded apologetic. She probably had to apologize to Raleigh on a regular basis. Her pretty, comically enlarged face blinked into view in the Number Seventeen square. Books teetered on top of a ladder in the background. I scanned the other camera views to see if there were any old men on the floor behind her, but they must be at home reading Grant's memoirs. She mouthed a "sorry" for the camera and resumed wedging books from the ladder onto the shelf. I couldn't swear to it from such a small vantage point, but her purple polka dotted dress appeared to fit like a second skin.

"Does that happen often?" I asked.

Jon A. Hunt

"What?"

"Cameras getting blocked like that."

Vice President Raleigh resented the question. A lot.

"It happens. The cameras are mounted on bookshelves. Sometimes a book gets in the way. We've quite a lot of the things here. I'm not going to dangle cameras over every aisle so customers wonder if they're going to be on the six o'clock news!"

"Then why bother with the cameras at all?"

He started up out of his seat like he'd developed a sudden allergy to it.

"Sit down, Raleigh, or I'll put you back in that chair myself." I said it low yet forcefully.

He hovered between standing and sitting. I hoped for his sake he took me seriously. Yesterday I'd flattened a guy's face with a shovel, and I'd used more of my limited supply of patience since then. He reconsidered and sat.

"I don't honestly care whether you like me," I told him. "A lot of people don't. But a little cooperation won't hurt you. The sassy attitude might. All right?"

"Yes, Mr. Bedlam." If stones could talk...

We stared mutely at the matrix of tiny unscripted movies for a while. The O'Dell family kept longer hours than their competitors, a fact that wasn't lost on the college crowd, but nervousness generated by the ice storm hadn't quite subsided. Aside from Raleigh and me, Darlene, a pair of clerks working the sales counter, and Meredith up in her bookless office, the store contained not more than nine or ten other souls. Except for Meredith, we saw every one of them. O'Dell's wasn't a good place to hide.

Darlene was easiest to follow. Her painted-on dress ensured that Raleigh and I weren't her whole audience. Whenever she moved out of frame, we need only watch for turning heads to locate her again. My brain was momentarily lured into a less

Flintlock

productive search, though when I caught myself, something I'd heard earlier about the security system popped to the forefront.

White shoes has been here before. Raleigh recognized him.

"How far back are the videos archived?"

Raleigh was okay with this question. It steered us safely away from my last.

"A minimum of thirty days. It depends on file size, how many cameras were recording, so forth. Usually it's closer to forty-five days. Then the system overwrites the oldest footage. I'm sure you already know that is typical."

"Uh huh." I let his dig pass without knocking his teeth out. I decided to make that my personal challenge, to see how long I could tolerate Raleigh without anyone needing to put him on life support. "The police confiscated the hard drives, correct?"

He frowned, not at me, not at the videos, just a general scowl. For a small moment, he felt we shared a common adversary. "The police have *copies* of the drives. Files are backed up in more than one place."

"So, you can access old footage."

"Not from that day."

"Why not?" Rafferty had mentioned this. I still wanted to hear explanations from the horse's mouth.

"The...system was down."

"You figure out why? It would be nice not to have a repeat occurrence."

"Yes," he said guardedly. "It won't happen again."

"I'll keep asking till you tell me."

Raleigh's expression hardened. Possibly he guessed my private goal not to damage him. "Mr. Bedlam, what are you doing here?"

I smiled sweetly.

"All right. Fine. The CPU got unplugged. Not from the wall outlet, from the power supply. We were down for two hours."

"You didn't notice?"

Jon A. Hunt

"If only you'd been here to advise, Mr. Bedlam..."

I dropped my gaze for a moment to the rat's nest of cables under the table, Raleigh's self-inflicted problem. Digging through that many cables *would* take a while.

"You have footage from *before* the outage, though."

"Yes."

"I'd like to see it."

"Retrieval takes a while."

I checked my watch. Meredith had been specific about my time. "I've got three hours."

"The full forty-five days——"

I held up a hand. The condition of my scabbed palm likely shushed him more than the gesture itself. "Not all of it. Meredith said you recognized the kid with the untied shoelaces."

Raleigh bobbed his curly head.

"Just look for footage with him in it."

"The police already——"

"I'm not the police. I'm not as patient as the police. And I bet you remember exactly when he was here."

Raleigh's jaw tightened sufficiently to affect his speech. "Give me two hours," he said.

• • •

My two-hour wait could be spent in better company. I left Raleigh to his onerous search and wandered the stacks. The place felt crowded even when it wasn't. Claustrophobia seeped with a heavy musk of decaying paper from between the books. Incongruous black spheres studied me from the ends of metal arms clamped to the uppermost shelves. My unshaven mug haunted the Vice President of O'Dell's long after I'd vacated the chair beside him. Served him right. He'd really get a kick out of watching me chat with his niece.

I caught up with Darlene in a section of the store I'd just as soon have avoided. Her dark eyes raised from the contents of a

Flintlock

book cart and said 'hello!" before I could retreat to a less awkward aisle. My old man would have described her as a "twenty-dollar date with a million-dollar smile." Whatever graceful manners I possessed came from the maternal side of the family. I did, however, appreciate my father's genes for excellent vision. I said "hello" back and strode into the *Sexuality and Erotica* aisle like I shopped there all the time.

"Here for the tour?" she teased.

"Maybe. How fascinating can a bookstore be?"

She winked. Purple eyeshadow again. This time, the only thing to match was the dress itself. Fabric that thin and tight concealed nothing lacy; what moved beneath was all Darlene. Meredith's warning yesterday about the girl had been vague. Even the most outspoken women of Meredith's age didn't discuss some matters.

"I *am* on the clock," I thought to mention.

"And Uncle Ral is watching!" she laughed.

Darlene's laughter was less reserved than Aubrea's, more sensual. The way her breasts danced must send men out of their way to share jokes with her. She'd probably heard more one-liners than Bob Hope. A limerick I knew about Irish Catholic cows clawed forward in my memory, though I remembered the four embarrassed old Confederate perverts quicker. She sensed my internal struggle and threw me a lifeline.

"Lend me a hand?" Her nails drummed the books atop the cart. "And Gram said you'd have questions?"

"A few," I confessed.

"I'm all yours." Her expression might or might not be intended only for the camera staring over my right shoulder. This aisle had an extra allotment of cameras, in spite of the fact that it ended against a wall and had only one exit. People might be less flustered stealing smut than walking up to the girl at the counter and paying for it. I didn't recognize the title on the covers of the six identical volumes she dumped into my hands.

Jon A. Hunt

"*The Fermata?*"

She leaned against the cart to start it rolling and deliberately bumped me with a hip. "Not a reader?"

"I am. Just, uh, different material. This any good?"

"Not bad, if you're into that sort of thing. Those go on the second row down. Smile for my uncle."

I grinned reflexively and popped the books into place. "I'm assuming you read plenty."

"That's one of your questions?"

"That's small talk."

"These go over to your left, next to Jong. Of course I read! I'm basically a librarian."

"Not a stereotypical one."

She used both hands to pass me an annotated *Kama Sutra Lovers' Companion*, and kept the large manual pressed tight against her midriff so I practically had to put my arms around her to take it. The real-life curves between me and the salacious cover art easily outscored the comparison. Her fingertips traced my sore knuckles as I withdrew the book.

"Because I'm not wearing....glasses?" she said.

"That must be it," I said. "Where does this belong?"

"On a bedside table," she whispered.

All that kept me from losing focus was Uncle Ral's digital glare on the back of my head. He had to have known what I was walking into when I got up to find Darlene. Her three-by-three pixelated likeness didn't wear musky perfume or radiate sexual heat. I understood why the old lady kept her on the payroll. She couldn't hurt sales. But the girl was trouble. I found a space for the *Lover's Companion* that wasn't a bedside table.

"Where does this all come from?" I said. "A whole aisle dedicated to sex and no mention of Hefner. I hadn't realized this stuff belonged in this kind of bookstore."

Darlene cooled all of three degrees. "Oh, people have been interested for as long as they've been having sex. None of ours

Flintlock

are *that* old! We have a few editions of *Fanny Hill* in the back from before the Civil War. Those stay locked up. Raleigh found them at an estate sale."

"He finds a lot of old books at estate sales?"

She kept one of her hands on mine. "Sometimes. He bids for books and other antiques at auctions, too, but usually it's book fairs. They're boring, but Uncle Ral only let me tag along for two. He says I'm distracting."

Uncle Ral and I agreed on something.

"Books make sense," I said aloud. "Antiques, though?"

She nudged the cart farther down the aisle. A man with something to be embarrassed about hesitated after stepping into the section; his face flushed, then he darted out of sight. Better to browse this aisle without company. Darlene grinned over her shoulder then dredged paperbacks from the cart to add to the shelves.

"Mr. Bedlam, what's so funny?"

The cover of the dogeared paperback in my hand displayed a woman in a doorway, visible as a bright-edged silhouette, naked, with a smoking pistol in her hand. I'd seen it before in Officer Smally's hip pocket.

"I know someone who read this."

Darlene stepped well into my personal space. She tipped the book toward her and made a face. "Really? We have the whole series and can't get rid of them."

I resisted a generous impulse to buy the lot as a present for Smally. His reading habits didn't need reinforcement. Either way, the girl's breath was warm on my chin. She hadn't gone back to the cart.

"You were asking about antiques," she reminded me.

"Um, yeah. Seems a bit off-topic for a book auction, doesn't it?"

I returned the paperback to its brethren, moving my arm so it widened the gap between us enough that we each used our

Jon A. Hunt

own air again. She noticed the effort without taking offense. She also found a way to take both of my hands in hers.

"You're hurt."

"It isn't as bad as it looks. Slipped on the ice."

"Big clumsy man."

"Why does Raleigh buy things besides books at the auctions?"

"Right. I didn't mean 'antiques' like old sewing machines or paintings. More like collectible papers. A lot of our books are technically antiques, too, aren't they?"

"You're the expert."

"Odds and ends turn up at the auctions and fairs," she went on, finally relinquishing my paws. "The second auction even had a table of old guns and knives. Bayonets, I think. Ugly—"

A puzzle piece snapped into place.

"That's how you know Tipper," I said.

A fresh smile warmed her face. "I like Tipper! Such a smart, sweet man." Then the smile was gone. "So sad about his family, though."

"Hmm?"

"I—I thought since you knew him..."

"We just met a couple days ago. What happened with his family?"

Seriousness wasn't an emotion Darlene had much experience with. For a minute her smooth confidence lost traction. "They were...murdered. His wife and a little boy. Back east, Boston or Philadelphia, I think."

"When?"

"A year ago. That's—that's all I heard. Rumors. He never mentioned it directly. Maybe you should ask him, instead of me?"

I let her have my hands again. Dragging the girl down hadn't been my intention. "Sorry. I had no idea. I didn't mean to upset you."

Flintlock

She accepted the apology as a means to move closer. "It's okay. I'm mostly just mad at myself for gossiping."

"That's something anyone would talk about."

"Not me. Everyone usually talks about *me*. So I try not to do it myself."

Back in his nest by the mezzanine stairs, Raleigh's miniature Darlene movie frowned furiously back at him. She might well have thought the cameras were there to watch her. The grip tightened on my fingers.

"How long have the thefts been a problem?" I asked, hoping to steer her from her gloom.

"Oh...a couple years now, I guess," she said, absently. "I mean, things get swiped from stores every day. People steal."

"Meredith said the thieves took parts of sets."

"Yeah. Pretty smart, huh? Nothing from *this* aisle," she giggled. Her solemnity had already fled. "This is just a target for ordinary shoplifters. We can go to the next row, by the way. Unless you want to read one of those paperbacks to me?"

I assured her I'd rather not. Who wanted to stare at printed erotica with Darlene right there in the flesh? But I kept her talking and was careful to keep her on task, which took some doing. She was a hell of a lot more communicative than her uncle.

The thefts had hit O'Dell's harder than Meredith's explanation let on. Employees were let go, especially when medical bills from Mr. O'Dell's long illness began to erode the family finances. Darlene and Raleigh worked Christmas season without pay. The store had weathered recessions, riots, economic downturns in the past, just not with a leader slowly expiring in a hospital across town, and not while hemorrhaging thousands of dollars' worth of irreplaceable stock. Words like *foreclosure* and *bankruptcy* became commonplace. The legendary shop was dying quicker than the old man who owned it.

Then Raleigh took the reins. Meredith was too busy,

Jon A. Hunt

waiting for time and cancer to make a widow of her, to manage the business. Raleigh found money somewhere, Darlene said. He paid bills that mattered, delayed those that could fester, stopped the downward spiral, and kept the store where it belonged, in the family.

"I think," Darlene whispered, "Uncle Ral sold some books that Gramps and Gram meant to keep for sentimental reasons. Gram would disown him on the spot if she found out."

We were alone at the dead end of the aisle. I doubted whispering was strictly necessary, except as a means of keeping her face near mine. I recalled Rafferty telling me about Shakespeare's *First Folio*. One of those ought to set any bookstore up for a while if the right buyer came along. Not Erik Jorgensen, I supposed, he preferred his collected items be lethal, but someone like him. I was forgetting something I should ask. Darlene had that effect on a man.

"The cameras were Raleigh's idea?"

She found my jawline interesting, stubble and all. Her fingertips traced heated trails there. "Oh yes. He loves to watch."

"I haven't gotten the impression the things have done much good," I managed.

"It isn't hard to outsmart them..."

I asked the question silently, with an arched brow. Darlene was only too happy to demonstrate. Using a yardstick from the cart, which she ordinarily employed to nudge books into place on upper shelves, she raised onto her tiptoes with one hand against my chest for balance, and scooted a tall leather-bound edition halfway out into space. The balanced volume acted as a shutter. Back in his nook under the stairs, Raleigh was probably tapping a black square on one of his computer monitors. The only camera with a view of the wall end of the *Sexuality and Erotic Literature* aisle suddenly saw nothing.

On her way back down to her heels, Darlene managed to

Flintlock

discard the yardstick, because both of her hands found the back of my neck and she hauled me in for a kiss. Her lips were incredibly soft, wet, very warm. Her breasts moved against me with each feverish breath—when our mouths finally parted so we *could* breathe—and if I hadn't seen the dress beforehand, I'd have sworn she was naked. That's how her backside felt against my hand.

Whether he meant to was debatable, but Raleigh saved me from hormonal stupidity. The wireless phone nestled among books on Darlene's cart vibrated furiously. She brought her hands around and pressed herself away from my chest. Bronze eyes smoldered beneath half-closed purple-tinted lids.

"The cameras don't see everything," she purred.

The phone kept grumbling.

"Better get that." I remembered how to make words. Impressive.

She scooped the phone up, pressed a button that unleashed her uncle's tinny wrath, held the device to an ear. While she apologized, grinning hungrily at me, I reached up and tapped the leather-bound book back into its proper seat. Problem solved. At least Raleigh's was. I might have just picked myself up another.

Darlene tapped the button and the squeaking ceased. Her face wore all the innocence of Sunday morning, if you didn't pay attention to slightly swollen lips.

"He said to tell you he found that video footage you wanted."

Jon A. Hunt

Chapter Seventeen

How was I supposed to find a red journal, if every book in the place wore the same crimson binding and none had titles on their spines? The shelves went on for miles.

It was no use asking Darlene. She was there, in her clinging polka-dot dress and brand-new Reeboks, but she was too busy to answer questions or even tie her shoes. She only wanted sex. Her manicured fingers deliberately worked buttons to free her breasts. I must have looked as stupid as I felt, because she laughed—except what I heard was too soft for Darlene—rain on summer leaves. Aubrea's laughter.

The dress fell away. I dove forward to Paradise.

Paradise looked an awful lot like a brick wall.

Massive hands grabbed both sides of my head and propelled me like a cannonball.

No smooth dark skin waited to receive me. Only bricks.

And there I was, crumpled at the base of the wall where a grisly vertical stripe of gore and tissue ended. I made a pretty ridiculous corpse in those crossword suspenders.

My long white shoelaces somehow remained unstained, even though they trailed across the fresh red puddle beneath me.

• • •

The bedside clock showed smaller numbers than I liked. It didn't matter. I was committed to the day now. Nightmares don't come with snooze buttons. I kicked the covers off and

Flintlock

barefooted out to the kitchen.

I'd slept—or tried to—in my condo. Aubrea hadn't been thrilled with my decision when I called after leaving the bookstore, but she felt safe where she was and tried to be understanding of a private investigator's long hours. I hadn't mentioned Darlene. The guilt made no sense. I wasn't committed to either woman; going straight from one to the other just seemed a colossally bad idea. Poole could keep an eye on Aubrea overnight.

A muted small-hours' city glow seeped through the living room windows, except for where the partial high-rise stood. I flipped on the lights over the breakfast bar. A fifth of Old Number Seven sparkled there beside the notebook I typically use to organize my thoughts. Neither had been opened. I'd gotten both items down for inspiration. My phone lay under the notebook. I touched the screen to rouse it. If I couldn't sleep it seemed reasonable to me that Rafferty shouldn't, either.

Rafferty's text message from two hours ago waited.

Call me.

How bad had *his* dreams had been?

The line rang enough times to suggest he wasn't desperate for my call, yet he picked up quick enough to prove he hadn't been asleep.

"Just went home for the night?"

"I checked in with Aubrea and Poole. A guy's got to make time to think."

"You do that often?"

"Occupational hazard. What did you need?"

"Our huge friend hit the girl's apartment. Lots of neat tidy piles."

"I thought you had someone watching the place."

"I did. Guess who turned up in the neat tidy piles."

I made a low whistle. The whiskey bottle began to look appealing.

"Poole and Miss Langston are fine," the Lieutenant continued, anticipating my question. "I sent a couple extra cars to Cool-Core. Nobody scary showed up."

"Sorry about your man."

A grunt was as close to a thank-you as I was likely to get. "Occupational hazard," he said.

"Smally's still offline?"

"He's tracking down some kids."

White shoelaces.

"There were three of them that hit O'Dell's on a regular basis," I said. "Boys, middle teens, they looked a little rough. Raleigh showed me the video footage."

"I thought he'd given it all to us. Little prig."

Raleigh's cameras had picked the trio up eleven times in thirty days. Three street toughs, homeless, or at least no one told them to shower or brush their hair. The brat in the Reeboks seemed younger than the others, but he was the only one I'd met in person. I could tell in the footage they were pros. They worked in unison: two distracted staff, even using Raleigh's frustrated awareness of them to their advantage, so the third could exit the building with the goods. I described them to Rafferty.

"That's them. Heavyset kid with the bad hair is Tom Dryden. Local, but no family will claim him. A self-taught electronics whiz with a knack for breaking home security systems. Tall one is Nathan Cole. Rich parents in Chattanooga want nothing to do with him, eighteen. All three have been hard as greased pigs to catch.

"The runt who never ties his shoes goes by Sal. No clue where he originated. Before the investigation went south, we kept an eye on them but didn't want to haul them in. Pretty sure they had big-time oversight. Getting removed from the

Flintlock

case meant we stopped watching. Used to be regulars at the Mission down on Eighth."

"'Used to be?'"

"Vanished after the raid. Folks at the Mission called yesterday to say three different characters have been around trying to pin the boys' whereabouts down. They caught up with one. Barge pilot found Cole last night, hung up in an anchor chain. Swollen like a party balloon and frozen stiff. .44 magnum made the hole in his stomach. Who knows where the bullet is now. Forensics think he was shot on the riverbank and fell in. If you want to eat again soon, don't ask for their explanation."

"Sounds like a connection," I said. "What, though?"

"Beats me. But we'd better get the other two off the streets or no one will find out."

"I bumped into Sal at O'Dell's on Tuesday."

"Christ, we've been all over town after him! Where'd he go?"

"I don't know. I caught him trying to swipe a book and ran him out. He was terrified. I gave him my name and let him split."

"Softy. He might live longer in custody. If he calls, I want to know pronto."

"Okay. Fair trade: what about Tipper's family?"

"Uh, why?"

"Unpleasant rumors."

"Uh huh. Wife and a son, murdered in Philly. Museum robbery. Wrong place at the wrong time. Killers were never apprehended."

"I don't think Tipper's left the Jorgensen estate since he got there.".

"He has nothing to go home to," Rafferty said flatly.

"Would you mind digging up the details? I realize he's been working for TBI and he's been screened. It might still be worthwhile to be sure of his motives."

"Sure, anything for you. What about the DA's girl?"

"I'll keep her in sight when I'm not at the bookstore."

"You're still helping Tipper?"

"Absolutely. Aubrea can tag along."

"Oh. Terrific."

"Any better ideas?"

Rafferty had already ended the call.

I thumbed the phone off and paused at the living room window in my skivvies. Golden winter sunlight flung itself down each visible east-west street and set the leading edges of downtown's glass towers aflame. A distant glint from West End must be the Cool-Core Tower. Aubrea might be looking back at me, probably wearing more than I was.

Down in the wet cold streets between us, maybe, two truant kids ran scared. Pros. Or they used to be. Something had gone wrong. The frightened scarecrow I'd caught in O'Dell's had lost his guidance, and he was smart enough to see the grownup world that once employed him wanted him gone. He couldn't run forever. He was a squirrel caught in a Mason jar.

Was my bullet-resistant big-footed foe involved? Was he even in town? Who all had he crushed into lifelessness besides Mitch and two police officers?

"Mitch," I breathed on the plate glass, "what in the hell did you drag us all in to?"

• • •

She'd escaped Tuesday's kidnappers in a fifty-year-old Volkswagen bus during an ice storm. Her Wednesday had been spent peering down from a disused penthouse suite atop one of Nashville's tallest skyscrapers. Now she flew along beside me in an overpowered American supercar on our way to a dead billionaire's estate. The absurdity of Aubrea's circumstances caught up with her three turns into the Belle Meade neighborhood. She laughed. For the first time I regretted the Viper's blatant exhaust note. I tried to keep the RPMs down

Flintlock

while she giggled. Newly thawed streets glistened, clean sunshine winked through the bare tree limbs, and if the day looked nothing like Christmastime at least it was pretty.

Then the estate's granite walls slid into view. Aubrea's mood cooled to match. I barely heard her above the engine. "This has something to do with Mitch?"

"It's connected."

"How?"

"I'm working out the details," I evaded.

The gate remained open. Vestiges of Tuesday's ice crusted the machinery on the wall's shaded inner face. No one could shut the gate if they wanted. The Viper burbled through and reclaimed the spot where I'd parked last time, next to a Metro cruiser instead of Smally's trash-heap pickup. Only cold and gray lived within the stone walls. The sun didn't like it there.

A beat cop emerged from the car to welcome us. His appreciation of my car was noticeable. He didn't mind the girl's looks, either. I completed his day when I popped open the trunk to release aromas of fresh deli sandwiches and boxed coffee.

"The Professor's still in the gun range?"

"He is," replied the officer. "He might finally be taking a nap, but he said to send y'all right on in. I'll be happy to pass around the sandwiches if you like."

I left him to manage the food and drink, and led Aubrea through the one functioning door. She clutched my jacket sleeve. The redistributed chaos inside what was left of Jorgensen's home would unsettle anyone.

"Tyler, can you just take me home?"

"Not now. Your apartment looks like this, too."

"My God—"

"I'm sorry, Aubrea. You wouldn't be safe at your parents', either. These people move quicker than the police. They don't have rules or procedures to follow."

Jon A. Hunt

"Who are you to say where I go?"

A second Metro officer came toward us. He had that wary look they all have when they approach anyone who is agitated. I turned Aubrea to face me. The blue eyes burned with helpless defiance; she was Eli's sister through and through.

"A cop died there." I said it quick and low. The officer didn't need to be reminded of what occupied every mind on the force. "Same way as Mitch. Same killer. He isn't afraid of the police. Do you understand?"

She shuddered. "How can *you* protect me, then?"

I didn't know that I could. I lied. "I don't have rules or procedures to follow, either."

Her eyes flicked to the hands that held her, torn and scarred from the last time I'd protected her.

"You two okay?" the cop wanted to know.

Aubrea caught her lower lip between her teeth, nodded faintly.

"Yeah," I said, "just startled at the mess. Tipper wanted to see us."

The officer forced a smile. Our problems weren't necessarily his. But cops die all the time because of problems that aren't theirs.

"Yessir," he said. "Follow me. Watch your step."

• • •

Tipper appeared as well-rested as when I first met him. Maybe he'd taken a nap, maybe he hadn't. He'd at least found a shower, shaved, and changed into fresh clothes under the lab coat. He didn't reek of burnt coffee, just spent powder. His handshake was as firm and warm as ever, his fingers steady as a neurosurgeon's. He'd crash eventually. It just didn't show.

His curly hair waved in greeting and when he saw I wasn't alone, he rose politely from his work table and wiped his hands on the sides of his smock. I let the cop excuse himself and duck out through the anteroom before I offered introductions.

Flintlock

"She's had her own run-in with the characters who did this." I gestured over my shoulder toward the mangled remainder of the house.

Tipper's face pivoted my direction with a nearly audible snap. For a fraction of a second his eyes went hard as flint. "Really!"

"Only nearly," she said, flushing. "I had help."

Tipper sandwiched her hands in his. The sharpness in his expression melted into poignant tenderness. He led her to his chair at the table, which she docilely accepted, then he walked me to the room's opposite corner, out of her hearing. I realized abruptly that the forensics tech from my last visit no longer shared the room. Neither did the contraption for capturing musket balls.

"Good Lord, Bedlam, why'd you bring her here?"

"Metro has its hands full," I said. "Whoever did this is a cop killer, too. They have some manpower to spare for watching her at night. The rest of the time, she's safer with me than anywhere else. She was a friend of somebody who tried to hire me before he died."

"I suppose you know what you're doing." Now Tipper looked tired. I understood his pain better than he realized. I wasn't ready to bring that up yet.

"Rafferty said to ask you about a red journal."

Tipper's voice regained its characteristic energy. "Did he? Is...Miss Aubrea party to this question?"

My attention skipped to the table by the shooter's bench. Aubrea sat with her pretty head tilted. The old weapons on the table beneath the swingarm lamps quite occupied her curiosity.

"No," I said.

A conspiratorial grin creased Tipper's ruddy cheeks. "Actually, if you paid any attention in high school, there's a fair chance you've both heard mention of the red journals. They're basic American history. Captains Meriwether Lewis and

143

Jon A. Hunt

William Clark wrote about their 1803 expedition to the West Coast in them."

High school seemed nearly as long ago as 1803.

"Rafferty talked about *a* journal. Not plural."

"That's because he meant the one that got away." Tipper rummaged through pockets of his lab coat and produced a small digital tablet. His dexterous fingers flew across the luminous screen to access a particular file, then he passed the device to me. "There's more to it than two well-mannered gentlemen would privately discuss while a lady waits in the same room. Here's my report to TBI. I can show your friend a few of poor Jorgensen's goodies while you read."

"Thanks. I have another question, though. Rafferty differed to you on this, too."

Tipper planted both hands in his pockets and rocked on his heels. "I'm flattered he sees me as knowledgeable."

"Fontaine and Jorgensen had some kind of disagreement years ago. Fontaine wasn't about to give me particulars, but bad blood wasn't hard to smell." Not even over the bourbon.

The bouncy curls silently laughed with their owner. "*Disagreement* would be a colossal understatement," he chuckled. "When Jorgensen was killed, Fontaine was an instant prime suspect. At least till the police confirmed there was no way he could have been here when Jorgensen was shot. I'm positive Fontaine made a point of celebrating the occasion."

"You mean he added an extra bottle to his nightly routine."

Tipper grimaced meaningfully.

"What happened?" I pressed.

"Jorgensen accused Fontaine of cheating in the pistol tournaments."

"Which ones?"

"All of them. He swore Fontaine was a fraud, in front of plenty of witnesses. Embarrassed the hell out of the man. He said Fontaine didn't deserve a single one of his trophies."

144

Flintlock

No wonder Fontaine held no love for his fellow old-fashioned marksman. His lake mansion brimmed with awards Jorgensen said he hadn't earned. That kind of thing drives plenty of high-society guys with no better hobbies to drink.

"*Was* Fontaine cheating?"

Tipper shrugged. "I can't imagine how. Weapons and targets are inspected before and after every round. People are watching the whole time. Jorgensen's accusations seemed pretty ridiculous. He never offered evidence, but he never backed down. The back and forth, the name calling, it got to be so appalling nobody wanted anything to do with either of them. It came to a head when Jorgensen challenged Fontaine to a duel."

"You're kidding. People don't have duels anymore."

"Well, it's against the law. Jorgensen told the world he wasn't concerned for his safety, because Fontaine couldn't hit a man-sized target at ten paces even if he was sober enough to hold the proper end of a pistol."

"And—?"

"Well, no duel took place. Neither man competed again. Years after, they at least decided to be cordial with each other. Common interests and all. Nothing like friendship, though."

It baffled me. Arthur Fontaine had enough character flaws, a person hardly needed to make any up as an excuse to dislike him.

"Some folks just live to argue, eh?"

"Or die trying," I said.

Tipper went serious again. "Read that report. Please point out spelling errors, of course."

• • •

I settled into the same chair and corner where I'd awaited my first audience with Tipper. He had a new student to awe and for the time being I could safely revert to a more relaxed observational role. Tipper's and Aubrea's personalities had

Jon A. Hunt

gotten familiar enough for me to anticipate their interactions. The girl who found emergency clothes and bagels enthralling couldn't help but be mesmerized by a tabletop array of vintage iron. And Tipper would never pass up an opportunity to show a willing audience how tangible history could be.

I followed their mutual distraction a while, then opened a packet of hearing protectors and pressed one into each ear. Tipper would remember his and the girl's protection, but I wouldn't blame him for forgetting about me. Sooner or later, Tipper was going to put one of Jorgensen's loaded antiques in her hands. I touched the tablet and dove into the report. For being so gung-ho about making the past entertaining, the guy cranked out a memo every bit as dry as those textbooks he abhorred.

Case No.: - - - - - - - - -

Incident: Homicide / Burglary

Location: Residence of Erik Jorgensen (deceased)

Item: BOLO Red Journal

Description: 8" x 5" book, worn red leather cover, bound on short edge (ie: flip book), metal clasp, visibly old. Hand-written entries in ink, severely faded and / or stained. May be in a protective bag or container.

Remarks: Dated by uncertified private assessment, c. 1808-1810. Allegedly hitherto unknown writings by Capt. Meriwether Lewis of 1804-06 expedition. If authentic, highly desirable to museums and collectors. Any entries penned by Capt. Lewis immediately prior to his death in 1809 would have incalculable value.

Item has not been mentioned by biographers or chroniclers of the Lewis and Clark expedition. Construction is identical to previously accounted-for 18 red journals. All knowledge thus far of this 19th journal derived from written correspondence by Robert Delphino of

Flintlock

*Louisville, KY, to the director of the American
Philosophical Society in Philadelphia, PA. The Society is
considered a foremost authority in the matter. Delphino
was found deceased before further communication could be
made. No such journal was discovered in his heavily
vandalized residence.*

*Decedent in this case, Jorgensen, was a collector of
early American items of historical significance, and prior
to death mentioned to other collectors he had acquired a
document connected to Capt. Lewis. Confirmation of
Jorgensen's statements have not been made. If, in fact, he
did possess the 19th red journal, item has not been found
on his property.*

T. Gering, PhD

I shut off the tablet. I wondered exactly when Capt. Meriwether Lewis died. The nutjob in the coonskin cap at the hotel had mentioned October. A quick phone search gave the answer: October 11, 1809.

He'd bought it while traveling on the Natchez Trace, in those days just a buffalo trail traveled by soldiers, trappers, robbers and the desperate, between Natchez, Mississippi, and Nashville. Lewis' grave and a memorial persisted in a spot in the forest where a crude inn had been, not far from present-day Hohenwald. Accounts varied. Plenty of period influencers benefited from his passing. No reliable witnesses, shady circumstances, no formal funeral or even a verifiable burial. Conspiracy theories abounded, hence the existence of modern-day phenomena such as the Meriwether Lewis Exhumation Convention. But the most widely accepted belief was that the despondent, financially ruined explorer blew the top of his own head off. With a .60 caliber flintlock pistol.

Earplugs didn't completely muffle the long-drawn

explosion. I'll own up to jumping in my chair before I remembered my surroundings.

Aubrea stood, legs shoulder-width apart, yellow earmuffs on that matched Tipper's beside her. They stared together down the target lane. The dueling pistol at the end of her arms smoked like a newborn volcano. I could tell from the shining eyes behind borrowed shooter's glasses that Tipper had won another convert.

I rose and moved so I could see the target without interrupting. If the paper silhouette six yards down the range had been a man, he wouldn't still be vertical.

Tipper grinned with sufficient admiration for both of us. He touched her shoulder to get her attention, carefully took the pistol, ran a cleaning patch through the barrel, reloaded, primed the pan. He explained each step through a sort of pantomime. Aubrea nodded attentively and smiled. Tipper returned the charged weapon to her.

I shouldn't be surprised. A district attorney's kids were more likely than most to grow up around firearms. She looked very much at ease for a girl handling unfamiliar iron. I blamed my father's swivel chair for deadening my grasp of the obvious.

Up went the pistol. Tipper stepped aside and winked at me over a shoulder. Our end of the alley flared with sudden brightness, but I heard nothing. Aubrea started to lower the muzzle and Tipper made an awkward lurch to stop her. He hadn't explained the proper procedure for a misfire. Now he held the weapon himself and kept the thing trained on the target, his eyes serious with warning. A second later the pistol bucked and flashed, and this time we all heard it. Aubrea's blue eyes widened in alarm. I had the first earplug out too late to hear their words, though I got the gist of Tipper's explanation.

"...count to sixty before letting the barrel down. Sometimes there's still flame on its way to the charge, it just takes longer than expected. You might still have your shot, a

Flintlock

little delayed. That's called a *hangfire*. You could accidentally shoot your foot or worse!"

Aubrea's expression was the precise opposite of a half minute ago. She apologized.

"Ssh, Miss Aubrea. No apology! I should have told you. You can never be too sure, though often a misfire is the end of it. Remember the phrase *flash in the pan?*"

She laughed nervously. This seemed as good a cue as any for me to step into the conversation. After Tipper laid the temperamental weapon on the bench, I returned his tablet to him. Aubrea sensed our need again for privacy and left the bench to study other interesting artifacts on the worktable under the lamps.

"How confident are you it was here?" I asked quietly.

Tipper cut too comical a figure for such a sober topic, with twin yellow earmuff bubbles clamped atop his head amid the curls. "Fairly confident."

"It's worth killing for?"

My question ruined the yawn he'd started. "To some people, yes," he said with sudden intensity.

"They're done with ballistics?" I asked, sensing a necessary topic shift. "I don't see the equipment."

His head bobbed mechanically. "Yes. Moved into the rest of the house. There's a lot to dig through. None of these were the murder weapon. I'd already told them as much, but they believe me now that there are no more guns to check."

"What's on the table, then?"

He successfully completed the next yawn. "A few I'm allowed to play with for, er, evaluation purposes. The rest are just loose bits and pieces, sights, ramrods. I'm going back through what we've inventoried to see if they were missed. These are all essentially custom works, so Jorgensen wouldn't have seen reason to keep extra parts around. I'll get them sorted."

Jon A. Hunt

"My advice stands. Take a break. If you like, I'll try and bring Aubrea back next time, if you promise not to be dead on your feet."

Tipper chuckled. "Fair enough. I'll grab those blueprints for you to take back to Fontaine. He'll fuss about them being gone long. And yes, I'd very much enjoy Miss Aubrea visiting again. This place isn't exactly cheery. It's nice having a girl around. Reminds me—"

He caught himself mid-phrase. The color drained from his face.

I'm no good at consoling people, but his misery, when it showed, grabbed a person's heart. "Get some sleep," I said, so he didn't have to carry the thought further.

He looked like a misplaced lamb when the girl and I left. I wasn't sure bringing Aubrea along had been smart.

Flintlock

Chapter Eighteen

The servant's resemblance to his master surprised me anew, though of course Fontaine wouldn't stoop to greeting his own mother outside his front doors. Gerard stepped smartly to Aubrea's side of the car and held the door for her. His coat, suit and gloves were immaculate. Only his lapels reacted to the breeze that sighed off the lake. Magic held every strand of his comb-over in place.

"Good day, Mr. Bedlam. Won't you come inside?"

"We're just returning Mr. Fontaine's blueprints."

"Indeed, sir. But we ought not risk precious documents being swept away in this wind."

"Is he home?" I asked without sounding insistent. Gerard, I liked; his master I could do without seeing.

"Mr. Fontaine is indisposed at the moment."

I didn't mind letting Gerard see my grin. He allowed me to reclaim my polish by introducing Aubrea, then glided ahead of us into the house. The palatial entry felt even grander than before, now that sunlight flooded in from either side. Aubrea exhaled more loudly than she intended. We turned left after the hydraulic glass panels and she got an eyeful of the great room. I was sure the thirty-second floor of Cool-Core Tower wouldn't impress her anymore. Gerard floated past an open vault door as big as any bank's, and when we stepped through in his wake we were surrounded by paneled walls and glass display cases. It had more class than a personal indoor shooting range, even if I never care for rooms without windows.

Aubrea raised on her tiptoes to peer down into the nearest case, which contained one of Fontaine's many antique pistols. How many of *his* had claimed lives?

"Your boss is careful with his collection," I observed.

Gerard accepted the borrowed envelope from me and touched a button on one of the cases. The glass lid swung up on tiny hydraulics. He slid the envelope beneath a brace of centuries-old weapons on a velvet-padded tray, a gorgeous set of old dueling flintlocks. The pistols distracted me for some reason that eluded me.

"Mr. Fontaine is exceedingly cautious," Gerard said. "The cases themselves need no locks because this entire room is quite secure. The lightest touch will open the vault door from inside, but from outside you would never guess it, would you?"

"Excuse me, what are the paper cylinders beside the guns?" Aubrea's excitement had gotten the better of her.

Gerard didn't mind explaining. "Those are pre-measured powder charges. The cases are humidity-controlled, so in addition to the proper caliber ammunition, is it possible to store several charges with each weapon. The ideal amount varies depending on the piece and manner in which it is shot, of course."

"In case he needs to fire them in a hurry?" I asked.

"Ah! Mr. Bedlam, precise measurements for so many weapons would be a great deal for anyone to remember. It is as much a precaution as a convenience."

Gerard and I both knew this wasn't as much help as his master needed. The liquor cabinet was too far away.

• • •

My phone vibrated as we climbed into the car. It was a missed call from an unfamiliar Nashville number, no caller ID. No one picked up when I returned the call. Usually I ignore

Flintlock

aborted calls. But I'd given that skinny kid with the incorrigible shoelaces my name for a reason.

Sal. At least that was how Rafferty knew him.

Three truants, the bookstore, the little demolition piles, the red journal, Jorgensen, Fontaine, Mitch…they might not all be connected, but my gut told me Sal was smack in the middle of it while I still nibbled around the edges. I needed to talk with him.

"Tyler?"

"Just thinking. Ready?"

"Back to Cool-Core?" she asked.

My focus ought to be closer. Aubrea sat beside me while Fontaine's all-observing butler watched us from the doorstep. One terrified street rat actually remembering my name was the longest in a world of long shots. I knuckled the starter button and let the Viper's rowdy ignition sweep away less immediate concerns.

"How about a road trip, instead?"

Her face lit up. She hadn't been looking forward to her gilded cage. "Where to?"

"Mule Town," I said.

• • •

Bright, clear, twenty-one degrees: it was an excellent driving day as long as the windows stayed up. The Viper coasted down the interstate in top gear so we could converse without shouting. We chatted about the incredible pieces in Erik Jorgensen's collection. I'd fired more of those than Aurea had, though she'd handled plenty of modern firearms growing up. I avoided mentioning their owner had had the middle of his face blasted away by a weapon of the same class. Mitch didn't come up, either. When not smothered under sorrow or fear, Aubrea's personality soared light as air. She was a rare adult who hadn't forgotten the thrills of seeing and doing. I hoped when our current business concluded she'd be the same girl,

153

unscarred by yesterday's ugliness.

Closer to Columbia, talk shifted to families, hers, then mine. Her father was a caring man, just too busy in his career to raise children. A constant rotation of stepmothers hadn't helped. Eventually, Aubrea's older brother Eli assumed the role of protector.

"I didn't need it," she started, but I glanced across at her to show I saw through the lie. "Okay. Maybe I did, but I didn't like it. Do you have any siblings?"

"Only child."

"Danny told me about your father. He didn't mention your mother."

"She died when I was little."

"I'm sorry. Miss her?"

"Not as much as Dad."

"But Danny said you didn't get along."

I laughed. "We didn't! But when Mom died, nothing changed that I couldn't handle. Dad went out before I was ready. Everyone saw it coming, then we blinked and he was gone. No one was as prepared as they thought they were. Especially me."

"But now you're...you're so——"

"Rich? Yeah. Now I've got a bigger audience than I ever wanted, and even if the board of directors leaves me alone most of the time, I still have to attend meetings once in a while. I couldn't care less about what makes a computer or a phone go. And regular people are a bit strange around me. I put a lot more effort into staying out of the limelight than you might realize."

Her blue eyes sparkled. "By being a private eye?"

I shrugged and swatted the turn signal for our exit.

• • •

Fir wreaths adorned the lampposts. Workmen in Santa hats were assembling a huge artificial tree in front of the gray stone

Flintlock

courthouse. Storefronts spilled holiday colors into the square and Sinatra gushed Christmas carols from outdoor loudspeakers. For all that, the square couldn't quite replicate its weekend charm on a Thursday. Foot traffic consisted of lawyers and accountants, not shoppers or oddballs in coonskin caps, and even the most personable merchants moved as if they had somebody else's schedule to keep.

I passed up empty slots outside the police station north of the square. I didn't want to give Chief Moran the impression I hadn't taken his warning seriously. But the mercury had sunk four degrees just since our arrival. Piercing breezes hustled pedestrians between Points A and B. Aubrea accepted the two-block walk back to the square on the condition that our first stop would be where she could pick up a warmer jacket. I didn't argue. Sellers and shoppers are usually talkers, and we'd have actually looked suspicious hurrying past the heated shops without ducking into them.

Aubrea attracted clerks like moths to a porch light. She was pretty, interested, and brought along a man with a billfold. I went with the moment. I'd paid more for information in the past. Mitch Braunfelter proved an easy topic to broach. His inexplicable slaying lingered near the surface of everyone's thoughts. There wasn't one place we entered where he hadn't been a regular.

It helped that *Tyler Bedlam* was as unknown in Mule Town as Mitch had been revered. Folks talked our ears off. They just weren't telling me anything I didn't already know. The same held true in shop after shop, from the corner café with the homemade crab bisque to the coffee boutique: everyone provided glowing yet uninformative assessments of poor dead Mitch's character.

Our final pause on the square was in a bookstore. I paid special attention. O'Dell's had made me something of a critic. This place had little in common with the Nashville establishment. Bright airy aisles kept every volume neatly corralled on the shelves, in alphabetical order by author. There was a mezzanine that beckoned shoppers up its antique spiral stairs. The "Christmas tree" in the front window, constructed of stacked books in diminishing concentric circles, must have taken days to create. The woman at the sales counter wasn't sick and tired of the books all around her. When Aubrea mentioned she was a friend of Mitch's, the saleswoman couldn't have been more sympathetic.

"I am so very sorry. We all miss him something awful. Such a sweet man! He used to buy a book a week, and I'm not sure if he had a moment to read. Just to help out. But I didn't know him well. You ought to stop in at the utility company. Mitch worked there for years and years. I bet they'd love to hear from a close friend of his."

• • •

We encountered a less talkative bunch at the utility company's main office. Mitch was missed as keenly there as downtown. He'd just been a lineman, not a desk guy, and those left behind still had phones to wrangle. A police cruiser idling outside after our arrival also distracted the woman at the information counter, and we never had half her attention. Aubrea and I left within six minutes. We did not, however, go empty-handed.

Mitch's former supervisor was out at the Riverside Drive intake facility, overseeing a pump replacement. We could catch him there if we hurried. Louis Aldritch. Nice man. Nobody in the company knew Mitch better. The intake facility was a half mile up from the old dam.

I made complete stops at intersections. The Viper languished at or slightly below posted limits. I employed the turn signal so consistently I risked being mistaken for an out-of-towner. The cop behind us didn't pretend to be subtle. All he needed was an excuse. Aubrea watched me as often as the

Flintlock

mirrors.

"Should I be concerned?"

"I'm not breaking any laws," I said.

The road curved left and we were treated to a view of the dam through barren tree limbs. It was a sight. Weather out east, past Shelbyville where the Duck River originated, had been wetter and warmer. *Flood stage* and the *Duck* weren't far from mixing in the same news story. Aubrea breathed a little "wow!"

A slurry of mud and half-formed ice pummeled the worn concrete structure, crashing over spillways and blasting spray twenty feet higher than the powerhouse roof. The spray seemed to hang forever in the air, though obviously it returned to earth: the little parking lot on the near bank, the security fence, the separate shed and the catwalk with the warning sign about aggravated criminal trespass were glazed with ice.

"You've never seen it like that?" I said. "Happens once or twice a winter."

"I'd never been to Columbia till the funeral. Mitch and I always met for coffee on campus. I didn't know where he lived and never thought to ask."

I resisted pointing out Mitch's home when it passed on my side. Two plain white official cars blocked the driveway and the front window had been boarded up. Otherwise, the place looked as dead as its owner and the neighbor's dachshund.

The patrol car lost interest a block afterward and veered onto a side street. Mule Town had plenty of local troublemakers to keep tabs on.

The Riverside Drive intake facility was a picture postcard from 1955. Three flat-topped structures with beige brick walls, white doors and window frames, each wore the utility company's 1955 name in individual raised metal letters. That style of blocky architecture used to thrill people in its time; I'd driven by days earlier without noticing. Two service trucks

Jon A. Hunt

filled the concrete apron between the street and the largest building. I parked in the lot for a closed restaurant next door. Pumping stations aren't designed with visitors in mind.

The Duck's fluid explosion out-roared the wind. Currents drove ferociously against the concrete footings of the pump houses where they extended down beyond the waterline. Two men in coveralls were locking hatches on the trucks. They looked done for the day.

Aubrea and I walked beside the street where we'd be plain to see. As soon as one of the men made eye contact, I hollered "Louis Aldritch" before we could be shooed off premises. The younger man turned questioningly to the older, who raised both shoulders. The younger man disappeared into the building through open barn doors. He dodged a dripping assembly of cast iron pipes that dangled inside the opening from a yellow I-beam. He returned with a third person who must be Mr. Aldritch.

Louis Aldritch stepped to our side of the trucks and, in a voice that held enough oomph to be heard over the river, asked if he could help us. I'd seen him before, in a suit at the funeral. He'd been squinting for decades; whatever his thoughts, I couldn't read his permanently narrowed eyes. He didn't *sound* excited to see us.

"We're friends of Mitch's," I said. That was sufficient to send the other men on whatever errands they could imagine. "Maisy at the office said you might talk with us."

Louis started to tug a cigarette pack from the front of his coveralls, glanced at Aubrea, decided a gentleman shouldn't light up. He put his hands in his pockets instead. "Pardon my sayin', but I never heard from so many friends of Mitch's as I have since he passed on."

I'd been around long enough to recognize the verbal stop sign. The living Mitch and I traded a few awkward words, once, in a venue where we couldn't hear ourselves think.

Flintlock

Before me stood his old supervisor. Nobody in the company knew Mitch better. To him I was yet another in a long line of cops, reporters and busybodies, and I wasn't likely to convince him I had any inkling who Mitch had been beyond a name.

"Is that the lift pump?" Aubrea asked the question abruptly enough to jog two men out of the beginnings of a stare down.

"One of them," Louis drawled.

"The one with the cracked the housing. The... the...oh..." She stammered, seeking an unfamiliar word barely out of reach. Then her eyes sparked. "The *impeller* housing! That's what it's called, right, Mr. Aldritch?"

If Aldritch *had* popped that cigarette in his mouth, he'd have dropped it. His jaw swung open like a trapdoor. "Miss, how'd you know about that?"

Aubrea's pretty face reddened more than the cold accounted for. "Mitch told me. He said you were having trouble finding a loss in pressure. The leak wasn't in the pipes. It was in a brand-new pump, right under the gasket, around back where no one could see. Water sprayed back down through the hole in the floor, out of sight. You had to wait for a replacement and it wouldn't ship till after he retired..."

The biggest, saddest smile I'd ever seen took command of Louis Aldritch's face. He was going to either laugh or cry if he didn't do something quick. The cigarette pack reappeared, and he got one between his lips just in time. His fingers weren't steady. He didn't light up.

"How 'bout y'all come inside? Awful cold out here."

Jon A. Hunt

Chapter Nineteen

The two workers were sent home with a word and what might be a warning glare. With Louis' perpetual squint, who could say? He hauled the barn doors together with the three of us inside. The room was tolerably warm, and emptier than I'd expected but for gray control panels on one wall and the pump hanging from the yellow beam over a large metal floor grate. Louis gestured ominously toward the grate. A mechanical rumble issued from beneath it. Around the far side of the control panels waited another door and a miniscule office beyond. Once he'd shut the door behind us, the little room was surprisingly peaceful.

I couldn't help but observe that even Louis Aldritch's field office in a pump house had more square feet than Jerry Rafferty's home base in Nashville. And a window. It smelled like grease and scalded coffee. There were only two chairs. He parked his backside on a metal desk that was as much a fixture of the Fifties as the building, and left the chairs to us. I had the impression Louis never used the chairs, anyway.

"You're spot on 'bout that pump, Miss—"

"Aubrea." She rose halfway to shake his rough hand.

I introduced myself as well. In spite of at least a twenty-year head start, Louis' iron grip warned me against arm wrestling. Then he dove right in, about the broken pump, how it had to be replaced today before the river broke flood stage, how no

160

Flintlock

one else spotted the problem, including himself, and *Old Mitch* found the leak right off by the sound. Louis' fondness for the man was evident.

"This was more his office than mine. Might've been Mitch's favorite part of the whole system. Used to come in on off days, sit in that chair with his feet on the desk, reading tech manuals for fun."

Aubrea laughed. She had no difficulty believing this. "No wonder he was so good with crosswords!"

Louis grinned expansively. "Ah! The old goat always had one of those magazines in his lunch box. But like as not, he entertained himself listening to pumps or checking on the dam."

"The one just down the road?" I asked.

"Down*stream*, Mr. Bedlam. Plumbing boys don't measure rivers by the roads beside 'em. But that's the dam. Was crazy about the old relic. Got his own key at retirement, so he could go visit her when he wanted—so long's he checked in with us still on the payroll first."

His weathered expression went downhill at the corners and he reached to the pegboard in front of the desk. A shiny brass key hung there on a black and white ribbon that reminded me of a dead man's suspenders. Engraved lettering on the key identified it as *Mitch's Very Own Dam Key*.

"Long as I'm here," Louis murmured, "that key's stayin' right where he left it."

The three of us hesitated, forward impetus lost. The same question dangled from our thoughts on a black and white ribbon.

Why would any person want to harm a man as universally loved as Mitch Braunfelter?

Aldritch's sliver eyes almost showed color when he rallied himself and found a smile for the girl in Mitch's chair. "I'd like to talk some more, Miss Aubrea, Mr. Bedlam, if you don't mind. Shift's over and it's too early for supper. If y'all ain't against a beer or two..."

• • •

Louis' beer or two resided a ten-minute walk toward town on Riverside Drive. That suited us all. Ferrying non-employees to drinking establishments in a company vehicle was against regulations, and my car had only two seats. He paused before our stroll with a gloved hand on a truck fender and contemplated the gleaming Viper crouched in the next-door lot.

"Yours?"

I fell back on my stock response. "Regular car's in the shop."

"At least it's American," he chuckled and offered Aubrea his elbow to lead the way.

The tavern hunkered at the far edge of an asphalt lot like an awkward teenager at his first dance. It was so low I spotted the storage shed beside it first. The block walls were painted white, window and door trims were garish red. Four pickup trucks out front emphasized the lot's relative emptiness. Wheelchair ramps climbed from either corner to a door in the middle. Handicapped access seemed out of place for a bar that probably had a lot of Harley-Davidsons out front in the summer. A neon Budweiser sign in the window all but said *y'all come on in*. We'd bypassed a newer bar on the same side of the road; Louis' crowd didn't go there.

A half dozen regulars greeted "Lou" at the same time, easily overmatching Hank Williams Jr crooning from unseen speakers. Neither the ballgames on two widescreen televisions over the bar, nor the unused pool table, held anyone's attention. Old-timers mostly came here to drink, smoke and talk. There were no beer pulls—Jimmy in the ballcap behind the bar was happy to pop the top off a cold bottle when asked—but the stale nicotine aroma was as stereotypical as any

Flintlock

well-used tavern's. Louis—*Lou*, here—waved us toward our choice of barstools.

We didn't leave till long after suppertime. Mitch was a subject everyone warmed to. Nine of us, including Jimmy who'd been in charge since 1965, gathered at the bar in long conversation. I covered their tabs. Nothing frees up tongues like beer somebody else buys.

Tales of Mitch's kindness and gentle humor touched more deeply in this relaxed setting than they had in the Arbuckle Brother's funeral sanctum. Louis often paused to smooth a hint of moisture from his eternal squint. And Aubrea's eyes shone with unashamed emotion. The memories shared were new to her yet heart-breaking in their familiarity. She had her own Mitch stories to tell, too. The kind-hearted retiree had attended yoga classes with his new Nashville friend and never missed a day in spite of an utter lack of coordination or grace. Louis laughed so hard at the idea of Old Mitch attempting the downward dog, he spilled one of his beers. I couldn't remember having a better time in a room full of half-inebriated strangers.

My slow realization, however, was that in many ways Mitch Braunfelter was as much a mystery to those closest to him as he was to me. Nobody was sure where the man came from, just that he wasn't a native. Any schooling or past employment remained a blank. None of tonight's cast of characters had any awareness of the house Mitch purchased up in Nashville. They'd only heard he'd died there. Mitch had just wandered into Mule Town thirty-odd years ago and then he was gone. Like a visiting angel.

Louis spotted the clock behind the bar and started. He was an hour late for dinner. Mrs. Aldritch was going to wear his ears out. I settled the tab. He and Aubrea and I said goodbye to the others, who were content to stay inside a while longer and buy their own beers. Out into the cold and dark we went.

Not much was said during our return to the pump station. The setting sun had taken back whatever meager warmth it provided. Bitter fog obscured everything except twenty feet of sidewalk and the pinkish-orange halos of the nearest two streetlights in either direction. No cars traveled Riverside Drive. At these temperatures, that fog would soon varnish the pavement with ice. We turned our collars up, jammed our hands in our pockets, withdrew every aspect of our beings inward as far as possible. A heavy rushing sound escalated as we went, enveloping us and yet distant: water crashing over the dam, a roar simultaneously deadened and amplified by the mists. Louis slowed and then stopped altogether. In the filmy aura of the streetlights I studied his face with its twin dark slots for eyes. Aubrea leaned against me. We watched Louis as a pair, neither daring to voice the question. We couldn't see the dam at all.

"Funny," Louis mused. His words might as well have been our own thoughts, so near and clear were they. "Ain't any of us been in the powerhouse since Old Mitch was last. Not like we're afraid of ghosts. Hell, he'd be the nicest ghost you ever saw. Just nobody wants to."

"I can't say I'd blame them tonight," I said.

The old lineman's head rocked an affirmative. "Sure, not now. River's not supposed to crest till sometime Friday. Would be a regular dumbass to try when the Duck's like this."

He muttered something intangible and resumed walking at a brisk pace.

• • •

Gauzy frost dressed the windshields of both vehicles. Louis and I fired up their engines to clear the glass. The clattering diesel engine made a lot of racket, but the Viper's thumping exhaust was what caused blinds to raise across the street. I let the Viper rumble and joined Aubrea and Louis beside his truck.

"Rowdy-sounding car you've got," he commented. Aubrea

Flintlock

giggled.

"I'll take you for a spin sometime, if you like," I said.

"Thank you, no. Don't look too safe. But then I got a bass boat near as fast, I reckon, and no brakes. Dial me up anytime you feel like fishin'."

"You mean it?"

A hint of reflected headlamps flashed in those creases Louis used for eyes. "Sure do! You're all right, Mr. Bedlam. Had my doubts when y'all first asked about Old Mitch. But Miss Aubrea, it's been a real pleasure, and even if you're a private eye—" here came that perceptive gleam beneath his brows again; I hadn't mentioned my profession "—I'd have a beer with you anytime. You're a far sight friendlier than the others."

"Cops, you mean."

"Well, them, too. But I meant the other detective. Didn't care a bit for that fancy pants asshole—beggin' your pardon, Miss Aubrea! He acted like he had plenty, too, but there was no chance of *him* buyin' drinks."

We found business cards to swap. I'd had fair luck with mine lately. Then we shook hands all around once more. Louis kept the girl's hands in his for several earnest seconds. He came the closest yet to an open gaze.

"Sorry for your loss, Miss Aubrea," he said. "Real sorry."

She pulled herself to him and embraced the old lineman fiercely.

We waited in the car till Louis backed his truck onto Riverside Drive and left. Before the fog digested the truck, a tiny red dot of a lit cigarette appeared in the side mirror.

"Missed call?" Aubrea forced the question. She needed to say something, or she'd stew in her thoughts.

"Not exactly," I said and dropped my glowing phone in the cupholder between us. It had begun pulsing the familiar purple warning by the second round back at the tavern. I needed to call O'Dell's and warn them I was running late, but not with lilacs blinking in my ear.

I eased onto Riverside. Black ice and the tail-happy Viper wouldn't play well together. The purple beacon in the cupholder kept on till after we passed the bar.

Four pickup trucks still loitered there with frosted windows. The rather nondescript sedan idling beside them with its lights off was new.

Was I on to something in Mule Town? Or was Keller Ableman?

We left Columbia as cautiously as we'd come. Stopped at every intersection. Obeyed every speed limit. The police car shadowed us to the city limits, then melted into the fog.

Flintlock

Chapter Twenty

The Viper spent that night under the money that bought it. Being watched came with the territory but now it made me especially uneasy, and no safer place to park existed in Nashville than the secured garage under Cool-Core. In addition to the usual gates, cameras and guards, Officer Poole and another plainclothes cop I didn't recognize waited to escort us to the elevator.

"Rafferty's orders," Poole said. "When Miss Langston's in the building, we all are, too."

"'We all'?"

"Yessir. A car at each entrance, plainclothes in every lobby. Which is why I'm here, actually. The building security people want your okay for us."

I tapped the elevator button. A lot of buttons here wouldn't work for Metro's finest without prior authorization. The four of us dutifully stepped aboard the cab, and I pressed Poole for an explanation as we catapulted serenely to the thirty-second floor.

"Yesterday it was scramble just to have you here. Now *your* help outnumbers *my* help."

"Daddy," Aubrea groaned.

Poole locked eyes with me and shared a quick shake of his head. Not in front of the girl.

"I'll ride back down with you in a bit and we'll get this

167

sorted," I told him.

• • •

We'd spent the day together; Aubrea wasn't in a hurry for it to end. Truth be told, I wasn't, either. But I had other commitments and questions that needed answers, not the least of which was understanding why Rafferty had multiplied Aubrea's official protection. A dozen or more cops watching over her ought to make me think she'd be safe. Why did it have the opposite effect?

Poole spilled the beans as soon as we were alone on our way down again. "Those buyers who were supposed to be at the bookstore when we raided it—Rafferty mentioned that to you, right?"

"The raid, yes," I said. "He didn't mention buyers."

"I got permission to explain," Poole said. "He says you should know."

"Talk quick. I'm on a schedule."

"Well, our plan went wrong when the expected people didn't show. They would have. Except they were dead. Just found them in a suite at the Lowes. Three men. Their necks were snapped. Whoever did it just walked in and…twisted…" He'd begun to toughen up finally but describing this made Poole's young face pale.

Between floors eighteen and twelve, I got lost remembering the dead undercover cop in the Crown Vic outside Mitch's house. He'd been killed like that, almost casually. Bigfoot had no problem killing armed professionals; three unsuspecting book collectors in a hotel room would be child's play.

"Where's Smally?" I asked. I really wished Smally could be there. Poole's inexperience made me nervous.

"He's beating streets around Germantown."

Smally had been after three boys, now down to two. We wouldn't know the extent of their involvement till they were found, and Smally wasn't the only one searching. Sal had my

Flintlock

name. I couldn't do anything else.

I used the phone at the doorman's desk in the West End lobby to make the arrangements with Cool-Core's security chief. Only Poole would be permitted inside the penthouse suite with Aubrea. His new sidekick waited in the elevator lobby. I trusted Poole to withstand that kind of distraction, not necessarily the other guy. Before hanging up, I cupped a hand over the mouthpiece and asked Poole: "Does her daddy know she's here?"

Poole said an apologetic "yes."

I discussed this with the security chief. Dear Old Dad was allowed into lobbies and common spaces, not on the thirty-second floor. He'd be upset about that if he came over. He'd also realize—I hoped—I was as serious as Metro about safeguarding his daughter.

• • •

I walked again to O'Dell's. The evening had softened, warmed by a transient front. By midnight it would be below freezing again. I dredged my phone from a coat pocket to see whose call I'd missed in the elevator. The Nashville number wasn't familiar. I tapped the callback button. No answer. I considered turning the ringtone on, but there are reasons I never will, places I shouldn't be caught with a pocketful of unexpected electronic music. If it was Sal, he'd have to keep trying.

The blocks went quickly. I walk fast when I'm thinking. Few pedestrians passed. Most of the cars that went by were crammed to their headliners with colorful packages. Why didn't I shop for presents? Who would I shop for? Maybe I gave in different ways. All of this might be a gift for a would-be client in no position to accept colorful packages from anyone. That, or I simply missed the point of the season. I hadn't made up my mind either way when I stepped into the bookstore on autopilot.

Jon A. Hunt

The door still didn't want to latch. The electric chime still irritated me. I assumed Raleigh still scowled at my likeness on his computer screen in the shadows. Darlene appeared, wearing a smile as warm as Palm Beach and a green dress that must have been applied from a spray can. Aware of how distracting her breasts would be with every cold breeze customers brought in with them, she'd added a crocheted shawl to the ensemble. I wasn't a customer; for me she had the shawl artfully draped over a forearm where it didn't hide a thing.

"Hey, Gorgeous." She said it, not me. "What're we doing tonight?"

I doffed my hat and dragged my gaze back up to her face. Same purple eyeshadow. "I'm after a random old book," I said. That sounded platonic. Trouble was, a girl like Darlene could turn dissecting frogs into foreplay.

She hooked her arm through mine and steered me toward the back of the building. Every other step brushed her hip against mine. "You've come to the right place," she cooed. "Not everything is a Google search away. Which book are you looking for?"

I timed my answer for Raleigh's benefit, too, waiting till we'd reached the sales counter. He was in his cubby hole, all right. The gray in his tight frustrated curls fluoresced as bright as the monitors that tethered his attention. He didn't say "hello."

"Meriwether Lewis' red journal," I said.

Darlene's doe eyes blinked, full of questions and invitation. "That's not very random."

"No, not really."

"It isn't very *specific*, either," she admonished. "There were several. Lewis and Clark both wrote in journals. You could've as easily said 'Clark's red journal'."

"You sound knowledgeable," I said.

"Not bad for a distraction?"

Flintlock

"Or a librarian."

Neither my mention of the journal nor the flirting elicited a reaction from Vice President Raleigh. I ought to play my hunch through, anyway.

"I'd still like to know more about the journals. Where are they now? What was in them? Have all of them been found?"

Darlene leaned in close. Whatever my opinion of her makeup colors, I liked her musky perfume. "Does this have connections to what you're investigating for Gram?"

I smiled for an answer to keep her and, more importantly, Raleigh guessing. He had to be searching for my expression on the visual for Camera Four, which monitored the sales counter.

"Let's take a look in our system," Darlene whispered.

I'd gotten there late. Maybe a half dozen customers grazed in the aisles. Meredith might be in her mezzanine office, though I doubted it. It was sufficient that Raleigh guarded the leather-bound flock from his lair, and Darlene disarmed the occasional wolf with her curves. For the time being, I was the only wolf present. She drew a keyboard close to her ribcage so I could watch her type. My eyes stayed on her fingers, honest.

The computer screen first scrolled through customer information. *Braunfelter* briefly appeared, with the words *backorder* and *deliver* next to his name. I didn't say anything. Then came rows of titles, authors, publishers, associated numbers that held no meaning for me. The crawl occasionally paused for Darlene to scrutinize particular items. She'd scoot the mouse over its pad, an exaggerated action that invariably pressed her closer to me, then she'd click and the gibberish resumed its upward march. For such apparent disorganization out in the shelves, O'Dell's possessed a hell of a lot of pertinent data. Now, instead of line upon line of digital records, there were block paragraphs on single topics with headers at each paragraph's beginning. This reminded me of Tipper's memo, right down to familiar names.

171

Jon A. Hunt

Jorgensen. American Philosophical Society. Delphino.
The Colonial Societists.

"Stop a second."

"Hmm?" Darlene watched me, lips parted, eyes hungry. She was less interested in books than me.

"What's this?" I asked.

The lips pressed together. The hungry bronze eyes refocused on the display. I found the girl most alluring when she wasn't throwing pheromones around.

"An estate auction," she said. "Mr. Delphino was a collector. Colonial American, maps and documents."

"Lived in Kentucky."

She scrolled farther. "How'd you already know that?"

"Tipper."

"Ah." She touched the screen with a sleek index finger to bring my attention to the highlighted words. "Says he wrote to the Philosophical Society about a red journal, but he was robbed and murdered, and no journal was found."

I'd already heard similar from Rafferty and Tipper.

No journal. A lot of tidy debris piles. A very dead collector.

I was surprised they'd pieced together enough bits for an auction.

"What do they look like?"

"The journals?"

"Yeah. There's got to be pictures."

Darlene rapped the keyboard. Pixelated text scurried again across the display. She read a lot faster than I did.

"Okay," she said abruptly, "c'mon."

Scooping up the ever-present cordless phone—God forbid Uncle Ral had a complaint and it got missed—she caught my arm with her free hand and led me from behind the counter out into the stacks. The aisle felt strangely vacant now. Without

172

Flintlock

people foraging, the shelves were merely storage. We passed *Early American Literature, Biographies, Sexuality and Erotica*. Her goal was a section not two yards from where I'd helped her sell half of Grant's memoirs to four randy old Confederates. She scanned the rows as if she relied on a secret cataloging system when I knew none existed.

The door chirped up at the front of the store. Raleigh had shooed the last shopper out into the cold. A deadbolt slid noisily home.

Darlene bent at her waist instead of crouching to reach the bottom shelf. The movement pulled the thin velvet most flatteringly across her curves when seen from my vantage point. She possessed an acute awareness of her appearance from any angle. She straightened and plunked a glossy textbook onto my waiting palm.

"We have a few picture books around," she teased. "More entertaining ones are in yesterday's aisle if you want to research there later." Her expression hardened and: "That'll be Uncle Ral. Don't go far!"

I hadn't noticed the handset lighting up or vibrating. My attention was elsewhere. Darlene sashayed from the aisle with the device to an ear. I leaned against the shelves to thumb through the book where Raleigh's nosy cameras couldn't read over my shoulder.

The photograph I sought was on page sixteen. A caption underneath credited the American Philosophical Society in Philadelphia, PA. The outside of a red journal from Lewis and Clark's expedition, one of eighteen extant volumes, matched Tipper's memo: five by eight, red leather, bound on a short side opposite a clasp. I wasn't sure what else I'd expected. Raleigh hadn't yet materialized to shoo me from the building, so I sacrificed myself on the altar of misdirected research and turned more pages. I even read some of the words.

Much of the history reminded rather than educated. Early

nineteenth century politics hadn't made much sense in school. I remembered my younger self wondering if Thomas Jefferson's pre-voyage micromanagement had gotten on Captains Clark and Lewis' last nerves. The President had been particular about every little thing, procedures, interactions with natives, note taking, protocol, every detail. He'd even worked out a secret code for correspondence, though neither of the men he'd commissioned for the journey was known to have employed the cipher. Then again, who advertised when they wrote coded letters? The textbook's authors devoted a full chapter to the Jeffersonian Cipher, which was based on a predetermined keyword only Jefferson and his trusty captains knew at the time. According to page forty, the keyword was *ARTICHOKES*.

Suddenly I wasn't in an old bookstore after hours. I stood in the shambles of a kitchen in a different corner of Nashville altogether, transported by realization, and stared again at a refrigerator door folded in half. Mitch Braunfelter was still a sticky pulp in the next room. Right up to the end, however, he'd been an excellent speller.

The word he'd left behind in those refrigerator magnets wasn't misspelled. It was just incomplete:

ARTIC...
ARTICHOKES.

The key to a two-hundred-year-old cipher, minus four digits Bigfoot had knocked off during his rampage, might have been plain as day in Mitch's kitchen.

...a doozy of a puzzle, he'd told me.

Even if I was a poor man, I'd have wagered a grand that puzzle came in a five by eight red leather wrapper.

• • •

Darlene reappeared draped in the equivalent of twenty synthetic foxes. I hadn't expected more practical outerwear.

Flintlock

She carried my gloves and hat, which I'd left on the back counter.

"Find what you wanted?"

I gave her the textbook to put away. Even smothered in imitation fur, she didn't disappoint in the process. "I did, thanks. Not as helpful as the real thing, but close."

Her fingers traced a tail up over my ribs as she straightened. "Silly, I'd have told you right off if we had the genuine article! What would I have gotten for *that?*"

I grinned. Stupidly. "Is your uncle coming soon?"

"No. He always stays late."

On cue, the lights popped out except for a fluorescent aura behind the rearmost shelves. Uncle Ral had important business to complete that didn't require our presence. I didn't see myself lasting many nights before I busted his jaw. The frosted storefront glass sparkled with borrowed illuminance from a nearby streetlight, brushing old book spines with enough luster to define the aisle. We found our way to the door without tripping.

"Walk me to my car?" Darlene prompted.

"Of course."

I thumbed the brim of my hat at a camera and pulled on my gloves. Darlene turned the deadbolt lever. The door yipped as we stepped through. She locked up again from the outside, dropped the keys in her purple leather purse, claimed my arm with both hands. The neon *O'Dell's* sign buzzed over our heads till Raleigh found that switch, too, and killed it.

The sidewalk was bone dry. The air gnawed our cheeks and burned our lungs. Nashville had slid back into the teens in less than three hours. Meters in front of the store were unoccupied now but hadn't been when Darlene arrived for her shift. Her car was a red Volvo two blocks distant. We walked close together so our breath mixed into a single cloud. It was late. It was cold. Nobody else was in the mood for a downtown stroll.

Jon A. Hunt

Except for two other guys.

They materialized from the shadows that framed the attorneys' office doors. One came toward us from the front. The other quickened his step behind.

Darlene gave no indication she noticed. I was the big paranoid private eye, that was my job. I slackened our pace incrementally. So did the man in front. Unless we stopped completely, all four of us were going to meet up where a lightless alley intersected the block between us and Darlene's waiting car. The alley probably held additional participants. It was embarrassing to have tramped so easily into such an unimaginative ambush.

"Have your car keys ready?"

Darlene release my forearm and opened the purse as we walked. I felt her tense with understanding that we were about to have unwanted company.

The man in front kept both hands jammed into his pockets, shoulders hunched, elbows locked. Cold makes you want to do that, though a professional resists. He at least had some street smarts: we never made eye contact because he watched my hands.

All that concentration didn't do him much good. When the alley yawned to my right, he stepped with purpose into my path and I kicked him in the nuts with one of the feet he *hadn't* been watching. The rest happened fast.

Darlene sprang out of reach in a swirl of artificial fur. The second man hit me in the ribs as I pivoted to meet him, his shoulder dropped in a solid football tackle. It didn't hurt enough to distract me from making sure he was on the bottom when we met the concrete. The first guy finished folding and his face slapped the sidewalk half a second later. I rolled over both of them. Concrete tore my knee and shredded the leather of my left glove as I used those knuckles for a fulcrum. My feet were mostly under me when the extras bounded from the alley.

Flintlock

There were two of them. They were swinging two-by-fours. Nobody invests in a decent baseball bat for assault anymore.

I ducked beneath one board and smashed somebody's jaw. Or maybe my fist. Either way, bones crunched. The other two-by-four caught me behind the knees. The indirect blow was sufficient to buckle my legs and topple me like a bag of rocks onto my weather shoulder.

Mr. Lucky Strike stood over me with his plank raised for another delivery. I took as long as any swivel chair addict to get off my damaged shoulder and onto my knees. He could have swatted my head across the street. Instead, he was yelling at the girl on my opposite side like *she* was the one who deserved his "what the fuck?!"

Then the center of his face pinched inward and every dirty joke and piano lesson he'd ever known escaped through the back of his skull. The roar of a gunshot filled my head as it emptied his, and he went down.

The Smith & Wesson finally flashed from under my jacket. Its muzzle pointed like a bird dog at the source of the explosion.

White terror ringed Darlene's bronze eyes. The purse lay at her feet, its contents vomited in a glittering mess on the sidewalk. Silver fur lashed at the breeze around her. Her dress had split from hem to navel and her spectacular legs were wide apart, tight, ready. Nothing cancels out sexiness, however, quite the way a snub-nosed .38 pointed at your groin does.

I eased my own gun earthward. No more sudden movements. The two-by-four slipped from a dead hand with a clatter. Only divine intervention prevented the ugly revolver in her shaking hands from going off again.

"All right," I said. "They can't hurt you now."

A glance confirmed this. One of the four lumps around me quivered and groaned. Two appeared to be out cold. The fourth sprawled grotesquely on its back beneath the streetlight, in the center of a broadening puddle of steaming darkness.

People under Darlene's kind of stress don't respond predictably to polite requests. I was all for predictability at the moment.

"Put the gun down, Darlene."

Her arms dropped to her sides. The .38 dangled loosely from the fingertips of her gloved hand. Blue flashes darted along the edges of things: the streetlight pole, strands of faux fur, the lumps of our defeated assailants, the boundary of pooled blood. I returned my unfired weapon to the shoulder holster. With luck, the police wouldn't confiscate it as evidence, especially if I got Rafferty's good word to back up my character.

"You have a permit for that?"

The whites of Darlene's eyes diminished. She started to shiver. "Gram insisted."

"Good. Nobody will debate self-defense. But that gun better be on the ground when the cops get here."

The revolver clunked onto the sidewalk. I winced reflexively but it didn't fire.

Four Metro cruisers slid to sloppy rocking stops all around us.

Flintlock

Chapter Twenty-one

We innocents had to stay put and answer a lot of questions. The dead guy left first in a coroner's van after the usual crime scene crew did their job; his accomplices preceded him in ambulances. Nobody mentioned my bloodied knee or knuckles, which didn't improve my opinion of the victim's role. They kept us separated so we couldn't corroborate each other's version of what happened. Standard procedure. Her account must have been more entertaining than mine: all but three of the officers hovered around her car.

I talked when I was supposed to and kept my trap shut when I should. I didn't complain. The plastic rear seat in the police car beat freezing my ass off outside.

Eventually I stood out in the cold again. Rafferty had been contacted, I was addressed as *Mr. Bedlam* and my .45 was handed back to me with the chamber cleared and the magazine ejected. Standard procedure. I holstered it and dropped the loose bits in a coat pocket. Mine and Darlene's stories must have matched.

Enticing calves extended from an open car door. The remains of her ruined dress rode dangerously high as she sat. Every item in her underwear drawer must be the same color. The girl loved purple. If the dozen cops guarding her noticed, they didn't say anything.

"You got a ride, Mr. Bedlam? Lieutenant says you need to

get yourself home directly."

I bet he did.

"It isn't far," I said. "what about Miss O'Dell?"

"We'll make sure she gets home safe."

"Uh huh."

I left Darlene in capable hands and pointed my shoes toward the Cool-Core Tower. Her bronze gaze swept from beneath long lashes to find me. The boys in blue could take her home if they liked. I was the one who got the smile.

• • •

The thirty-second floor still blazed like high noon. Aubrea and Poole hadn't found any wall switches and the voice controls only obeyed Jack Bedlam's son. I wondered how Dad had accomplished this without my involvement.

"Lights to twenty percent," I commanded

Poole and the girl turned to squint at me, through the fireplace's gaseous cascade, from the red leather couch. They'd been talking a while, yet Poole maintained as much distance between them as a ten-foot couch allowed. He also had a hand on the service automatic under his jacket till his eyes adjusted and he recognized me. He got up and came around, took in the overnight bag under my arm and the dried stains on my jeans. He let go of his weapon and smiled amicably.

"Dispatch said you were running late. I'm supposed to let them know you arrived."

Them meant Rafferty.

"That's fine," I said. "Go ahead and report on your way down. It's late."

"Will do. 'Night, Miss Aubrea." He didn't have his Predators hat on to tip but collected it from the entry table on his way out.

I'd hoped to excuse myself and clean up before she got a good look at me. She already had the route to the bathroom blocked when Poole shut the door. Her expression was one of

Flintlock

concern or disapproval or something else I couldn't identify.

"I see better in the dark than you think," she said. "Are you staying this time?"

"Sure. Cabs aren't crazy about fares who look like they've been in fights."

"Have you?"

"Just the one."

"Come here."

I let her lead me to the glass desk and the swivel chair, and for the second time the District Attorney's daughter played nurse to me. My knuckles hadn't mended much from Tuesday's adventure, though this time they weren't peppered with rock salt, and the vodka bottle remained in the cabinet. I administered an oral dose, instead, of damned fine bourbon my father had set aside for medicinal purposes. We cut the leg off my jeans on the injured side with my pocketknife, since the overnight bag I'd brought from the Viper had a change of clothes. It also yielded bandages and antibiotic ointment. Experience has taught me when I stay away from home unexpectedly, I generally also need first aid.

Downtown's skyline glittered beyond plate glass, a sprawling diorama for the elevation privileged. Tiny Christmas trees twinkled in distant windows. The space between looked plenty cold. We sat above the world, beside a shimmering wall of gas flame, further heated from the inside by indecently rare liquor from a bottle with the name *Old Fitzgerald* on the label.

"Does this happen often?" She daubed a cut on my jaw with gauze. I hadn't noticed the cut earlier. Her eyes shone with miniscule copies of nighttime Nashville.

"Usually just when I'm on a case."

"'Usually'?"

"Once in a while I piss somebody off for free."

Her eyes didn't shift from the task at hand. *Old Fitzgerald* didn't entirely mask Darlene's perfume.

Jon A. Hunt

"Should I ask what this fight was about?"

"You're going to either way. Damsel in distress, regular PI stuff. She'll be okay."

"Mm-hmm."

"I didn't get the girl."

Her finger brushed my lower lip.

"Do you ever?"

"Get the damsel in distress?"

"Mm-hmm."

"I wouldn't be the one to tell. I'm a gentleman."

I felt her smile rather than saw it. And more than Kentucky bourbon was to blame for my pulse rate. "Tyler, do you think I'm in distress?"

"Not up here. I suspect I'm in more trouble."

She confirmed my suspicion with a kiss.

It was just a kiss. Maybe several. But our brains recognized what our bodies wouldn't, hands met, fingers meshed, and we clung tightly to the space between us. Her cheek touched mine and stayed there. I felt her breath, her pulse, the contrast of soft feverish skin and cool descending tears.

"I can't hide like this forever," she said. "My life isn't supposed to be up this high."

"Mine, neither," I said.

"Tyler—"

"Ssh. I'm working on it."

We'd made progress. Or I had. Things had rattled loose. Those gorillas with the dimensional lumber hadn't really set their trap for Darlene. Maybe I'd asked the right questions in Columbia, though my money was on overheard conversations in my favorite bookstore. Uncle Ral and I needed another chat soon. *Then* I'd bust his jaw.

Aubrea leaned away first. She released my hand and allowed me to brush the moisture from her face. Those eyes outsparkled any city skyline I'd ever seen. My bandaged

182

Flintlock

knuckles made a poor substitute, but I focused on them instead. I hadn't gotten the tar beaten out of me for two women, not really.

This was for Mitch.

"Get me some ice?" I said.

"For your drink?"

My internal chuckle never quite surfaced. Aubrea and I belonged to different universes.

"In a towel, for my shoulder," I said. "I'd better check in with Rafferty or he'll get impatient and come up here himself."

• • •

"What happened to keeping this all low-key?"

I raised my glass to eye level. Viewed through coppery liquor, the AT&T building dwindled to insignificance. I bet my old man had studied the skyline through similar optics.

"I was just walking the girl to her car."

Rafferty's growl didn't daunt any less over the phone than it did in person. "Does she *always* dress that way?"

"She wasn't who attracted attention tonight. Who were they?"

"Locals. I'm surprised you didn't recognize Chad Walker."

"Which of the four?"

"The dead one."

"I didn't get a look at his face, while he had one."

"Been in and out of the system. Shoplifting, public intoxication, minor assault, possession. Pissant stuff but always looking for worse. He was a guy to call if you needed a group collected to do bad things. No appreciable time served, no sense to keep his nose clean. Sooner or later, he'd have stepped in over his head."

"I'd say he did that tonight."

Rafferty made an affirmative grunt. "Miss O'Dell did the rest of us a favor."

"I doubt she feels it was a public service."

183

Jon A. Hunt

"Scared shitless."

"You talked with her? I thought Langston——"

Aubrea glanced across the half-darkness from the couch. She was folding ice cubes from the wet bar refrigerator into a hand towel. The fireplace painted undulating oranges and blues around her and rendered her expression impossible to read.

"——weren't you pulled from the investigation?" I rephrased.

"That business at Vanderbilt was a game changer. We were told to start back up. Yeah, I got the story directly from Darlene. And I checked Walker's mobile phone."

"You enjoy snooping through people's electronics."

He ignored the dig. "Last received call was from the O'Dell's landline. When you and her left the building."

"Raleigh!"

"Had him hauled downtown. Swears up and down he didn't make any calls."

"I'd be happy to jog his memory."

"I'm sure. My way is admissible in court, though. He *may* be telling the truth. Their system can route calls through like a switchboard. Officially, it's for family use to offset long-distance expenses, but anyone with access can use it and the outbound number shows up as the store's. Old lady Meredith could've triggered the hit."

"That's legal?"

"It's a gray area. It's also a great way to launder phone traffic."

Shady collectors named Jorgensen and Fontaine would appreciate perks like that offered by their favorite bookseller.

"Okay," I said, "but tonight took planning. These weren't pros. They needed every step mapped out for them by a smart person. And it's a jump from assault to murder. I'm not sure killing me was the idea."

"You worked them over pretty well for just a wrestling match."

Flintlock

"Nobody stopped to clarify intent."

Rafferty must be in a fairly good mood to be so chatty. He was glad to be working again. I should keep him talking while the information flowed.

"What else?"

"Uh, your guess about Tipper's family was on the money. Great big killer, little piles. That makes it more than just a robbery. Never disclosed that to TBI, and TBI avoided asking. I'll get him downtown—"

"Let me talk with him first. You're not always that good at conversation."

"You're quite the fucking diplomat yourself."

"See what I told you?"

"All right. Just don't dawdle. And are you giving me anything new for all this? I'm assuming people aren't just wanting to club you to death for the fun of it."

What *had* I found? I turned my back on the city lights and leaned against chilled plate glass five-hundred feet above West End. My injured shoulder let me know its displeasure. Aubrea started toward me with the towel full of ice and sensual deliberation. I was ready to finish my conversation with the large cop in the tiny office.

"I'm not sure," I admitted. "Braunfelter looks to have had the missing red journal in hand at one time. He may have been trying to decipher the thing."

Rafferty grunted again. Aubrea was beside me. The iced towel lay over my good shoulder. She started working my shirt buttons. I held a phone and glass of very good bourbon, which effectively incapacitated me. The Lieutenant's gravelly voice reengaged my attention.

"Interesting theory, except I didn't think those journals were ever coded, and whoever busted his skull is still looking. We're down to just one of those kids now."

Somehow the glass wound up in Aubrea's hand. I reflexively

Jon A. Hunt

grabbed her wrist, too hard.

"Sal?"

"The other one. Tom. His top and bottom halves were distributed between two dumpsters back of Cool Springs Mall. Dumpster lids were folded shut."

Like Mitch's refrigerator.

"Jesus…"

Aubrea whimpered. I remembered her and loosened my grip. I whispered I was sorry.

"I've heard worse," Rafferty responded. "You get that call from Sal, I need to know. That boy's got a lot of trouble on his tail. Your buddy Keller Ableman is even asking about him. Who do you think *his* clients are?"

I couldn't imagine anyone with the boy's well-being in mind and said so.

"Got another call," Rafferty said. "Talk again soon."

A click put the period at the end of his sentence.

Smooth hands eased upward over my forearms. Aubrea's breath warmed my bared chest. A muted bit of swaddled ice gently pressed my aching shoulder. I winced in spite of years of practiced machismo, in spite of *Old Fitzgerald's* finest Kentucky bourbon.

"Tyler, are you all right?"

"I'm better off than some people," I told her.

• • •

We safeguarded each other's dreams. Confusion and ugliness had piled in too many layers to share or ignore, and weariness alone guaranteed no peace. The short-term cure was a warm trusted body held close. Anything more physical was neither prudent nor necessary. I slept better for five hours with Aubrea in the crook of my good arm than I had since Mitch died.

Only for five hours.

She didn't wake when I eased from beneath her; she just

Flintlock

squirmed deeper into the warm couch cushions. The blinds hadn't lowered and the penthouse was as dark as a high-altitude fishbowl in a city ever got. Aubrea's shoulders wore a glow from lights in other windows blocks distant, and her pale bra straps seemed the brightest components to the room. She'd had a blouse on when my eyes closed. Unsure who deserved credit for that, I shed my own shirt and draped it over her.

Most of Nashville wouldn't wake till dawn. There was no activity in the streets below, except flashing traffic lights and a few slow vehicles, most of which carried watchful cops. They were awake on purpose. I crossed the plush carpet to one of the bathrooms. A shower couldn't hurt.

Where is it? I silently asked the steaming spray.

Mitch had been killed—I guessed—for a five-by-eight diary once owned by another puzzle solver, who'd died just as violently centuries earlier. Mitch was smart enough to understand its value, smart enough to ask for help, smart enough to recognize Jefferson's cipher and maybe solve it. He was smart enough to hide the journal.

Mitch was gone. The journal was still missing. The searching and the killing would continue till it was found.

I couldn't begin to think like a man who wore crossword suspenders.

I toweled off, padded back out to the main room in my spare jeans and a fresh shirt. There was no reason not to rejoin the girl on the red leather couch and watch another Nashville sunrise. The glass desk distracted me from my new plan. It pulsed with dim green light. My phone on the charging mat had an incoming call.

I got there late again. The unidentified caller had hung up. I took the phone into a bedroom and redialed. Three rings. A descending trio of beeps. Silence.

Someone had lifted a receiver and put it back in the cradle unanswered.

Jon A. Hunt

I dialed again.

This time I got a man's voice. His "hello" sounded more like the color than a greeting, and was louder than normal people are at five in the morning.

"I just missed a call from this number."

"Wasn't me. I'm just frying donuts."

"Did you see who it was?"

"Prank call. Kid snuck in and grabbed the phone, that's all—"

"Skinny? Reeboks with the laces untied?"

Suspicion crept into the voice. "Hey, if this is some kinda joke, I got work to do."

"Police," I said. Desperation made me do it.

"Kid slipped in here and called the *cops*?!"

"Please answer the question. It's important."

"Okay, okay. Yeah, he's a beanpole. Shoes like you said. I figured he was stealing donuts, but he went for the wall phone. Uh, you're really the cops?"

"Cars are on their way. You can ask them. Confirm your address?"

"Shouldn't you already know it?"

There wasn't time to salvage my lie. I hung up and called Rafferty. He picked up on the second ring.

"How quick can you do a reverse look-up from a phone number?"

"Sal?"

"Probably. He got run off before we could talk. Someplace with fresh donuts."

"Gimme the number."

I did. He told me to hold. I did that, too. Then he came back and told me cars were on the way and Smally had been notified. That canceled out my earlier untruth.

"Darrywimple's Donuts on First," he confirmed. "Apple fritters are as good as anybody's. Maybe we can pick up a dozen

188

Flintlock

and the kid."

"Go for it," I said. My gut told me Sal was blocks away by now.

"You're still up in the Tower?"

"Sure. Why?"

"Was just on the line with Tug Moran. He asked about you."

"I've been good."

"That's what I told him. Somebody broke into the water company's pump station not far from Braunfelter's place. You and the Langston girl were there earlier."

"We were. Do you mean vandals, or burglars?"

"Burglars. Vandals don't deactivate security cameras. No windows broken. Lock was picked. They hit the office in back, made a mess, but there wasn't anything of value to steal, just papers and keys—"

Two hours before sunrise, I'd already hung up on two people. Rafferty might call me back on the road. I jammed on shoes, shrugged painfully into the shoulder rig, checked the Smith & Wesson, snapped my hat and jacket up from the chair where I'd left them, and was hissing groundward in the elevator before Aubrea could notice I was leaving.

Cool-Core had a helicopter on the roof, mine to use if I wanted, but that took more time to orchestrate than I had to spend. I had a fast car and I needed to get to Mule Town. Now. Before the sun came back.

...the little office in back.

...just papers and keys...

One key that used to hang on the pegboard in that office had been *Mitch's Very Own Dam Key*. My guess was nobody'd yet looked for any red journals there.

Aubrea, Louis and I had been watched. Keller Ableman had guessed ahead of me.

189

Jon A. Hunt

Chapter Twenty-two

The Viper emerged from Cool-Core's garage, snarling in a cocoon of exhaust, a newly hatched dragon. I wasn't counting on stealth. The unmarked car near the exit wouldn't follow; the men in it had orders to stay put and use the radio. Contrary to what Poole said or believed, the Tower was watched round the clock whether I was present or not. I knew Jerry Rafferty.

Speed limits were agony. Every flashing red light chewed up vital seconds. I fought an instinct to fly and kept the supercar reined in on city streets right up to the ramp onto I-40. Then I floored the accelerator and made sure nobody within a quarter mile remained asleep.

Night stretched bone dry and bitter around me. A bloated moon rode the horizon. The Viper's back end wagged. The tires were cold. I'd be okay unless I needed to stop suddenly. The broad southward sweep into I-65 was doable at 150.

Aubrea's mobile number scrolled across the central dash display. I upped the volume so I might be able to hear her over the engine.

"Where are you?" Even against the explosion of ten cylinders, she sounded anxious.

"Sorry, there wasn't time to wake you," I shouted. "I'm going back to Columbia."

"*Now?*"

"I'll explain soon." I bopped the end-call icon on the touch

Flintlock

screen. Nothing I could tell her now would ease her nerves.

180.

Semis trying to overtake each other filled the headlamp beams. I stomped the brake pedal. Tires protested, the front end dipped, the tail stepped out but didn't quite let go. I got around the leftmost truck on the shoulder. The rumble strip had more bark than bite, but it was a hell of a bark. Traction felt vague. I lifted my right foot till gravity remembered me, then pressed down again. High-mounted truck lights shrank frantically in the mirrors. The moon stood directly ahead, a fat radioactive orb blocking my way, insisting I'd go no farther than a quarter million miles or so. Fine. I only needed to get to Mule Town.

150 again.

I couldn't easily read the next number on the dash. Who else could it be, though?

"Hey," I said.

"What the fuck is going on? Where're you headed?"

"Columbia."

"Not like that, you aren't!"

165.

"Jerry, I gave you some great leads. And you can't get there quick enough."

"You act like I've got favors left to give——"

"I know where the red journal is—but not for long."

The speedometer flashed its trademark red serpent's head during the final upshift. I wasn't sure whether my news or how fast he'd been told I was traveling generated Rafferty's "shit!" but he was ready to listen. "Talk fast, you're all over the radios."

Blue roof lights filled my mirrors.

• • •

He had to play along. I was right, Rafferty wouldn't get where I was headed in time to be useful. Cops need permission.

Me, I was just breaking the law.

He threw me every ounce of clout he owned. The pursuing troopers fell back—they couldn't match the Viper's speed if they wanted—and the only roadblocks I encountered were at the on-ramps, sideways cruisers keeping innocents away from my reckless passage. The interstate was mine as long as deer paid attention.

197.

The mechanical roar that propelled me tore my senses. Green mile markers winked past every eighteen seconds. Solid and dashed lines were indistinguishable, and what few other vehicles hadn't been ushered out of my trajectory shot by in twin red blurs.

203.

Rafferty had warned me the state troopers were more cooperative than county sheriffs or the Columbia police. I was on Tug Moran's list.

· · ·

I came off Exit 48 hot, but the brakes scrubbed illegal velocity before I joined Highway 99. All I passed were trucks, evenly spaced, travelling with as much purpose as me, just less urgency. The American road freight system never sleeps. A state trooper SUV watched my turn southward onto 31 without reaction. Riverside Drive arched to my left. I followed it.

The moon's edges blurred till its position in the sky became questionable. Streetlights exhaled yellow glares that never found the asphalt beneath them. Leaden fog pressed upward and outward from the Duck River and defeated both heavenly and artificial lights. My headlamps dazzled more than illuminated. Ten miles an hour now felt suicidal; I strained to keep between painted lines I could barely see.

The crime-scene tape helped better than anything. It stretched across the street edge of the concrete apron where Louis Aldritch's work truck had been parked the prior night, a

Flintlock

wavering yellow boundary. The police had gone home. I didn't need them as long as I could keep the crime tape in my peripheral. The dam wasn't far.

I doused the headlights and relied on the less distracting running lights. I rolled my window down. Mist crowded into the cabin to join me, dense, painfully frigid. My breath mixed with it. The Viper's exhaust was a dull thump-thump-thump. Water crashed beyond the mist, a lot of water, so much I could hear it over the car. I sensed pavement sloping away to my left. That had to be the parking lot beside the dam. I cranked the wheel.

Crumbled asphalt beneath a tire alerted me to an unseen edge. I adjusted the wheel and eased forward more. The side reflectors of a colorless sedan jumped at me and I dabbed at the brakes. I'd have plowed right into the other car if I hadn't already known it would be there. A familiar purple pulse on my phone had warned me.

Keller's field agent was a few steps ahead of me.

• • •

Alternating applications of salt and sand by day, and freezing mists by night, had left the lot an amalgamation of rough and glossy. With a careful gait it was passable. Pressing the driver's side door shut gently was a wasted precaution: icy cascades thundering over yet unseen spillways dominated the aural landscape. The other car was empty, not yet cool. The red blip of the security system warning light inside was almost startling. There was no telling how far purple flashes from my phone might travel if I let it out of my jacket pocket.

I crouched beside the rear wheel well and felt for the tiny GPS device. Dirt and ice crusted its edges. I used my pocketknife to pry it loose. I used the knife on the tires as well, and watched with satisfaction as the car settled heavily on that side. One way or another, tonight would be the end of my unplanned working relationship with the Keller Ableman

Jon A. Hunt

Agency. I got up, pocketed the tag, crept toward the wet roar of the old dam, which I still couldn't see.

For all the larger landmarks, what first resolved into familiarity was the zigzag of the chain link gate that used to bar access to the dam's crosswalk. I hooked gloved fingers through the wires and the gate obligingly swung toward me. An open padlock rattled from one end of the loose chain. Whoever opened it must have missed the sign warning about aggravated criminal trespass.

The old powerhouse almost solidified when I squinted in its direction. Hints of darker right angles formed. Once, briefly, a hard bright corner appeared. Keller's man had forgotten to keep his flashlight beam below the window. Then the window melted into the mists again, leaving only much closer aspects visible: a rounded cliff, at once constant and in violent downward motion—a whole river instantly changing elevation—and the near end of the catwalk. The catwalk didn't pass more than three feet above the water. It had looked more substantial in daylight. Icicles drooped from the handrails. Ice covered the walkway, a foot thick and humped higher in the middle. I'd seen more inviting bobsled runs. Keller's man would have to come back that way. Waiting at the gate was more prudent.

But Mitch hadn't tried to hire anyone prudent. I shouldered past the gate and out onto the catwalk.

The decision proved as rewarding as I expected. Steps one and two went as planned. The third went fifty miles an hour sideways. I hugged a railing and my lower half spun out into nothing. The river reached for me. Spray slapped my kicking feet. Swinging my legs back onto the frictionless walk took more tries than I could count. Ice smashed the Smith & Wesson into my ribs.

Light swept along the glazed concrete again. Another window appeared in the powerhouse, an array of panes

Flintlock

brightened from within by Keller's man. The moment revealed red dots frozen into the walkway ice. He'd fallen harder than me and torn himself to keep going. Nothing but the best for the Keller Ableman Agency.

The light and the window vanished.

I dragged myself the rest of the way on my stomach.

• • •

Deadbolts give one advantage to the professional trespasser: they can be locked again from the inside. But the Columbia dam's powerhouse deterred honest visitors the same way the catwalk gate had, with a simple padlock. I shivered outside the double doors while the gap between them brightened, darkened, and brightened again. Keller's agent wasn't finding the reason we'd both come here. He saw the place only through the eyes of a professional trespasser, not a former utility worker. I eased the doors apart during a dark interval and ducked through. A draft wouldn't give my entrance away. The building was no warmer inside than out, and mists oozed in through many other openings.

The interior reminded me of the pump station half a mile upstream. A lot of overbuilt structure wrapped around a lot of nothing else. High windows interrupted the bricks on all four sides. That's how places were lit in the Twenties. The windows were black now, their sills several feet above my head, panes broken or missing, especially on the upstream side. From the floor's center rose two rusty domes, each twelve feet in diameter, six or seven high. Sheet metal cabinets lined the upstream wall, high-voltage control panels. None of the equipment seemed to have been operational in my lifetime. Higher even than the tops of the windows, a grated walkway ran the perimeter, accessed by precarious iron stairs that went up beside the doors. My competitor rummaged up there with his flashlight. If he glanced through the grate, he'd spot me, but thus far his attention was elsewhere. I kept my back to the wall,

195

moved when he did, made what use I could of his fitful flashlight aura.

The building groaned around us, withstanding the Duck River's ferocity as it had for decades. I was less likely to be heard than seen. The.45 waited under my left arm as a last resort. Ricochets here could be equally unhealthy for shooter or target.

The flashlight painted walls and trusses. My reflection stared at me from glass in the partially open door. Then the light shifted, the reflection vanished, and I took another step. Something clanged. The guy upstairs swept his light angrily across the ceiling. I grinned at the thought of him rubbing a dented shin. Mitch's personal key had so far been his *only* lucky break.

But he *was* on the right trail. The red journal was here. I hadn't been surer of anything except sunrises in the last two weeks. Where in the powerhouse a retired city plumber and puzzle fanatic would hide it...that was the tricky question.

Weight ground across overhead iron. Looking high made sense. The Duck had overrun the dam dozens of times during Mitch's tenure, filling associated structures with mud and debris. Playing safe seemed too obvious, however, for a man who wore crossword suspenders. Where would he have stashed the journal?

The downstream wall could be immediately discounted. Too vulnerable, even for someone avoiding the obvious, and too bare. Time and unmanaged waters had scrubbed all but the window frames away. Unfortunately, the other walls were no more promising.

Maybe I should just go upstairs and buffalo cooperation from my competition. The stairs were starting to lose contrast with weakly illuminated brickwork beyond. His batteries were running low. We could team up, share the fresh penlight in my pocket, except he'd probably shoot me before I could offer.

Flintlock

Such irony, handicapped by darkness in an old powerhouse...

Dim saucers hovered far above me, antique industrial lamps. When the flashlight beam grazed them, blackened glass was revealed, or corroded threads of empty sockets. There hadn't been electricity here for a long time. The metal cabinets watched me with their dials, useless indicators serving no more purpose than eyes in corpses.

A hinge shrieked on the catwalk and what sounded like a bucket of wrenches clanged onto the grate. The light fluttered out for a moment, then stuttered halfheartedly to life again. Keller's man had taken to shaking the flashlight to keep it going. He'd be in the dark soon. I hustled myself to the cabinets.

They weren't tight to the wall as I'd supposed. A three-foot space separated the panels from the bricks, interrupted every few paces by metal supports. While the other guy banged around on the mezzanine, I risked the penlight, clamped in my left fist with my glove off. The thin glimmer wouldn't catch anyone's attention who wasn't looking straight at me. I hoped. More dead dial faces occupied the backs of the cabinets, some ponderous levers. I stowed my other glove and ran my hand over the metal. It was cold and pitted with neglect.

Feet jarred the mezzanine above me. I slipped the penlight into my jacket. The tiny familiar square of the GPS tag brushed my knuckle as it adhered to the light. Footsteps continued, firm hammer taps that overmatched the general roar of things; their distance and direction were impossible to judge accurately.

The flashlight failed altogether.

The ring of shoes came more slowly now. I didn't blame Keller's man for his caution. It was a long way to fall in the dark.

My touch met irregularities that touch alone would have to identify. A raised circle and glass—or sharp chips of it—meant a dial. A recessed vertical crevice meant the start of another

Jon A. Hunt

cabinet section. There were levers, frozen switches, coarse protrusions, all crusted with oxidation, corroded into a single unassailable mass. No nooks for hiding a journal.

The footsteps ceased. For a while only the booming river outside seemed to keep me company. This would be quicker if I could see. Would Keller's professional trespasser really opt for violence if I made myself a target? How many people had died already because of the thing we both wanted to find before the other guy?

I passed my open palms over the frigid metal.

One footfall only came from the catwalk, then I heard only river noise. He knew I was there.

I left the .45 holstered. I needed both hands.

Another bolt head dented the half-numb pads of my fingers. It was one of thousands, yet the corners were smooth and there were too many of them: earlier bolts had had sharp coarse corners, old-fashioned squares, not modern hexagons. The other bolts sure as hell hadn't turned freely under my fingertips.

Iron popped, the weight of a man shifting.

I almost dropped the bolt when it twirled loose. There were more, five more. They outlined a brick-sized rectangle if I connected the dots. Like a puzzle.

Another stair squeaked. He wouldn't announce himself between levels. Keller didn't hire morons.

The second and third bolts spun free. I dug my fingernails under the metal edge that had lifted. It didn't relent. Every screw must be undone.

"Hello."

Social hour had begun.

I ignored the summons and focused on the last screws. Keller and his fancy tracking equipment and his professional trespasser weren't going to beat me to this. The final bolt evaded me and plinked onto the concrete.

Flintlock

Fuck it.

I let the metal panel fall, too, with a jarring clang. My hands found the opening.

A rumble came from the doors. The other private eye was pulling them shut to prevent my exit. I couldn't feel a damned thing in the hole.

"You won't leave without my help," Keller's minion coolly informed me. It wasn't quite a shout, just a carefully modulated statement.

"I'll manage," I growled under my breath.

I dug out the penlight again, pushed it into the opening, which was at eye level for a man of Mitch's height. I thumbed the light on. A partial rectangle of betrayal warmed the bricks beside me. The cubby was deeper than I'd guessed. Rust lined the inside and there were fat cloth-wrapped wires at the back. A clear waterproof bag was wedged among the wires. Something red was in the bag.

The other guy headed my way quickly now. I had a fifty-fifty guess at which end of the control panels he'd come around, and no guess at all what he'd do then. I shoved the penlight and my entire left arm into the cavity. Soft plastic kissed my fingertips.

My right hand groped for the Smith & Wesson. Ricochets might be the least of my worries.

The edge of the bag caught between my fingers and the barrel of the penlight. I had it! I withdrew my hand.

My opponent stamped into the slender canyon. He was behind me, of course, and caught me with my paw in the proverbial cookie jar, shining my tiny light into the bag to confirm its contents. A flare hurled my shadow, hunched, distorted, far across lumpy bricks. I hadn't given the guy proper credit: he'd brought spare batteries.

"Your right hand, Mr. Bedlam. Please remove it slowly from your jacket, where I can see. Empty would be wiser. My

Jon A. Hunt

preference is not to shoot you, but..."

I followed directions till a more creative approach occurred to me.

"Leave your light in the bag."

"I was using it," I said.

He stood near enough for me to hear his taut chuckle. I also caught a glimpse of shadow shaped like a pistol barrel. "Please," he insisted.

I flicked my penlight off again and dropped it in alongside Meriwether Lewis' nineteenth journal. I compressed the bag's seal between my thumb and forefinger. No sense letting it get wet now.

"People know I'm here."

"That wouldn't surprise me," he said. "Leave the bag on the floor. No sudden moves. Take five steps forward and stop. If you turn, I'll shoot."

"That wouldn't surprise me," I said.

"Bag on the floor. Five steps."

I did as directed. Playing meek didn't do my disposition any favors; neither would a bullet in the back.

"Hands over your head. Thank you."

"You're welcome for the help finding the prize, too."

"Of course." His voice receded into the fluid snarl around us. For all the bravado, a quiver of excitement sneaked through. "Face the wall. Watch those hands."

The door rattled again. My shadow darkened the bricks in front of me. He was directly behind me with his flashlight.

"Be careful out there," I said.

His response was immediate darkness, steel door edges slapping together, the metallic snick of a padlock closing outside. I'd gone to an awful lot of trouble just for some bastard to lock me inside the powerhouse.

Flintlock

Chapter Twenty-three

Waiting was pointless. Keller's flunky had what he came for. He couldn't afford to stand around and make sure I continued to stare at a wall. I fished my phone from a pocket, powered it on, watched for the telltale purple. It pulsed briefly, then reverted to an ordinary glow. The journal, my penlight and Keller's tenacious GPS marker had traveled out of range.

Light from my phone got me to the doors. The glass framed into each section's upper third wore too much grime to see through. It broke the same as clean new glass when I applied the butt of the .45. Fog tumbled in past ragged edges like something had spooked it. Orange halos from streetlights on Riverside Drive didn't offer much assistance. The padlock outside clutched greedily at my fingers. It must have torn the hell out of the other guy's hands. I found my gloves and searched for something to use as a pry bar. A stretch of iron stair rail had fortunately fallen loose and worked to bust the hasp off the doors. I lost a good six minutes in the process.

The ice-coated bridge to shore hadn't improved. Violent quicksilver curling beneath it flipped a fresh wave over the catwalk, just for my benefit. How any man had crossed so quickly was beyond guessing.

I removed my belt and wrapped a couple turns around the railing before I started. Mitch would never have ventured out here in conditions this bad.

Jon A. Hunt

My shoes skidded on the glossy surface. All the concentration in the world didn't prevent me from going down hard several times, usually ending on my belly with the river's nearby slithering surface promising swift escape from worldly cares. Only the leather around my wrist and the railing kept me from becoming a water safety object lesson. Pain gnawed my weather shoulder.

My ordeal didn't last as long as it seemed. Dawn still hadn't broken when the chain link gate met me. The diamond-weave pattern switched back and forth between a mere hint and sharp distinction. I was happier to grab the thing than I'd ever admit publicly. I was also surprised to find *two* cars still frozen to the parking lot.

Keller's man might have tried driving off even with two flat tires. He hadn't. His sedan glittered under the streetlights, resplendent in a fresh dressing of ice.

The Duck churned relentlessly back where the fog lay thickest. The powerhouse was imperceptible, though the catwalk to it etched a pale line outward from the near bank, that gradually succumbed to the mists.

The gate hadn't been locked again.

Was I the only one to make it back to shore?

• • •

Discernable edges didn't persist downstream of the dam. Instead, earth and water merged in a shifting no-man's-land two feet lower than the parking lot. The sidewalk lay underwater. Restless logs, debris and ice dared any fool to approach. The fog thickened to a veritable paste. If the man with the red journal had fallen in, the river wasn't about to share its secret. I searched anyway. Stubbornness runs in the family.

The sky lightened and I still couldn't see farther than I could reach. I watched my phone for the purple warning light I used to loathe, but that never happened; finally, a different warning

Flintlock

about battery life filled the touchscreen and the device shut itself off. My weather shoulder and my back ached. My knees wobbled. Both feet were well on their way to frostbite in soggy shoes, and I stumbled through bleak surroundings with barely more visual awareness than Stevie Wonder. I'd misjudged Keller's man once. He could have simply abandoned his crippled car and walked away into the mists across Riverside Drive. I wouldn't have heard any dogs barking from the bottom of the riverbank. Either way, I wasn't going to find him now.

I turned, disgruntled, back upstream.

The lot where I'd left the cars wasn't difficult to find. A lot of flashing blue lights had arrived. Shadow puppets of uniformed officers materialized as I stepped over the guard rail. I saw them a second before they spotted me. They swung their lights onto me as a group, better lights than either of us PIs had brought. A familiar stocky silhouette approached. Red stubble by his ears glowed in the hazy brilliance behind him.

"Don't you sleep?" asked Chief Moran.

"Not much," I admitted.

"I'm obliged to ask…"

I kept my hands in plain sight and indicated the sedan with a tilt of my head. "Looking for this guy," I uttered, the Gospel truth.

Moran's breath billowed around him and stayed weirdly separate from the fog. "Looks like you've been at it a while. Where do you think he is?"

I shrugged, which hurt. Moran never glanced back at the road. That suggested he hadn't passed anyone on foot there, nor had any of his troops. That left the river.

"Did anything I said the other day sink in, Mr. Bedlam?"

My kind of person rarely delivers a convincingly innocent smile. I tried my best.

"I'll take your gun," he said. "We can talk in my car."

• • •

Jon A. Hunt

This new habit of warming my toes in police cars needed a cure quick. Nothing good would come of it. At least this time I sat up front.

Tug had questions. Had I actually seen the man from the four-door? I suggested he'd been on the dam, inside the powerhouse. What time? I gave a fair estimate. Had I noticed the damaged tires? I lied. More telling, though, were the things *not* asked. My reasons for tailing Keller's man, or who he was, never came up; nor did the chief press for my location during the supposed break-in. He danced around topics, which wasn't at all in character for an official who'd personally dealt with me the last time just to make a point. The charade sapped our conversational energy and we devolved into one silent cop and one taciturn professional trespasser with wet socks, who just happened to be in the same car. Our attention wandered to searchlights carving the mists outside. Columbia's finest had taken up looking for what I couldn't find. Minutes came and went. Finally, Moran passed my unloaded .45 and its magazine across the cab.

"Rafferty says you can't discuss much while the investigation is active. I prefer knowing what's happening in my jurisdiction. But orders are what they are. Thanks for helping me keep up appearances in front of my boys."

"Not a problem," I said. My brain scrambled for a foothold. How many favors did I owe Rafferty now?

New headlights descended from the gloom of Riverside Drive. A Mercedes, another marked car, then another Mercedes. With no view of the old dam available, the overlook lot had never been fuller. Moran's eyes echoed the dash clock.

"How are your feet?" he asked.

"Better."

We climbed back out into the cold, because we were supposed to expect whoever had arrived. I recognized the first Mercedes, which was something, since they all look alike. The

Flintlock

doors popped ajar and out stepped Eli and Aubrea Langston. Her eyes found me. She staggered on an icy patch, mastered her composure, took more anxious steps toward me. Little Eli bounded between us. Just like at the funeral. Moran and his bunch apparently knew who Eli was and kept out of his way.

Eli punched me. In front of God, the police and his sister, he threw his weight behind a furious uppercut to my jaw. I let him. My teeth clacked and my head rocked back. He hit pretty hard for barnyard fowl. Aubrea yelled and he ignored her. Stupid kid. It was her honor he protected. His elbow ratcheted back for another. I'd rather not knock him cold in front of family, but he'd used up his freebie. My right fist balled, shoulder tensed.

"Eli!"

That voice stopped him. People listened to DA Langston, especially his kids.

"Go over by your sister. I want a word with this man before he loses patience with you."

Eli's frame slackened. He drifted backward. The pale ferocious eyes bored through fog as sharply as any searchlight. He didn't blink during his entire retreat.

The man who stepped into Eli's footprints brought no height advantage. While the younger Langston compensated with rage, his father understood how large character made a person. He'd spent decades whittling giants down to manageable size in courtrooms. Eyes reached up and grabbed mine, pale as the son's, burning with steadier fire. The voice was equally steady.

"I wanted a good look at you in person."

"You didn't catch me at my best," I said.

"You're treading mighty fine lines, Bedlam. With the law. With my daughter."

I studied him. My words needed careful choosing and it was an excuse to rub my sore chin. Langston looked like more money than I did, even if he wasn't, but the veneer had flaws. The tailored suit under the trench coat was unbuttoned, he wore no tie, no hat covered the salt-and-pepper hair. He'd left home in a rush.

"No one's finding answers playing safe," I said. "I'm being as cautious as I can be and still get results—"

"'Results'?"

Not careful enough words. "I mean the investigation, sir."

Langston moved no closer. His voice could do that all on its own. "I understand you're a civilian consultant, assisting the law. I am not naive about perceived gray areas, especially in undercover work. Lieutenant Rafferty filled me in on the particulars. But you must be quite clear on two risks, Mr. Bedlam.

"First, if you break the law, it is my duty to see that you pay what's owed. That could easily be more than even you can afford.

"Second, hurt my little girl and any laws you broke will be the least of your problems."

He had me convinced. What *had* happened to Aubrea's old lovers? But I wasn't that kind of boy, and I had bruises and smashed knuckles from keeping her safe. Langston got no verbal acknowledgment. I just matched that goddamned glare with my own.

His sigh escaped in a small frustrated puff. He had nothing further to add. Closing statement. He walked back to his idling Mercedes, driven all the way from Nashville in the dead of night so I could disappoint him. Maybe he said something to son and daughter as he passed; maybe his force of presence didn't need to be heard to be understood. Aubrea's face bent downward and Eli's jolted up with renewed outrage. The big German car backed from the crowded lot onto Riverside Drive, headed home. I watched the taillights dissolve into the fog. I had nothing better to do just then.

Flintlock

Doors slammed, nice solid German car doors that hardly needed that kind of persuasion. Aubrea stood alone in the middle of the lot with a duffel bag at her feet, my overnight bag from the penthouse. Her brother had enclosed his wrath in the remaining Mercedes and was attempting to leave. The police cruiser which had accompanied them blocked his exit. Because Eli Langston didn't give a shit whether people in houses across the street might still be trying to sleep, he laid on the horn.

Moran reappeared beside me. Or he'd been there all along. I was too tired to remember.

"He's pleasant."

"Uh huh," I said. "Mind if I go, too?"

"Not if you try a lot harder to stay off my radar."

Eli maneuvered around the police car. He left some gray Mercedes paint on the curb. Angry people pay higher insurance premiums for a reason. The cop car backed serenely onto Riverside Drive and headed home to Nashville; it was a Metro car, not local.

"Sorry," Aubrea said when I got to her. "There wasn't anybody else I felt safe calling. Officer Poole insisted one of their cars follow us."

"Waiting where I left you was an option," I said.

"You're welcome," she snapped and shoved the duffel into my hands.

• • •

Moran initiated a limited search: vehicle patrols of roads above and below the dam, searchlight scans of the river from what currently constituted its edges. The sheriff's department in nearby Williamson County had boats and water rescue equipment, but that wouldn't be available for hours and he couldn't justify risking personnel with neither a missing person's bulletin nor certainty anyone had ended up in the water. The river wouldn't crest till six-thirty. The air temperature wouldn't get above thirty degrees. If Keller's man *had* gone in, he didn't need rescue, just recovery, and that could wait.

I'd done my part. For better or worse, whatever baloney Rafferty fed the locals kept Aubrea and me out of the process…mostly. Two Columbia police cars stayed outside the hotel where I slept for nine hours.

I opened my eyes in familiar beige and brown surroundings. I'd stayed in the same hotel after Mitch's funeral, in spite of better options since the Second Annual Meriwether Lewis Exhumation Convention had wrapped. Pleasant warmth streamed slantwise across the room, rays from a beginning sunset that had slithered beneath the clouds. It made even the dreary little mall across the street more inviting.

"What's funny?"

I sat up on top of the covers and wiggled my bare toes at the girl in the beige desk chair who'd been watching me sleep. One or the other of us had removed my shoes and socks.

"The last time I was here, I'd considered buying new shoes," I said. "I should have."

Aubrea laughed. Her features were drawn and weary. Her laugh was still summer rain on the roof. "We can if you like. I hadn't made plans."

I swung my legs off the bed, a little stiffly, and raised my shoulders as a test. The pain was tolerable. Soreness in my back came mainly from sleeping in a shoulder holster, something I usually only do in alleys or drainage ditches. The overnight duffel waited on the second twin bed, which hadn't been slept in. When I unzipped the bag, I saw some clothes that didn't belong to me. Her statement about not making plans rang a tad hollow. I excused myself to shower without mentioning it.

I rarely enjoy long showers. After ten minutes under hot water, the usual guilty images of thirsty African children intruded on my thoughts and I had to shut off the tap and grab a towel. Aubrea had ordered room service coffee and the aroma

Flintlock

drew me out into the main room still buttoning my shirt. Coffee uses water, and thirsty Africans for that matter, but my conscience is more flexible where caffeine is concerned.

She helped me with the buttons. My hands were still ragged from fighting with rock salt. But I checked the Smith & Wesson's action without difficulty; buttons and firearms use different muscles. Then we slurped from Styrofoam cups and avoided eye contact. Checking my phone alleviated some of the awkwardness. A day on the charger had given the device a new lease on life. A week's worth of messages and missed calls had collected.

Rafferty preferred to leave text messages rather than voicemail, and I had three from him. Smally had narrowed his hunt for Sal to the area around Harding Place and Grassmere. He'd keep me posted.

There was a message from the dealer about my car.

There was a missed call and a voice message from Mr. Tiffany on the Cool-Core board of directors. I hadn't been to any meetings for a while. It *was* my company. Blah blah blah...

Evan in the West End lobby wanted to make sure I knew of Miss Langston's departure early that morning.

Tipper had phoned and left a voicemail wondering if I planned on coming by the estate, but it was late, so he supposed not.

And Darlene had called. All four of her attempts ended in a new voicemail. Even over a cell phone she seemed to exhale pheromones.

"...hadn't mentioned whether you were coming in tonight. I owe you a proper *thank-you*..."

I felt guiltier than a three-day shower listening to her breathe in my ear while Aubrea nursed second-rate coffee in the same room. I hung up, knuckled a quick text to Danny about the GPS tag, and stowed the phone. The girl with the coffee lifted her eyes expectantly.

Jon A. Hunt

"Let's go buy me some dry shoes," I said.

• • •

Aubrea and I returned to the hotel on foot with my new shoes, fresh socks, and a police escort following at a polite distance. Between the four of us, we'd doubled the mall's evening population. How the place kept its doors open was a mystery I'd never solve.

An easier riddle loitered outside the hotel. His shoes were nicer than mine. Keller only wore the best.

"Wasn't he at the funeral?" Aubrea whispered and took hold of my arm.

"Yeah," I told her, "but he's no friend of Mitch's."

We detoured to pause beside our other guardian police cruiser, the one that had idled at the hotel while we shopped. The officer inside lowered the passenger window. Warmth spilled outward from dash vents.

"Mr. Bedlam?" Now everyone in Mule Town knew the name.

"Would you mind keeping Miss Langston company while I chat with my acquaintance?"

"He's been hanging around an hour. A problem?"

"Nothing I can't handle. Hanging around is what he does. He'll leave after we're done."

"Okay. C'mon in, miss." The cop cleared paperwork from the front passenger seat and unlocked the door.

Aubrea's expression couldn't be read under the dim parking lot lights. Anxiety doesn't need to be seen to be recognized. I applied reassuring pressure to her hand, shut her inside the cruiser, and crossed the asphalt.

For all his efforts to track me, Keller and I hadn't been face-to-face since before Mitch Braunfelter went into the ground. He leaned against a light pole with rehearsed nonchalance, after having brushed that side of the pole clean. He didn't so much wear his slate gray suit jacket as he was embraced by it. Deep

Flintlock

shadows under his brows and cheekbones made him look as exhausted as I felt. His eyes glittered as usual, though, and his shoes glowed bright as burnished Italian bronze.

"You worry about the wrong people, Bedlam. I wouldn't lay a finger on the girl."

"Your clients might try," I said.

He shared half a smile, pretty generous for him. Was that stubble on his normally polished chin? We'd both put in long hours. He'd likely already billed for his.

"I'm not inviting you in for a drink, Keller. What do you want?"

The smile went out like a spent match. "Just an antique."

"I don't have any." I'm not bad at poker. But the truth was I didn't, even if I'd held exactly what Keller wanted—what Keller's clients wanted—in my hands hours ago.

His words dripped with oil. "I'm willing to offer my resources. Whatever's necessary. We can work together. The value of this thing is—it's astronomical!"

"What do I care? I'm a fucking billionaire."

Keller's posture sharpened. His voice went from slippery to razor-edged. Every facet of his personality became menacing, a Damask dagger in a Brioni scabbard.

"There's only one! Not just any billionaire can have it. And no one's safe who's touched it! Not you, not that idiot Braunfelter, not the rats downtown, not the girl—"

A sudden breathing difficulty cut him short. I relished the delicacy of silk as it twined through my fingers, luxurious yet strong enough to strangle a man. I twisted Keller's pale green tie farther. My knuckles dug under his jaw. His eyes glittered less and bulged more.

"You *really* want to work together?" I growled in his ear. He shuddered and gagged. His hands flopped for the metal defense inside his tailored jacket, but my other fist held the lapels tight. "You'd do anything I asked, in return for your damned antique?"

He couldn't say "yes" or "no." He needed air to do that. But his head bobbed wildly against my fist.

"Tell me who killed Mitch Braunfelter," I said and dropped him on his fancy ass.

He wheezed and scrabbled for an elegant way to lift his artisan-stitched britches off the pavement. Halfway into a crouch his hand dove toward his open jacket.

"I'll kill you in self-defense. Right in front of a cop."

He hadn't been moving all that quick, not if I'd gotten in two whole sentences. I shouldn't let it go to my head that my .45's blunt nose already pointed at his chest. On cue, the patrol car's lights flared, propelled my shadow in front of me and to the left of Keller. A door catch released. From that angle the cop wouldn't see my gun, but he'd spot Keller drawing.

"Everything okay, Mr. Bedlam?"

Forcefully illuminated, Keller looked like hell. He looked like a dead man who just hadn't found the right place to fall. His feet got the rest of the way under him, slowly, while he held both hands far from his sides.

"Mr. Ableman is leaving now," I said over my shoulder.

And he did. With his thoroughbred tail between his legs. The wrong clients will do that to you.

Flintlock

Chapter Twenty-four

This time Aubrea slept in a bed. She would have even if there hadn't been two in the room. I didn't need to be horizontal to rest. I propped myself against the box spring, dressed except for my new shoes and socks, facing the door, waiting.

I waited for answers to one phone call I'd made and one email I'd sent before the lights went out. My phone lay tethered to its charger on the carpet beside me.

I waited for anybody to enter the room uninvited. Specifically, I waited for a grotesque colossus who smashed houses and people for fun and sorted the bits into piles. For all the good it would do, my .45 rested next to the phone, a round in the chamber, the safety off.

I'm the worst kind of cat-napper.

Nothing I waited for happened. The girl breathed tranquilly behind me. Her hand slipped from the covers onto my shoulder. I didn't mind. All the wariness in the world couldn't long postpone the inevitable and the night outlasted both of us. Sometime well ahead of dawn, the phone roused me. I'd been dreaming about Meredith O'Dell's office, with the file cabinets and the wastebasket full of junk mail and no books.

Steady patient pulses grazed carpet tufts. It could have been going for an hour. I tipped my head to one side then the other to stretch my kinked neck, blinked the fuzziness away and eyed

Jon A. Hunt

the bedside clock. No, not an hour. One of those blinks signaled Danny Ayer's response to my email, and it was only 4:18. The other was a missed call and voicemail from Louis Aldritch. That *was* an hour old, but linemen never sleep. I eased from under Aubrea's caress and took the phone and gun into the bathroom. I reset the safety while I was at it.

Danny must be at his workstation beneath Cool-Core. He never carried a phone and rarely logged in remotely. The Vanderbilt security upgrades had eroded his sleep patterns. His uncharacteristically terse answer to my question practically read like a yawn:

Up to 2 weeks. 10-20 feet of water, max.

I called Louis again.

Aubrea's eyes met me on my return to the bedroom. Bringing her along wasn't ideal, but she was here now, Keller knew it, and so did Keller's clients. Columbia's finest couldn't protect her any better than I could.

"How soon can you be ready to go?" I asked.

She shrugged partly free of the covers and hesitated when cool hotel air touched her bare shoulders. Neither of us had brought pajamas.

"Ten minutes, I guess. Why?"

"We're going fishing," I said.

• • •

Nobody sneaks away from anywhere in a GTS Viper. Louis and I arranged alternate transportation to shake watchers, well-meaning or otherwise. He sent Mrs. Aldritch.

"Look for a white Aerostar," he said.

"You don't have anything else?"

"Not that fits three. Y'all dead set against Fords?"

Not Fords. Just white minivans like the one every cop in Middle Tennessee and Kentucky was looking for. But there

Flintlock

wasn't time for a perfect plan.

"The Aerostar's fine," I said aloud. "See you soon."

The right white minivan pulled into an empty lot north of the hotel at 4:40. Aubrea and I exited via a side door; cops trying to stay alert inside warm cars out front and back were watching for trouble going *in*, not on its way out. The air felt sharp against my nose. Mrs. Aldritch's old economy van whirred in a wreath of well-earned exhaust. She reached across the cab and popped open the passenger door. She wore a red down jacket, a scarf, gloves, round bifocals, and white hair up in a bun. Her cheeks glowed. If I hadn't already shared beers with her husband, I'd have sworn our chauffer's last name was Claus. The van interior even smelled like sugar cookies.

"Hello, Mr. Bedlam, Miss Aubrea." Her spectacles shone like tree ornaments in the turquoise dash lights, and something in her manner betrayed amusement at Aubrea's disheveled beauty. Louis may have mentioned the girl a few times more than a married man should.

We climbed in and the Aerostar bumped out onto the highway. Mrs. Aldritch drove the posted limit, no more, no less.

"Would you believe I was pulled over?" She seemed pleased with the adventure.

"Not a ticket, I hope?" Aubrea had taken a seat in the the second row and leaned forward to be heard.

Mrs. Aldritch tittered. "Good heavens no! I'm the most boring driver in town. I thought a brake light must be out, but they were just checking white vans. Apparently, criminals use them. The officer was very polite. He asked where I was headed and sent me on."

"What did you tell him?" Keeping tension from my question wasn't easy.

Louis' wife shot me a sly little wink. I bet Louis had had to knock a lot of competitors' molars loose back in their dating

Jon A. Hunt

days. "I had a craving for cookies, of course. They're in the box on the back seat. Help yourselves!"

• • •

Columbia's primary streets carried a fair amount of traffic despite the hour: panel vans delivering cookies to gas stations, semis bypassing a snarl on the interstate, early commuters. Not so, Riverside Drive. It didn't go anywhere other roads couldn't get you quicker. The final stars dimmed, overhead blackness paled, and the world around us leveled to a homogenous gray as we neared the river. Mrs. Aldritch slowed the van to keep between the lines. Aubrea and I quietly chewed cookies and let her concentrate. An occasional street light burped orange over us, then dissolved again into the ravenous mists. Mrs. Aldritch was unfazed. She'd travelled this road thousands of times. By ten after five, the Aerostar rolled to a stop. Crooked lines in the murk beyond the headlight beams reminded me of tree limbs.

"Well, here we are," our driver announced. "Louis said he'd tie up downstream of the ramp till I called." A cheap cellular phone appeared in her gloved hand.

We thanked her earnestly and opened our doors.

"Oh, Mr. Bedlam?"

"Yes, ma'am?"

"Y'all be careful out there and get my Louis home for supper this time, okay?"

• • •

Fog trumps blackness when you're without a light. Sounds are wrong. The Aerostar's tail lights faded well before the charismatic rattle of the engine. Yet I couldn't detect my own breathing. Aubrea's fingers found mine.

I sensed the river. No rushing, it merely lapped at unfamiliar tree trunks concealed by the fog. The Duck still crashed over a dam nearby. I didn't hear that. A new noise

Flintlock

arose, though, starting as a hint then growing steadily to a low mechanical gargle. The girl's grip tightened; she heard it, too. A single star flitted past twists of saplings we hadn't realized were between us and the water. The star swelled and was mimicked by soft reflective ripples, till larger shapes filled in the gaps. A chrome-plated pole connected the star to the prow of a low, flat boat. The bow light—not a star—revealed wet brown weeds, glistening mud and a grooved concrete ramp that led from our feet to the river's edge. A bouquet of cigarette smoke and two-cycle exhaust touched my nostrils. Aluminum grated on the concrete. The outboard motor adopted a more furious pitch as the human in charge reversed for a couple seconds, then it resumed its slow popping purr. A second light dazzled us. Louis Aldritch raised a travel lantern above his frayed canvas fishing cap and grinned.

"Hello again!" he said.

• • •

The attic of the Aldritch home had to contain a faded sash adorned with merit badges. Only an old Boy Scout would have come so prepared. In addition to tackle and spinning reels, Louis' nineteen-foot bass boat carried tow ropes, rain gear, tarps, blankets, flashlights, spare batteries to last till the Second Coming, a cooler full of peanut butter and jelly sandwiches, Thermos containers of coffee and hot chocolate. He presented us with our own life preservers. There was a wide-brimmed fishing hat for Aubrea. The only item we didn't leave shore with was the cigarette Louis had been puffing prior to meeting us. He flicked the half-burned butt overboard. Louis didn't smoke in front of the womenfolk.

"You want to start by the dam?"

"Yes, please," I said.

"Grab those flashlights," he said. "We've got a couple hours. Then Williamson County will be out with their search and rescue crew. What're we looking for?"

Jon A. Hunt

I brought out my phone and did what I could to maintain his ignorance a while longer. "A purple light."

Louis grimaced, swiveled his captain's chair back to the wheel, grabbed the throttle lever. The low-sided craft burbled backward into the main current. He aligned the hull with riverbanks we couldn't see and nudged the 150-horse Yamaha outboard from a growl to a quick rumble. Filthy water charged past on either side. We didn't seem to move half as fast as the river.

Much of yesterday's excess had already flowed beyond the city limits. The Duck's sodden fringes began to withdraw toward its centerline, which moved fast but with less discipline than a dog hunting a new field. The flat hull slapped over sheets of grimy ice. As the current eased nearer the dam, Louis backed off the throttle. Things banged against the aluminum under us. We heard water crashing over spillways, though the fog resisted our lights. Branches shuddered beside the boat.

"That's as close as I dare," Louis announced. "There's an island under us. Water's still higher than you think! Don't want to foul the prop."

Aubrea played her flashlight beam across liquid murk and quivering twigs on her side. I'd instructed her to watch for anything red. Thus far, my phone detected nothing. The odds were long that Keller's GPS gimmick still shared a waterproof bag with the stolen journal. I had no better options.

The journal hadn't made it back to Keller, or he wouldn't have turned up outside our hotel. Either his man had split with the goods, or his man and the journal were in the Duck River. I'd realized, before nodding off last night, why my competitor never deactivated his little magnetic beacon after I stopped driving around with the thing. He didn't trust his own guy.

The river pouring over the old dam was close, alarming, deafening, hidden behind its own vapors. My face felt stiff and numb in the spray.

Flintlock

"How far do you think something man-sized could've gone in twenty-four hours?" I yelled.

"Maybe miles," was the unwelcome, pragmatic reply. "But stuff tends to hang up in the back-currents. Tough to say."

"Let's try downstream. At least for an hour."

"Alright."

• • •

Daylight must be creeping over dry land. We couldn't tell from the Duck's mist-smothered surface. Flashlights were necessary just to avoid ramming barely submerged deadheads. The outboard motor ran backward more often than forward. Louis' demeanor never varied from cool and focused. He also rarely let go of the steering wheel or throttle.

Aubrea huddled under a blanket in the stern and doggedly attacked the pea soup with her light. Her wan smile when our eyes met belied determination. It's hard to look for anything in the water when you can barely see past the gunwales.

I wiped my phone on a sleeve. No purple light. The hour I'd given Louis was nearly up.

Fog brightened off starboard. Not daylight, this was a series of focused spots that flared when directly before me. Other flashlights. I shut mine off and reached forward to cover the bow light with my hat. My comrades understood: Aubrea's light went black the same time the motor fell silent. The lights on the not-quite-visible shore turned often in our direction, never certain. They couldn't see us, either. The bass boat drifted past them like another slab of dead wood. It started to rotate sideways in the current.

Louis released the wheel and crawled forward. He unlatched a small electric trolling motor from the deck at my feet. Ice flaked from the shroud when he pivoted it upright and snapped the motor into operating position. He flipped a switch and the thing softly whirred. Then he retrieved my hat from the now dark bow light.

Jon A. Hunt

"Best let me sit up here and run this," he whispered. "It'll keep us straight long's the current is steady. We'll need the big motor again for faster water."

I relinquished the bow chair. "What's over there?"

"Boat ramp. Not the one I used. The one where you two got aboard."

"Where'd you leave your trailer?"

"Down at Chickasaw Trace. About six miles."

I worked my way astern to sit beside the girl. She passed me a Thermos.

"Who is it?" she breathed.

"Not police." My best unspoken guess was Keller. There were worse guesses, though.

Louis' silhouette in the bow resembled a hood ornament on an antique car. I suspected he missed his cigarette. I poured some coffee and watched the fog absorb the mysterious lights. We appeared to have the river to ourselves again. I checked the phone.

Nothing.

• • •

Half a mile farther downstream, Louis flipped the trolling motor back onto the deck and scooted aft to rouse its big two-cycle brother. We'd found that faster water he warned me about. For the first time since boarding, we were treated to both river banks, because they were vertical and only sixty feet apart. Scraggly pines clung to the starboard shore, only grass and dry vines attempted the limestone cliffs on the opposite side. The river gathered itself and hustled us along. The outboard's sputter reverberated off stone.

Louis lit the bow light again. We had more immediate concerns than who might see us from shore. He gestured for me to lean in, so he didn't have to shout.

"No use searching here. River never got high enough to spread outside this little gorge. Nothing slowed down—and it's

Flintlock

all easier to see."

A heavy dark stripe separated the overhead gloom. We passed under a bridge.

"Street runs 'tween the square and the farmer's market," he explained.

Aubrea had time for an exclamation before the bridge, pine trees and steep banks slipped into obscurity. I sneaked a look at my phone, which proved Louis' point. Nothing purple about it.

A second, larger, bridge appeared and disappeared in similar fashion. This one had pole lights and rumbled with passing trucks.

"412," Louis said.

Then the river ran straighter and faster. Neither flank was visible, nor did the usual debris bob alongside or in front of us. Only flat swirling water reached beyond our lights. Louis held our speed slightly higher than the current—to keep the boat straight, he said—and a lot of featureless gray hurried by. That was all. No floating junk, nothing red, nothing that made my phone blink. The Duck wasn't out to impress.

Louis pointed out yet another approaching bridge, except this one never solidified beyond a vague stripe. It must be quite a lot higher than the others.

"Highway 43." He seemed to know the undersides of area roads better than I knew their tops. He knew, too, that it was time to ease off the throttle.

The outboard motor shuddered and assumed a bubbling simmer. The river arched gently to port. No shore came into view, but a massive logjam did. Floodwaters had washed every loose thing from the old dam down to this point, where the river ran shallow and the current momentarily forgot where it wanted to go. Our flashlights played across sodden hardwood trunks, planks from runaway boat docks, vibrating branches with dead leaves, and more trash than the local landfill collected in a month.

Jon A. Hunt

"Here you go, Mr. Bedlam. If it didn't head all the way to the ocean, chances are whatever you're looking for stopped here. I'll fire up the troller again."

We wouldn't be alone much longer. The Williamson rescue crew was on their way. I trained my light on the nearest junk. There were more trees than anything. Their limbs tangled hopelessly, riding higher than their heavier root ends. Litter collected among the branches, held in place by glassy ice. The little electric motor tugged us closer. I recognized labels on beer cans. I've sometimes resorted to digging through people's garbage for clues; pride has no place in a private eye's day-to-day routine. But this was a whole county's trash. On ice.

Aubrea got to her feet, still swaddled in a wool blanket, and bumped me with her shoulder to let me know she was still in the game. A third light snapped on and joined ours. Louis flashed us that squint-eyed grin. He could help, too, because for the time being, he steered with his foot pedal.

The next thirty minutes crawled and raced by at the same time. It was tedious. A lot of the trash was red: beverage cups, smashed ice chests, plastic bags, a lot of beer cans. We couldn't pause and study each item. We were running out of time.

Aubrea shut off her light and plunked onto the deck to unscrew the battery compartment. We'd gone through a lot of Louis' battery stash. I narrowed tired eyes at the patch she'd left.

"Louis, bring us in tighter. Over there..."

The electric motor buzzed more urgently. A party of bobbing Budweiser cans clattered against the aluminum prow. I clicked my light off, too. Something still glowed among the logs.

"I see it!" Louis said. He paused the little motor and was instantly beside me with a long-handled fishing net. Then his voice sank to a coarse "oh."

The bright circle was a flashlight lens. It shined from

222

Flintlock

beneath an overthrown sapling and half a foot of cold muddy water. A bloodless hand still clutched the flashlight's body. The rest of the corpse was held just beneath the surface by the dead tree. I thumbed my light on again for closer inspection.

Keller's man hadn't made it ashore.

Jon A. Hunt

Chapter Twenty-five

Aubrea's reaction wasn't much of a reaction at all. She wavered between Louis and me, the blanket draped over her shawl-fashion, her flashlight unlit in at her side.

Louis' working life involved rivers, weather and idiots. He'd found cadavers before. His only outward distress was the fresh cigarette that magically appeared in a corner of his mouth.

"Beg your pardon, Miss Aubrea," he said and snapped a flame from a lighter and drew in a calming puff. "Now what do y'all think *he* was looking for?"

I wouldn't insult a friend with senseless evasion. Any person who'd drown without letting go of his flashlight must have been searching for something important.

"Same as us. A little red book in a Ziplock bag."

"Worth dying for?"

"Mitch did. Until that book is in the right hands—or the wrong hands—no one close to him will be safe."

"No one," the girl murmured.

Louis retreated in silence, briefly, behind an orange tobacco ember. People who'd shared his association with Mitch— friends, neighbors, family, Mrs. Aldritch—were on his mind. So was that unfortunate "old goat" whose personal key used to hang inside the Riverside pump station. He tugged his sleeve away from a wristwatch.

"There's a little time yet. We can use the oars to poke

224

Flintlock

around."

. . .

Eventually the underwater flashlight would go out and Keller's man would sink. We emptied a red gas can into the boat's fuel tank and tied the can to the sapling for a buoy. Louis said the Williamson County guys could use the hint. He guided the boat tight to the logjam while Aubrea and I pried interlocked limbs apart with backup paddles. The gloom lessened. Trees beyond our clouded breath and the flotsam showed as a backdrop of dark lace. We put the flashlights away. I consulted my phone often without success. Keller owned better equipment for tracking his own GPS tags. We hadn't invited him along.

Coffee in the Thermos was still hot, the sandwiches had frozen, we didn't linger over either. Louis resisted a third cigarette. My phone announced an incoming call, which I ignored. Only twenty minutes of battery life remained. Darlene would leave a message. Aubrea peering over my shoulder made me uncomfortable.

"Purple," she said.

"Louis! Hold up!"

Our captain jumped to reverse the trolling motor and hold the boat in place. A hundred jumbled yards of logs and junk separated us from an almost visible shoreline. I asked Louis how deep he thought the river might be there. His face furrowed with amusement.

"Y'all don't fish much?" He locked the trolling motor in place, returned to the captain's chair, tapped a button to wake a display mounted near the steering wheel: the standard-issue depth finder every bass fisherman east of the Mississippi used. "Eleven and a half feet," he said.

Up to 2 weeks. 10-20 feet of water, max.

Danny's text message was less encouraging now. If the bag hadn't stayed sealed, that red book Keller's man died trying to

Jon A. Hunt

retrieve could be on the river bottom.

"Follow the logs, try to narrow our search," I said. "The big motor's fine if it does the job quicker."

My phone had eighteen minutes of battery left.

The Yamaha snorted awake and Louis tested his piloting skills to their limit. Sodden hardwood thudded against the hull. I consulted my phone.

"Too far. The signal's gone."

Louis pushed the throttle lever forward. The bow dipped, then leveled again with the furious corrective burble of the outboard. He spun the wheel like he was competing for cash and prizes on a television game show. The boat carved a tight semicircle to face upstream, then the motor shoved us in that direction.

The purple warning flashed again. The battery warning popped onto the phone's screen, also.

"Wait!" Aubrea shouted. She'd abandoned any semblance of stealth in her excitement.

Louis throttled down again.

A red corner inside clear plastic bobbed behind a rat's nest of branches, forty feet away. Hulks of trees filled the gap between us. Plowing through them would be a quick way to capsize.

I asked if we could tow the intervening snags aside. Knowing boats and rivers better, Louis shook his head.

"They're all stuck in the bottom or to each other. All I've got is a bit of spinning propeller. That wouldn't move this boat, either, if it was anchored like that. We could try snagging the book with a big spinner bait..."

"No, tear a hole in the bag and it'll sink. I'll have to try crawling out to it."

His eyes emerged from their usual squint. "Isn't that how that fella over there died?"

"He didn't have help," I said and shrugged out of my life

Flintlock

preserver, coat and gloves. The still air around us gnawed through my shirt sleeves. Aubrea pleaded against the idea as I unbuckled my shoulder rig.

"It's just a book! It isn't worth dying for."

I glared at her. Mitch had died for it. Who knew how many others had perished trying to protect or obtain the missing red journal? Unclaimed in a river full of trash, it would continue to be a reason for someone to kill. She at least suspected as much.

Tears glittered on her cheek. Yeah, she understood.

My phone with its portentous violet eye went into a cubby under the dash. My coat, hat, and holstered .45 landed on a swivel chair—bass boats aren't so much different from offices, their chairs are just waterproof—and that was enough. I had no intention of stripping further. Louis bent and looped a nylon tow rope around my waist, without asking. He secured my lifeline with a running bowline, a proper Boy Scout knot.

"If you fall in," he warned, "the shock of the water'll hit you quicker than hypothermia. Keep your mouth shut or you'll drown too quick for anybody to help. Keep your arms clear of the branches. You go under, we'll haul you in. We'll haul you back after five minutes, either way. Put your life vest back on."

"Aye aye, sir," I said. Louis' boat, Louis' rules.

Then he concentrated on piloting. A fat round dead oak screeched against the aluminum hull. The thing wore ice as clear as varnish. I shot a quick look at the girl without allowing myself to focus on her expression, then I clambered over the low gunwale onto a wallowing ice-glazed log on the Duck River in December.

I kept my eyes locked on the red speck floating beyond distant branches and started crawling. I let myself think only about the journal and keeping my mouth shut.

• • •

The river supporting the logjam seemed less menacing, at first, than the river that had roared under the catwalk out onto the old dam. I wouldn't fall far if I lost my footing. Nearly placid water lay between tree-corpses. But it was just an act. Powerful undertows had herded all those trees together, and the river had all the time it wanted. It could wait for my mistakes.

Saturated hardwoods rolled or sank beneath my weight. The more stable hulks proved no easier: every one was slick with slime and ice. Crawling was no less reckless than trying to run. I only made progress by squirming on my belly, as snake-like as the yellow lifeline that slithered behind me. My new shoes were full of ice water. Rough frozen bark grated across my hips. The life vest shielded my torso from the bark but didn't protect me from the cold. My fingers hurt beneath hardening skin. The lone remaining comfort was a steady putt-putt of a 150-horse Yamaha behind me in the fog; my friends wouldn't let the river have me without a fight.

The waterproof bag with the red journal played peek-a-boo with me through the branches. It wasn't as close as it had seemed from the boat. Louis might reel me in before I got to the thing.

Another mechanical sound answered the outboard. A faint yet dense popping, it felt far yet approached steadily from downstream. More boats? The Williamson County water rescue squad? I tried to turn that direction and nearly went into the drink for the effort. Misery knifed into the already strained tendons in my bad shoulder. I did my best to ignore the pain.

Where had the journal gone?

The approaching sound competed fully with Louis' motor now. *Pop pop pop pop.* It urged my chilled emotions toward panic.

Not boats.

A helicopter.

This time I succeeded in looking toward the noise. Very thin, almost imperceptible lines of relative brightness battled

Flintlock

downstream mists. Twin searchlights traveled up the river. The authorities had finally gotten hold of some real equipment.

Assuming I made my way off the Duck River alive, a new, third possible scenario came to mind. Either I grabbed the floating journal; or Louis and Aubrea dragged me against my will back to the boat without it; or the next county's marine rescue experts would bravely snatch my sorry ass off those logs from the air.

I didn't want rescuing.

I wanted that damned red book.

There it was, right ahead of me.

"Mr. Bedlam!" Louis hollered. "Time!"

I wriggled my feet onto the log beneath me and sprang forward bullfrog-style. My wild grasp met soft plastic in the middle of the splash, then my ears and nose filled with icy brown water. The Duck swallowed me. But I didn't swallow the Duck.

Louis had undersold the shock's magnitude. I only kept from screaming because he'd warned me not to open my mouth. Jolts from every nerve ending shot straight to my brain, a million tiny agonies that joined in a colossal symphony of pain, roaring toward the inevitable decrescendo of unconsciousness and death—

—except for the rope around my belly that interrupted the dying process and yanked me like an outraged bass into gray winter daylight.

Jon A. Hunt

Chapter Twenty-six

My next moments passed with no more clarity than the river's syrupy depths. Sheet ice alternated with frozen trees and branches, pummeling me in turn. Then hands clawed me into the boat, hands sharp as talons, hot as branding irons. I sensed voices. They sounded frantic. Next came the outboard motor's straining staccato, the slap of aluminum against choppy waves.

"The journal!" I yelled. "Did you get the journal?"

No one acknowledged. My words might have been too slurred to understand. Wool blankets and a tarp were thrown over me. Soft, searing skin pressed against mine. Aubrea had stripped to her underwear and wrapped herself with me inside the blankets to share her life-giving warmth. I couldn't fully appreciate the gesture because shivering rocked my whole frame. The Yamaha thundered in our ears. It stank of burning oil and gasoline; my nose, at least, worked fine. My ears functioned, too, though I struggled to comprehend them. The outboard motor battled other sounds, even the girl's voice when her incandescent lips touched my cold cheek and she called my name, begged me to stay awake. What wasn't overpowered was that other sound, that heavy, thumping, hammering noise.

"Where's the book?" I was awake, damn it! Why didn't they answer?

"It's here, Tyler!"

Flintlock

My first clear sensation was of that red leather rectangle on the deck, under my wet shoes. The plastic bag still protected it. My penlight still kept it company.

The thumping sound made sense again. The helicopter. It sped over us. Searchlights swept other details away. Louis' third cigarette singed my ear as it spun off into the gloom. The cigarette's owner waved the men leaning out of the chopper's open sides away. Nobody here needed help. Searchlights and rotors charged upstream and let us continue, unmolested.

"Any hot chocolate left?" I stammered.

Aubrea laughed or cried. I couldn't tell which.

• • •

The boat ramp at Chickasaw Trace State Park must have been built on a dare. Its location was a narrow steep-banked straight, through which the river ripped authoritatively, whatever the season. The ramp stabbed down from the trees into that torrent, sheltered only by a breakwater of broken concrete slabs salvaged from a previous ramp the river had obliterated. Louis' predawn launch, in the fog, would have been akin to merging onto a busy interstate in reverse with his eyes closed. He didn't think this feat any big deal, however, and prepared to repeat the process in the opposite direction.

He allowed the current to rotate the boat's tail downstream, then gunned the motor. The bow light pointed at the ramp's center. Barren old trees with their toes in the water leaned far out over us, and from one of their sturdy limbs dangled a yellow rope like the one Louis and Aubrea had used to drag me back to the boat. The loose end trailed in the water. Louis never asked for a hand—I was too chilled to make my fingers work, and the girl under the blanket with me was too naked—but he'd done this often enough on his own. He secured the wheel with a Velcro strap, stepped to the port side, scooped up the rope and tied it to a cleat on the gunwale. The rope tightened to a bright vertical line. Rope and motor held us

Jon A. Hunt

in place against the speeding current. Then Louis took another rope from a floor hatch up front and tied it to another cleat on the bow.

"Y'all sit tight," he told us with a wink. "We'll get you in the truck and crank the heat—"

"Who's that?" Aubrea smashed her body even more firmly against mine.

I flexed every muscle then relaxed in an effort to ease the shivering. It worked enough for me to concentrate on the ramp, trees, riverbank. As Louis moved to grab the rope descending from above, I spotted the gray form beyond him.

Keller Ableman sat near the upper end of the ramp with his back against a filthy slab of edgewise concrete. His legs stretched leisurely in front of him, knees slightly bent, the heels of his Italian shoes pressed into cold mud. His dark hair was tousled. His jacket had wrinkles. I remembered that jacket from the previous evening. Same went for the pale green necktie.

"Louis," I said, "not here!"

"Has to be! My truck and trailer are here."

Louis was used to people watching the river from that spot. They needed to work up their nerve before they dumped their boats in. And from a distance Keller seemed harmless enough, if overdressed. But this made it twice I'd seen that man on the ground in twenty-four hours, I hadn't put him there this time, and he wasn't getting back up again. Keller would have rather died than be found so dirty. Someone had obliged him.

"Get us back out on the river!"

Whether my tone, or the well-dressed stranger on shore who hadn't blinked once, did the convincing, Louis bent to untie the yellow mooring line. Not soon enough.

The sudden racket on shore reminded me of Mitch's place when I'd interrupted his killer rearranging walls. Saplings and underbrush sounded about the same as framing studs when the

Flintlock

brute smashed through them. My friends heard, too, and each reacted according to their understanding of our peril.

Aubrea jerked the blankets from our shoulders so I could move. Her slender torso showed pale in the half-light, but she ignored the cold. Freezing would take longer to kill us than that monster on the riverbank.

Louis battled the mooring line knot, which had cinched tighter. A fist as big as his head grabbed the rope from the shadows. Another massive paw snatched the yellow nylon farther down then, hand over hand, the giant hauled us closer.

I kicked the red book in its bag up under the steering console. Something told me it needed to stay out of sight. Groping on the boat's wet floor netted mixed results: I found my holstered .45, but my chill-deadened fingers struggled to separate steel from leather.

Ice water sloshed over the gunwale as the boat dug in against the irresistible force dragging us shoreward. The Smith & Wesson scuttled out of its holster and disappeared behind me. Men shouted from the ramp. There were three or four of them, normal-sized, still no friends of ours. Keller's chic corpse toppled and slid on its face into a swirl at the river's edge.

I found my gun again. My thumb couldn't operate the safety release. The first shot came from shore. Louis' clever electronic depth finder blew to pieces. Aubrea screamed and dove to the floor beside me. There's nowhere to hide on a bass boat.

Louis let out an impressively vulgar curse and the mooring rope parted with a sharp bang. He'd given up on the knot and hacked the nylon in two with a filet knife. The boat lunged backward. The outboard's propeller ground on something hard underwater.

I rapped the gun's safety off with the knuckles of my left hand and finally made the gun roar as I wanted it to. A man on the ramp spun and went down.

Jon A. Hunt

Louis scrambled to the steering wheel. The Yamaha rumbled, its throaty call altered by the damaged prop, and the boat surged out into the current.

I pivoted on a knee and warned the girl to stay low. Another of the men on shore had his arms out toward us, fists together. Classic shooter's stance. I fired again. My fingers weren't cooperating and jerked the trigger. The shot went low. The man toppled anyway, maybe not dead, but he wouldn't be fathering any children.

A four-foot triangle of broken concrete hurtled after us from the trees. Bigfoot's parting gesture splashed in our wake. Louis kept the throttle fully open and the injured outboard flung us around a curve of the river. My last sight of the Chickasaw Trace boat included twin red flares, taillights on the back of a white van.

• • •

Louis had sustained our trio's only injury, a three-inch gash along his jaw. The mooring line had snapped back in his face after being cut. Aubrea offered to doctor the wound, but he was more concerned about what Mrs. Alritch might think of his receiving an incompletely dressed girl's attention. Her wet bra clung to her like a translucent second skin.

"Just sit back with Mr. Bedlam and cover up, Miss Aubrea. I've done as bad shaving in a hurry. And I 'spect we'll have more company soon."

He was right. Our retreat had been upstream for good reasons. The next river access downstream was miles away in Williamsport and Louis had no idea of the river's condition there. Upstream, he knew there'd be a logjam, bridges, fog, a body marked with his red gas can, and the water rescue team from Williamson County.

We met up with them at the logjam. There were two red and black inflatable motorboats. One burbled up alongside us; the other continued its business in the debris field. Men in wet

Flintlock

suits were heaving Keller's dead agent over their craft's sides. I wondered if the Keller Ableman Agency had enough moving parts left to compete with me for clientele. We let Louis do the talking. He'd been cautioned against mentioning our real reason for being on the river, and obviously the part about me trading fire with attackers was omitted. The deputies in the rubber boats had heard shots, regardless. Units had been dispatched to Chickasaw Trace.

From prior experience, I suspected they'd find nothing except blood and one deceased Nashville private eye, immaculately dressed, with his head in a puddle.

After brief conversation (Louis said we were looking for a lost dog) and a recommendation from a deputy that Louis get his cut looked after soon, we were directed to proceed upstream to the launch ramp in Columbia. More deputies there would help secure the boat till Louis' truck and trailer had been examined and retrieved from what must be considered a crime scene.

• • •

Our last minutes on the Duck River passed with little discussion and less to see. Thoughts retreated inward. The fog nearer the dam hadn't lessened and Louis' nautical memory took over where the bow light failed. Aubrea and I dressed. I was getting tired of wet feet, but my shivering had subsided. I stowed the journal in my waistband at the small of my back, under my jacket. Keller's GPS tag had done me more favors than it had him; our relationship, though, had come to an end, and I tossed it overboard. I returned my penlight to its usual coat pocket. Louis had another cigarette. He made a point of apologizing to Miss Aubrea when he lit up. I resisted an urge to bum a smoke for myself.

A veritable welcoming committee of deputies, Columbia police and EMTs ushered us ashore. Louis made a quick call to his wife then received a well-earned bandage from a fully clothed professional. We talked about nothing important during the repair job. The old lineman's squint wandered often to his battered fishing boat, banging dully against logs in the shallows. I mentally added one extravagant Christmas gift to my shopping list for the year.

Our reception puzzled me for the same reason my earlier conversation with Chief Moran puzzled me. Nobody ever cut to the chase. Questions put to Louis were minimal and barely touched on events at Chickasaw Trace. I knew these people had radios, yet the girl and I were largely ignored. I'd steeled myself for final awkwardness regarding Keller. Even dead, he'd be a pain in my ass. Local law enforcement had witnessed our altercation hours before he died, and my shipmates would be considered dubious alibis. But the topic never came up. For that matter, Tug Moran wasn't there.

Mrs. Aldritch arrived in her cookie-scented Aerostar to fetch her husband. We thanked the couple warmly, and I pulled Louis aside to warn him about possible repercussions. He and his wife should get away from Mule Town, go someplace with a lot of friends or family for a while. I apologized for not having considered that before accepting his help.

"The Missus has been wanting to visit her sister out in Jackson," he said. "We'll leave this afternoon and I'll square it with the company from the road. That little book will really help you track down whoever done in poor Mitch?"

"There's a good chance," I said.

"Then don't apologize, Mr. Bedlam. Go get that son of a bitch."

• • •

My phone had given up out on the river. I flagged down a Columbia cop who didn't seem as busy as other emergency personnel and asked if he wouldn't mind calling us a cab. He smiled, said there'd be no need for that, Chief Moran was arranging our transportation back to the hotel. Aubrea and I

Flintlock

hadn't pulled wool over the local boys' eyes by sneaking out any side doors.

The arranged transportation was Moran's own late-model Tahoe, which crept down from the blur of Riverside Drive into the crowded parking lot.

"There he is now, Mr. Bedlam. He said on the radio he'd like a word with you in private. If the lady doesn't mind waiting..."

The lady didn't have a choice, really. I didn't need to remind her or the officer to stay close till Chief Moran and I had finished.

Moran waited inside his SUV. He rolled the window down so my tired cold face could see his tired warm face. I must have looked in bad shape.

"Get in," he said.

I did.

The leather seats were heated. Moran had my rapt attention as long as my butt was warm.

"You should give my team more credit," he said. "We aren't big city cops, but we aren't bumpkins, either. There's been a tail on you all morning, except when you were on the river."

My toes and fingers experienced the usual stabbing-throbbing reward anyone gets for narrowly avoiding frostbite. I tried hard not to let him see me grimace. The red journal into my waistband dug a corner into my back to warn me against saying too much.

"The Aldritches?"

"I've still got a car behind them."

"I'd suggest keeping one there till they leave town. They aren't as safe as they think."

"I plan on it. Did you find what you came back for?"

I rubbed my fingers together in front of a dash vent. One benefit of climbing into the police chief's personal vehicle was being allowed to keep my hands in front of me and my firearm stowed. The Smith & Wesson had two rounds missing from its magazine I'd rather not try to explain. "I think so," I said.

"Then you'll be leaving soon, too?"

"You always seem ready to hold the door for me." I was too exhausted to be diplomatic.

"That's because every time you're in town, somebody turns up dead. I don't think you're directly responsible. A regular man doesn't snap vertebrae like that. Still, you're the common denominator, aren't you?"

Aubrea's silhouette in the mists, dutifully waiting beside one of Moran's non-bumpkins, distracted me. Even freezing my ass off, I'd appreciated how she looked in a wet bra.

"Hmm? I suppose. My plan is to go back to the hotel, get some sleep, head into Nashville in the morning. I don't expect my current business will bring me back."

"Good," said Moran. "You're likeable, Bedlam, and I'm all for intercity cooperation against crime. But whatever you and your Lieutenant are up to, all it's generated here is fillers for body bags. My first duty is to the people who hired me. Set foot in town again before Christmas, I'm locking you up for everyone's protection. Your friends in Metro can raise a stink about it if they like. You'll still be in jail. Clear?"

"Yep."

"Okay. Let's pick up Miss Langston and get you two back to the hotel. You look pretty rough."

• • •

Away from the Duck's perpetual fog, lofty clouds with clear air beneath them almost gave town a high-noon flavor. Colors failed to extend the illusion. Everything wore grays, tans, browns, hues of decay. The police cruisers in the lot were as bright as tree ornaments by comparison. I recognized their car numbers from that morning. This time, Keller didn't decorate any light poles. Now he just filled another of those body bags Chief Moran lamented.

Flintlock

Five minutes after our arrival, the room door was bolted and a brown upholstered chair was wedged up under the doorknob. My jacket, hat, pants and shoulder rig lay over another chair to dry. My new shoes and socks steamed atop the window heater. The red journal rested in its bag across a corner of the bathroom vanity under a Smith & Wesson paperweight, and I stood in the shower worshipping the hottest water the hotel offered.

I'd neglected chivalry. I hadn't asked Aubrea whether she'd like the first shower. She wasn't the idiot who'd jumped in a half-frozen river. I only wanted to be warm and to think. Thinking wasn't in the cards just then, because I wasn't left to shower alone.

I felt the curtain drag aside. My head was under the spray. Gentle hands traced my bruised ribs from behind. The hotel water heaters ran a few degrees cooler than her fingertips.

"Ssh," she breathed on my neck, "it's just me."

A step backward was necessary to get my face out of the spray and she expected that. Her arms came up under mine. She locked her slender wrists across my chest and pressed her naked warmth against my back. I consciously relaxed the shoulders I'd tensed with a wince.

"Does it hurt much?"

"Aubrea, there's no one alive who'd think this is a good idea. Not even me."

Her voice was honeyed weariness, a strangely erotic mix. Soft lips brushing the .38 caliber scar on my weather shoulder woke more sensations than the original bullet had. "Isn't that what you call avoiding a question?"

I shut my eyes again. Yes, the usual pain persisted, deep beneath the muscle. Separating it from her delicate kisses on the surface proved difficult.

"It comes and goes," I said. "Cold makes it worse."

She unlocked her wrists so her hands could follow her

mouth. "I don't want you to be cold," she murmured.

"Aubrea—"

"Oh, they all think we are already!" Her voice hardened with bitterness, only for a moment, then softened again. "Would it be so bad if they were right?"

I reached over the shoulder, twined my salt-damaged fingers with hers, turned. Her short jet hair glistened where the spray touched, barely ruffled after the morning on the river because it was shorter than mine. She didn't look in any way boyish. Nothing about Aubrea was less than feminine, not even her hair, especially now. Other senses begged for indulgence, but I made the effort to focus on her face, because she needed me to. Her blue eyes held mine. Beneath a sheen of tears, I found fear, loneliness, something intensely primal.

"Don't let what people think drive you," I said. "Most of the time you're reading them wrong, anyway."

"Am I reading you wrong?"

"Probably not."

Triumph brightened her eyes. Her strength surprised me when she drew my hand to a breast. Steam swirled around us, its sole purpose to encourage intimacy. Neither had any trouble reading the other's desires; they transferred as easily as heat skin to skin.

Flintlock

Chapter Twenty-seven

Sunset was worth sleeping through. Nothing colorful, the overcast sky just got tired and went dark. Streetlights tried to compensate. Whatever their success outside, the glow filtering through our third-floor hotel room's gauze curtains barely warmed the ceiling, sufficient to reveal form and shadow, not color. A five by eight Moroccan leather rectangle looked no redder than the scandium alloy pistol on the desk beside it.

I'd been sitting in the swivel chair, wearing a hotel bathrobe, staring at Meriwether Lewis' nineteenth journal, since an hour before nightfall. I hadn't opened it.

Our lovemaking had distracted me for a while and let exhaustion have its sway. Aubrea and I slept in a luxurious tangle through the afternoon, oblivious to traffic on the street, voices in the corridors, everything. But one question came back and put me in the chair.

A lot of people had died for a two-hundred-year-old diary. Two billionaires, two hired guns, two—maybe three— homeless boys. A few men I'd put in the ground myself. It wasn't farfetched to include Tipper's wife and son. And Mitch Braunfelter. Mitch's *doozy of a puzzle* was the only connection I could see between them. That wasn't what kept me awake.

I could buy into someone with means wanting the journal badly enough to kill to obtain it. A veritable army had come after Aubrea at Vanderbilt. People like that never come cheap,

241

especially when they pick up after themselves. Transporting and hiding the behemoth I'd dubbed Bigfoot would be no small expense. And fewer clients could afford Keller Ableman than could afford me. The money behind the effort didn't prevent a full night's rest.

What interrupted my sleep was a question about the murders that was too callous and pragmatic to ask out loud:

Why bother?

If getting hold of the red journal was the primary goal, what made killing so many people necessary? Taking life complicates things. Regular thieves prefer to avoid it where possible. Something forced the issue.

Men cut from Mitch Braunfelter's cloth are never so married to possessions that they'd die trying to keep them. He'd have told a wall-smashing six-hundred-pound gorilla the journal's hiding place, without even a "please." He'd looked me up because he was afraid of someone who wouldn't bother asking at all. Unfortunately, he'd been right.

I hadn't yet verified my suspicions regarding Tipper's involvement.

I couldn't vouch for the personalities of Jorgensen or the Kentucky collector before him.

But Keller, I knew. His motivation was profit. His instinct for self-preservation was strong. He wouldn't have sullied his beloved Italian footwear on a muddy riverbank searching for any old thing.

And Tom, Nathan, and Sal made less sense as victims than anyone. By Rafferty's account, the boys were hunted by practically everyone. I had no doubt they were involved with the stolen journal. I was equally certain none of them would dare hang onto anything so valuable. They'd get rid of it fast. They wouldn't bargain. Any offer that put food in their bellies

Flintlock

and kept them off Metro's radar would do. They were just boys. A determined interrogation would yield any information desired from the first one caught, yet *two* had been brutally dispatched. The third now flew from friend and foe, because he couldn't tell one from the other—if he hadn't also run out of time.

Whether they'd held it, seen it, or not survived trying to claim it, the reason those people weren't alive rested on the desk in front of me. A superstitious person might convince himself the red journal was cursed.

I stood, crossed to the window, drew the curtain aside. The cruiser down in the lot didn't blend in. Nobody parks next to a cop car. There were no white vans. I was pretty sure we were pushing our luck staying as long as we had, though.

"Tyler?"

Aubrea sat upright in the center of the bed. White sheets and the twisted brown duvet wrapped her from the waist down, for decoration, not for warmth or modesty. The outer curves of petite breasts mimicked her shoulders, all gently delineated by trespassing city-glow. Her eyes showed only as dark pools.

"I can't sleep," I said.

"That's okay."

The invitation wasn't subtle, but my thoughts were too dark for that now. I let the curtain settle back into position and brushed her cheek with the back of my hand. We shouldn't have. We both knew that. We weren't what each other needed, only what each other had.

"What now?" she asked.

"I'm trying to decide."

She knew I wasn't talking about us. She caught my forearm and held my hand against her face anyway. While the river's chill was just a memory, her touch remained fiercely warm.

"Have you read any of it?"

243

Jon A. Hunt

"I'm not sure I should," I said.

Aubrea laughed. My first impression had yet to find a better comparison than summer rain on a roof. "You'll jump in the river for it, but you won't look at it?"

I grinned while she couldn't see my face well, then reached for the desk lamp.

• • •

The journal sidestepped most of my expectations.

Instead of coming apart in my fingers, the metal clasp operated as smoothly as when new. The cover flipped open noiselessly. Yellowed pages inside weren't especially brittle or crammed front to back with encrypted gibberish. About a third were blank; the rest bore plain nineteenth century English. The writer's hand traveled with such discipline I half imagined guidelines integral to the graceful faded ink, though lined paper hadn't existed back then. I recognized Lewis' penmanship from reproductions in the textbook Darlene had showed. If this was a fake, it was a damn convincing effort, right down to the period materials.

"The date!"

Aubrea's eyes echoed tiny copies of the desk lamp. She hadn't drawn the front of her robe shut and the heat of her torso against my elbow threatened distraction. But the date on the first page's upper corner excited me, too.

Wednesday May 23rd 1804.

The narrative described a river and a cave. The river must be the Missouri. The cave had French names carved inside. Thrilling as these descriptions might be, they were standard expedition fare. The O'Dell's textbook had mentioned gaps in Lewis' record-keeping, including a period from May of 1804 to April of 1805. If genuine, this red-bound treasure had eluded every one of his biographers. That made it valuable, certainly,

Flintlock

just not worth killing anyone who'd seen the thing. Information from Lewis' hitherto unknown entries had been gleaned elsewhere, probably from Captain Clark's logs; this wasn't fresh news. It didn't explain those magnetic letters on Mitch's refrigerator.

I let Aubrea lean closer. Any man with a pulse would. I turned pages.

We read entries for that long-gone May, some for June, none for July, two for August, a half dozen through autumn of 1804. Then the blank pages started. I went farther. I found Mitch's fatal doozy of a puzzle.

Two thin jaundiced sheets that didn't match the rest of the journal, folded into thirds like any modern correspondence, hid between unused pages. They'd been pressed so long the creases had split cleanly as scissor cuts, and instead of two pages there were six shuffled rectangles. Except for a small ink sketch of a muzzle loading pistol in one corner, Lewis' strong handwriting marked both sides densely. But this time, the words were *not* plain English. They appeared to be random letters separated by spaces. The author found what he'd written as alien as we did; his script had none of the earlier rhythm and I could tell from repeated dark blotches that his quill had paused often.

Only a date and a name remained comprehensible.

Aubrea's exclamation barely exceeded a whisper. I wouldn't have heard her if our cheeks weren't touching.

"*The* Thomas Jefferson?"

"Yeah," I said. "But it isn't his signature. See? Lewis' handwriting. This was to be sent *to* Jefferson and never got delivered. Jefferson invented a lot of codes like this."

"You think it's real?"

"All these people dying over a phony letter wouldn't make sense."

"Mitch had this?"

I nodded. Emotion silenced her for a moment. She tried

again to speak without success. I turned the chair and she sank onto my knee. She buried her face between my shoulder and neck. Her reaction never reached sobbing this time. She'd looked on a friend's death warrant. A person needs time to process that.

My right hand stroked her black hair, but my left went to the desktop. Captain Lewis' undelivered letter felt rough and primitive.

No, I corrected myself, not *Captain* Lewis. He'd been appointed Governor of the Louisiana Territory in 1809. And if historians were to be believed, by October 11th of that year, Governor Meriwether Lewis was dead and buried in a forest grave, beside an old buffalo trail south of Nashville.

But the letter was dated, in Lewis' own hand:

Saturday October 28th 1809.

Seventeen days too late.

Either the letter was an unimpeachable fake, or a two-hundred-year-old chapter of US history had been written wrong.

• • •

The Langstons were accustomed to matched china and hand-polished silver. Meals I offered Aubrea came in cardboard boxes. I might be living down to her DA father's probable opinion of me, but we'd missed two meals each, the hotel didn't have room service, and when we left the red journal would have to go with us. That meant getting in the Viper and driving the hell out of Mule Town. Tug Moran's non-bumpkin crew weren't our only watchers.

Aubrea insisted on giving me cash for the delivery driver. Eli had brought an old purse and a new (filled) wallet from home when he picked her up at Cool-Core. Her regular purse hadn't escaped Vanderbilt with us.

Flintlock

"I don't make much, but I can afford this," she said.

I didn't argue. After the door was locked and we sat cross-legged on the unused bed in our bathrobes, with the open box steaming at our knees, I asked what she did for a living. The question hadn't come up earlier.

"I've been wanting to ask you the same thing," she said between mouthfuls of pepperoni. "Or almost the same thing. Why do you work at all?"

"I'm fortunate enough to do what I want."

"This is what you want to be doing?"

"Yes." Twenty-four hours earlier, I might have said something else.

"I teach yoga. Three days a week—what's funny?"

"I'd assumed you were a student."

"Are you sure you should be a private eye?"

"Shut up and eat your gourmet meal."

She did. We did. We'd done nothing but burn calories since before breakfast. Still, that poisonous bit of Americana on the desk didn't relinquish our thoughts for a single meal. Both of us wound up staring past the pizza box, across the bed, to the red journal.

I'd progressed beyond searching for a reason for the slayings of Mitch and others. A crumbling coded letter to Thomas Jefferson would have to serve as the motive. Now I needed to figure out *whose* motive.

"Can you read it?" she finally murmured.

"No."

I might research Jeffersonian ciphers if we had time. We didn't. I might ask Danny to feed the digits into Cool-Core's mainframe, season it with algorithms, and make sense of the babble that way. There wasn't time for that, either. And this wasn't Danny's puzzle to solve.

"I know who can," I said.

"Tipper!"

247

Jon A. Hunt

"Uh-huh. He lives and breathes this stuff."

• • •

If you have it, take it to Tipper.

Rafferty's eight-word text message spoke volumes. Rafferty's tenuous standing with Metro wouldn't tolerate much more string-pulling. I'd given him next to nothing in return. I shouldn't expect any more favors soon. At least we agreed about the journal.

I unplugged my phone from the charger. There was also a missed call from O'Dell's standard number and a subsequent voicemail. Aubrea was in the shower. I walked to the window with the phone to my ear.

Sunday morning was lightening at the edges the same way Saturday had ended, without color. Parking lot lights below the window still burned. A new police cruiser squatted on the lot's far side, glowing inside as the driver busied himself with the computer. No white vans.

Meredith O'Dell's recorded voice came on the line as I let the curtain fall again. She hadn't tried my number at any exotic hour. She'd called about the time people her age typically finish supper. Aubrea and I had been too occupied to notice. The old woman's message was no more amicable than Rafferty's.

Mr. Bedlam. You haven't set foot in the store or communicated your progress in any way in the last two days.

I don't mean to tell you how to do your job. However, I cannot understand how it is possible to accomplish without a reasonable amount of time spent here.

Kindly contact me or the store at your earliest convenience to discuss, or I must assume our association has concluded.

Meredith never shied away from making valid points. Verbal pink slips are common in my chosen profession, but I

Flintlock

wasn't ready to burn this bridge. I redialed the number to at least leave a message at the store. The line rang till the answering system engaged, I gave my name and started an impromptu excuse, and a human intercepted the call. Darlene was the last person I'd have expected before seven A.M. She could just as easily have picked up from inside the store or at home; she always had a bedroom voice.

"I've missed you."

"Sorry," I said. "It's been a crazy couple of days." My eyes were on the strip of light under the bathroom door. Aubrea still had the water running. Why did I feel like the proverbial kid with his arm up to the elbow in a cookie jar? And whose cookies?

"Come see me?" Darlene purred.

"I thought the store wasn't open on Sundays."

She giggled. She didn't *sound* like she was in the bookstore wearing her nametag. She sounded like she was at home in bed wearing nothing except maybe a purple ribbon around her neck. "Who said anything about the store? You can buy me lunch. And I still owe you a special thank-you for the other night."

"Today might be tough. I'm running down some new leads." This was a stretch. My leads probably had nothing to do with why Meredith hired me. Now was just not the time to learn Darlene's definition of *special thank-you.*

Her voice conveyed a playful pout. "Sure? I found something about that red journal."

"Did you?"

"Uh-huh. It's not here now, but in Uncle Ral's shipping records. I can show you..."

The five-by-eight red leather rectangle on the desk stared back at me. Raleigh's thoroughness could backfire on him if he'd left a trail others could find. How had Rafferty's bunch missed that?

Jon A. Hunt

"I'm three steps ahead of you," I said, "but I'm still interested in the paper trail. Tipper needs to see this thing first. How about tonight? I'll call."

"Okay. I'll wait. Not very patiently." Even her good-byes came across as invitations.

I tapped the phone to end the call and immediately felt less guilty. Water had stopped flowing in the bathroom. My attention returned to the journal resting atop its clear protective bag. It *had* passed through O'Dell's, then. Interesting. I stepped to the desk and opened the well-aged clasp, flipped to the letter, arrayed the pieces on the desktop long enough to photograph all sides with my phone. Then I emailed the images to Danny's secure Cool-Core account. Danny's regular projects, delayed by his Vanderbilt consultations, were certain to drag him down to his basement lab even on a Sunday, but he wouldn't be out of bed this early. I'd have to trust my luck till he sent confirmation.

In the meantime...

The bed we'd slept in seemed the safest option. I shoved the mattress off the box spring and opened my pocketknife.

Flintlock

Chapter Twenty-eight

Two patrol cars escorted us beyond the city limits. Chief Moran's orders. Their roof lights winked blue farewells as I turned onto the I-65 ramp. I let the Viper reply with an accelerating roar, and Aubrea and I sped northward to lives in some other precinct.

Traffic was sparse. A mixed palette of evergreens and somber winter decay rushed past the windows. Today was shaping up to be December's warmest yet, without sacrificing an iota of the month's accustomed dreariness. Taut gray sky stretched between horizons. Pillows of fog sulked in low pockets beside the interstate.

The red journal rode between us in its clear plastic traveling garb, one corner down in the cupholder. It might as well have been a slab from Erik Jorgensen's granite perimeter walls; the separation was as complete. Aubrea's regal profile didn't alter for miles. She just stared ahead. Neither of us wanted to speak first. I started to take the initiative, not out of lost patience so much as the realization this wouldn't get easier if we let it percolate. I got as far as opening my mouth.

"Daddy would never approve of you," she said.

"Does he need to?"

A quick glance verified she was watching me now. Her eyes showed blue as the roof lights atop those Mule Town police cruisers. "No. One day he'll have to try. I won't always go out

251

of my way to make it so difficult."

"I know."

"Tyler, I—"

The old journal wasn't really as impassible as it seemed. I reached over it for her hand.

"I'm farther than you are from wanting parental approval," I assured her.

She surprised me with a laugh. A lot of the girl's responses surprised me. She didn't let my hand go and wasn't planning to for a while yet.

"We weren't...close...in the same way," she said, "but you aren't so different from Mitch."

I took that as a compliment. Mitch Braunfelter was the kindest soul I'd ever met.

• • •

Sunday morning impressed none of Belle Meade's denizens sufficiently to lure them outdoors. They could afford to wait for better. Drapes parted to glare at my ten-cylinder noise ordinance violation rumbling past their dead lawns, still devoid of inflatable snowmen and reindeer. I might've liked the neighborhood, till Jorgensen's dismal estate poisoned my outlook. I kept coming back anyway. There were the dull stone walls.

I'd called ahead to make sure Tipper would be there. I'd also warned Aubrea that Tipper might not react well to the surprise we brought him. When she asked what I meant, I could only shake my head.

Tipper's sedan was exactly where he'd left it a week ago. The tires probably had flat spots. A different Metro car sat in Poole's old spot, and now there were *three* white TBI vans. I missed Smally's dilapidated pickup truck. Except for the girl beside me, this business felt more isolated than usual.

At least Danny had my back. My phone lit up in the cupholder next to the journal a few seconds before I killed the

252

Flintlock

engine. His text message was brief, just a web address. A uniformed cop watched the Viper from the granite front steps without moving to approach; he'd been warned. I touched the link in Danny's message and asked Aubrea to find me the pen, notepad and paperclips in the glovebox. The web page loaded. The photos I'd taken were on it. I deleted the originals from my phone, closed the browser, took the pen and paper from Aubrea.

"What is that for?"

"Insurance," I said.

• • •

The door warden checked my license. I'd internally rehearsed what to do if asked for Aubrea's photo ID—lost with her last purse at Vanderbilt—but it never came up. Even though we weren't going to be an *item*, she held my hand fast as we stepped into the foyer.

The mess had evolved. Every loose bit had been carted from the foyer and adjoining rooms to forensics labs north of Nashville. We threaded our way between bare studs into the next spaces where work hadn't progressed as far. Another regular officer met us and said the Professor was in the indoor firing range. He accompanied us as far as the trophy room and excused himself, but he didn't leave us alone. The place was a sea of white frocks. TBI's hordes had finally finished sniffing around the edges and now attacked the estate's core. Camera flashes pulsed. Nobody said hello. Aubrea only released my hand after we'd dodged every rubbish heap, spotlight, and evidence bin between Points A and B. I couldn't decide which bothered me more: her reliance on me for security, or my willingness to accept it.

Both doors into the firing lanes were wedged open. The green *ENTER* sign in the anteroom glowed. We obliged. The only person in there was who we'd come to see. He wasn't ready for us. Tipper was, in fact, asleep.

253

Jon A. Hunt

The familiar worktables blazed beneath adjustable lamps. Plastic evidence tubs were arrayed in a semicircle behind the Professor's chair. He must have placed them that way for quick reference; a casual observer might suspect the *tubs* of watching the *man* instead. Tipper's multi-lensed jeweler's glasses sparkled near his left elbow. Curls showed like ringlets of flame in the light where his head rested on crossed forearms. I had never encountered soft snoring in a gun range till now.

"Can't we leave him be?" Aubrea whispered.

I shook my head. Waiting for anything was perilous now that the journal had been found.

Disembodied gun components—trigger guards, brass fittings, a short ramrod—covered the table. The surface where Tipper had laid his head bore an open but dark laptop computer and otherwise softer fare: paper and parchment fragments in clear plastic bags. Few of the scraps were large. Most wore the jaundice of extreme age and probably had been valuable before being shredded along with everything else. Directly under one of the lamps lay a lone intact sheet. This was neither bagged nor old. I'd seen the embossed letterhead before, the hammer and anvil logo.

"Tipper."

Only someone used to perpetual exhaustion wakes like that. Soldiers on front lines. Emergency room doctors. A man who hadn't really slept since his wife and child were murdered. He just sat up and opened his eyes.

"Tyler! Miss Aubrea! Sorry, I lost track of time. You, er, caught me resting my eyes."

Self-deprecating humor was within the bounds of Tipper's character. But he also had a subtler nature I'd grown aware of with observation. The hand we weren't supposed to be watching scooted the newer letter beneath older bagged items. I trapped the document under a fingertip. Tipper had no opportunity for protest, because at the same time I plunked the

Flintlock

red journal onto the table in front of him.

The man stopped. He stopped talking, stopped moving, stopped blinking, damn near stopped breathing. Firing range or not, I'd visited noisier morgues. The hiss of air drawn through ceiling vents by unseen motors, Aubrea's restless shift of weight from one foot to the other, the tiny ratchet of a wall clock's second sweep, all transformed to huge sounds compared to his silence.

At last he said: "Please close the door."

Aubrea turned, nudged the rubber wedge with her toe from under the inner door, pressed it shut. If the TBI crew on the other side paid attention to things above seven feet, they might notice the *IN USE* sign light up.

My gaze traveled from the man beside me to the letter I pressed against the table. I had time. Tipper was a still-life again. The letter came from the same *Colonial Societists* whose correspondence I'd ogled on Art Fontaine's desk. What I read now bumped me nearly as off-center as the journal had Tipper.

Mr. Gering,
Please accept our heartfelt condolences for your loss...

"Where did you find it?"

Tipper's voice maintained an eerie steadiness when his fingers could not. He had to lay both hands across Meriwether Lewis' red diary to settle them. His eyes, red-rimmed and whatever color I liked except blue, implored me to answer.

"Fished it out of the Duck River," I told him. "It was only there by accident."

The most miserable smile on earth crossed Tipper's lips. "I suppose it would have to be accidental. Yet, in a way, that's closer to home than it's been for a long time."

He didn't ask for details. Finding things was my specialty. He tried the clasp. Aubrea pressed against me, mesmerized by

Jon A. Hunt

his every shaky page turn. Tipper wore no protective gloves. History was meant to be touched. For Tipper, those dry pages represented both centuries-old history and a more painful recent past.

He reached the coded letter. Half of it, anyway. Three of the six pieces kept company with a sheet of modern lined paper, the web address Dany provided scrawled thereon in ballpoint pen, all parts corralled by a shiny silver paperclip.

"This isn't the whole letter."

"The rest is safe," I said.

Tipper remembered how to move all at once. He sprang to his feet so ferociously that Aubrea jumped backward and my fists balled on instinct. His chair crashed to the floor. Till now I'd never have guessed Tipper had that kind of energy in him.

"You *separated* the pages? They aren't *yours* to manipulate—"

Impressive. I'd just had more practice losing my temper. "What are we supposed to do?" I snarled. "Wait for Jefferson to read it first?"

He stepped squarely into my space, a man who'd never thrown a punch in his life. "That letter belongs to the people! *All* of it, to *all* of them!"

"Is that what you insisted on in Philadelphia?"

It tore my guts to say. It hurt him a lot worse to hear. Tipper staggered like I'd busted his jaw. He felt dazedly for his upended chair, found nothing, sank instead to his knees.

"We worked hard to stay alive and bring this to you," I said, softly. "If everyone deserves the whole letter, don't you think we deserve the whole story?"

His second silence was brutally concentrated. I held my place till he spoke. He'd lived with the truth this long without help, he'd last a bit longer. Aubrea peered over a shoulder at the door. No one came in to see what the fuss was about. The room had been engineered to contain more decibels than one falling chair made.

256

Flintlock

"I don't understand," she murmured. "Tipper?"

He sank onto his butt on the floor. He ignored the sideways chair. He didn't make answering Aubrea's question a priority, either. He had his own question: "How did you know?"

"The basics are public record," I said. "Guessing the rest wasn't hard. I prefer answers to guesses, though."

Without his customary warmth Tipper looked haggard, pale. Even now, he battled to retain secrets he'd carried for a year. The struggle showed in his eyes.

"This isn't just your fight," I said. "There are other casualties."

The girl tensed. She was thinking about Mitch, too.

"The rest of the letter—"

"—isn't where anyone can touch it." I hoped that was a promise I could keep. "The website has photographs of both pages and is locked with a password. If we need them for backup or negotiation, there they are. Maybe half of the physical letter isn't worth killing for."

Only one side of Tipper's mouth attempted an unconvinced smile. He patted the floor, though, almost playfully, an invitation from the Tipper I remembered.

That's where the three of us sat, beside perfectly serviceable chairs no one wanted to fetch. Tipper had things to get off his chest. We weren't about to interrupt that for better seats.

"Finn. Huck Finn Gering. That was my boy's name. Marie had a sense of humor like that, and we couldn't imagine other kids teasing him about it later. He learned to walk in the museum. Pulled himself up by a Yorktown caisson wheel and off he went. That's what we did, together, we ran a museum, or tried to..."

His odd-colored eyes stared through me to happier times. Tipper hadn't always been so carefully contained. Pulling rocks out of his emotional dam was perilous.

"Six years," he continued, "the last three with my new

Jon A. Hunt

family. Ours wasn't the main History Museum, it was an offshoot focused on Colonial and Revolutionary eras. There's an audience for it. Getting that audience through the doors— tough. Funding was always iffy, and what we got channeled through the larger museum. Keeping the lights on could be a struggle. Then, a week away from bankruptcy, we had a windfall.

"I'm no fan of this—" he stretched both arms to encompass the room, the estate, the idea, "—private hoards that hide people's best stories from themselves. History nobody knows might as well be fiction, right? But everyone dies sooner or later. Even billionaires."

I couldn't decide if that was meant directly for me. A hint of mischief briefly deepened a crease on the left side of his mouth, similar to his expression when he'd set that first loaded dueling pistol in my hands. Then absolute seriousness returned.

"The third-richest Colonial antiquarian in New England bequeathed his whole collection to us. We had met the man once, never had a subsequent conversation. Who knows why? It was a lifetime's worth of fantastic exhibit material. At the bottom of one of the crates I found that journal, overlooked for two-hundred years. And the day kept getting better. That same afternoon, two men representing interested philanthropists came to see me about bankrolling the museum. Fully. For the next decade. Marie and I were beside ourselves! I agreed to a second meeting the following evening with Mr. Ray and Mr. Delphino."

"The Delphino in your report," I interjected, "from Kentucky?"

Tipper responded with sudden coldness. "Yes. I can't honestly say I was surprised or sorry about his murder. He was an emissary of the Colonial Societists."

The letters to Fontaine and Tipper.

Flintlock

The embossed hammer and anvil stationery.

"Who are they?" Aubrea asked.

Tipper startled us with a laugh. The sound didn't match his character, at least not the character I'd convinced myself I knew. It was harsh, mirthless, bordering on madness.

"Who are they?! Don't you think I want to know? Who are they!"

His face contorted as if an invisible demon was tickling him to death. Too many rocks taken from the dam. I leaned forward as the girl recoiled.

"*Tipper!*"

My shout got through. He fell silent. Tears on his cheeks sparkled in the work lights' aura as if he wept molten gold.

"We can help," I said, "*if* you keep it together. I don't think there's much time."

His words came now with strained discipline. "They'll find it. They always do."

"Who are these people? What have they done?"

"They're an association of experts, collectors, supporters of research and historical education. The Societists promote themselves as guardians of the original American culture."

"Doesn't sound very sinister."

The miserable half-smirk returned. "Of course not. That's why I agreed to the second meeting. Ray and Delphino and their wonderful Societists were swooping in at the last minute to save us. The museums future—mine, Marie's, Finn's— would be secure. For a price."

"Isn't that the point of negations?"

"When the terms are reasonable," Tipper snapped. "Theirs were not. A controlling majority on the museum board. Final say on all exhibits and procurements. We were to turn over certain items to the Societists for safeguarding and make absolutely no mention of those items' existence to anyone."

"The red journal?"

"The first item on his list," he muttered. "I couldn't accept. That wasn't getting help, that was selling out. I thanked them for their offer, said I couldn't in good conscience present it to the board. I never voiced my opinion that it was all a very extravagant ruse to obtain the lost journal. Buy a whole museum to get one old book. Even now, it sounds ridiculous, doesn't it?

"Mr. Ray politely insisted the Colonial Societists' offer was sincere, and he would give the museum a week to reconsider. But the red journal, in particular, was not to be opened, examined, or revealed to other parties. He added that there were worse things in life than losing controlling interest in a museum."

Tipper hesitated. I understood he had to pace himself. My services don't include leather couches or inkblots, but my role does require some sense of what makes people tick. I waited.

"You can't imagine how often that warning plays through my head now," he said.

He steeled himself for a punchline no one would find funny, plowed on.

"I called Marie. She was at the museum. After hours. She'd promised her mother pictures of Finn...standing by the caisson. Moms love mementos. Marie was disappointed but completely in agreement with me. The Societists' insistence that the red journal be untouched baffled us both. Neither of us had yet opened it, you see. I...I think..."

Aubrea sensed his agitation. She reached for Tipper's nearest hand. The girl had the makings of an excellent counselor, or even a PI. Tipper's eyes went to the floor.

"The museum was robbed that night. Smashed into so many pieces there was never any question about attempting to reopen. It was as much vandalism as a simple robbery. And Marie and Finn..." Tipper's eyes came up and locked onto

Flintlock

mine, full of anger and anguish and tears. I'd asked him to share; he was going to make damned sure I felt as much of this as a listener could. "The police didn't want to tell me. They said I didn't want to know those kinds of details. I demanded them anyway. They were my life, I deserved to know!"

"Tipper——"

"You said you needed to know, too!"

"All right."

"Finn died first. Those monsters...took their time, made her watch. Then they killed her, too."

Chapter Twenty-nine

I had no suitable consolation. Aubrea's handholding was as effective as anything. She communicated more through contact than most. She knew the futility of words.

Tipper's voice started again, small, slowly gaining volume and impetus. "Now...I'm here. Marie's gone. Finn is gone. The old museum is a shell no one will buy. But the Colonial Societists are around still, and I'm watching from the trenches. You'll want to know why."

Tugging his fingers away from the girl with noticeable hesitation, he pressed himself up from the floor. He stooped to right the fallen chair. We followed him to the table and leaned beside him over the scraps and the leather book which had cost so many so much. He separated papers with the fingers of one hand, fingers that no longer shook. He caressed an edge of the partial coded missive that peered from between red Moroccan covers, decorated with my offending paper clip.

"The letters," he said. "Especially what the Societists sent me. You can guess how much mail I let pile up at home. I didn't open it for ten days." He tapped an ominous drumbeat on the intact letterhead with the embossed hammer and anvil. "It's dated the same day as their murders. Hand delivered to my box."

"Tell me you showed this to the police," I breathed.

Tipper shrugged. "They said they couldn't use it. The

Flintlock

Colonial Societists aren't a den of thieves or murderers. Each member has always been beyond reproach. The offer was withdrawn—no museum was left to support and the journal was taken—but the organization cooperated fully with the authorities, posted a million-dollar reward for information leading to convictions, offered all possible help to me and the other surviving staff, assisted in trying to trace what had been stolen. The police confirmed that the letter's date was an unfortunate clerical error. The only fingerprints were mine and a secretary's at the Societists' Boston office. Harmless."

Tipper fanned another fragment from under his letter. This one was bagged, dusty, a torn third of a sheet of stationery. There was the embossed hammer and anvil. It was addressed to Mr. Erik Jorgensen, Belle Meade, Tennessee. Everything else had been ripped away.

"Now what do you suppose they wanted from Mr. Jorgensen?" Tipper's sarcasm bubbled like simmering grits. "Always protecting our fragile heritage. Exhibitors across the country have the Societists to thank—for *money*—never artifacts. What the Societists find, the Societists keep. And their influence isn't limited to museums and collectors. Remember a few years ago, when Lewis' descendants wanted to exhume his remains and finally settle the question of suicide or murder?"

I remembered the people in the Columbia hotel after Mitch's funeral, in the coonskin hats, there for the Second Annual Meriwether Lewis Exhumation Convention; I said nothing aloud. Aubrea shook her head. Tipper scowled disappointedly.

"He's supposedly buried just off the Natchez Trace Parkway, down by Hohenwald, on National Park land. The National Park Service had to give its consent. After years of cajoling and pleading, they agreed to it. Then, before anyone could grab a shovel, the Park Service reversed their decision and forbade any digging for perpetuity. Concerns were

263

Jon A. Hunt

mentioned about disturbing nearby pioneer graves. Come on! Archeologists have been carefully digging around remains for decades. Somebody just didn't want those bones brought into daylight. I looked into the records and found the Colonial Societists had quietly met with park officials the day before they changed their collective mind. That's just one example. The organization openly funds exploration into our past, and selectively smothers what's discovered."

"Why?" I asked.

Tipper's face colored with frustration. "I have no idea! I mean to find out. You might say I've a score to settle. My one break since...since Philadelphia...was being hired as an expert by the police in matters involving stolen artifacts from the same time period. I'm able to pay the bills and continue the hunt."

"Till someone decides to stop you."

"Till then," he agreed soberly and laid a hand on the old red journal.

"What does the letter say?" Aubrea wondered aloud.

A frown briefly clouded Tipper's features. Then he realized which letter she meant and found a warm smile for her, warm enough I felt a pang of guilt for what I'd done with the girl earlier. "This is the first time I laid eyes on it. Delphino seems to have had it since Philadelphia."

"Writing that he possessed the journal might count as an admission of complicity," I pointed out.

"He said he had *a* Lewis journal. Not specifically *this* one. But that's moot. He's dead. The journal and letter are found."

I wished I'd been nosier about Fontaine's mail when I had the chance. What did the Colonial Societists want from *him?* And how honest was Tipper being now, really? He hadn't been forthcoming about his past till I forced the issue. For some dumb reason, I believed him now. It was the same kind of faith that gave me a shoulder that ached whenever the weather changed.

Flintlock

"Is the journal genuine? And the letter?"

"Obviously someone thinks so."

"Then Lewis' death—"

"—didn't happen as the history books tell it. Only President Jefferson, Captain Clark and Governor Lewis knew this cipher, if it is in fact the one Jefferson cooked up for their expedition. He survived long enough to write his old Commander in Chief in code."

"Can you read it?" Aubrea pressed.

"Anyone could, with the prearranged password."

"Mitch thought it might be *ARTICHOKES*."

Both the others assaulted me with startled looks.

"It was on his refrigerator door," I said.

"Every biographer and historian knows that," Tipper said. "Pretty obvious."

"Obvious *today*, sure," I agreed, "but who would have known in 1809?"

• • •

For all the admirable qualities Mitch Braunfelter took to the grave, some of his guesses were no more on the money than his fashion sense.

I'm okay to wait a week for my bodyguard to start.

ARTICHOKES must be the password to Meriwether Lewis' letter to President Jefferson.

Nobody wanted Mitch's guess to be right more than Tipper. He pulled up a spreadsheet on his laptop computer, already loaded with formulas specific to Jefferson's cipher. His fingers attacked the keyboard as I read off individual letters from the three yellowed fragments. I was prepared to do the same from the images Danny had digitally stowed of the second page, but Tipper sank back disgustedly and stopped typing.

"That isn't it," he groaned.

265

The "words" on the screen were still gibberish, though, just arranged differently.

"Can't we figure it out without the password? Mitch and I used to solve puzzles where we looked for familiar patterns, repeated letters, things like that."

Tipper appreciated Aubrea's enthusiasm. But his smile now was more weary than warm. "Unfortunately, no. You're thinking of one-for-one letter substitutions. This isn't that. Jefferson's trick was to use a predetermined codeword, one only the writer and intended reader knew, to locate substituted letters on a grid. *H* might equal *E* in one place, then it represents *R* the next time, *W* after that, and so on. If you have the same letter repeated like *OO* or *TT*, they won't be represented by two identical characters in the coded version. Without the proper codeword, this is virtually impossible to crack."

She murmured "Oh. What could the word be?"

"Pretty much anything, I'm afraid, as long as the same twenty-six-character alphabet is used. We might reasonably assume an English word (or maybe French), and generally a longer word was employed—but that hardly narrowed the options."

"Mitch died...because of a letter no one can read..."

She'd uttered my own sullen thoughts. The ransacked homes. The broken, torn, waterlogged bodies. For what? I glared at two-hundred-year-old rectangles of nonsense, meaningless except for two names, a date, and Lewis' strange pistol doodle. The date had significance, I supposed. If genuine and correct, it meant Governor Lewis hadn't met the dismal end we'd all supposed. Still, without a legible explanation...

My jacket pocket whirred. I backed from the table and extracted my phone. The name *C Smally* glowed on the display. Rafferty's hulking right-hand man, with the rusty pickup truck and the six-paperback-a-week drugstore smut habit, had never

Flintlock

called me directly till now. I put the device to my ear and immediately regretted it. The shriek came through so piercingly, Aubrea and Tipper both whirled to face me. A voice that sounded like Smally's yelled "Hang on!" as I pressed the phone to my chest.

"I'll take this in the anteroom," I told my fellow decoders, and stepped through the steel door. I thumbed the volume button down on my way.

"Smally?" I tried again as the door shut and the red *IN USE* sign glowed. I kicked the wedge from under the outer door to avoid annoyed expressions from the forensics herd in the trophy room.

Metallic screams persisted in the background, albeit somewhat muted. "Trains," he explained. "I'm at the Radnor railyard. Rafferty said to call you. He's in his office with the DA—"

I'd seen Rafferty's office. If he and Langston were in there simultaneously, I hoped Aubrea's old man wasn't prone to claustrophobia.

"—I caught up with the kid."

I forgot about Rafferty's office. "Sal?"

More screeching, then: "Yeah, him. Says he'll only talk with you."

"Fine. Hang onto him and—"

"I, uh, never said I had him in custody," Smally interrupted before another train could. "He's twenty feet from me. Closest I've been able to get. Only way I'll have that twitchy little snot in my car is if you convince him it's okay, or I shoot him. I showed him my badge. He says I'm not as big as the other guy after him. He'll wait twenty minutes. I just texted the address."

...*not as big as the other guy.*

Smally was plenty large. I knew exactly who the boy meant, then.

The phone's chime got overmatched by train brakes, but I

saw the blink. I recognized the address. It was doable in fifteen if I didn't get lost on my way.

"Tell him I'll be there."

"From where?"

"The Jorgensen place."

"It's foggy as shit, you won't make it."

"Kid doesn't have a watch on, does he?" I remembered skinny *bare* arms.

"Not that I can see."

"So lie about the time. Just keep him there."

"All right." The call ended with a mechanical wail.

Flintlock

Chapter Thirty

"You can't watch over me twenty-four-seven, Tyler. Go! Just make sure you come back, okay?"

Aubrea was right. I'd told Mitch myself it wasn't possible for a single man to completely protect anyone. The best way to keep Aubrea and others safe was to find the danger at its source. A scrawny kid with untied Reeboks, staring down Smally at a railyard, was closer to the source than anyone. That was why his friends were dead. It wasn't like I'd left the girl by herself, either.

Tipper promised me *he* wouldn't let Aubrea out of his sight. He'd used the paperclip to fasten Lewis' unreadable correspondence and the paper with the web address together, slipped it all back inside the Moroccan leather journal, and stowed the journal inside his coat.

"We're a team." The wink was quintessential Tipper. "If the letter's a dead end, I've got my own lead to follow: this loose ramrod here doesn't have a matching pistol on site. I'll have a description of possible weapons it fits tonight, if I have to get it myself from Fontaine."

"He'd help?"

"He's not pleasant, but nobody knows guns better. Even Jorgensen wouldn't have disagreed, regardless of what he thought of the man's marksmanship. I've had conversations with him about the collection already, and if he's, ah,

269

Jon A. Hunt

indisposed, Gerard has access to his notes."

I didn't have time for better assurances. The Viper rocketed through the estate's front gate shortly afterward with eighteen of Sal's twenty minutes remaining.

Smally's fog existed in patches. None crowded the estate's granite battlements; the intersection with Harding Place proved nearly invisible except for traffic lights; two miles farther east the air cleared again. I pushed the car hard when I could see to compensate for stretches when I couldn't. I hoped Smally managed to keep that kid in sight till my arrival but wasn't counting on it. Twenty minutes is a long wait for a fourteen-year-old on the run.

Headlights flared within another fog patch ahead. The driver either recognized my speed or heard ten cylinders hammering: he pitched to a stop. That worked in our favor, since I hadn't considered braking. The route needed more of my attention than I gave it.

Sal was the last of his tribe.

...not as big as the other guy...

Where was Bigfoot now?

The Hillsboro light created blood red haze beneath it. A wall of blushing moisture churned up from a nearly-frozen pond beside the road. Braking made the Viper's tail shudder. Oncoming cars on either side weren't there yet, so I catapulted through without waiting for my turn. Let them honk. I couldn't hear over the engine.

My memory saw better than my eyes: hand scribed letters, illegible in their arrangement. *ARTICHOKES* wasn't the keyword. History books were wrong about that, too. But when had Lewis and Jefferson been able to choose another, and with the expedition to the west coast over, why would they? And why the pistol doodle?

The exhaust snorted as I jerked my foot up.

"Call Tipper Gering!"

Flintlock

The handsfree system obeyed. Two ringtones sang over the speakers as I accelerated again, then Tipper's recorded greeting replied. I realized by comparison how weary his voice had been back at the estate.

"Hey, it's Ty. We're on the wrong path. Try *PISTOL* or *FLINTLOCK*—something that sketch in the letter might represent. It's got to be a hint for Jefferson."

I hung up via the steering wheel button. A speed limit sign flashed by. The number was half of what the speedometer showed.

Why didn't Tipper answer?

Arthur Fontaine. Tipper must be calling him about that orphaned ramrod.

The light over Franklin Pike was green. I could see across that intersection. The Viper's undercarriage banged and sparks flooded my side mirrors. 104 was too fast for the grade change. I switched to the middle pedal.

Whiteness filled the windshield. My foot stamped reflexively; muscle memory wrenched the wheel. The van cleared my front end but clipped the rear. The Viper spun through the next light at the I-65 overpass, tires shrilling. It took two complete revolutions to regain my bearings, then I mashed the gas pedal to launch the car forward. The taillights swept through my peripheral and washed me with angry red. Then the van was gone, bouncing recklessly northward on Sidco Drive. Whoever had the wheel never slowed.

I ground into the left turn lane. My heart drummed as fiercely as the Viper's pistons. The final mile was all mine. My dance with the van must have caused a pile-up back on Harding that choked off northbound traffic. Nobody went the other way, either. I couldn't much capitalize on it: the Viper barely managed legal speeds, with bodywork scraping across the pavement. Fog, too, hampered my progress. The headlights clawed away no more than thirty feet at a time; details to my left and right failed within half that distance.

Another white van grew out of the vapors. This one leaned, motionless, half off the road's left flank, facing the wrong direction. Open rear doors revealed an empty interior. It couldn't be the van I'd tangled with minutes ago. Now any white van worried me.

I had four of Sal's minutes left, if the boy even had that much patience.

Smally's derelict truck wasn't visible in any of the lots I scraped past. Two tons of rust wouldn't exactly stand out in the fog. The lots were empty. It was Sunday. It was dusk. It was almost Christmas. Smart people had better places to be.

A square-shouldered form appeared at the roadside. Smally recognized what was left of the Viper and waved me to an entrance I wouldn't have found otherwise.

He was alone.

• • •

"You missed him," he said flatly and reached through the old pickup's side window for something on the seat. "Took off like a scared cat down the hill."

What Smally called a *hill*, others might call a *cliff*, a brambly fifty-foot tumble down to the nearest tracks. The bottom was farther than earsplitting howls of steel on steel let on.

"Why are *you* still up here?" I yelled.

"I've got helpers waiting below," he said.

The offered binoculars resembled a Cracker Jack prize in his grizzly-bear paw. I took them and stepped to the drop-off. The railyard wasn't socked in after all. Fog caught on the high edges and hovered there, a damp indistinct ceiling. Floodlights on dizzying steel towers had come on, but they *were* in the mists and glowed decorously without illuminating anything solid. The yard stretched beyond clarity, line after line of parallel rails, some bare, most laden with lumbering rectangles and long black cylinders: containers on flatbeds, petroleum tankers,

Flintlock

boxcars, tall car carriers with perforated sidewalls, thrumming diesel-electric locomotives. Everything that moved did so with a godawful noise. If Sal somehow managed to evade Smally's trap and get to the far side, his hearing would never recover. His odds of escaping weren't good, though, and not for reasons Smally supposed.

I spotted the kid first. *Scared cat* would be an accurate description for a police report. He'd lost his jacket since our encounter at O'Dell's. He was running like hell and had nothing to fear from at least one of the plainclothes men down there with him. It was my turn to pass the binoculars and point. Their magnification was sufficient to recognize a dead detective.

Smally mouthed a four-letter word neither of us could hear over the train wheels.

• • •

We took the pickup. My car was in bad shape and Smally wouldn't fit inside anyway. There was no point in one of us staying on the bluff with binoculars as spotter: whoever went into the valley couldn't hear phone directions. That might be why one of Smally's plainclothes cohorts never answered his status request. We already knew the other guy's reason.

As we left, I noted a white van bouncing over a dirt access road by the tracks. It didn't belong to the railroad. The rear fender was crushed.

Smally used an incongruously modern police radio under the faded steel dash to light up the airwaves as we lunged on two wheels onto the street. The nearest way into the railyard was a mile north, which didn't take long. Whatever Smally had under the hood wasn't stock. Raw-edged paperbacks flopped around my feet, castoffs from his deplorable reading list. A southbound Metro cruiser passed en route to the wreck on Harding, roof lights flaring, siren singing. I watched the driver execute a U-turn at speed to join us. Nothing alters police priorities like the radio call *officer down*.

"Yessir. Yessir. No, he's here with me."

Rafferty's voice burst from the radio a bit louder than whatever roared in the engine bay. I heard my name, a lot of colorful descriptive terms, then Smally thumbed the mic to concur with more *yessirs* and the radio conversation was over.

We'd collected a second car with flashing lights. That practically made a parade. The truck wallowed through a hard left, asphalt gave way to loose gravel, the bed wagged like an excited Weimaraner. Smally slapped the shifter into a new slot and stamped the pedals to death. He heaved on the wheel. The pickup skipped sideways till the tires on the high side bounced back to earth. The Metro cars halted nearby with similar finesse.

A hell of a lot of screaming metal crawled before us.

My companion slapped the glovebox lid in front of me. It flopped open to disgorge another tattered drugstore novel, a box of 9mm shells, and cellophane packets of foam earplugs he kept for spontaneous firing range visits. He snatched a packet. So did I.

"Lieutenant says this is your show!" Smally shouted between brake screeches. "What now? Grabbing the kid before the other guys won't be easy!"

"They don't want to take him anywhere," I yelled, "they just want him dead."

"Witness?"

"Sort of. Look between trains and try not to shoot each other. And steer clear of anybody bigger than you!"

"Huh?"

I waited for another sound opening. My unshielded ear must be bleeding by now. I remembered the kid's ears and took some more earplugs. "Sal's got the same character who made the mess at the Braunfelter and Jorgensen homes on his ass. Same one that broke the officer's neck in Columbia. If you're

Flintlock

close enough for a clean shot, you're too close!"

"Got it!"

I pushed the box of extra cartridges into his hand. He finished cramming the last earplug in place and shared a perplexed glare. But he took the box. I had every spare magazine I owned in my pockets. We thumbed our guns' safeties off and opened the doors to the noise.

Jon A. Hunt

Chapter Thirty-one

The floodlights on their towers couldn't be counted on. They might dribble a helpful glow from the high fog to reveal railcars, but a runaway kid would disappear when the sun did. And if we waited for backup, we might as well just shoot Sal ourselves. Four of us ventured immediately into the yard: Smally, me, two regular cops. A third cop was tasked with finding someone who could stop the trains. We didn't have grand expectations—the trains never paused for holidays, dinner or bedtime—but trying couldn't hurt. The best plan I could conceive was to alternate between rails, each man pausing to survey the alleys between cars, then continuing westward. The trains traveled slowly and stepping up and over couplings was doable, though a misstep could be fatal.

Balance became a special challenge. Great shuddering steel hulks created the moving walls of each slender canyon, traveling at different speeds. The sky was a stripe of blended yellows and grays. Hardpacked gravel and ice underfoot were just a darker version of the sky, with no horizon for reference. I crouched and touched a gloved hand to the ground to orient myself. I couldn't imagine anyone getting used to the noise; even with ear protection it was excruciating. Less affected senses adapted to compensate: the earth shivered like a breathing monster, dusk's renewed chill stung my cheeks, there was a tang of diesel fumes and grease. None of these would

Flintlock

warn me of danger on two legs.

The people I'd battled to extricate Aubrea from Vanderbilt were here. *He* was here, *Bigfoot*, or whatever his real name was. That dead detective's head had been twisted like a jar lid, just like the dead man's outside Mitch's Columbia home. They were searching, same as us. Our dancing roof lights hadn't scared them off.

I held my breath so it wouldn't obscure my view, looked north, looked south. No Sal. No one else. The Smith & Wesson's checkered grips bit through my clenched glove. I straightened and faced a westward wall of black petroleum tankers. A red warning sign winked for every coupling that passed.

Gauge speed. Get ready. Jump up. Gauge speed. Jump down again on the far side.

I landed in another crouch in another gravel-bottomed alley. The motion around me only contributed partially to my vertigo. Piercing shrieks messed with my equilibrium as well.

Somebody stepped into the corridor, a hundred feet away. The .45 came up.

He was big. An easy target.

Smally paused and let me decide not to shoot before waving me on.

It occurred to me to peer *under* rolling cars before crossing this time. With a grimace Smally couldn't read at that distance, I unbent my knees—then froze again.

A third form had joined us between the cars. Not in uniform, instantly stationary, he stared around Smally and waited. Warning Smally without being seen was impossible. It was a weak point in our rushed strategy.

The third person melted into the shadows seconds after I'd spotted him. Smally didn't twitch till I nodded an all-clear. He'd sensed trouble without seeing it, a seasoned cop's intuition. He snagged the ladder on a passing railcar and hauled himself aloft to ride southward. I followed his example and crept the opposite direction to make my own crossing someplace else.

A fresh glare stabbed underneath reverberant steel. A diesel-electric locomotive followed its sun of a headlamp ahead of a procession of black cylinders. Ice sparkled. Gravel danced. Bright and dark sides of every pebble were crisply defined. Discarded bottles flared. Twin ribbons of silver fire raced down the rails.

Even in the added light, organic signs I hoped—or dreaded—to find didn't materialize. No feet could be seen under the cars, small or large. No white shoelaces. I supposed by now Sal's Reeboks wore the same gray dinge as everything else. Either way, I didn't see him.

I got myself onto a coupling, hesitated to assess my resolve, dropped again from between cars into a new gravel-floored canyon. That narrow slot felt uninhabited. The tanker cars hustling along its western flank moved too quickly for a casual hop between them. My only choice was to wait for the iron parade to pass. When it finished, I stepped over empty tracks left in its wake. Then someone shot at me.

Train brakes and gunfire were all the same to my stopped ears. A bullet skipping off metal beside my head, though, was hard to mistake for anything else. My knees and elbows plowed up frozen gravel. The semiautomatic bucked and spat half-audible flames as I slid. I had no time to dial in a target. Whether I hit what I needed, or two jacketed .45 caliber slugs pinballed between trains till gravity overpowered them, no one returned fire.

This hadn't been a friendly accident. Our band of four had agreed not to shoot first, only in defense. Chivalry was another weak point in our plan, even if it kept us from killing each other. I pressed the ground away with my free hand. The semiautomatic jutted ahead of me. Of course, my next foe

Flintlock

might be *behind* me.

I accelerated to a jog, keeping as tight to boxcars on one side as possible without tripping over tie ends. Dim graffiti traveled beside me, extending from the car's lowermost edges to as high as amateur spray cans could reach; some of it was good enough to be called "art" in a different setting. I caught the ladder welded to the mural, pulled my feet up, rode the route my bullets had taken. The edges of shadows began to merge. Lofty floodlights only made the fog more apparent. I remembered the penlight in my jacket, as good an invitation for foes to blow me full of holes as I'd ever find. Too bad. Once the sun completely failed, we'd all be blind as well as deaf.

More concentrated brilliance argued the point, slipped between moving parts: another locomotive. Where had the cop sent to stop these trains gone? Were engineers *that* oblivious to a railyard full of trespassers?

I used the next interval between cars like a door. Another passage opened. Pebbles turned again beneath my shoes. The same illegal frescos lurched past me.

There was the usual noise.

Always the noise.

A relentless aural agony of steel gnawing steel that all the hearing protection on earth couldn't mitigate, I felt it through my soles and exposed skin. And beyond this iron canyon lay another, then dozens more, all of them full to their lumbering brims with that goddamned shrieking. The Radnor yard might as well be a million miles across.

My distraction almost got me killed. He capitalized on it and rejoined me from an unexpected direction. The character who'd tested me already for target practice stepped from the same train segment, four cars to my right, and fired at me again.

What might count as bad luck another time saved my life. The cars pitched without warning as I jumped. I landed on ice and stumbled. A bullet intended for my head ricocheted from metal inches above it.

I embraced the fall and scrambled for cover that didn't exist. More shots chased me along the rough ground, carving angry furrows and spitting gravel around me. Another locomotive headlamp half blinded me. Alternating brilliance and blackness ruined whatever sense of direction I still had, but it also disoriented my assailant and he let go of his trigger. I pivoted on a knee. Massive rusty wheels—gigantic meat slicers—squealed a lot closer than any sane person would've let them.

When he wasn't actively trying to kill me, I couldn't find the man. I kept my left hand over the .45's tritium front sight. Lining a bead on anything here would be tough, but a pro only needed the tiniest betraying gleam.

A finger of light stretched between cars to touch my enemy's pale face. A new flame stabbed out from a new angle. Somebody else took advantage of the moment before I could. The pale face disappeared in an ugly wet mist and the man spun permanently into the shadows.

The rectangle of light found me next, the Metro cop a half second later. He stood twenty steps to the south. At least, I thought that was south. We were close enough to recognize each other. He nodded grimly, lowered his service weapon.

A hand like a steam shovel shot from a passing gap, cupped the officer's head and slapped it flat against a spray-painted boxcar.

• • •

Getting farther from that monster had always been the sensible thing to do. Till now. This time, he and I had the same reason for being there. I wasn't happy about it. I waited for my Goliath to stomp clear of the shadows.

He was wrapped in dark colors—*dressed* seemed too civilized an adjective in his case—and his only weapons were

Flintlock

those prodigious hands. The six .45 caliber stones in my sling didn't concern him as long as he wagged a Nashville policeman as a shield between us. The brute possessed enough guile to understand I wouldn't risk shooting even a dead cop.

The cop certainly was dead. Railcars hadn't paused for our little drama; the steel where his brains were smudged bounced through my peripheral vision. A man doesn't lose that much of himself and talk about it later.

Vertical bars of stray light dimmed as the locomotive that cast them pressed deeper into a restless steel forest. Murals and gore lost resolution. My final sight in that narrow corridor of anything smaller than a train was grotesque. Bigfoot smiled at me.

It was my turn.

I spun, groped for a handhold, lucked out and caught a ladder rung. Bigfoot hurled his lifeless burden, a two-hundred-pound knuckleball with whirling limbs. The body crashed into the car behind me, tangled in the wheels and vanished. I was glad I couldn't hear that. But I did sense the steam shovel hands reaching for me next.

My options were limited.

I pivoted on the ladder and fired. One, two, three shots went squarely into the space between the arms. A hideous brick-browed grimace flashed into view with each pull of the trigger. The expression showed more rage than pain. But he fell back without grabbing me.

My chest slammed against the ladder rungs again. I scrambled upward. There was nothing on the ground I wanted any part of.

• • •

The gloom was less pronounced above the trains than between them. Mists gnawed inward from the perimeter, but I could see farther there than I could shoot. Red and white streaks betrayed the interstate's elevated route. Rectangular halos fringed billboards, all featureless from my vantage point, because advertising is wasted on freight trains. Nearer at hand, boxcars and tankers jostled along in tight protracted columns, huge bleating inorganic sheep hustled toward unseen corrals. I rode like a clever herd dog atop his subjects.

I wasn't the *only* dog.

Packs of us prowled the train tops. The other predatory shapes weren't close enough to identify as friend or foe, though there were too many to be only my associates. No doubt they wondered about me, too.

We all recognized the rabbit.

Sal had reasoned that higher might be safer. Bigfoot hadn't yet ventured topside. I was aware of him barreling alongside me at a shocking pace, but so far, he stayed on the ground. The kid ran quick as his twiggy legs could go. When he leaped the gaps between cars, his flailing limbs reminded me of a dandelion seed. He often slipped on ice or tripped over his own shoelaces. Those undone laces were going to kill him before the hunting pack did.

Chance had put me on top of the same line of cars. I couldn't get Sal's attention even then. Shouting wouldn't work. Waving my arms would attract the wrong eyes. I'd have to manage what Smally hadn't: I'd have to outrun the kid. I holstered my gun and sprinted.

He moved pretty fast. I ran faster. I hadn't skipped as many meals and when I did sleep, it wasn't in unwatched doorways or behind dumpsters. There are reasons most prey animals have short life spans. And even squirrels don't run with their hands over their ears.

New colors touched my senses, a lot of reds, even more blues, ill-defined beyond the fog. Their sources were obvious.

Officer down.

Metro police descended on the Radnor yard from east and west. Smally's war cry had summoned them.

Flintlock

The boy must know they were present. He scrambled onward just the same. So did the other shapes hunting on top of the trains. Predators and prey were running out of time.

Brightness lanced inward from the valley edges. Spotlights. The beams didn't quite reach us. I imagined somebody calling over a loudspeaker for us all to stand still, drop weapons, raise our hands, except that nothing could possibly be heard above the rending screams of a thousand scraping wheels. No one had stopped the trains.

My toe found a raised hatch that my eyes missed and I belly-flopped onto corrugated steel and skidded. Only by throwing my arms wide was I able to keep from tumbling off the railcar altogether.

Sal darted out of focus while I reacquainted myself with my knees. Another hunter earned my notice: he'd also stopped running. He might have shot me between the eyes while I waited to see whose side he was on, but he didn't.

They don't want to take him anywhere.
They just want him dead.

He raised his weapon and aimed it at the boy, something no cop would do. I hauled out my gun and blasted him off the top of his train.

Pain repaid action, a burning dragon's claw scratching my neck. There was nothing mythical about it; I'd been creased by bullets before. No muzzle flash. Must be from behind me. I twisted, lined the .45's sights up on the only possibility, fired again. The second shooter left his perch like he'd been yanked away on a string.

There weren't any immediate others. Trading fire with me lost appeal as the valley began to sparkle with blue lights. Trouble was, I'd look just like another bad guy to newly arrived law enforcement. I got up and followed the kid. He'd shrunk

Jon A. Hunt

with distance, but the last car in the line was visible. He'd have to stop and climb down—

Massive dark shoulders interrupted my passage. Bigfoot had overcome his dislike of heights. He popped up between us, right behind Sal, and swatted the boy off the undulating steel as casually as flicking a spider off a porch rail.

With the boy out of the way, I had a clean shot. The Smith & Wesson's lone remaining round put a .45 caliber dent between the bastard's shoulder blades.

This perturbed him mightily. Ferocious little eyes glittered in the police lights, tiny blue electric sparks. It didn't matter whether he remembered me. Either way he meant to do to me what he'd done to Mitch Braunfelter. He lowered his head and charged. I didn't feel those piledriver footfalls because he'd climbed up two cars away; the separation wouldn't last seconds. I stayed on my knees—no way in hell would I outrun him—ejected the spent magazine, rammed in a spare from my jacket pocket, snapped the slide forward to seat the first round.

He bounded across the first coupling as if there was no gap at all.

Maybe before he tore my head off, I could put a slug in his eye. None of the other times I shot him had gone my way. Bigfoot could be made of cast iron, for all I knew. No Achille's heel.

He cleared the last gap. Now I felt his approach through my kneecaps, cold steel slamming my nerves in time with those giant stomping feet. Too bad I couldn't hear him. I bet he was yelling really poetic stuff.

A wall of blackness shut out my forward vision.

I leveled the gun, for all the good it would do me.

No Achille's heel.

Realization hit me before Bigfoot could. The .45's barrel dipped. The brute's arms reached for me. I didn't care about his arms.

Flintlock

1-2-3-4-5-6-7.

I kept pulling the trigger till the slide locked back. Saving one reserve shot wouldn't help me if blasting the shit out of Bigfoot's *feet* didn't stop him.

The contracting universe between us blazed with staccato flames. My would-be executioner lunged weirdly. Jolts like simultaneous sledgehammers assaulted both of my knees. Bigfoot toppled so violently he caved in a portion of the railcar's roof. He slipped, tried to regain his balance, then vanished in the gap between cars.

• • •

I had to climb back down. The kid was on the ground. People who wanted him under it were there, too. Their goal may already have been accomplished but Sal had tried to ask for my help; I couldn't fail him like I'd failed Mitch. I stayed on top of the train long enough to feed the semiautomatic my last spare magazine.

The train hesitated also. It still trembled with potential and its iron neighbors hadn't stopped moving. This one wouldn't linger long. The high floodlights stained coagulating vapors beneath them, burning soft-edged circles centered on the bases of their steel towers. Everything within the circles turned unflattering hues of cheap lager and urine; beyond the circles lay black featurelessness. The interstate and billboards were smothered. Blue pulses danced among crawling hulks, though lights and obstacles were equally blurred and blended by the fog.

I guessed at the ground and dropped from the ladder's last rung, essentially into a sea of India ink. Between trains, my eyes had nothing to adapt to. Coarse gravel stopped me a foot sooner than expected. I reluctantly reached into my jacket for my penlight.

The little electric beam played across greasy ties, clean-scraped steel, ladders, levers, chains, bolt heads. The .45's nose tracked with my eyes. I was mighty unpopular to be waving a flare around in the dark. But this alley felt lonelier than the high places I'd just quit.

When I did spot another person, I found no comfort in it.

Bigfoot dangled in a knot of limbs, chains and hydraulic hoses, between the boxcars where he'd fallen. He was nowhere near as dead as I'd have liked. At least he was upside-down. I studied him in the penlight beam despite my loathing. Beady savage eyes glared back at me from above a brow like a sidewalk curb. He thrashed against his accidental bonds, but chains are sturdier than 2x4 stud walls and held.

No wonder our earlier encounters hadn't fazed him. I'd seen jackets like his before, chunky bulletproof Kevlar. His obviously was custom-fitted and extra layers had been added. The thing must weigh as much as a small pony. When someone Bigfoot's size comes after a person, instinct never opts for the head shot. I noted with morbid satisfaction that his gargantuan unprotected feet were messes of torn leather, blood and splintered bone.

The train lurched. He settled till his head was within a foot of the rails. A mouthful of chipped teeth opened in a roar my deadened ears couldn't hear. Huge fists closed over sections of hose, ripped them free. Black hydraulic fluid spurted in frantic strings. Chains lost their grip. Legs like dock pilings wriggled earthward and the bloodied feet touched down.

My gun sights lined up between the ugly pig eyes. I'd only get to pull the trigger once more.

The assembly shuddered into motion without further pause. Someone half a mile away had decided a thousand tons of steel ought to be farther down the tracks.

Bigfoot surged a final time against his failing restraints. It doesn't take a PhD to calculate your odds against a loaded gun versus a moving train. The last loops gave way. His crippled feet caught under a rail and, big as he was, the train neither

Flintlock

noticed nor cared. He clutched at rusty couplings, then the car's undercarriage, as he was dragged inexorably beneath it. The first set of double wheels slowly carved him and his Kevlar jacket into smaller thrashing pieces.

Not being able to hear wasn't such a bad thing.

I averted my eyes and the penlight beam as the train gathered speed, and wheels after wheels after wheels repeated what their brethren had done.

Jon A. Hunt

Chapter Thirty-two

Eleven steps from the subdivided remains of his fearsome antagonist, my penlight found a lump wearing filthy untied shoes. The kid lay in a heap of filthy leftover snow, where he'd landed, curled into a fetal position with both hands over his ears. The fall hadn't broken him. He'd just decided flight held less promise of escape than death did.

I closed a glove over the light, so a trickle escaped between my fingers. The .45 went back into its holster. If anyone in the shadows wanted to take a potshot at me there wasn't a damn thing I could do about it here. I rummaged in my pockets for the second packet of disposable earplugs. With the penlight propped between us in the gravel, I pantomimed an explanation, then set the packet within his reach.

Wide, wary eyes glittered. For all the resignation in his posture, he reminded me of a cornered ferret. I let him have the time he needed to recognize me. His hands stayed clamped to the sides of his head. The shrilling of train wheels made *my* skull ring and I had protection. The boy had to be in agony.

Twiggy shivering fingers reached for the plugs.

• • •

Sal had a twisted ankle from his fall and little energy left to walk. I swaddled him in my coat and carried him in my left arm, against my hip, the way a mother might lug an outsized

Flintlock

infant. A fourteen-year-old ought to be much heavier. The Smith & Wesson returned to service and pointed down our path, northward, between trains. We'd have to find unoccupied tracks to cross. I'd seen the results of getting tangled between cars.

New lights blazed ahead, more rooftop blues, and high-powered searchlights, the kind affixed to police cruisers. Another ominous broad-shouldered shape stepped into the alley to meet us. I lifted the .45's muzzle skyward so anyone could tell I didn't mean to shoot. Smally's was a familiar silhouette.

• • •

Our situation changed rapidly once Smally reentered the picture. Cops in tactical gear stepped from the mists to encircle us. They bristled with assault rifles and discipline. We were herded across empty tracks and around now idle trains: the necessary railroad exec had been contacted at last. A big white van waited, not an unmarked mystery vehicle, an official police rig decked out in more blinking lights than a Dollywood Christmas tree. Smally held the back doors open and a uniformed EMT helped Sal aboard and sat him on one of the lengthwise bench seats. The guy had the best bedside manner I'd ever seen. He administered a bottle of water and a granola bar, both of which the boy inhaled.

Smally and I parked ourselves on the opposite bench. Somebody banged the doors shut and off the van went, bouncing up a dirt road to speed us away from rails and noise and death. We pried the foam plugs out of our ears.

The ride didn't last five minutes. Tire roar softened when asphalt replaced dirt beneath us. Then the driver pulled off the street, doused the lights and set the parking brake. Sal's eyes found me in the soft glow of cabin lights. That trust he placed in me was wearing thin. The EMT gave his bony shoulder a reassuring pat that didn't reassure and exited with Smally through the rear doors. A damp chill reached inward for a few seconds. When the doors closed again we shared the space with Jerry Rafferty and a tantalizing aroma of fried chicken.

"Figured you'd be hungry."

Rafferty plunked a cardboard bucket full of greasy decadence, a bag of apples, and a six-pack of Coke onto the seat within Sal's reach. It was just us three and fried chicken. The driver had strategically excused himself.

Sal hesitated. A single granola bar couldn't compete with the feast Rafferty offered, but this teenager's wariness was the only reason he'd survived to join our little get-together at all. He also couldn't hear a word. I tapped my earlobe to remind him. His eyes widened and he dug grubby fingertips into his ears.

"Sal, this is Lieutenant Rafferty. He's a friend." I spoke up. My voice probably got to his brain with all the clarity of fish burps. "He brought the food for you."

Hunger won out. Sal tore the lid off the bucket and attacked its contents. Rafferty shot me an I-told-you-so look, when he knew damned well neither of us had many chances lately to tell the other anything. The smell was maddening. I'd missed a meal or two myself. But there wasn't enough to share with a famished street rat. We watched and waited. Before progressing to an apple, Sal employed paper napkins in a way that demonstrated civilized upbringing. He'd escaped clean linens, regular meals and daily baths for this paradise.

"Thanks."

His volume was more appropriate for a hockey match than the inside of a vehicle. Damaged eardrums would have to relearn indoor dynamics. He bit into the apple and chewed deliberately. Bandaged knees, a taped ankle, weeks' worth of grime, in the back of a police van, he was already developing a swagger. Tough kid.

"Am I under arrest?"

Rafferty wagged his close-cropped head. "Just want you to

Flintlock

answer a few questions."

"What if my answers are wrong?"

"You aren't under arrest. No cuffs, right?" The Lieutenant sounded weary. The DA's voice must still be echoing in that miniscule downtown office of his.

"I can go whenever I want? Now?"

Rafferty's eye twitch might not convey full meaning to the kid. Teenagers under the best of circumstances can be pretty clueless. It made *me* wince. I played diplomat, because we needed Sal's cooperation as much as he needed ours.

"People died on your account tonight," I said.

This tempered his attitude. He hadn't considered events down in the railyard from others' perspectives.

"I'm sure you didn't ask for any of this," I continued while Rafferty held his tongue. "The cops who died were doing their jobs. Those men chasing you would've done so no matter what you did. But it isn't over till we find them all, find out why. Jerry, was everyone in the railyard accounted for?"

He gave a terse "no."

I looked Sal in the eye. "We can't protect you unless you talk with us. Do you have anywhere better to run?"

"Your two friends didn't," Rafferty added.

"I—I don't know," the kid stammered.

"What? Who?" Rafferty's impatience got the better of him.

Sal's expression personified loneliness. "*Any*one," he said. "I don't know anyone here. Not now. Was just me, Tom, Nat. Nat set up the jobs. *He* knew people. My job was to read the notes left in the book. I can read, you know! But there weren't friends to make, and new people are dangerous. I never saw who left the notes. I never talked with anybody in the store. I don't know who those men by the trains were, or that...that..."

Once unleashed, his words came in a flurry. He missed plain conversation. Only the hardiest fugitive can deny a

291

Jon A. Hunt

hardwired need for human interaction, certainly no fugitive in his teens can. But Sal ran out of steam when he tried to describe the behemoth who'd crawled out of his nightmares and swatted him off a boxcar. He hadn't seen Bigfoot's exit.

"You don't need to worry about him now," I said.

Funny. The savage who fed Mitch Braunfelter to his own brick wall was now a similar mess down in the Radnor yard. Justice doesn't get more complete than that. Why didn't I feel even a hint of resolution?

"What notes? What book?" Rafferty persisted.

The boy hesitated.

"Sal, we're on your side. We aren't here to judge or punish. Okay?"

He nodded dazedly. Then he remembered the apple. He took another bite. His ability to dart between wariness and casual irreverence was impressive, for a charade. He finished chewing, then: "Which book, which shelf, which aisle. Where to take it. Our orders were typed on a loose sheet inside the big green book."

"Poe. *Tales of Mystery*."

Rafferty stared. Sal understood. I'd retrieved that big green book from him right inside O'Dell's chirping front door. I'd tapped the loose page in. I'd handed the book to Raleigh while he yelled at me. Maybe tonight could have gone differently, or been avoided altogether, if I'd been more curious about the book.

"That's the one," Sal admitted. "It was Nat's idea. Or his boss's. He took credit, but he didn't read so well. Sometimes there were other instructions, like stay away till a certain day or where to go besides the store to...get things. A lot of times there wasn't a note at all and we had to keep coming back to check."

Rafferty's face might as well be chipped from limestone now. I knew from experience the less he showed on the

Flintlock

outside, the faster his brain was going. We were thinking alike.

...get things.

Poe's *Tales of Mystery* acted as a dispatch system. Sal and his ill-fated comrades had been contract thieves. Nothing else explained how they kept getting into the store, kept finding such valuable books to steal in a place where only the staff had a clue how to find anything. Rafferty's unspoken hunch had been on the money. Sal's bunch had help on the inside.

"How'd you get paid?" he asked.

Sal didn't seem to mind explaining for the time being. He'd decided to take us at Rafferty's word on that Get Out of Jail Free card. "We left the books different places. In cemeteries, under the bags in city trash cans, in parks—never the same place twice. There'd be a bag with cash in it waiting. Only at the times in the notes. If we got there early or late, nothing."

"You always left the right book when you took the money?"

Sal pried a Coke loose from the plastic rings and popped the tab like he was who'd bought them. He downed half the can in one go. Running for your life is thirsty business. He finished the Coke and set it empty on the bench seat.

"What kinda thief do you take me for?"

Rafferty's patience slipped a cog. "You tell *me*," he snarled. "It took seventeen live cops and four dead ones, not to mention your new best friend Bedlam here, to get you out of that yard alive. I'm just trying to figure what you did that so many people want you dead."

That let some of the air out of the kid. "We—we wouldn't dare skip out on a drop," he stammered. "They were always watching."

"How do you know?"

"Same way we knew cops were watching."

I stowed my grin before Rafferty spotted it. Their cat-and-mouse game was almost worth the price of admission.

"What about the other stuff?"

293

"What other stuff?"

"When you were sent places besides the bookstore."

Sal clearly regretted his earlier mention of *getting things*. Fried chicken had distracted him. He was smarter on a full stomach. He shrugged.

"Been to Belle Meade lately?"

Sal shrugged.

"You have. I talked with the Uber driver who took you, to an estate with high stone walls. People saw the three of you wandering the streets after dark before that. That's weird in that neighborhood. Folks notice. They described Tom, Nathan and you accurately enough."

No shrugs now. The boy wore that haunted wariness I remembered from our first encounter in O'Dell's. Rafferty's zinger was only a surprise to me.

"The guy who lived there was killed that night," the Lieutenant added, almost as an aside.

My brain raced at least as fast as the kid's. I'd assumed the three boys played a transitional role; I hadn't considered Sal and his cohorts might have stolen the red journal from Jorgensen's estate in the first place. They couldn't have been the ones who turned the mansion upside down looking for what wasn't there. And Sal didn't strike me as a killer—an assessment Rafferty plainly shared, or he'd already be in cuffs—which meant the estate had had *three* unwelcome visits by the time the alarm finally went off.

Connecting the men who'd killed Keller Ableman on the Chickasaw boat ramp to the men in the railyard wasn't just a reasonable deduction. It was the only one. They had a better idea than Sal where the red journal was now. What had he and his friends done that still merited death?

Not what they'd *done*… Smally's guess might be closer than anyone's.

Witness?

Flintlock

"We never hurt anybody."

Rafferty's gaze narrowed to a pinpoint at the end of Sal's freckled nose.

"You were there, though," I said. "You were seen."

Sal's nod was barely perceptible.

"And you saw something a person would kill to keep hidden, didn't you?"

No nod this time. No response at all. Rafferty supplied the final impetus.

"As long as you're the only one who knows, you're living on borrowed time."

"I don't—I don't want to go to jail..."

"Being dead is one way to avoid it."

"Cooperation now goes a long way toward keeping you free *and* alive," I suggested.

Wide terrified eyes studied me. Trust is a risky venture. The whine of a siren rose outside, sped nearer, reached a crescendo then diminished again, a reminder of the cold dangerous world outside. Much of it never got any friendlier just for the holidays.

"Okay," Sal said.

• • •

His voice softened as his hearing recovered. He probably hadn't ever been a loud boy. Rafferty and I leaned forward to understand. Fear edged the narrative, though the immediacy of that night weeks ago had been tempered with weariness.

"Nat got us the ride. He was tall and had an ID that said he was older. He had one of those prepaid phones. I think somebody we never saw paid for the car. The driver didn't ask for nothing but directions."

"Uh huh," rumbled the Lieutenant. I could tell by his tone he'd found only dead ends in that regard, except for the ride share driver.

Sal blinked at him and continued.

Jon A. Hunt

"We were early. We were excited. This one should pay enough we wouldn't have to work again for a long time. The trick was getting inside. Nat took us out that way a few times and we looked around and found the back gate. The plan was to come back a different night, but then this big fancy car drove up. The man in the car talked with the intercom and the gate opened. Tom said we should go in now. So, we sneaked in behind the car before the gate shut."

"Did you see who was in the car?" Rafferty asked.

"No. Mostly we just saw the lights."

Sal's eyes ping-ponged between Rafferty and me. Neither of us gave any indication we'd heard all we wanted. He went on.

"Tom figured out the door lock in the dark after the man from the car went in. He said the alarm wouldn't reset for a while. There weren't any cameras. We knew from watching the place everyone who worked there had left for the weekend. We just had to be careful inside.

"The...things...we were sent for were in a desk drawer in an office—"

"Not locked up?" Rafferty interrupted. "Just in a plain old drawer? The little red book?"

Sal tilted his head slightly, like a hound listening for rustles in the brush. "Top drawer with the other stuff. Just like the note said."

Rafferty's features weren't outwardly readable. But he must be wondering who among Jorgensen's ill-used household staff had outmaneuvered his team during questioning. O'Dell's had no monopoly on inside theft connections. Someone out there seemed to know all the pertinent details and we'd learned next to nothing.

"My job was to keep watch on the men in the back room," Sal went on. "I couldn't see, I just heard them talking. It didn't last long."

"What did they say?" Rafferty pressed.

Flintlock

The boy's complexion paled. His voice wavered. "I couldn't hear words. One of them sounded angry. I thought it was the man from the car, but it could have been the man who lived there, too. The other man...he...laughed."

"*Laughed?*" I blurted the word with enough force to make our youthful narrator jump.

"Yeah," he said after a tense pause. "Not like he heard a joke. It was a mean laugh. Like a mad scientist in an old movie, over and over and over—and then there was a loud bang."

"A gunshot?"

"I guess. Except it didn't *sound* right. Kind of like when they shoot up fireworks on the Fourth, you know?"

"Black powder," Rafferty growled.

"Sal, did you see either of the men's faces?"

He'd gone quiet. I realized the van's police radio had been shut off. All I heard was my own pulse and a faint whistle of air leaving Rafferty's nostrils.

"Sal?"

The boy shifted in his seat. What seemed an eon later, he said: "I was too afraid to move. I just froze in the hall. Nat and Tom ran out where I could see them. Tom knocked over a little table. A man came out from a door between us. He had an old-fashioned wooden gun. Smoke came out of it. He looked right at me!"

"Describe him!" Rafferty barked. But Sal's nerves had tightened to the snapping point.

"I...I...we ran! As fast as we could. His face was all hate and I thought he'd kill me, kill us all, but he didn't and we ran! We ran..."

"You're safe now," I soothed. It took effort to tamp down excitement in my words. "Tell us what you can."

The boy swallowed and bobbed his head. He seemed in need of another granola bar. Rafferty's looming presence didn't help. He rallied anyway.

Jon A. Hunt

"I didn't know him," he said. "I don't know anybody. But his clothes were fancy. Same as the car. Wedding clothes. He was kinda bald…"

The rectangle of my phone dazzled all three of us in the darkened van. I squinted and tapped in the search. Something would come up. Important people are always getting their pictures taken whether they want it or not.

"This man?"

If he hadn't been contained, we'd have lost the kid again. He shot a couple feet to the left when I showed him the news photo on the little screen.

"Sal?"

"Yeah! Yeah, that's him!"

I didn't put my phone in Rafferty's outstretched paw. Danny Ayer's trick electronics would shut the device off if I let go of it. But I turned it in his direction. The Lieutenant's words traveled on a hiss.

"Arthur Fontaine!"

"Or his butler," I said.

Flintlock

Chapter Thirty-three

Rafferty drove. Not his personal Cadillac, this was an official unmarked Dodge. He pushed it like it belonged to someone else. Two standard Metro cruisers kept us company, lights and sirens and everything, and once we swept onto I-65 all three cars hurtled northward in excess of a hundred miles an hour. Nashville drivers, not normally the best at getting out of emergency vehicles' way, took the hint tonight. Probably they thought Rafferty and I were in the getaway car. The fog from above the railyard couldn't quite hold onto the interstate. A mile after we shot across the river, clean black skies and stars as sharp as pinholes in velvet spread before us. The fog would be thicker than anywhere by the lake in Hendersonville, though.

"Any luck?" The Lieutenant had to shout over radio chatter and engine howl.

I mashed my phone to an ear and concentrated on the same unanswered ringtones I'd already heard two dozen times in the last ten minutes. I hung up without leaving a message. Tipper had six from me already. Aubrea wasn't answering her phone either.

"No," I said.

Rafferty was pissed. I liked to think he was mad at the circumstances, but I had my fingers on everything that was suddenly wrong. Tipper had the ill-omened red journal, half of Lewis' coded letter, the DA's daughter, and probably a ramrod

299

Jon A. Hunt

from the antique pistol that had killed Erik Jorgensen. And if Sal's account was to be believed, Tipper had taken all of those directly to the murderer to ask damning questions.

One of the Metro boys babysitting the estate had escorted Tipper and the girl out of Belle Meade. Then a traffic accident diverted him. Tipper and Aubrea continued to Fontaine's lakeside property by themselves.

"What do you really know about Fontaine?"

"Not a goddamned thing more than I'm told," came the reply. "But if you're wrong, showing up in a huff at dinnertime will sure as hell get me fired. Kid didn't have any *names*. Could've been anybody Jorgensen let in."

He plainly didn't agree with his own words. The boy had been sent downtown under protective custody. Rafferty had made certain Smally would be with him the entire trip, then we were going like hell toward Hendersonville.

"It's a foolproof alibi," he muttered.

"Ever meet that doppelganger of a butler of his?"

"Gerard. Sure. Questioned him myself. They could be twins, except the one's always drunk off his ass."

"What if he's just drunk for show?"

"Fontaine's acting was so good we had to pour three pots of coffee into him to get a statement. But he had a houseful of guests drinking with him that night. All told the same story. What's your point?"

"Did you ask if they ever saw Fontaine and Gerard in the same room together?"

Rafferty swore like a sailor with a stubbed toe.

• • •

The parkway through Hendersonville might as well have been a parking *lot* after a quarter hour of triple-digit speeds. Nobody drove fast in that smothering lake fog, not even the police. The cruisers doused their roof lights and blended into the gloom behind us. If this turned out to be a wild goose chase,

Flintlock

Rafferty preferred his embarrassment served with less fanfare.

"We need them, I'll call them," he said.

Traffic was minimal on the main drag except at intersections. There, headlights and tail lights passed meekly beneath red, amber and emerald glares that seemed to hover unsupported in the vapors. Residential streets lay emptier still and amounted to a slow motorized crawl into blindness. Signposts melted to invisibility before they got to their signs. The only way to identify our path was the five-inch navigation screen on the dashboard. Rafferty confirmed street boundaries more times than he liked by bouncing the tires off curbs.

I tried my phone again. Tipper's and Aubrea's numbers, once each. Nothing. I traded the phone for my gun and checked the magazine.

"Glovebox," the Lieutenant said.

Behind the little hatch, between an owner's manual and a flashlight, I found a full seven-shot magazine for a bobtailed Smith & Wesson .45 semiautomatic.

"I confiscate your sidearm often enough, it was bound to happen," Rafferty said.

I stowed the .45 and the extra magazine inside my jacket.

Fog lathered the car windows. It skulked with increasing reluctance from the headlamp beams as we approached the unseen lakeshore. Festive colors pulsed a few times—unlike Jorgensen's stuffy neighborhood, this one hadn't entirely shunned Christmas lights—but these attempts at cheer eventually ceased and inky dampness reigned supreme. The navigation screen showed a familiar Chinese dragon shape. Rafferty twisted the volume knob on the radio till the crackle of remote conversations became digital mice rustling. He also unholstered his service weapon and set it muzzle down in the cupholder.

Wavering yellow smears bracketed the car minutes later. Rafferty pulled between the gas lampposts into Fontaine's

Jon A. Hunt

driveway and levered the transmission into park. He extinguished the headlights but let the motor idle. For fifteen seconds we sat without speaking, our faces outlined by the aura of gaslights, waiting for our eyes to adjust. Sounds seeped into the cabin to compete with the radio's muted scurries, our breathing, the hum of the engine. Ragged sputters of gas flames became discernable. A door shut somewhere ten yards or a mile away; fog made distant and near noises indistinguishable from one another. A motor growled and tires rolled on a coarse surface, out of sight yet close enough to hear.

We'd have seen a glow from Fontaine's showy front entry if it weren't for the fog. Moon and stars glittering on the lake beyond the mansion's silhouette wasn't too much to expect, on a clear night. I hadn't yet been here during one of those.

"I'd rather neither of them was down there."

Rafferty's voice jarred me from my thoughts. The other vehicle was nearer. How much nearer, I couldn't say, and the mirrors were all dark. "Me, too," I said.

He grunted and unlatched his seatbelt.

"Hit the lights!" I yelled.

Rafferty slapped at the lever and the headlamps flared. The car I'd heard moved too fast and came from too low to be anywhere except flying up the rough-paved driveway from the lake. Sudden brilliance exposed both vehicles so abruptly that Rafferty and I dived for our doors. The other car's lights were off. Instead of plowing head-on into us, the driver swerved. The car skidded on wet dead grass and slammed into the stone base of a lamppost on my side.

• • •

The car was a ten-year-old station wagon. The men inside it reacted faster than typical crash victims. In fact, the front passenger came out shooting. Rafferty's windshield fractured and sagged inward. Neither of us were waiting inside to catch bullets. Rafferty's 9mm spat twice from behind his open door

Flintlock

and the man from the station wagon spun like a dreidel and went down. He didn't stay down. When he reappeared, he was shooting again from behind the undamaged lamppost across the driveway. Rafferty returned fire, a dozen paces away now, where a stacked stone wall afforded better shelter. The useless radio winked tiny indicator lights at me through the open passenger door.

I kept the car between me and Rafferty's gun battle. I had other worries. Just beyond my .45's tritium sights was the station wagon's cracked windscreen. Two persons remained inside, pale faces in the glare of Rafferty's high beams.

The driver wasn't anyone I knew but the other face belonged to Tipper. There was no mistaking those curls, even when the features beneath them had been bludgeoned past familiarity. The lids of both eyes were purple and swollen so only a thin glint between them proved either consciousness or death. I guessed the former. Otherwise, the driver's hauling Tipper forward from a back seat by his hair and pressing a revolver muzzle to his bloodied temple made no sense.

Rafferty and his sparring partner had gone silent. One or both might be down, or maybe neither dared pop up from behind his chosen rock to find out. They didn't matter now. The men in the mangled station wagon mattered. Especially the one with the gun to his head.

Tipper's antagonist never looked my direction. He wasn't expecting either of them to live through the moment, because he didn't intend to negotiate with Tipper as a hostage.

They don't want to take him anywhere.
They just want him dead.

It was no ordinary gun. I noticed, the way I tend to notice details in a fraction of the usual time when room for action is compressed into pieces of seconds. The weapon was a Civil

Jon A. Hunt

War era revolver with a smooth cylinder and a barrel too long for concealed carry. Colt Army Model 1860, black powder, percussion type. A soldier's pistol. Tipper had let me shoot an identical specimen from Jorgensen's collection. It was plenty lethal at close range, but so is a baseball bat, and a bat doesn't need to be cocked before you can use it.

If the guy in the station wagon understood how a single-action revolver worked, he'd have pulled the hammer back.

I lined up my sights on the driver's profile from thirty feet away and killed him with one shot through the windshield.

• • •

A lamppost tilted from the front corner of the station wagon where a wheel used to be. The sheet metal from there back was buckled, and only pure determination could wrench the pinched door open. I had a lot of determination. A fresh corpse toppled out at my feet. Hard-edged shadows, where Rafferty's headlights didn't reach, either created the illusion of the body having no head or concealed the fact. The dome light came on inside the car and showed me more than I wanted to see.

Tipper slumped over the center console. He'd survived a hell of a beating, had a gun against his head, and heard a loud nasty bang. Passing out was as graceful a reaction as could be expected. Most of the blood wetting his shirt belonged to someone else. Rough crystals of safety glass sparkled in his curls. I kept low and touched his near shoulder. A blackened eye tried to look at me.

"You aren't dead," I assured him.

"Good to know," he quipped softly. His lips were split and a tooth was missing from the attempted smile.

"Aubrea...?"

The smile vanished. Smiling had to hurt. "He...took her. I don't know..."

"Who? Fontaine or Gerard?"

Flintlock

He weakly turned his head side to side. Tipper couldn't tell them apart, either.

"Can you walk?"

"I think so. Hands tied."

"Hang on."

The doors on the passenger side worked better. Using them meant more exposure but we needed to hurry. Two more gunshots assaulted the fog farther down the driveway: Rafferty and his opponent were still at it. I switched off the dome light. Tipper squirmed down to the chilled pavement with my help. His wrists were secured with zip ties. An avalanche of wood and metal clattered out with him. I holstered my .45 and dug for my pocketknife.

"What's with all the guns?" I asked.

The station wagon's splattered interior was littered with antique firearms, none newer than the first World War, except for a Glock 21 on the front seat.

"From Fontaine's collection," Tipper said. He leaned back against the open door and gingerly kneaded circulation into his right wrist. The fingers of that hand pointed the wrong directions, all broken. "They just heaved the lot into the car. I doubt any are loaded."

I wondered if any court of law would fault me for killing a man when I knew his weapon wouldn't fire. It wasn't worth mentioning.

"You'll have to use it left-handed." I pressed the Glock into his good hand. This one *was* loaded. Tipper's would-be executioner must have simply grabbed the wrong gun. "Stay low. Crawl if you have to, just get away from the cars and keep out of sight. I'll and yell for you when all is clear. Rafferty is here. So's the character from the front seat. Please don't shoot Rafferty and don't pop up waving a gun, or pretty much anybody will mow you down. I'll go find the girl."

I tugged my gloves back on. My semiautomatic came back

305

Jon A. Hunt

out of the shoulder rig.

"They have the journal, Tyler. And the paper with the website address."

"I know." I started to leave.

"Not the letter." He almost grinned at my hesitation, thought better of it. "She worried about it when we lost our escort. It's in my shoe. They never looked."

"Tipper, you're amazing. Keep it. Don't get killed."

"I'll try. Same for you."

• • •

The most direct path to Fontaine's home seemed the least sensible. Combatants who couldn't see each other didn't let that stop them from trying to shoot across the driveway. I took a perpendicular route, downhill in the fog toward the lake. Fontaine owned lakefront property. I'd follow the lakefront to him.

The headlights of Rafferty's car flung my wobbly stick-figure shadow far out into the mists for a while. Then the fog dispersed everything in a billion useless directions, never permitting total blackness, still rendering any fool who dared to challenge it essentially blind. I heard only frost-crisped grass crunching underfoot. If anyone on the other lakeshore properties had called the police about those gunshots, there were no sirens yet. I was on my own.

Surprisingly, the air cleared by the time slick polished river rocks supplanted the brittle grass. Breezes out on the lake hustled the fog landward. Stars peered through cracks in the gloom. The water itself remained black, featureless, except at the edges where paper-thin layered ice glittered back at the stars. The rocks marched in a tight blanket of rounded lumps, millions of sleeping beetles. They weren't indigenous. Fontaine had had truckloads of stone applied to his allotment of lakeshore. Rich people detest mud. A fresh glimmer grazed the farthest stones: outside lights from the house.

Flintlock

I paused to listen. Still no sirens. I heard no gunshots, either. What I *did* detect was a familiar liquid burble. After my fun on the Duck River, the pulse of a boat engine was still fresh in my mind. Who would take a foggy lake cruise after dark, just before Christmas?

I went on. Concentrating on sounds was difficult while traversing an icy, uneven lakeshore. I'd have upped my pace in spite of the ice, except I'd found a body.

• • •

Maybe he'd hoped to follow the lake's edge back to the house as I did. For him, though, flight had degenerated to a crawl, then a slither, then he'd stopped altogether as an inanimate lump on the rocks. Another animal had dragged itself to the water to die.

I squatted beside the still form and assessed its condition as well as I could. No pulse. You need blood in your veins to have one, and the last of his faintly steamed on the rocks beneath him. He was probably the man from the station wagon who Rafferty had shot. I had no way of being certain. The semiautomatic he still held wasn't warm, nor was it as cool as the hand grasping it. Even in half-assed starlight, the dark wetness beneath the unzipped jacket was obvious. There was also a spattered plastic bag jammed into the waistband of his jeans, containing a familiar dark rectangle.

They have the journal, Tyler.

I left the gun. I left the red journal, too, for someone else to find. It hadn't brought luck to anyone. And I had more important concerns.

He took her.

I tramped again toward the lights and boat motor.

• • •

Mansion, stairs, a dock, and a yacht resolved into solids as I approached them. Light came from ovoid glass lamps with cast cages, fixed at regular intervals to the stair rail that descended from the house to a floating dock. Access to the dock was restricted by a high fence that extended outward from the base of the stairs. The dock was huge because the yacht was huge. It looked like a set-piece for a Bond movie. The yacht itself had no lights going. It just rocked patiently on Old Hickory's lazy offshore waves and purred.

Any goings-on happened upstairs in the house. Two tall windows showed hints of illuminance deep within. Noises of heavy items scraping across floors, and doors opening and shutting, leaked through the cedar walls. Last minute packing for a boat trip.

If roads leaving the estate were watched—let alone blocked by wrecked cars—the only quick escape would be over the lake.

The fence out past the shoreline would be impassible any night of the year when the lake hadn't frozen. Tonight, though, ice extended around the fence's end, left over from the earlier cold snap. I let the fence bear most of my weight and shuffled atop the ice to the outer terminus, then back again on shore to the dock. A gate across the bottom of the stairs was locked and its hinges had a squeaky look that warned me off. I hadn't come for the stairs. Just two ropes and simple knots tethered a multi-million-dollar getaway vehicle to the dock.

No ice collected around the sleek fiberglass hull. The boat hadn't been there long. Yachts have cozy winter nests and this one had only just returned to the water. The ropes quivered at my touch. The dock vibrated with the massive engines' breath. If anyone up in the house came running, I wouldn't hear them.

The freed craft moved easily. Lake water sloshed along her profound length as she responded to my tugs. Then the yacht drifted leisurely away, mooring lines trailing, and gave herself up to the returning mists. She was out of reach except by swimming, yet sounded as close as she had on my arrival.

Flintlock

I eased myself down from the dock, worked back along the fence atop creaking ice, then started up the steep grassy hill. The only doors I'd seen on the lake side opened onto high decks or gated stairs. The bottoms of the windows were at least ten feet above grade. Invited or otherwise, my only way in was through Fontaine's fancy glass-walled front entry.

• • •

Fontaine's property wore more cameras than O'Dell's bookstore. Raleigh would have approved. I'd spotted one on a post staring at the dock, two peering down from the top of the stairs. Others dangled like one-eyed bats beneath the eaves. Mists would hamper them, maybe, but anyone watching security monitors inside would see enough of me to arouse their suspicions. My gamble: maybe nobody *was* watching. They were busy packing. And if I guessed wrong, so what? I doubted the police would be notified. I kept tight to exterior walls, regardless, and avoided sudden movements.

The thrum of boat engines felt nearer than ever, as if the yacht had waded back ashore and followed me up the hill like a dog. I sensed something akin to sirens, thin reedy howls that came from half a county away. Thuds and scrapes heard through the cedar wall at my back, were rushed, incautious. The banging around reminded me of grisly scenes in the house where Mitch had died. Even though the monster who'd killed him was just as dead himself, I couldn't stop myself thinking Aubrea might be receiving similar treatment.

Yellow points with blue fringes danced ahead of me: gas lanterns. I'd slinked around to the half-circle drive with its attending parade of iron lampposts.

One car occupied the drive, Tipper's. It had a dejected, vulnerable appearance. All four doors hung open. The trunk lid and hood were raised. The little sedan had been searched as thoroughly and brutally as men without tools could manage.

I kept the .45 poised. I don't know why. Nothing waited

around to shoot. I followed memory to the high cedar doors of the vaulted entry. The glass felt warm even through my glove. No lights glowed inside. The mirror glass only repeated my face and the smudged glimmers of gas lamps. My reflection looked worried.

A pulsing red dot beckoned, the digital touch pad Gerard had used to unlock those doors on previous visits. He wasn't there tonight to let me in.

I eased the glove off my left hand, stuffed it in a coat pocket, rummaged for my phone and turned the device on by feel. I hated how obvious the phone made me feel. Adjusting the display brightness failed to mitigate the LED that blinked for missed calls and unread messages. O'Dell's number, four calls. Darlene had also left a text message from her personal phone.

What time? You haven't called.

I'd all but told her I already knew where the red journal was. Her persistence must mean something, however, and her boss *was* my only paying client.

8:18.

The night was young. If I survived my business here, Darlene wasn't the kind of girl who minded waiting up late. I replied with a message about *11:30* and activated the phone's *Do Not Disturb* setting.

Using the widget Danny had installed meant breaking the law. It might also get me inside without breaking glass. I held the phone against the touch pad.

It worked. Danny's gizmos usually did.

One cedar door clicked open and swept inward under its own impetus. The touch pad continued winking a blind red eye at me. I stepped through, pushed the door shut, powered my phone off before it made me a target.

Sirens and yacht engines ceased with the latching of the door. The glow from the gas lamps followed me inside, a little. The glass gallery felt neither spacious nor welcoming tonight. I

Flintlock

sensed nothing except a soft rhythmic scratching somewhere ahead of me. At least I was no more visible than my surroundings. I waited behind the Smith & Wesson for my eyes to adjust.

Meager warmth gradually became noticeable beyond the glass at the gallery's far end: the thin lights over Fontaine's Wild West paintings in the great room. I wondered if that room was ever fully illuminated. My feet started toward the glow, toward the soft scratching. Something hard and mobile met my knee and toppled with a clatter. I crouched, groping with my free hand. A chair lay on its side on the flagstones, a simple wooden chair, smack in the middle of the entry corridor. I picked it up and set it to one side, but the damage was done.

I wasn't alone.

A man's silhouette waited for me at the glass hall's other end, upright, unspeaking.

Jon A. Hunt

Chapter Thirty-four

Neither of us made the next move for a full minute. My heart flopped around in my chest in spite of the .45's being centered on the shadow in front of me. If he was armed, I could only assume he did likewise.

Nothing happened besides the strange scratching.

"Well?" I breathed.

That got no answer.

I wrestled with options, none of them good, decided I committed myself and took a wary forward step.

The other person *was* moving. He swayed. Side to side, barely an inch each direction. He still said nothing. His head canted quizzically to the left.

"I'm here for..." Words wandered off before they could coalesce into a full sentence.

The tall upright shape wasn't listening.

Against my better judgment, I brought out my penlight and snapped the beam on right in the other guy's face. He didn't blink. Corpses don't.

What struck me as uncharacteristic about Gerard's jacket was its unbuttoned state. The gloves were missing, too, from fists which were permanently clenched at the ends of ramrod straight arms. The body remained vertical because it dangled from a rope which had been tossed up through the iron framework of one of the chandeliers, then tied off to a cedar

Flintlock

post. The scratching noise came from shoes that almost, not quite, reached the flagstone floor. They'd started higher, but nooses slip and necks stretch. The ridiculous comb-over remained plastered in place, scant black strands contrasting grotesquely with the pallor of the tilted, bloated face. A black tongue protruded between tight blue lips.

I risked the quickest glance back at the chair I'd stumbled into. Eight feet from the body. That wasn't a jumping platform for a suicide; it had been seating for an audience of one.

The rest of the entry was as I remembered, cedar ceilings, timbers and beams, chandeliers, flagstones, glass walls on either side. There was just no humble Gerard gliding through to guide me to his master.

Should I cut him down? Despite the jacket and missing gloves, his tie was perfect. *Too* perfect. Hanging victims don't straighten what's around their necks.

Standing close wasn't pleasant, only necessary. I sniffed. Decomposition hadn't made yet the kind of headway vultures appreciate. I detected traces of sweat and urine. But mostly what I smelled was bourbon.

• • •

Glass panels at the foyer's inner end parted for me as they used to for Gerard. Perhaps they automatically opened for anyone who'd passed the front doors. I turned a final time toward Arthur Fontaine. I hadn't cut him down.

The corpse was definitely Fontaine's, draped in his butler's clothes. You had to drink harder than Gerard did to smell that way in death. When I found Gerard, he'd be cold sober, and I'd insist on an explanation.

But first I meant to find Aubrea.

There was a map of the house, with amber lights telling where people moved, on the wall in Fontaine's office. That was as good a place to start as any.

Paintings of gunfights watched me cross the darkened great

room. Each glossy scene was a bright canvas window into a dusty violent past. Unshod hooves hammered through my imagination, a whiff of smoke, the snap of pistol fire, shouts of dying cowboys; but when I paused to contemplate the pony soldier with the arrow in his back, my ears detected only drawers and cupboard doors banging in a distant room.

No tumbleweeds here, no lucky shots.

The office wasn't locked, and the owner was beyond caring. The banker's lamp had been left on. The room reeked of high-dollar bourbon. I checked the etched floorplan over the door. Letters glowed for a room at the back of the house, and of course for the office where I stood, not for any other rooms. Not even for the fancy entry. Infrared sensors saw Fontaine only as furniture. Were they seeing Aubrea the same way? Or was she in the back of the house where the drawers and cupboards banged? Was she in the mansion at all?

I should have searched the yacht before I set it adrift.

A crunch interrupted my self-critique. Glass ground between my heel and the shag carpet, which was damp and the source of the room's alcoholic bouquet. Wainscoting across from the desk was dented. On the floor nearby lay the concave base of a broken bottle. Wild West gun battles had been easy to imagine studying Fontaine's art collection; I had trouble picturing him so upset he'd throw a full bottle at a wall.

I looked again at the map. The lights hadn't altered. Another minute or so, and I'd need another strategy. In the meantime, I investigated the desk more quietly than whoever was throwing things around across the house.

Believe what you like in the movies. Desks are usually uninteresting. I only search them because I've seen too many movies. Fontaine's had no concealed compartments or weapons. He hadn't kept a liquor stash there, unless that was what he'd pitched across the room. The most damning items I found were envelopes from the *Colonial Societists*. Seventeen of

Flintlock

those. Not a letter in any of them. Most contained blank stationery with the hammer and anvil embossed at top, never so much as a typed word, folded in thirds the way you might wrap a check to keep the postman from seeing it through a sealed envelope. The most recent correspondence lay in the bottom of the drawer where Fontaine had dumped his mail during my first awkward visit. It hadn't been opened. I assumed he wouldn't mind now and slit the short end with my pocketknife.

A check was folded up inside, all right, made out to Arthur Fontaine.

$475,00.00

A fat lot of good it had done him.

The floorplan plaque above the door changed. Instead of in the back room, gold letters for a corridor next to it shined. So did letters for the vault.

The security system saw at least *three* live bodies in the house now.

• • •

When I ducked back through the office door, the banker's lamp pushed my shadow ahead of me to merge with the general darkness in the rest of the house. I hoped it didn't matter. According to the metallic blueprint in Fontaine's office, I had that side of the house to myself. I kept low through the great room, holding tight to walls and furniture. My silhouette showing in front of a lucky shot painting wouldn't do me any favors.

A furtive click admitted fresh sounds into the gloom: internal combustion grumbling out on the water, a dim yet strident symphony of sirens. The former felt near when I knew it wasn't attainable; the latter, closer yet not close enough. An exterior door had been opened, probably the one at the top of the dock stairs. I couldn't see from my position behind a sofa that smelled like cowhide. The door closed immediately. The deadbolt slid home, outside sounds ceased, security system electronics beeped. Soft-soled shoes moved inward.

The other person walked with a self-assurance of someone familiar with his surroundings. I followed more deliberately. The footsteps paused every few seconds.

Listening.

He knew I was there.

Not all of the plans derailed in the last few days had been mine. He still meant to leave. Staying wasn't an option. Only now he had no hope of leaving alone.

For a minute—a damn long time in the dark, behind a .45—nothing happened. I visualized the electronic map of the house in Fontaine's office, and decided the soft soles had stopped at the massive steel portal to Fontaine's weapons vault.

I eased around the sofa. The brim of my hat brushed the carpet. I didn't need to see a flawlessly pressed jacket or hear the modulated voice to know him. There were just two comb-overs that laughable in Middle Tennessee, and the other bobbed on the end of an extra mooring rope in the foyer. He was lit faintly by the vault's lock interface. His expression still radiated humility. Draped over his left arm were jeans, a torn blouse, the winter jacket I'd bought for Aubrea in Mule Town.

I waited till he'd coaxed the keypad lights from red to green. Then I said:

"Where can you go, Gerard?"

He spun fast and shooting, atypical reactions for a butler. But then, Gerard wasn't as ordinary as he'd first seemed, and I wasn't there on a social call. The space between us erupted with furious sound and fire. I kept the Smith & Wesson barking as I tumbled through a blizzard of stuffing blown from the cowhide sofa.

It stopped with equal abruptness. Now I hunkered tight to the cushions of a different couch in the room's dark center. My left bicep burned where a bullet had creased. My hat hadn't stayed with me and my ears rang. Miraculously intact plate glass

Flintlock

reverberated with the memory of gunfire. Wild West paintings reflected in the glass, but not the walls behind the paintings, which made each framed piece seem to hover in blackness. One of the paintings swayed. I recognized my own reflection, as well, crouched, hatless in a den full of Remingtons.

Gerard's reflection watched me. His retreat had deposited him behind a hulking cabinet. The cabinet remained featureless, but the man partially glowed in the spill of a picture light. His dark informal attire was less appropriate for answering doors than for sneaking past them. At least I'd gotten him away from the vault. We waited, our mirror images in each other's plain sight, twenty physical feet or less apart. Standing for a shot would be volunteering as a point-blank target.

Keeping Gerard's copy in focus, I eased the magazine from my weapon. It was empty. The slide hadn't locked back. One round remained in the chamber. I swapped the empty magazine for Rafferty's spare.

Where had Rafferty gone?

I couldn't hear sirens now.

Across the room, Gerard chuckled. "We seem to have achieved an impasse," he said.

My peripherals sensed a vertical stripe of brightness beside the half open vault door. Aubrea had to be in there, naked, judging by what Gerard carried when he activated the keypad.

What had he done to her?

"I'll wait," I growled.

Brass rattled on the floor. My opponent had to reload, too. Loose shells might mean his was a revolver. Counting to six is harder than you think when you're being shot at.

There were the sirens again. Louder. The sound didn't offer comfort. Metro's finest had lost some of their own. Once they worked themselves up to entering without permission, Gerard and I were equal threats, two nameless suspects in the dark with guns.

If I stayed low and safe, if Gerard reached the vault, he'd emerge with a valuable hostage.

If I had the cajones to try and stop him during a raid, we'd likely both end up dead.

He tried to crawl toward the open vault door.

"I'm not too chivalrous to shoot a killer in the back," I cautioned.

Gerard's reflection resumed its original position behind the cabinet. He squatted like a cowboy at an imaginary campfire. The revolver dangled over a knee with deceptive casualness.

"Presumptuous, isn't that?"

"Who else would straighten that dead asshole's tie, besides the person who poured his drinks all those years?"

Gerard smiled. It irked me that I didn't entirely hate him. I'd kill him if I had to. Unless he finished me first.

"Servants must be impeccably dressed, Mr. Bedlam."

He hadn't meant his words to carry the value they did. Gerard had snapped a vital puzzle piece into place.

Servants...
Seventeen envelopes in Arthur Fontaine's desk...
A check for $475,000.

I'd had their roles backwards. Everyone had.

"Aren't there cheaper ways to get things done than renting a billionaire?" I said.

"That depends on what needs to be done."

A shadow interrupted the light from the vault. Gerard raised his voice for her benefit and mine equally.

"The exterior doors are locked. None will open until I enter the code to release them. Surely you recognize the need for security in a home such as this. Do feel free to join us in the great room, Miss Langston, if you wish."

The opening became an empty bar of light again.

Flintlock

"Shy, I expect," Gerard quipped.

I appreciated his humor only because it made the prospect of shooting him more appealing. He was baiting me. Hoping I made the first mistake. Anyone who could weather Arthur Fontaine's acidity day in and day out could outlast me in a waiting game.

The assumptions added to my handicap. Crazy hypotheses. They'd never stand in court. I hid behind that cowhide sofa and strung them together anyway. Ludicrous as the assumptions were, they worked. Gerard had given me just enough.

He'd strangled his supposed employer. The comment about impeccably dressed servants invited no other interpretation.

He'd shot Erik Jorgensen. Fontaine and his house guests provided the night's alibi. God, what a trial that must have been for Fontaine, pouring other people's booze while he soberly *played the roles of both servant and master!* Jorgensen would have let Gerard in at the gate if he heard Fontaine's voice over the intercom. They hadn't liked each other but they still interacted. A quick call from Fontaine to the limo phone would suffice.

It followed that Gerard was the actual contestant who won Fontaine's pistol tournaments. Jorgensen must have seen through the charade, but there was another reason for Gerard to blast a .60 caliber hole through his skull: the red journal.

Nathan Cole and Tom Dryden died because they'd seen Gerard holding the proverbial smoking gun. Sal was supposed to have been eliminated for the same reason. And it wasn't just Gerard's horror show: Bigfoot joined in. *He'd* come with an entire support team.

Maybe it didn't matter who Keller Ableman's clients were. Fontaine, Gerard, Bigfoot, the Colonial Societists, all might be different tentacles of the beast that ultimately destroyed him.

So many lives cut short. There was also Tipper's family and poor innocent Mitch Braunfelter.

But *not* Governor Meriwether Lewis. He, at least, hadn't

Jon A. Hunt

died in October of 1809.

He'd written a letter.

"You've all gone to an awful lot of trouble," I said aloud, "for a letter no one can read."

The false cordiality left Gerard's voice. He got easier to hate by the minute. "The point is," he said slowly, "nobody *will* read it."

Just like that, I had confirmation.

"Are you so sure?"

"Come now, Mr. Bedlam! Persistence brought you this far, but you lack imagination and a longer view. All you accomplished in the end was to deliver the journal directly to me, in the hands of the one person outside our organization who understood its importance. We were prepared for his arrival. Before that, you left other documents to be easily found in a hotel mattress. You act as if we only started looking for these things yesterday instead of two hundred years ago. Photographs on a web page! Without physical proof to back them up, they're no more to be believed than the rest of the Internet."

...outside our organization...

Even as the enemy Gerard couldn't avoid being helpful. But time was short. Aside from our conversation and a soft whir from unseen ceiling fans, there were no other sounds now. Everyone was waiting. Either Gerard, or the police positioned outside, would make their moves soon. I had a bigger hunch to play and should do so now.

"By 'we' I assume you mean the Colonial Societists."

No response. I didn't expect an instant admission.

"You're going to hide the letter again. You don't kill people to get hold of something like that and think you can let it be seen again. You aren't collectors. You sure as hell aren't philanthropists. Your organization isn't interested in preserving or promoting history at all."

320

Flintlock

The reflection with the revolver on its knee watched me mutely for a while, measuring the worth of dialogue. Ultimately, he replied. He meant to kill me, anyway.

"Preserve, yes. Promote...*selectively*. Our driving purpose has always been to ensure *responsible* exploration of the past. These are pivotal times, Mr. Bedlam. We are a nation of sheep guided by idiots. All that keeps the system from flying apart is the supposition that the system works. The ordinary voting American needs to believe the founding fathers were better men, larger than life, not petty or selfish..."

"Uh huh," I said.

Gerard's tone sharpened. "Your skepticism is the Societists' reward for a job well done! You believe what you're taught. Even a man who makes a living second-guessing doesn't bother to confirm some things. But what if Benjamin Franklin was only the village drunk? What if Adams, Revere, Washington were common crooks? What if proof existed that Jefferson was a schemer and a murderer? What citizen benefits from such a discovery so late in the game?"

"That's what this is about?" I said. "Public relations for dead people?"

"We safeguard the nation's roots. Protect the heritage. If you can't trust your beginnings, how can you have faith in your future?"

I couldn't stop myself from seeing his point. Trouble was, my unimaginative, short-sighted view didn't go as far back as Gerard's. I saw my father in a dead heap under a bar stool. No. I was better off knowing the truth.

"You're full of shit, Gerard. And you only have *half* the letter. Tipper hid the rest in his shoe. The police have him, his portion of the letter and the journal. Your accomplices never made it past the gate. You heard the shots."

His voice tightened. "This is bigger than either of us. The authorities have relinquished material to the Societists before."

Jon A. Hunt

The silhouette returned to the vault door, tentative, feminine, I assumed terrified. Gerard's attention only recognized me now.

"I wonder," I said, "if you really intend to relinquish *your* half of the letter to them."

I'd planned for diplomatic failure. I got it. Gerard's patience abandoned him and he fired two rounds at my reflection. The windows didn't shatter—Fontaine's palace was wrapped in bulletproof glass—but my opponent's true goal grabbed me with the second shot. Spiderweb cracks obliterated Gerard's mirror image. I could no longer see even a copy of him.

I didn't wait for the third round, because it wasn't meant for any windows. I pivoted instead, fired blind into the shadows *opposite* fracturing glass. My instincts hadn't been off by much. Flames passed each other. The couch that once shielded me lurched and splintered. Large fragile objects crashed in the blackness. The revolver bellowed twice, deep shattering explosions. My retreat didn't figure in unseen end tables. I tripped over one and somersaulted backward onto a stone floor. My gun spun free of splayed fingers. The tumble ended with me flat on my belly, defenseless, no longer in the dark.

Light flared through every window. The great room blazed in an artificial sunrise that entered from three directions. Police floodlights.

My chin lifted from the floor toward a familiar metallic shape. The Smith & Wesson lay on the stone, just out of reach. I started to press myself upward.

He chuckled.

I locked my elbows and raised just my eyes the rest of the way to meet Gerard's. He knelt twenty feet past my weapon in a well-balanced shooter's position, one he'd employed thousands of times to win Fontaine's undeserved trophies. This time the target was a real man and his breathing was labored. Even against his dark shirt, blood from my rib shot glittered in

Flintlock

the silent barrage of spotlights. But he wouldn't miss.

I saw a dull glint of copper, one last .44 caliber slug with my name on it, waiting in the barrel's depths.

"Not good enough, Mr. Bedlam."

• • •

"Gerard."

Her voice was small. Our condensed battlefield still simmered with memories of fire and thunder and rage; a name called out so softly should have been overwhelmed. But she was there, and we heard her.

Gerard's revolver turned till the muzzle centered between two houseguests, one unwelcome, the other unwilling. I didn't take that as an invitation to move. The tiniest twitch in his peripheral senses would give him all the excuse he needed to finish me.

Polished steel, the door to Fontaine's gun vault, gleamed behind Aubrea. The rest of the corridor overflowed with brightness. Shadow hid her right half, but bare skin shone on her left. Curves of breast, shoulder, hip and calf on that side were gilded with the brilliance of the floodlights. If Gerard hoped modesty would keep a nude girl in place, he'd miscalculated. Her feet pressed into the flagstones, shoulder-width apart. The short hair was a feral mess. Her left eye sparkled like sapphire. One of Fontaine's antique flintlock dueling pistols jutted from the ends of her outstretched arms.

Awkwardly for Gerard, he'd put himself exactly between Aubrea and me. It was his own fault for leaving her in the vault.

"Put down your gun," she said. "Please."

Gerard shook his head. I doubted he knew about her time with Tipper in Jorgensen's gun range. Regardless, he brought up an excellent argument.

"That is a complicated weapon, Miss Langston. Not just anybody can load one. Even for an expert it isn't reliable. I suggest you stop playing with toys you don't understand, or I'll

Jon A. Hunt

kill Mr. Bedlam here and take care of you with my bare hands."

Aubrea's visible eye flashed. She held her ground. "Put the gun down," she repeated.

"Have you ever killed a man?" Gerard sent her the wickedest, least butler-like grin imaginable and moved the .44's muzzle.

Aubrea pulled the trigger.

A miniature Fourth of July engulfed that end of the corridor, a sparking flurry of ignited black powder. But there was no loud boom.

The girl still held the weapon before her, arms locked, waiting as Tipper had taught her to do when an old gun misfired, counting in silent helplessness to sixty.

A flash in the pan.

Gerard laughed, brought the revolver's snout back toward me for the kill. Then his head disappeared in a horrible scarlet blossom with a center of flame.

The old flintlock in Aubrea's hands had finished firing after all.

A delayed rush of violent sound surged over me. I sprang upright at precisely the moment the girl sank and Gerard's truncated corpse toppled.

Flintlock

Chapter Thirty-five

11:23.

I was going to be punctual. Meredith O'Dell appreciated punctuality. Too bad this wasn't her meeting and she'd never accept my reasons for being there.

I passed Darlene's frosty Volvo half an empty block from the bookstore. Sharp winds scythed around me, scraped across darkened storefronts, hacked the rhythm from my stride. Streetlights shivered. I was glad I wouldn't be out in the weather for long. Sort of.

The neon sign greeted me hours after its bedtime. The front door wasn't locked. Either transgression would dangerously elevate Uncle Ral's blood pressure if he found out, not that I minded anything that upset him. I laid a hand on the door's crossbar and peered inward through my sherbet-tinted breath.

• • •

I'd been warmer an hour ago. Whatever Arthur Fontaine's disdain for comfort he couldn't pour from a bottle, he'd kept his lakeshore home balmy as a Malibu beach. I missed my jacket less than the girl I'd wrapped in it before the EMTs escorted her dazedly away.

Lieutenant Rafferty kept his own coat on. He and I crouched like cowpokes in one of Fontaine's spotlighted paintings, except my six-shooter had been confiscated and a corpse, not a campfire, occupied the space between us. I asked Rafferty why he wore that grim smirk.

"Appreciating the irony," he said. "Tipper says that loose ramrod he found at Jorgensen's matched a gun in Fontaine's collection. Didn't realize it till he made the mistake of telling Gerard. Tipper and Aubrea came in the front, so Fontaine must not have been dangling yet. If Gerard had done away with them on the spot he'd have escaped. He stayed. And of all the ways to die, he gets his from an identical gun—*the other half of the matched set*—to what he used to off Jorgensen. Funny."

"Hilarious," I muttered.

He wasn't listening to me. He fished a pen from his pocket and employed it to flip open Gerard's unbuttoned jacket. A cellular phone tipped out and thumped, whirring, into the gruesome pond beneath its owner. Rafferty stretched a knuckle toward the pulsing screen.

The scene was an unwelcome echo from Mitch Braunfelter's ruined second home weeks earlier, right down to my knowing the number of the incoming call.

"Don't answer that," I suggested.

• • •

The electric chime and a rush of warmth greeted me. I stepped inside and dropped both gloves from my other hand onto the aluminum threshold. The door pinched leather without quite latching. Noise of wind squealing through the gap didn't persist more than ten steps in among the books. No overhead lights were on; only a low intimate something beckoned from the sales counter in back. I made for it. Some hints can't be ignored.

That absurd guilt nagged me again. Every time I talked with, or put myself in the same room with, Darlene, it happened. Like I was a kid flipping pages of his big brother's dirty magazine stash. I'd originally chalked it up to nascent feelings toward Aubrea. I realized now Darlene would be just

Flintlock

as guilty a pleasure if there were no other women on the planet.

To be fair, Aubrea was one reason I'd bothered keeping this appointment. She, her daddy, Tipper, and Rafferty all had different claims on my responsibilities. They were still at Fontaine's, would be for hours yet. People don't normally stroll away from that kind of a crime scene once the police step in. Rafferty had made an exception in my case. He debriefed me and sent me the hell away before the DA found me there. He never asked what was in my pockets, he just took my gun like he usually did. Smally arrived, having delivered the boy, Sal, wherever he needed to go. The Lieutenant reassigned him to chauffer duty.

"Anywhere but here," Rafferty growled as Langston's Mercedes slalomed past blinking roof lights and shushed down the driveway.

I checked my watch and told Smally to take me downtown.

• • •

The sales counter blazed under artfully positioned desk lamps, less a transactional surface than an improvised burlesque stage. The bright rectangle of a computer monitor might have captured my attention if it hadn't shared billing with the only woman I'd ever met capable of employing an entire room as a fashion accessory. Darlene O'Dell perched on the counter, bare feet swinging beneath long, smooth shins. I bet the girl didn't even own a pair of stockings. The artificial fox fur I remembered from the other night draped over her shoulders, open at the front for my appreciation of the interplay of shadows beneath her chin and between her breasts. A hint of purple showed at her throat.

"You came!" she purred.

"I said I would."

I removed my hat, circled to the employees' side of the counter. The security displays in Raleigh's cubby under the mezzanine stairs were black, dormant.

Unplugged.

Uncle Ral couldn't very well be allowed to view what his niece had in mind.

A lot of hardwired biological programming needed to be ignored for me to play cool. I managed. I reached past her to bump the mouse and wake the computer. Of course, O'Dell's network demanded a password.

"You said you had something to show me." Not the wittiest phrase I'd ever turned.

Darlene giggled, pivoted on a hip, swung her feet above the counter and over a familiar purple leather purse. I remembered what used to hide in that purse the night we'd been ambushed outside. I wondered if she'd gotten that wicked little .38 back from the police. Mostly, though, I tried to keep my eyes above her exquisite collarbones. A dozen artificial silver foxes slithered from her bronze curves.

Somehow, she got both legs around my ribs. Her heat pressed through my shirt. My jacket flopped down around my shoes. Fingernails etched searing trails down my shoulders, paused a thoughtful moment at the lump of fresh medical gauze I'd earned at Fontaine's place, moved to tease the leather of my empty gun rig.

"Password?" I rasped.

Why did I need a password again?

She gave it to me. She breathed it into my ear, accompanied by a playful nibble. Meredith and Raleigh plainly had their own access codes, because Darlene's was downright pornographic. I struggled with whether to type the thing or perform it.

I'd come here with loftier goals than sex.

• • •

A last puzzle piece...

Aubrea held my hands as I said it, stared into my eyes with a haggard expression. Tipper's wounds were being dressed in the

328

Flintlock

ambulance behind me. He'd gotten the rough treatment he had trying to defend her. She wanted to be near him. But I was there, too.

"Be careful, Tyler."

"Always—"

"I mean it! Mitch wouldn't have wanted all this if he'd known. He wouldn't want anybody hurt, especially—"

I did her the favor of not brushing away the tear. If ever a person needed a good cry, Aubrea did. And mine wasn't the shoulder she needed.

"—especially you," I said.

Then I got up and followed Smally to his rusty pickup truck without looking back.

• • •

The keyboard squeaked across the countertop as I clawed it toward me. I tapped in Darlene's dirty password. She busied herself with the buckle of my shoulder holster, unhurried. The empty rig wasn't going to buy me much extra time. Her warmth and her scent were maddening. Raleigh had proclaimed her too distracting for auctions. I agreed. Part of me recognized the distraction as deliberate; part of me didn't care.

Customer names appeared on the screen, same as last time. The girl murmured that I could skip those, her breath heating my neck. The shoulder rig thudded in defeat on top of my fallen jacket. I did move past the customer names, once I'd scrolled through the B's.

M Braunfelter was no longer a database entry.

Purged.

Again.

"Inventory," Darlene whispered, "special items. It's there."

Her breasts crushed against my chest without even my shirt to separate us. She'd unbuttoned that as well. Her lips moved up my throat, soft, damp, hot. The only anchor that kept me from being swept away was the reason I'd come downtown.

329

Jon A. Hunt

Mitch Braunfelter.

Who wasn't listed in O'Dell's computers anymore.

The time at the bottom of the screen was *11:39*. That was the most important thing there. The time. For the hell of it, I found the reference:

Journal, Lewis, M.
Hold for auction. Bolton, Jorgensen, Andrews, Fontaine.

Now why hadn't anyone found that till now?

Jorgensen presumably had been the high bidder. He'd bought himself one old red diary and one .60 caliber lead ball through his brain. Oops.

Who had the seller been?

Darlene's hands slid with purpose down over my ribs toward my belt.

"You like?"

I grinned in spite of myself. The information on the computer was interesting, sure. I'd already guessed most of it. I doubted that was what Darlene meant.

The clock on the screen changed to *11:40*.

Her fingertips curved over my waistband—and stopped. The purple purse against her bare thigh buzzed. A hint of electronic brightness leaked from the opening.

She wanted sex. Hell, *I* wanted it. But she'd been waiting for that phone to ring all night.

"Go ahead," I told her.

She leaned back, supporting herself from my belt, and smiled wickedly. I allowed my eyes to fully admire her beautiful uncovered body. There'd be no other chances. She let go of me, opened her purse. I had to give her credit for her confidence. But the number on the glowing device confused her. I recited the number without needing to see it.

"Gerard won't be calling. He's dead. That's Lieutenant

Flintlock

Rafferty, Metro Police. I'm sure he's got a lot of questions."

Darlene dropped the phone back into its den, unanswered, still whirring.

"No one else could've suggested to Gerard that Tipper might have the red journal."

I spoke to a beautiful mahogany statue, immobile yet warm, with mahogany thighs encircling my waist.

"Just theories now," I continued, "but easy to confirm. You were the inside person helping the thieves. Uncle Raleigh really is as clueless as he seems. You probably used his typewriter for those notes you left in *Tales of Mystery* for the kids. You unplugged his cameras before the raid, didn't you? Just like you did tonight."

Big bronze eyes raised to study my face. Nothing like passion showed in them now. Fear did. A bit of anger. A lot of desperation.

I can't imagine the nice girl who rang me out would have missed it.

Mitch hadn't known it at the time how right he was.

"You dropped the journal into Mitch Braunfelter's bag when he wasn't looking, to get it out of the building before the police found it. You passed his address to Gerard. How long have you and Gerard been together? Somehow I doubt it was all work and no play——"

She *had* gotten her revolver back. In a blink, the stub-nosed metal beast pressed against my sternum. I'd much preferred her breasts there.

"Now's a good time to plan for your future," I said. I made damn sure my tone stayed even. "So far, premeditated murder isn't on your list of sins. Mitch is dead because you ditched contraband in his bag and told somebody where to find him. You didn't kill him yourself. Two of those kids you helped steal from your family business are dead, but someone else got credit

Jon A. Hunt

for that, too. I suspect you blew away Chad Walker to keep him from spilling the beans that you'd hired him to attack me the other night. Lucky for you, there's no reason a decent lawyer can't convince a jury that was self-defense. There are likely others. Never direct involvement.

"But if you shoot me now, in front of a cop, that's pretty much a first-class ticket to death row. Isn't that right, Smally?"

I'd never been happier to see that mountain of a Metro man. I'd already collected more .38 caliber holes than I needed. He stepped forward from the shadows, on cue, having slipped through the door I wedged open, unseen by the deactivated cameras. His expression could best be described as embarrassed. Smally preferred his smut safely contained between the dog-eared covers of drugstore paperbacks.

"He's right, ma'am," he said. "It'd be best to put your gun down."

Darlene's features softened again. She was relieved, pretty again, desirable.

"Fuck," she exhaled.

I shook my head. Not tonight. Not ever.

To be honest, I was a little disappointed myself.

Flintlock

Epilogue

"You okay?"

Tipper's clenched teeth had nothing to do with the cold. His frame had tensed so abruptly I heard the crackle.

"I know that man," he hissed.

"Go off-script now and we're both dead," I warned.

"I won't."

We came to our predetermined standstill on a gray-brown lawn. Small weathered stone squares, discrete testaments to forgotten pioneer lives, marched through the grass in ordered rows from our shoes. A less subtle chiseled monument rose from the meadow's center. The broken marble column signified a life full of promise cut short, an after-the-fact headstone for the graveyard's one prestigious resident. Governor Meriwether Lewis was supposed to be buried beneath it.

Hard December winds scrambled through the bare trees around the meadow. Sapless branches rattled like grasping finger-bones. A high sun in the pale sky had no power to temper the chill.

The man Tipper recognized approached. He was portly and dressed in expensive clothes that weren't ideal for the weather. He must have been waiting behind the monument, watching for us, the same as his compatriots in the trees. In spite of the wind he managed not to step on any grave markers. I guess that made

Jon A. Hunt

him reverent. He stopped an arm's length from Tipper. His tiny eyes glistened, droplets of molasses in a wad of fleshy dough.

"Hello, Tremaine."

"Mr. Ray." Tipper's voice carried no inflection at all.

The beady-eyed man extracted one hand from his coat and thrust it toward my friend. He didn't wear ordinary gloves. His were dainty white cotton, curator's gloves, intended to protect what he touched not what might touch him, the kind of gloves Tipper never wore.

Tipper's expression startled me. I hadn't thought him capable of such enmity till I realized who Ray was.

Mr. Ray and Mr. Delphino.

From the Colonial Societists.

They'd offered to bankroll Tipper's museum, but Tipper wound up losing instead of gaining. Tipper handed over the red journal. His taped and splinted fingers barely quivered.

Ray accepted the book. Wind notwithstanding, he popped the clasp and thumbed pages with his delicate white fingers. The journal's age showed in the harsh winter sunlight. An ordinary plastic-handled utility razor appeared between a gloved thumb and forefinger. Ray deftly slid the blade across selected pages, close to the binding, and removed them. He collected every page dated after Lewis was supposed to have died. Then he shut the journal, latched the clasp, returned the mutilated artifact to me, not to Tipper.

"For posterity," he said. "And the letter?"

I didn't respond promptly. I let Tipper glare at him. This needed to be awkward to work.

"Mr. Bedlam?"

"No letter," I said.

Ray calmly stowed the journal's cut pages inside his coat. His molasses-drop eyes never changed. The guy would be murder in a poker game. "In light of your recent experiences,"

Flintlock

he said without the tiniest hint of exasperation, "you must realize this is no joking matter."

He was right, there was nothing to kid about here.

"The only funny thing I see," I told him, "is that you think your people can be trusted with secrets. We wouldn't be here now if Delphino had kept a lid on it."

Ray had nothing to say to that. I said more.

"As far as we're concerned, all of Governor Lewis' letters were found generations ago. That's what the Societists want, correct? And as long as none of the living people associated with this mythical letter you mentioned are molested, that won't change. But if any of them get worried, turn up dead or disappear, I can be worse at keeping secrets than Delphino. Preaddressed packages, donations only billionaires can make, all the related publicity, one very pleased public museum—all that happens if I'm convinced it needs to. Or it'll happen automatically if I'm not around to prevent it."

The molasses-drop eyes didn't change. The puffy face around them reddened, though. "Others have tried—"

"I doubt they had my resources or my bad attitude."

It wasn't a bluff. You don't bluff with organizations like the Colonial Societists. The package was already addressed and buried in Cool-Core's multinational network, poised in one of a thousand obscure mail rooms, waiting for the right—or the wrong—signal. Jerry Rafferty should have checked my pockets when he found me stooped over Gerard's body.

"Have it your way," he relented. "As long as no letter surfaces—"

"—and no one is hurt," I added.

"No one."

"Not even Darlene O'Dell."

"Prison is a dangerous place, Mr. Bedlam."

"It better not be for her," I told him.

• • •

Jon A. Hunt

That was the end of it. All the loose ends weren't tied. Justice had been incomplete. The coded letter Meriwether Lewis had penned to his former Commander in Chief, after Lewis was supposed to be dead, held all of us hostage. I didn't dare play my best card and the Societists didn't dare force me to.

Ray turned and walked back across the meadow to disappear among the gray trees. Tipper and I watched him pass the simple pillar that represented the tragic unfulfilled life of a great American explorer.

"You read it?" I asked quietly when we were alone.

"I did. The keyword was *flintlock*. Like you thought."

"Who do you suppose is buried under that thing?"

Tipper shook his curl-topped head solemnly.

"Not Meriwether Lewis," he said.

• • •

Rafferty waited in his enormous Cadillac, parked sideways across the monument's only access road. He'd insisted on driving. I hadn't found a good reason to deny him. It was Christmas Day, after all. In minutes we were swaddled in warmth and leather, floating northward in excess of the posted limit over the sinuous Natchez Trace Parkway. Nashville was a long quiet hour away.

Tipper passed a small box to me from the back seat. Glossy red paper, a gold ribbon and a bow, the works.

"From Aubrea," he said. Tipper and the DA's daughter had been seeing a lot of each other. They were fixing up the Nashville home Mitch had willed to her. To sell. Aubrea couldn't bear living where her friend died. "She says you deserve it and you'd understand."

Rafferty turned his placid eyes from the road long enough to grin as I opened the package.

Mitch Braunfelter hadn't been given the very last set of crossword puzzle suspenders on earth, after all.

336

337

338

Acknowledgments

I'll own up to Google searches and window peeping for much of my research. Being able to jump in a car and go see helps. But nothing's as effective as asking people who know better. The author wishes to express his gratitude in writing, to the people who know better.

Lieutenant Carl E. McCoy II, with the Sumner County Sheriff's Office, has been a terrific resource for police procedural questions. I still wing it too often, but Carl's input has hopefully kept my efforts believable.

Beau Campsey, with CSX in Nashville, was kind enough to explain basic scope and operations of the Radnor railyard to me. Before our discussion, pretty much all I knew about the place was that it was loud.

Scott Lunsford, Dan Erickson and Adam Miller, of Envision-Advantage in Nashville, I thank you for, respectively: patient explanations of security systems, a diver's understanding of hypothermia, and emergency transportation so I lived long enough to finish the book.

Special appreciation is due my favorite proofreader and wife, Rachel Hunt, who had to wait this time till the *whole* book was written to read it.

My ultimate gratitude, as always, goes to the reader. Nashville might linger a while without an audience, but Tyler Bedlam and his associates could not. Thank you!

Jon A. Hunt
September 18, 2019

Printed in the USA
CPSIA information can be obtained
at www.ICGtesting.com
LVHW091923061023
760214LV00008B/170/J